Also by Alice Kellen

Let It Be

All That We Never Were

All That We Are Together

only after we met

ALICE KELLEN

sourcebooks
casablanca

Originally published as *Nosotros en la luna*, © Alice Kellen, 2020 (represented by Editabundo for Spanish language and c/o Planeta Book&Film Rights for worldwide translation and audiovisual rights). Translated from Spanish by A. Nathan West.

Published by Sourcebooks Casablanca, an imprint of Sourcebooks
P.O. Box 4410, Naperville, Illinois 60567-4410
(630) 961-3900
sourcebooks.com

Originally published as *Nosotros en la luna* in 2020 in Spain by Editorial Planeta, an imprint of Grupo Planeta.

Cataloging-in-Publication Data is on file with the Library of Congress.

Printed and bound in the United States of America.
MA 10 9 8 7 6 5 4 3 2 1

For Leo.

Hopefully one day you'll be hanging upside down from the moon,

fearless, with a huge smile on your face.

As if you could pick in love, as if it were not a lightning bolt that splits your bones and leaves you staked out in the middle of a courtyard.

—Julio Cortázar, *Hopscotch*

Part 1

—

MEETING. FRIENDSHIP. CHANCE.

"Baobabs start out by being little."

The Little Prince

1

Ginger

WHEN YOU MEET A PERSON, there's no way of knowing all at once that they'll turn your world upside down. In the blink of an eye. The way a soap bubble pops. The way a match catches fire. In the course of our lives, we meet thousands of people: at the supermarket, on the bus, in a café, in the middle of the street. Maybe the person who's meant to shake things up for you is standing there in front of you at a crosswalk or grabbing the last box of cereal off the top shelf when you're out buying groceries. Maybe you'll never meet that person; maybe you'll never even exchange a word. Or maybe you will. Maybe you'll lock eyes, run into each other, make a connection. It's just that unpredictable. That's where the magic lies, I guess. For me, it happened one freezing night in Paris when I was trying to buy a ticket for the subway.

"Why aren't you working?" I moaned to the machine. I pushed the button so hard it hurt my finger. "Stupid piece of trash!"

"Are you trying to kill it?"

I turned around when I heard a voice that spoke my language. And I saw him. I don't know. I don't know what I felt just then.

I don't remember clearly, but there are three things I can't forget: the collar of his jacket was turned up, he smelled like spearmint gum, and his eyes were a bluish gray like the London sky on one of those leaden dawns when the sun tries to break through the clouds but can't.

That's all. That's everything. And that's all I needed to start shivering.

"I wish. But for now, it's winning. I can't get it to work."

"You've got to choose what kind of ticket you want first."

"Where...uh, where do I pick?"

"On the start screen. Hold on."

He stood beside me, pushed the buttons to get back to the main menu, and looked at me. And it was intense. Like when someone arouses your curiosity, but you don't know why. Or when you wake up in a cold sweat.

"Where are you trying to go?"

"Well...actually..." I was nervous, and I tucked a strand of hair that had come loose from my ponytail behind my ear. "Downtown?"

"You're not sure?"

"Yeah! No! I mean, I don't have anywhere to stay tonight, so I was thinking, like, I'd get to know the city a bit. Any place you recommend?"

He leaned against the machine and arched his eyebrows. "You don't have anywhere to stay?"

"No. I just caught the first flight out."

"Just like that, throwing caution to the wind?"

"Yeah, basically. Like that."

"All by yourself...?"

"So what?"

"No, I get it. I do the same sometimes."

"Great, congratulations. So, getting back to the ticket..."

"What's your name?" he asked.

"Ginger. What's yours?"

"Rhys."

His accent was American. And he was so tall he made me feel tiny. But he had something. That something you can't always put in words when you meet someone. It's not that he was handsome or that I felt lost in the city I'd just arrived in. It was that I could read things in him. I still wasn't sure if those things were good or bad, but when I looked at him, the very last thing that came into my mind was *empty*, which was funny, because I'd find out later that the emptiness was one of the things Rhys feared most. But I didn't know that yet. We were still two strangers looking each other in the eye in front of a ticket machine for the subway.

"Do you have any advice for me?" I said, getting back to the subject.

He hesitated but didn't look away. "Yeah. I could show you Paris."

"Look, before this gets uncomfortable, I might as well tell you I just broke up with my boyfriend. We were together a long time, so I'm not into getting to know someone else or having a one-night stand..."

If only someone had told me what a fool I was being then.

"I offered to take you to see the city, not to bed."

He crossed his arms with a wry grin. I blushed like a fifteen-year-old.

"Of course. But, like, just in case..."

"Right. You're planning ahead."

"Exactly. I try to, anyway. I mean, actually, at this moment, I've obviously done anything but plan ahead, but fuck it, I'm trying to get...to get my life in order. And everything..."

Rhys didn't seem bothered by my momentary insanity. That should have been the first sign. I should have known right then he would be different. I was talking nonstop, the way I usually did when I felt nervous, and that was what was special in that moment, the way he just listened, nodded, and agreed.

"...everything's just chaos right now, you know? This situation. My life. Maybe I'm here in the middle of an unfamiliar city as a kind of symbol of what I feel like right now. Sorry, I don't know why you haven't turned around and walked off yet."

"I like people who talk."

"Why, to fill the dead air?"

"Maybe. I haven't really thought about it."

That was a lie. I'd later learn Rhys was a good talker, the kind who asks questions others don't even think of, the kind who can stay up all night rolling over whatever's in their head and never get bored of it.

"The thing is, my flight back leaves tomorrow."

He looked at me a few moments, tense, interested. "You want to do this visit or not, Ginger?"

I remember all I could think right then was, *Why does he say my name like that? Why does he sound like he's said it a million times before?* It scared me, but I liked it in equal measure. Or no. I liked it more than it scared me. Because he uttered it delicately, and I've never liked my name. Ginger's a spice or a root, not something romantic or spiritual, but when Rhys said it, it sounded different. Nicer.

"You're a stranger," I said.

"We're all strangers until we meet."

"Yeah, but..." I licked my lips, nervous.

"Whatever. It's your call." He shrugged.

Then he wished me a safe trip, his face brushing the collar of his jacket, and he walked toward the tunnel that led outside.

I weighed my options. I was lost in Paris because I'd just broken up with my boyfriend and I thought I was being a rebel by buying the first ticket I could find, even if it was a round trip with a quick turnaround and I had nowhere to stay and nothing on me but a backpack with a pair of panties, a change of socks, and a pack of crackers. And I didn't know where to go. And I couldn't ignore the shiver I felt when I heard his voice the first time.

I don't know. It was an impulse. A sudden attraction.

"Wait!"

He stopped.

"Where are we going?"

"We?" He turned around.

"I know I just told you I don't know you, but if you turn around and leave right now... I think I'll follow you."

Rhys looked surprised.

"I mean, yeah, let's go. Because I don't know where I am and I don't have any data on my phone because the company sold me this garbage plan and... I feel like if I stay, I'll end up getting eaten by a bear or whatever happens when you get lost in a city instead of an enchanted forest. You know what I mean."

"I don't have the damnedest idea what you mean." He smiled.

"Whatever. Just...don't leave me."

"Fine, but you need to relax and go with the flow."

I nodded and he laughed. And I followed him. I followed him without thinking another thought, bought a couple of train tickets, and cut through the crowd to get into the first subway car that stopped there.

I didn't know then that my life was going to change.

That Rhys would be a before and after.

That our paths would join forever.

2

Rhys

WHAT WAS I DOING? NO fucking idea.

Ten minutes before, I'd gotten out of the subway ready to go home (if I could call it home), thinking I'd heat up a cup of noodles and eat it while I mindlessly watched TV without sound or put on some music and read.

But instead, there I was, sitting on the subway next to a girl who looked even more lost than I did, which wasn't an easy thing to imagine, our legs were rubbing against each other's, and I still hadn't decided where to get off, because I was making it up as I went along, as always.

"I don't like not knowing where we're going."

"Two more stops and we'll get out," I said with a smile.

She made me nervous. Every inch of her, from her feet in her red Converse to her brown hair pulled back carelessly in a ponytail. Maybe because I hadn't found a label for her yet. *Ginger*. That was her name, I kept telling myself. She was a complete blank to me, I guess because she seemed to have everything under control, but she'd actually just hopped a plane a few hours ago for no reason.

And that didn't make sense. Nor did the unexpected tremor I felt when I saw her cursing in front of the ticket machine. So short. So funny. So pissed... She reminded me of a child's cartoon.

"Where are you from, exactly?" I asked. It was obvious she was English, but I couldn't tell from where by her accent. Her voice was soft, almost raspy.

"London. You? No, wait, let me guess."

"Fine." This amused me.

"Alabama?"

I shook my head.

"You've got a Southern accent though."

"Try a little further north."

"Tennessee."

"Yep. That's it."

"What are you doing in Paris?"

"It's not a forever thing."

"What do you mean?"

"Get up. This is our stop."

I stood, and she followed me to the doors as they slid open. We cut through the people walking back and forth and went out onto the street. It was bitter cold. Ginger was hugging herself, and we were walking fast, hoping to get somewhere warm before long.

The Eiffel Tower stood there in the distance.

"Is that what I think it is?" She smiled. And it was a smile so precious, I wanted to frame it. I would have if I didn't hate photos. Ginger was one of those girls who deserved to be immortalized, not because she was especially pretty or unusual, but because of her eyes, the way her lips curved upward without her even thinking, the little contradiction I could sense inside her, even if I didn't know her yet.

"Yeah, that's it. One of the iconic sights of Paris. I realize I'm not much of a tour guide, but in my defense, we've only got a few hours. Anyway, I wanted you to remember this."

The Seine flowed to our left as we walked under the starless night sky and the full moon. I remember all I could think about was how it had been worth it to trade my cup noodles for the smile on her face.

"It's beautiful. Thank you."

"Have you had dinner?"

"No. It's been forever since I've had anything to eat. I had a coffee this morning, but then the drama happened this afternoon, and it was bye-bye to my everyday routine. I couldn't have gotten anything down, anyway. I'm doing it, I'm talking too much again, right?"

"Yeah, but I like it."

She looked away.

Was it embarrassment? Shyness? I didn't know.

"Shall we go eat then?"

"I know a place nearby."

"Good, because I'm dying of cold."

"I would've thought you'd be used to it, living in London."

"Nobody ever told you there are people who never get used to the cold? 'Cause I'm one of them. It doesn't matter how much I bundle up; I can have two scarves on and three pairs of socks; still, I'm like a block of ice. When we used to get in bed, Dean would…"

She stopped and shook her head.

"Let me guess: Dean's the guy you just broke up with, and he used to warm up your feet?" I couldn't help but crinkle my nose. "That's disgusting."

"What? No, it's not, it's super romantic."

"Feet gross me out. I can't even touch my own feet. And I'm not sure about your ideas about what's *super romantic*..."

"Fine. But you know what? I don't know you." She giggled. I liked it: soft, sweet. "So I'm not going to worry about your opinions as far as what is and isn't romantic. Plus, you look like the typical guy who...you know."

I stopped, even though we were across the street from the place I was planning to take her for dinner. I stood there, looking at her sternly. I was almost two heads taller than her. She looked up defiantly. I liked that too. "Aren't you going to finish your sentence?"

"Maybe I was getting ahead of myself."

"Damn right. You just saw me for the first time fifteen minutes ago. But who cares? I want to know what your impression of me is. I won't let it affect me, I promise."

"You look like the type of guy who doesn't give a shit about romance. The type of guy who bangs a girl one night, and then it's adios. The kind who's allergic to commitment."

"You're being redundant."

"Sorry. I was trying to make a point."

"Sure."

I started walking again. We crossed the street. Once we were inside, I noticed the smell of freshly made crepes. I babbled in French and ordered a couple with cheese, tuna, and mushrooms. From the corner of my eye, I saw her take off her backpack and settle down at a corner table near the window.

"Hey, beer or Coke?" I asked.

"They don't have water?"

"Yeah. Water then?"

"Actually…maybe a beer."

I shook my head. The girl was a walking question mark even when it was about something simple. I turned back to the guy behind the counter, who didn't seem in the mood to wait. Soon afterward, I grabbed the tray with our drinks and the crepes off the counter and carried it to our table.

"I could eat a baby elephant," she said, her eyes devouring our still-steaming dinner. Then she looked at me. "Thanks. For real. I haven't said that yet, have I? The truth is, I just felt like it would be a good idea to do something crazy for once in my life: catch a plane without thinking about it, you know. But then I got here, and… I was terrified. I'd have probably ended up spending the night in the subway station next to whatever kindly beggar would clear off a nook for me, waiting for the sun to rise so I could fly back to London and, dammit, I just can't stop talking. You say something."

"Be careful with the crepe. It's hot."

"No. I mean, say something about yourself. You know enough about me already. You know I left my boyfriend, you know I'm nuts, and you know I can't figure out how to use a ticket machine."

"Okay. What do you want to know?" I took a bite of my food.

"You never answered me the first time."

"I don't follow."

"You do though. You're lying. And you're bad at it. You're one of those people who looks the other way when you're lying. I like that. It could be useful. So tell me: Are you a stalker or a serial killer who preys on girls in subway stations?"

"No." I suppressed a smile.

"Good! See? You didn't look away."

"I suppose that's a relief to you."

"You better believe it. Now, let's find out if you're one of those guys who's into one-night stands and doesn't go for romance."

I grinned. It had been ages since I'd had so much fun. When was the last time I'd met someone who threw me for a loop like that, someone I couldn't take my eyes off of? Especially without having to do anything special, just being herself and blathering on and on like a caffeinated parrot.

"By romantic, you mean stroking people's feet?"

"Ugh. I mean, it does sound gross when you put it that way." She laughed and covered her mouth with her hand.

"Maybe *warming up someone's feet* sounds better, but it's the same thing, Ginger."

"You're fucking up one of the few nice memories I have of Dean, just so you know." She took a bite of her food and chewed thoughtfully. "Damn. That's delicious. This cheese is just...mmm."

She licked her lips slowly, not thinking, not trying to make an impression.

"Tell me about Dean," I said, forcing myself to look away from her lips.

3

Ginger

DEAN, DEAN, DEAN.

Where should I start? What should I say?

Rhys was waiting impatiently while I tried to decide if it was worth it to talk to a stranger about my ex. Rhys was a guy who was nothing like Dean, a guy who hadn't bothered combing his wild, dirty-blond hair, whose eyes were intense, piercing my skin instead of lingering on the surface. I don't know, I feared that a person like Rhys wouldn't understand my story, but even so, I wanted to share it, to let out all the things I felt in the hope that the knot I'd had in my throat for hours would finally disappear.

"It's a long story."

"Great. Your plane doesn't leave till the morning, right?"

"Very funny."

Rhys could tell I was struggling to jimmy the box where I kept everything pertaining to Dean, so he rested his forearms on the table and bent forward, making me feel closer to him. I noticed the almost invisible dusting of freckles around his nose. And his eyelashes. And the small imperfections in his skin. Those, too, were somehow attractive.

"Can I tell you a secret? I studied psychology."

"Come on! I don't believe you," I responded.

"Why not?"

"Let's see. You don't look like a psychologist; you look like a rock guitarist. Or a movie star who's trying to pass unnoticed. Or a melancholy writer who's come to Paris looking for inspiration."

"Okay, you caught me. I dropped out before my second year, but I still know how to listen." He gave me a patient, good-boy smile. It made me laugh.

"You're not an easy person to read. Anyone ever tell you that?"

"A lot. In a bad way."

"I think it's a good thing."

"You must be the first."

"Great. So, getting back to the *Dean Files*...that's what we'll call it, okay? Where should I start? We've known each other forever. Since we were kids."

"Interesting." He took a sip from his bottle of beer.

"We went to private school in the center of town, and our parents are really close, so we also saw each other outside of class. Then we got older, went to another private school, started going out, and that probably explains why we decided to attend the same university, and..."

"So you're like Siamese twins."

"What? No! Of course not!"

"Can I ask you something then?"

"Sure. Shoot."

As he stared at me, I noticed the blue points in his gray eyes, like brushstrokes of light in an ashen sky.

"This trip…all this nonsense about catching a plane without thinking…is this the first time you've ever done anything totally on your own? Without Dean, I mean."

"Well…I…I mean, I do a lot of things on my own. I paint my nails. I go to the bookstore; I love doing that…" I sighed, defeated. "Fine. You got me. It's the first time I've done anything without him. And I think that's why I'm so scared and why I feel so lost. But I had to do it. It doesn't even make sense."

"It does though."

His voice was hoarse. Sincere. I was grateful as I took another bite of my crepe, enjoying the melted cheese and sauteed mushrooms. He was distracted as he chewed, and his knee struck mine once in a while, moving to the rhythm of a song coming from a radio on the counter. Something in French. Slow, pretty, soft.

"Where'd you learn French?" I asked.

"I don't speak French. I can get by. Same with German and Spanish. You live somewhere, you wind up picking it up. But don't change the subject. We were talking about the *Dean Files*, and you didn't finish. Why'd you leave him?"

I stirred uncomfortably in my chair. "Let's just say after five years together, Dean apparently wants some time for himself, to have new experiences in the year and a half we have left of school, before he settles down or whatever. Honestly, I feel cheated."

"Cheated?"

"Yeah. Just think: it's like if you buy a gorgeous sweater, bottle green or that mustard yellow everyone's wearing this year…"

"Where are you going with this?"

"Imagine the salesgirl is like, *Oh, it looks perfect on you,* and you save for it for months and months. You wear it, you're like, *Wonderful*, and then you put it in the washer, and it comes out all covered in little balls of fuzz."

"That's quite an image, Ginger."

"I just wasted all that time."

"I don't believe in wasted time."

I took a deep breath. He got up to break the silence. As I finished my last bite, I watched him at the counter paying and ordering two more beers. I didn't even bother offering him any money. I was still thinking of that damned raggedy sweater. When Rhys motioned for us to go outside, I followed him. I followed him like it was the most natural thing in the world, taking the bottle of beer he offered me and walking along the Seine toward the bright lights of the Eiffel Tower. We were two strangers in the middle of the city under a dark winter sky, strolling as if we had all the time in the world. I liked it. I felt good.

"Weren't you ever tempted to do the same as him?" he said, picking up where we'd left off. "You never wanted to have new experiences? You thought you'd just, what, finish college, marry Dean, have kids, and that's that? I'm not judging you. I'm just wondering."

"When you put it that way, it sounds boring."

"Those are your words, not mine."

"I don't know. I guess. I'm a simple person."

"You don't seem simple to me at all."

He turned and walked backward. It looked funny. I laughed and took a sip of beer.

"What kind of person am I, then, Rhys?"

I could tell he was thinking. I could feel it.

"Contradictory. Sweet. Clever."

"Anything else?"

"Yeah. Complicated."

I almost savored that word. No one had ever thought of me that way. It was probably the last word my friends or family would use to describe me, and I was surprised it struck me so much. My eyes stung.

"Thanks, Rhys," I whispered.

"Hey, what's up? Are you crying? Shit…"

He set our beers on the ground and grabbed my shoulders. It was the first time he'd really touched me, and his hands felt firm on my green army jacket as his fingers squeezed softly and he crouched down to my height and looked me in the eye, and I stopped running from him.

"Sorry. You must think I'm crazy."

"No." He slid a thumb over my right cheek and wiped away the tears. "You want to know what I actually think of you?" We were very close, and his other hand was still on my shoulder. Our breath was turning to vapor in the cold and mingling with the darkness. "I think you want a lot more than you know. I think you're the kind who says they just want one piece of candy, but you really want to close the shop down and grab handfuls of everything you want and throw it all up in the air."

I laughed despite my tears. It sounded so stupid, so childish, but there was so much truth in his words. We looked at each other in the silence. Intensely. Intimately. I blew my nose. Nothing could have been less attractive, but it didn't bother Rhys.

"I guess you're the type to be happy with just one piece?"

"No." He smiled, a dangerous sort of smile, wry, the kind that burns into your memory forever. "I robbed the shop a long time ago, and I took everything I found there."

"This is nice. You not knowing me, I mean."

"Yeah." He took a breath. So close...

Then he looked away, helped me take my backpack off, and threw it over his shoulders without explanation before bending over to retrieve our beers and passing me mine. He walked, I followed him, and I asked myself how long it had been now since our paths crossed for the first time. Two hours? Maybe. Maybe less. And I thought of something I'd heard of so many times and that I never thought had anything to do with me. How you could *know a person*, supposedly, even when you barely knew a thing about them. What other way was there to explain something so strange, so magical, and so unexpected? Behind him, I tried to catch certain details: the way the damp wind blew his hair all over, the sharp masculine outline of his features, the way his threadbare jeans hung off his hips, or his long steps, hard for me to keep up with even if he seemed to be just ambling.

He turned and caught me looking, and I blushed.

"What time's your plane leave?"

"Eleven thirty tomorrow morning."

Ten minutes later, we were in front of the Eiffel Tower, which stood just past the river that cut through the city. I leaned my elbows on the wall in front of me and exhaled, satisfied. I was here; I was in Paris. A few hours before, I'd been crying into my pillow, regretful, and now I was here contemplating one of the most famous monuments in the world with a guy with gray eyes and a mysterious smile who had effortlessly managed to make me start to forget Dean. Or at least to make me able to think of him without feeling sorrow.

It was the most wonderful madness I'd ever known.

"You know the Nazis almost destroyed it?"

"I heard that," I said, not looking away.

"It was in August of 1944. The Allied troops were approaching, and Hitler knew they would lose the city. So he ordered it destroyed. He and Choltitz came up with this complex plan to demolish it, but fortunately, the Swedish ambassador intervened. Imagine. And here we are now."

We looked at each other and smiled.

4

Rhys

THAT WAS THE PROBLEM—I couldn't stop looking at her.

I couldn't, and I knew that soon I'd have to. And weird as it seems, I think that was what I liked the most. How ephemeral the moment was, Ginger and me under the moon, which cast a reflection on the gleaming water, showered by the glimmering lights of the city. Talking. Getting to know each other. Observing each other. Touching without touching.

I'd never met anyone who shared so much with me and was so transparent, so ready to open up to me without expecting anything in return. And it made me want to know her better. I looked at her from the corner of my eye as she took the last sip of her beer. The wind was tossing the strands of hair that had come loose from her ponytail. Her eyes were still swollen. She must have cried the whole flight. I asked myself what she'd be doing in a few days. What I'd be doing. What we'd be doing.

"Is this your favorite place in Paris?"

"No. I like Montmartre. But I wanted this to be the image you held on to, I don't know why. It's simple. A memory. You can't ask for more with less than twenty-four hours in the city. Or wait—I'm trying to think of how to make it better."

"I doubt that's possible."

"You'll see."

I finished my beer and put my bottle down next to hers before looking for a song on my phone and turning up the volume. I set it down on the wall as the first chords of "Je T'aime…Moi Non Plus" began to play.

I reached out toward her. "Here, dance with me."

"Are you crazy?" She looked around. I didn't know if her cheeks were red from the wind or from embarrassment, but she looked unsettled. A couple passed us, and some tourists who didn't pay us any mind.

"Even if someone notices us acting stupid, they'll forget it five minutes later, but you'll remember it for the rest of your life. And just think, you'll never see me again."

She looked wary as she stepped forward and took my hand. Her fingers were soft and cold. I squeezed them and pulled her close to me, resting my hand on her waist. She looked at me and laughed shyly as we started dancing, enveloped in the voices of Serge Gainsbourg and Jane Birkin.

"Why'd you choose this song?"

"I can't tell you. I'd scare you off."

"Rhys…" I liked how she said my name, the way the final *s* slipped through her lips, which puckered as she heard the moaning of the melody.

"Because this song is like making love."

Now she really was blushing, but she didn't look away. Her

eyelashes were long and dark; her eyes were staring straight into mine. Like embers. I pulled her closer. I had no idea what I was doing. When I decided to put the song on, I disconnected. All I knew was that I wanted the memory of those notes to belong to this stranger named Ginger, and maybe in ten or fifteen years, I could look back and remember the moment with joy. Tell someone else about it, maybe. *I met this girl who was lost one time in Paris, and on the spur of the moment, we danced together.* One of those incidents you collect in the course of your life.

But it wouldn't be like that. Even if I didn't know it yet.

Ginger wouldn't be just another story.

I hummed to the tune of the song.

"I don't understand. What does it mean?" she asks.

I leaned closer until I touched her ear with my lips. Ginger shuddered when I translated a few sentences for her. The words floated around us: hips, wave, naked island, I love you, you come and go...

I went on whispering the lyrics. Maybe because it was one of the most sensual songs ever written. Or because it was romantic. Special. Or just for her, for that girl. She was different. Unique. I guess that's why the moment felt more intimate than so many other nights I had spent in bed caressing another person's body, another person's skin. I didn't need to touch Ginger to feel her on my fingertips, as if we were reaching through each other's clothes, through each other's skin. Turning the present to a memory.

When the song ended, we parted slowly, but her hands remained around my neck, her lips a few inches from mine.

"How many girls have you done this with?"

"You want me to tell you that you're the only one?"

"Yeah. That's what I want."

"Just with you."

"I changed my mind. Tell me the truth."

"Just with you," I repeated.

"I don't know you."

"Ginger, Ginger…" I laughed, reached behind my neck to grab her hands, and held them as we studied each other in silence. Then I cocked my head to one side. "I think I know what your problem is. You think too much. You think all the fucking time. You're doing it now, aren't you? I can see the smoke coming out of your ears."

"I can't help it."

"Wait. Let's try something."

Before she could put up a fight, I told her to turn toward the Eiffel Tower and just look at it without thinking. I stood behind her. I surrounded her petite body with my arms and rested my hands atop hers on the low wall.

"Just look. Are you doing it? Are you looking at the lights, the way the moon reflects off the water like a mirror, the way the cold makes your skin swell? Do you feel the breeze on your skin? Do you feel me? Enjoy it all. The crisp sounds of the wind. My chest against your back. The mist escaping your lips. You can even touch it if you like." She laughed and reached out into the nothing. Then she turned.

We were together then, me in front of her. And I wanted to kiss her. Ginger. Her lips were flushed from the cold.

"I was right. You wouldn't answer, but I hit the nail on the head. You're a one-night stand kind of guy. Fess up. You're too good at this."

"Guilty as charged."

"The thing is…"

"Nothing's going to happen." I was being serious.

"Okay."

"Okay then."

"You up for a walk?"

I nodded, smiled, and stepped away, heading down the street the opposite way we'd come. We walked. And talked. And went on walking. And kept talking and had no idea where we were going. Our destination didn't matter, even if we did cross a few bridges and Ginger stopped on them, needing to think. She chatted away, looked all around, and told me more details about her relationship with Dean, the years they'd spent together and the plans that no longer existed.

"What will you miss most about him?"

"Mmm…our routine?" She bit her lower lip, reticent. "Yeah, that, I guess. Our everyday lives. Him just being there every step of the way, from early morning until sundown."

I leaned back against the wall of the bridge and crossed my arms, grinning and watching her, I don't know for how long. "How is it possible he doesn't miss listening to you?"

"Are you sucking up to me?" She scowled. Angry. Or cautious?

"No. I'm being serious."

"You're not funny, Rhys."

"Good. I wasn't trying to be."

She sighed. Confused. As if she couldn't believe what I was saying was true. But it was. It was the first thing I thought when she told me her story, that if I'd gone out with her for five years, with the girl who made me smile every time she spoke, I'd miss her voice, its soft, firm presence that never went away. I'd never met a person who had so much to say and whom I wanted so much to listen to.

"Where are we? We got off track."

I shook my head and looked up. "I live there. In that gray building. On the corner."

5

Ginger

"YOU WANT TO COME UP? And just to cut you off before you start making excuses, I'm not asking you if you want to go to bed with me."

Funny enough, I didn't feel that way. And yet I was excited. I looked up at the outline of his building beneath the streetlamp while he waited for a reply.

"Honestly… I've been in need of a bathroom for a while now, but I didn't want to ruin the magic of the moment. You know, a walk at night through Paris and all…"

He laughed and shook his head. "Come on. You need some rest."

He opened the door, and we took a narrow stairway up to the top floor. He put the key in the lock and invited me in, apologizing for the sorry state of the place and its small size. It was an attic studio with a mattress on the floor and the kitchen on the other side of the room. I say *kitchen*; what I mean is a hot plate on a wooden counter someone had tried unsuccessfully to sand down and varnish. The walls were bare except for a few spots of damp, and exposed beams crisscrossed the ceiling. Rhys pointed to the door of the bathroom after leaving my backpack on a chair with threadbare upholstery.

"It flushes weird," he warned me.

"I'll keep that in mind." I went in.

I washed my hands and face before coming back out. When I did, Rhys was in the kitchen area boiling a pot of water. Glancing over, he opened a creaky cabinet.

"You in the mood for some noodles? I didn't get full."

"Sure. Nothing spicy though."

"Nothing spicy. Got it."

I walked over beside him and stood there shoulder to shoulder, watching the noodles go limp as he stirred them in the pot.

"What are you thinking?"

"Just how weird this all is," I said. "Don't you think? I mean, I was in London in my room a few hours ago. And now I'm in the apartment of some guy I just met in Paris. But the weirdest thing is..."

I wasn't sure if I should say it. He turned, and I saw his eyes were lighter than I'd thought at first: the color of icicles. And that made me think of winter.

"Spit it out. What's the weirdest thing?"

"I don't even feel uncomfortable."

"Just like home, huh?"

"I'm serious, Rhys. I feel like I've known you a long time, but I don't actually know anything about you. We haven't even told each other the basics, the stuff you have to type in when you open an account on a dating app. Hey—don't look at me like that." I slapped his arm when I saw his mischievous smile. "That's not what I meant. It's just weird that we've been talking for hours, and we don't even know how old each other is or what each other does for a living. Do you have a job? Are you studying? What are you doing in Paris?"

He reached up to grab bowls off the upper shelf, and his white shirt rose up a few inches. I looked away quickly, almost wishing he'd just kept his jacket on.

"That's what I like the most."

"What? Not knowing?"

"Yeah. That you didn't just come out and ask me that stuff. If the first things you'd wanted to know about me had been my job and my age, we probably wouldn't be here."

"No. Right. It was better for me to ask if you were a player. How magical." We laughed. Then I thought of something. "Have you ever read *The Little Prince*?"

"No, why?"

"It's my favorite book. It was even when I was little, before I could understand it. I have a copy full of underlines, marks, and notes in the margins. I reread it all the time. One of my favorite parts is where he's talking about adults and how they like numbers, and he says: *When you tell them that you have made a new friend, they never ask you any questions about essential matters. They never say to you, 'What does his voice sound like? What games does he love best? Does he collect butterflies?' Instead, they demand: 'How old is he? How many brothers has he? How much does he weigh? How much money does his father make?' Only from these figures do they think they have learned anything about him.*"

"Interesting," he whispered, serving the noodles and taking two beers from the fridge. He walked off to the mattress on the floor and set his bowl on his lap. Then he took a sip of his beer.

"You eat in bed?"

"Where else?"

I sat down in front of him.

"You can take off your shoes."

I did it because my feet were killing me after all those hours walking. I crossed my legs and picked up my bowl. I twirled the noodles around my chopsticks as we ate, looking up occasionally and laughing for no reason. None of it made any sense, and at the same time, it meant so much... I still had beer left over when I was done eating. I took little sips and looked around, memorizing every detail. The piles of books. The stacks of records on a table full of cables and electronics. The half-dead plant on the kitchen windowsill.

"You know what I liked most about tonight?"

"You'll break my heart if you don't say me," he joked.

"You're part of it... Have you ever had the feeling that all the people who know you think you're someone else? I mean, maybe that's my fault. Sometimes it's like time sets a pattern for you and you can't change it. Like everyone thinks I'm so understanding. *Oh, tell Ginger; she'll get it. Ginger won't get upset.* And I don't get it. And I do get upset. But I've spent so many years pretending to be the person others say I am, the girl who never loses her grip, who always thinks of others first... I've been doing that so long that I don't know where the real Ginger is. Maybe I killed her. Maybe she'd dead and buried. What do you think, Rhys? Because I'm scared to think about it."

I don't know where all that came from, and all of a sudden. I just know I was thinking that since Rhys didn't know me from Adam, it meant I could be myself in a way I didn't allow myself to be with the people who had gotten used to the fake, stick-on Ginger, who never said what she thought, who always put other people first, the good girl who was never selfish.

"She's not dead. She's here, with me."

"I think I'm going to cry again, Rhys."

"No, please. Shit. Don't cry."

"Like, how's it possible I can tell you this and not my sister or my friends? It should be just the opposite. It should be harder with a stranger. And you still haven't told me anything about yourself, and I've been talking all night without stopping."

"If that bothers you, I'll tell you something about myself."

"Something you can't tell anyone else?"

"Okay." His expression changed. He seemed nervous. "My dad. I haven't talked to him for more than a year. Lots of people know that, basically all my friends do. But they think I hate him. That we had a fight over something dumb. But that's not true. He's always been the person I love most; it's just that something happened…and we argued…and we said stuff neither of us can forget. We haven't seen each other since last Christmas."

His eyes were glowing as I bent over—I don't know why; it just came from inside me, spontaneously—and hugged him, so tight that I almost fell on top of him. Rhys held me in his arms. I was wrong when I first met him: it wasn't his gum that smelled of mint; it was his hair. His shampoo. The smell surrounded me as I sank my nose into his hair.

We separated slowly until our noses were touching, and he held my hand in his. The hours were slipping by.

"Look, to hell with all this sad stuff; let's talk about something else. What do you do?"

He smiled, and his look was sweet and tender like a caress. "I'm a DJ and a composer. I make electronic music."

"You're fucking with me."

"Why do you say that?"

"I don't know; I just didn't expect that. It's like if you told me you were a beekeeper or something. I didn't imagine you listening to...that kind of music."

"I like all kinds of music."

He got up and turned on his stereo. A song began to play, sung by one of those women whose voice feels like an embrace. Soft. Low. Rhys danced his way back to the bed. He looked silly. He didn't care. I laughed.

"So that's how you make your living? How old are you?"

"Now this does feel like a date."

"Stop joking. I want to know."

"Make a living, not really. I get by. Basically I travel, and then I stay a while in whatever city offers me opportunities. Right now I've got a gig at a club in Belleville for two months. After that, we'll see." He shrugged. "And I'm twenty-six. I hope that satisfies your curiosity, Ginger Snap."

"No, dammit! Don't you dare!"

"What, Ginger Snap? I like that. Ginger snaps are my favorite. You are literally one of my secret vices," he confessed.

"I hate you right now."

"I like you every bit as much as I did before."

"You're one of those people who can't take anything seriously."

"Maybe. You'll have to find out."

I sighed when I saw he was just playing along.

"Okay, your turn. Now that we've gotten all serious, what's your dream?"

"My dream?"

"Or your job then?"

"Right. You're one of those idealists who thinks I should be living my dream. I'm sorry to disappoint you. I don't have one of those wild fantasies I have to fight to make come true. I'm studying marketing and business management. Same as Dean."

"Were you two separated at birth?"

"Don't start. It's simpler than that. My father is the owner of one of the biggest cabinet companies in Britain. He does all types of designs and materials…"

"Are you trying to sell me some?"

I laughed and took a sip of beer. "I'm trying to explain why I'm studying business. The idea of running a company, I don't know, it's always seemed cool to me."

"What about Dean?"

"I told you, our parents are friends. He was always going to work in the family business when school was over."

His eyebrows furrowed. Just for a second, but I saw it, the doubt, the urge to contradict me. Then he smiled the same old smile again, the one that made me breathless if I looked at it too long. He finished off his beer and left the bottle on the floor next to our dishes. Then he lay back on the bed, bent his arm behind his neck, and looked up coolly.

"How old are you, Ginger?"

"Twenty-one. As of last month."

He turned serious, and I felt his fingers wrap around my wrist and pull me gently toward him. I didn't stop him. I lay there next to him, my head resting on his pillow. On the sloping wall of the attic was a round wooden window like a porthole on a ship. It was right above us, and the moon was looking at us through the glass. I shivered. I knew this was a significant moment, but I still didn't know why. I took a deep breath. *One, two, three.* The music was floating in the background. His hand was on top of mine. He'd let my wrist go and was tracing circles on my skin with his thumb and following the lines of my veins.

He turned off the lights.

I was sinking down into his mattress.

Everything else, the whole outside world, suddenly ceased to matter. Because he was there. I was. We were. And a French song I couldn't understand. And a window to the sky. And the feeling of ease, of being able to breathe. Excitement.

I closed my eyes and focused on his fingertip as it traveled over my skin.

"Rhys." I whispered in the darkness.

"Yeah." He took a deep breath.

"What I'm about to say is going to sound crazy, and I know it doesn't make sense, we only met each other a few hours ago, but I promise you I'll remember you. And even many years from now, I'll still remember you and this night that happened out of nowhere."

I didn't see him smile, but I felt it.

"Okay. I hope that when you think of me in that moment,

you've made all your dreams come true." He covered my mouth with his hand. "Don't laugh, dammit. I'm being serious, Ginger. I'm trying to be deep, like one of those intellectuals who spouts stupid shit that sounds smart because of who it's coming from."

"Sorry, you're right."

"Damn straight I am. A day will come when you won't feel like you have to hide everything in front of people, you know? You'll be able to just be yourself. It sounds easy, but it's actually like utopia. I know the people around you push you to be different, but just tell yourself they're numbers, like you said about the Little Prince, and they're down on earth, not up where we are."

"Where are we?"

He looked out the window. "Us? On the moon."

"I like how that sounds."

"It's the truth. Aren't you feeling it right now?"

"Yeah," I admitted. "I feel like I'm on the moon..."

"Get some sleep, Ginger Snap."

"I hate you, Rhys."

"Good night."

"Good night."

6

Rhys

I LOOKED AT HER AS the sun rose, glowing through the window, brightening her face. That was the thing I liked most about the apartment I'd called home those past two months—the one I'd go on calling home until I had to pack my bags again, because the idea of remaining still while the world turned terrified me.

But not in this moment.

In this moment, I wanted to stay for a long time next to Ginger's warm body, while she was curled up next to me, hands clutching my T-shirt as if she feared I would escape in the middle of the night. I was nervous. I was feeling…things since I met her in front of the ticket machine in the subway station. Good things. Tenderness. Curiosity. Desire.

Her nose was roundish and slightly broad, her lips were half-open, and her hair tie had fallen out, letting her brown hair spread and tangle. She was like that too, I thought, tangled up inside. Complicated. She had cried when I told her that, but they weren't tears of sorrow. And I thought I was starting to understand why. Probably I was the first person who'd ever thought Ginger wasn't as simple as she seemed at first sight. That she wasn't just the girl with an eternal smile who always tried hard to make everyone else happy. To the contrary, she was someone who swallowed her fears. Who let her wishes pile up. Who struggled to see herself when she looked in the mirror.

And I adored her. Tangled up as she was.

But she had to take her road, and I had to take mine.

I moved slowly, trying not to wake her, but in vain. As soon as I was a few inches away, she blinked and opened her eyes, almost panicked.

"What time is it?" She sounded like a mewling cat.

"It's eight. You can stay a few more minutes."

I got all the way up and smiled as I saw her curl into a ball. I turned on the coffeepot and got into the shower. When I came out with a towel around my waist, she was sitting up in bed, hair a mess, looking at my bare torso. *Fuck. Fuck.* I wanted her. Bad. I took a deep breath, thinking if only she hadn't just broken up with that dumbass, if only she wasn't about to hop a plane to another country, if only we had met at another moment, another place, another time...

"The coffee's almost ready. You want a shower?"

"Do I have time?"

I nodded.

"Okay then."

"You have clothes in that bag?"

"Just underwear. And crackers."

"Always thinking ahead, I see."

I opened the small closet where I kept all my clothes, grabbed my smallest sweatshirt, and tossed it to her. She looked doubtful.

"I can't give it back to you."

"I already figured that."

"Okay. Thanks, Rhys."

She disappeared into the bathroom. I heard the pipes banging as she turned on the hot water. I wished I was in there with her. I wished…I don't know…that I could lick her skin. Kiss her. Know what she tasted like. I shook my head. That was crazy talk.

I buttoned my jeans and walked barefoot to the kitchen. I poured two coffees with milk and dug out a chocolate croissant left over from the day before in case she wanted to eat something before leaving. She emerged from the shower a little later in the same jeans as yesterday and my sweatshirt.

"I don't think I thanked you for everything…"

"You did," I cut her off. "Coffee?"

She looked at me cheerfully and nodded. The silence was comfortable as we ate breakfast together, and even later, when we got on the bus. I decided to go with her to the airport. Surrounded by people coming and going, by loud voices over the PA, up to the security checkpoint, I began to realize how real this was. I was there, saying goodbye to a girl I'd just met…and I had a knot in my throat, and I didn't want to think about it.

I handed her backpack to her, and she slung it over her shoulder.

She had a hard time looking up from the floor. "I guess this is goodbye."

"Yeah." I sure as hell didn't want it to be though.

Our eyes stared into each other's so long that the rest of the world seemed to become a blur. I tried to sharpen my idea of her. She was a normal girl. Just a normal girl, I tried to tell myself to convince myself she wasn't the most beautiful, funniest, craziest girl I'd ever met, the most…I don't know, just *the most*, period. It's not that we'd done anything crazy special together. I hadn't had incredible sex with her; she wasn't some guru who'd introduced me to a new religion that had brought me inner peace. But I didn't care. For me, she was *different* from the first moment I looked at her, and that was enough. I couldn't help but notice how my heart was pounding rhythmically like a song crying out to be written.

Fuck it. Fuck it all.

I wanted to kiss her. I was going to kiss her.

"Rhys…" she whispered. Barely.

"What?" I swallowed.

"Thanks for last night."

"Stop saying that."

"It's what I feel."

"Goddammit, Ginger."

"I need to go."

"I wish you didn't."

"Yeah." She waited a moment. "It's been fun."

"Fun," I repeated, ill at ease.

Fuck that. It had been real. Authentic.

I was tense, but I didn't know what to say.

And then it was like words weren't needed, because she stood on her tiptoes, hugged me like an old friend saying goodbye, and kissed me softly on the cheek before pulling away brusquely.

"Bye, Rhys."

"Take care."

She nodded, turned, and walked into security. I probably should have turned around then and walked off until I vanished into the crowd. But I didn't. I stayed there, hands in my pockets, contemplating her matted hair—I hadn't had a decent brush to offer her that morning. My sweatshirt was wrinkled and hanging loose over her back.

Ginger had already laid her backpack on the conveyor belt when she turned back toward me. She seemed surprised that I was still there. And then I knew it. I knew she was going to do something crazy. I almost smiled as she started shouting at the other passengers asking if anyone had a pen.

I struggled not to laugh.

People watched her squeeze out back through the line, dodging those waiting and running toward me with a pen in her hand. She was so nervous...so gorgeous.

"I know you must think I'm nuts, but I don't know... I don't know, Rhys, just...if you ever get bored or you're looking out that window of yours into the sky and you can't figure out anything else to do, write me."

As she babbled those words, she grabbed my hand and wrote out a series of letters I soon figured out was her email. Again, I wanted to kiss her, but instead, I just stared. She walked off again and vanished from my line of sight, crossing through the scanner and into the airport.

I don't know how many times I've asked myself what would have happened if I'd kissed her that day. What would our lives have been like? Would anything have changed? Yes, but that *yes* was filled with unknowns that would never stop pursuing me. Or her. Two roads came together, hers and mine, and even if they weren't meant to run side by side there in Paris, where we were then, they were still the beginning of a far longer path: a detour to the moon.

7

Ginger

I SAT THERE AND WATCHED the planes waiting to take off on the runway, thinking to myself, *I should be sad*. I should have been missing Dean, trying to figure out why he'd left me and what was going to become of my life from then on. But I wasn't. All I could think about was memorizing every detail of Rhys that I'd learned in those few hours. I could recall every touch and the gravelly tone in his voice. The way he looked at me. The way the corners of his eyes crinkled when he laughed. The lightness in my stomach when his thumb followed the course of my veins, as if he were feeling my pulse. And the moon I could see from his window. And us on the moon.

Can you fall in love with a person after just a few hours?

Can you forget them a few hours later?

8

From: Rhys Baker
To: Ginger Davies
Subject: [No subject]

I don't really know where to start. I just wanted to see how things were going and let you know the ink in the pen you used was permanent. It took days to disappear. I was all careful on the bus in case it blurred or something, but no need to worry about that. I guess I should say semipermanent, but either way, you chose a good one.

Well, I hope you're good, Ginger Snap.

From: Ginger Davies
To: Rhys Baker
Subject: I'm not crazy

Okay, so it's been four days since I left, and I guess I can admit I didn't think you'd write me. I mean, I'd get it, after seeing me run at you with a marker in my hand like a knife-wielding psycho from the movies. But I don't know, I just realized then that it had been so long since I'd met anyone I felt so good with and I was sad when I thought we'd never learn any more about each other. And I thought about all the things I didn't have time to ask you, all the things we didn't talk about, and you know, the rest is history. Do you think I'm spinning out?

P.S. I'll ignore you calling me Ginger Snap.

From: Rhys Baker
To: Ginger Davies
Subject: You're not crazy

You're not spinning out. We can talk sometimes. Be friends. Don't leave me hanging: What were those questions you wanted to ask me?

BTW, did you ever see Dean again? How are you handling it?

From: Ginger Davies
To: Rhys Baker
Subject: RE: You're not crazy

Yeah, I saw him. Didn't I tell you? We're in all the same classes except for two electives *and* we've been assigned to a project together in one of them. Brilliant, right? It's going to be hell. At least I'm in the dorms, in my own room, safe and far from my parents.

You can already imagine how they reacted to the breakup. Bad. At first, at least. Then my father surprised me, like, "Most men want to have a little fun before they settle down." You know what, Rhys? I think you'd be proud of me. In any other moment, I'd have just swallowed my anger, but this time, I didn't. I remembered what we'd talked about, how it's so hard to be yourself, and I wish you could have seen my dad's face when I started yelling at him about how stupid and sexist what he said was. He was freaking out.

I know I write too much, the same way I talk too much.

As far as questions, I don't know... Just everything. I need to know everything about you, Rhys.

From: Rhys Baker
To: Ginger Davies
Subject: RE: RE: You're not crazy

You're right. I'm proud of you. And you're also right about what he said. It was stupid. You know what I think? *You* need to have fun and experiment and go on a million adventures. Did that ever occur to you? I'm going to ask you a question. Here goes (I can almost imagine you blushing): How many guys have you slept with? Or girls?

From: Ginger Davies
To: Rhys Baker
Subject: You're an idiot

I didn't blush and you're an idiot, just so you know. Now that we've got the important stuff out of the way, I may as well say yes, just as you guessed, I've only been with Dean. What did you expect? I started going out with him when I was sixteen. I've never even kissed another guy. There. I said it. And worst of all, I don't know if I could. I mean, I could. But I couldn't. You know what I mean?

From: Rhys Baker
To: Ginger Davies
Subject: RE: You're an idiot

I admit it. I'm an idiot. And no, I don't know what you mean, and I couldn't unless someone invented a machine for translating feelings that don't make sense. What does that "But I couldn't" of yours mean? Because I don't get it. You're very much on the earth right now.

From: Ginger Davies
To: Rhys Baker
Subject: RE: RE: You're an idiot

I don't get what you mean by "You're very much on the earth right now."

As far as the other thing… I don't know, Rhys. Like I want to, okay? I do want to experience freedom… Do you ever just want to be someone you're not? I do. For example, I'd like to not be embarrassed by my body. I mean, I'm not embarrassed; I'm like…shy. Don't laugh. I know you're laughing. I'm thinking about girls who go around without a bra on and don't care, or those people you see in Europe sunbathing without a top. Or who wear some piece of clothing they love, even if it doesn't look that great on them. Isn't that wonderful? Doing whatever you feel like without thinking twice; it must be so liberating.

As far as going out with other people, I don't know...

What's your story? Do you date or whatever? I never asked.

Is there someone special in your life?

From: Rhys Baker
To: Ginger Davies
Subject: RE: RE: RE: You're an idiot

No, there's no one special. I do go out though. I know chicks; we have fun together. What's wrong with that? You should give it a shot, Ginger. You don't have to spend your whole life waiting for Dean to get bored and come back.

Why can't you be the type of girl you were talking about?

I for one fully support not wearing a bra.

Not to mention going topless. Don't stop yourself.

From: Ginger Davies
To: Rhys Baker
Subject: Let's change the subject

Look, maybe it's best to put aside the liberation of my breasts and my nonexistent sex life. Especially since yours must be way more interesting. Whatever. Right now I should be studying for this week's exam, but I decided I'd rather write you. I have a confession to make: I googled "DJ and electronic music composer," and I know now what all those gadgets you had on your table in that attic were. How did you get into that?

From: Rhys Baker
To: Ginger Davies
Subject: RE: Let's change the subject

You honestly don't want to go on talking about your sex life and liberating your breasts? I don't find the subject uncomfortable. I mean, boobs are boobs. And sex is sex. They should teach us about it differently in school, show us that it's something normal. Maybe that way, girls like you wouldn't blush when they said the word *fuck*. Before you chew me out, I'm not making fun of you, Ginger. It's just an observation. I like imagining a parallel reality where you adore every part of your body and enjoy it.

At least tell me you masturbate.

Denying yourself that is a sin.

At this point you're probably banging on your computer screen, so I'll answer your question: I ended up doing electronic music by accident. I was lost at the time and didn't know what to do with my life. I'm talking about a year ago. I met a friend of a friend who was into it and let me try. And I just loved it. I don't know. I just disconnect from everything, and all I'm paying attention to is the music; that's all there is. I'm going to tell you a secret: it's not my favorite kind of music, but it's the one kind I know how to make. And when you're doing it, it's yours every step of the way, from the composition to the mixing to the recording. I like that. I don't know why.

What kind of music are you into?

From: Ginger Davies
To: Rhys Baker
Subject: RE: RE: Let's change the subject

One thing at a time. Yes, Rhys, I masturbate, even if I can't believe you asked me that. You can rest easy; I know what I'm doing and I'm quite satisfied in that regard. I hope you're not smiling stupidly while you read this. That's not what I wanted to write about though. I mean, it is, but it isn't. I apologize in advance, but you're going to have to get used to me saying things like *It is, but it isn't*, because lots of things are just like that, contradictory. What I was trying to tell you the other day was that it would be weird for me to sleep with a guy who wasn't Dean, because I've never done it before and it would mean breaking with everything I've ever known. But I would like to know what it feels like to be with another person.

You and my sister would get along well. You think the same way, basically. Her name's Donna; she's three years older than me. She finished college last year, so that means everything's kind of come at me all at once: she's not in the dorm anymore, Dean's off doing his thing, and I don't know if the other girls in my year like me. They look at me weird when I talk so much. I get it, of course. There's one who's nice though; Kate, she sits next to me in statistics. I don't even know why I'm telling you all this.

I like what you say about your job.

Honestly, I'm not very musical. Don't hate me. I mean, I know the major groups. I don't know what makes a song great or terrible though. I put on the radio sometimes, that's all. Why don't you send me some of your stuff? I'll probably like it.

From: Rhys Baker
To: Ginger Davies
Subject: Listen to your sister

Seriously now, I hear you when you say it's hard for you to imagine sleeping with another person after being with him so many years. I can't know what you feel, Ginger. I'm trying to cheer you up, but I've never been in a relationship for five years. I imagine you can't just erase that though.

Don't try and make me get all deep.

But listen to your sister. She sounds like the kind of smart girl who's always right about everything. Anyway, it's a good thing there's not much left of this school year. You should go out and try to meet more people like Kate.

Didn't you have friends before you broke up with Dean?

Does he not even try to stay in contact with you?

I can't believe you're just not into music. It's weird; I thought you'd be one of those girls who goes everywhere with her headphones on. I don't know why; it's just what I imagined. I'll have to show you the basics at some point. I apologize though: I'm not ready to send you one of my songs. Don't get mad. I will later, maybe, okay? I promise. When I have one I think you'll like.

From: Ginger Davies
To: Rhys Baker
Subject: This is unfair

What do you mean, maybe later? This is unfair. I know we barely know each other, a month has passed, and now I think back to that night in Paris, and it almost seems like it wasn't real. But still, I won't judge you. We're almost friends, right? Or trying to be friends if that sounds better to you. I know I'll like anything you do.

Send me a song, please, please, please.

From: Rhys Baker
To: Ginger Davies
Subject: RE: This is unfair

You didn't answer me about Dean…

From: Ginger Davies
To: Rhys Baker
Subject: RE: RE: This is unfair

You didn't send me a song…

From: Rhys Baker
To: Ginger Davies
Subject: RE: RE: RE: This is unfair

Are we really going to fight about this? I admit it, it sounds fucking crazy, but it feels weird not hearing from you for the past four days. Ginger, Ginger Snap, I'm working on something, I'll send it soon. Deal?

Say yes. I miss your messages.

Did you get your grades back yet?

From: Ginger Davies
To: Rhys Baker
Subject: RE: RE: RE: RE: This is unfair

Have you ever seen one of those cop shows where there's hostages and they bring in a negotiator to keep the guy from killing all the people he's got locked up in a supermarket? Because you're one of those. And that's cheating. I'm not saying I'm on the killer's side, but it's not fair for me to tell you things and you just listen like this was confession and don't give anything back.

Are we friends or not? Because friendship is reciprocal.

From: Rhys Baker
To: Ginger Davies
Subject: Friends 4ever

Yes, Ginger, we're friends.

And you're right, it's hard for me to talk about myself and I really like learning about you. I won't argue there. But I promise I'll try harder. So let's see. What can I tell you? Right now I'm at the airport. My plane leaves in three hours. I'm going to New

York for a month. I'm nervous. It's weird. I might see my mom. Maybe. I'm going because a friend got me a gig in a bar. I'll be filling in for someone. You know what? I feel strange leaving Paris. I've never had this feeling before.

I hope you're well. Look on the bright side: one day we might be shopping and wind up in a hostage situation. And you'll live, thanks to me being there.

From: Ginger Davies
To: Rhys Baker
Subject: RE: Friends 4ever

I like this subject line so much that I don't think I'll ever, ever change it. Yeah, we're friends. I admit it: it's weird for me to go too many days without hearing from you too. Strange, right? Getting so used to looking at my email in bed right before going to sleep every day and finding one of your messages there.

It's hard to imagine you in New York. I always have this idea of you walking the same streets in Paris we saw together, but I'm glad you'll get to see your mother. How long has it been? You seem a little sad, or am I just making things up? Ignore me. You know I've got that tendency.

I got an A on the exam. So I'm happy. As far as Dean and our friends, I could write a book about that. And I don't want to bore you.

From: Ginger Davies
To: Rhys Baker

Subject: RE: Friends 4ever

I forgot to ask: Why did you feel weird leaving Paris?

From: Rhys Baker
To: Ginger Davies
Subject: RE: RE: Friends 4ever

I've gotten used to seeing your emails too…

Yeah, you're right. I'm a little sad. I don't know if my writing shows it or if you just know me better than I thought possible, but traveling to America makes me feel nostalgic. I guess it's the thought that I could just rent a motorcycle, hit the road, and go home. To my real home. When I'm far away in Europe, I don't think so much about my family. It's almost like that ocean between us makes me feel secure. Does that make sense? Probably to you. But don't overthink it, Snaps.

Tell me all about Dean and your friends, please. I love reading your emails. And it's good for me at times like these, when I feel like this. I'm writing you from a tiny bedroom in an apartment I'm sharing with five people. I don't know if I can take it much longer. I like traveling the world and laying my head wherever, but once a few days pass, I need my space, my solitude, and having too many people around makes me feel like I'm drowning. I suppose you get that too.

As for Paris… I don't know…

When I left, I felt like I was forgetting something.

Don't try to figure out what that means, Ginger.

From: Ginger Davies
To: Rhys Baker
Subject: RE: RE: RE: Friends 4ever

Oh, Rhys, I can't stand thinking you're sad. And so far away! What I mean is, if I was there, we could see each other for a coffee, and I could cheer you up and make some dumb remark, the kind only you don't find embarrassing. I think I understand what you're telling me. You're there; it makes you feel closer to home. I'll bet you can't stop thinking about it. I don't know what to say to make you feel better, but I'll do what you say and tell you about Dean.

I had friends, but we always went out with the same group. And it's not like he just wanted to drop me; I had a hand in it too. It's no fun going out with your friends one night for a drink and having to watch your ex try to hook up with the waitress and even getting her number, you know? And that happened the first time I decided to go out. Look, I'm not one of those strong women who's all brave and can leave her boyfriend of five years, and then two weeks later it's like nothing ever happened. Now I'm starting to feel better though. I'm finding myself. Don't laugh. You were right. We *were* like Siamese twins; we did everything together. Maybe that's why it was so hard to get used to being without him. I mean, getting up every morning and reminding myself I didn't need to call to wake him up because he always shut off his alarm, or standing outside the door to his dorm waiting to walk to school with him and get a coffee from the corner shop where they make the best cappuccino in the world (you can't even imagine how good it is). Then there's the classes we share. Then there's our social life. I've had to cut the cord. But I feel better. Actually, you know what? I think I'm going to go to a party Kate invited me to next week. It'll do me some good.

Tell me how things are in New York.

From: Rhys Baker
To: Ginger Davies
Subject: RE: RE: RE: RE: Friends 4ever

Dean's an idiot. You don't have to be a genius to know how to use a little tact. I have no idea what it was you saw in him for so many years.

I'm glad to hear about the party. Have fun, Ginger. Go crazy. Throw on something you feel insanely sexy in, don't think about anything, dance, and talk to any stranger you come across (even if obviously he won't be as awesome as me). Be the girl you want to be. Dare.

I'm better now. I'm going to LA in a few days. I've got friends there. When you travel as much as I do, you end up with friends all over the world. I don't talk to them every day, obviously. We have a different kind of friendship. Anyway, I'll stay there awhile and see if I find work or something. Making it up as I go along has its benefits.

Before I leave, I'm going to see my mom. She's coming to New York next week. I didn't answer when you asked, but I haven't seen her in more than a year. Not since last Christmas, when I got into it with my dad. It wigs me out just thinking about it. But

I also don't know how to wriggle out of it. I feel like I've gotten into something, and there's no turning back.

Keep me up to date on your next steps, Ginger. And have fun.

9

Ginger

ALL MY CLOTHES WERE ON the bed. Dozens of garments I had tried and rejected, because none of them looked right on me. Or at least not *insanely sexy*, to use Rhys's term. And for once, I wanted to think that when I looked in the mirror. I wasn't trying to impress anyone. I just wanted to see myself looking like that.

I scowled as I looked at my dresses and opened my closet again. I put on some tight black pants with zippers on the side and a see-through top that showed off the dark lace bra I bought a week before on an impulse as I passed by a lingerie shop. I liked it because I'd never treated myself to anything like that when I was with Dean. It was nice to do something for myself. I threw on a pair of boots too. Then I took a deep breath.

I didn't look elegant, but I did look *insanely sexy*.

I smiled, trying to decide whether to pull my hair back or leave it down. I went for the second. Kate knocked at my door. I grabbed my bag and opened up.

She looked me up and down, smiling. "Man, you look amazing. Gorgeous!"

"Thanks. You too. Shall we?"

"Yeah. I parked right outside."

I followed her, and she brought me up to date about all the people who were going to the late-night party. It was outside of town, at a house with a big yard that belonged to a former student. Kate kept her eyes on the road.

"How are things with that friend of yours?"

Lately we sat beside each other in all our classes, so she knew all about Rhys and his emails. She was a nice girl, the kind who always saw the glass as half-full, and she didn't assume she knew who I was based on past experience. We both had made an effort to start from zero, as if we hadn't already passed each other in the hallways at school dozens of times that year.

"Rhys? He's good. He's in New York right now."

"That's not what I mean, Ginger. I'm asking, are you really not planning on telling him you have feelings for him? You talk every day. That has to leave a mark."

"Yeah, but it's not like that."

"What's it like then?" she asked.

"Okay, I do feel something for him, but I can't explain it. Our relationship is perfect like this, platonic, with our emails and each of us on a different side of the world. I don't know. It's nice. It's one of the nicest things I've ever had in my life, and I'm not about to screw it up, especially because there wouldn't be any point."

"Who knows? Maybe he would stop flitting around and move to London. He'll have to do it one day, right? Hit the brakes, I mean?"

"You don't know Rhys." I smiled and sighed.

I was starting to understand him, from one email to the next. But I still had the feeling, after three months of daily contact, that I'd only seen the tip of the iceberg. I didn't care though. I liked him. With problems or without, with love or without it. I couldn't explain to anyone else what we had, how hungry I was to reconnect with him through email when nighttime came, our closeness, how easy it was to talk about everything, the important stuff and nonsense too. Even intimate things I wasn't used to sharing. That meant Kate thought I was in love with him, and my sister did too. But they were wrong.

I was only in love with the young man I'd met in Paris. With a fleeting memory. Because that young man didn't exist. He was just a tiny piece of Rhys. I repeated that to myself every day under the covers, remembering the feel of his fingertips on my wrist, looking for my pulse, his caresses. Those hours together had been special, and I had the feeling they'd never return, and that I'd better keep them tucked away in my memory, where I could cherish them, let them out from time to time, polish them, savor them. And I asked myself if he would ever do the same.

"It's that house over there, with the lights in the garden."

"Jesus, it's huge. How many people are there?"

"More than I thought. Half the college maybe? There's barely even anywhere to park." Kate giggled.

I didn't remember the last time I'd gone out, and I felt something funny in my stomach when we crossed through the doorway and greeted a few people we knew. The Killers were playing loud, and all over there were people dancing, laughing, drinking, acting stupid. I smiled without thinking.

"There we go," Kate said, wrapping an arm around my shoulders, looking content. "It's about time you take your life back, isn't it, Ginger?"

"I think so." I sighed.

I hadn't tried yet. For three months, I'd taken refuge in my studies, Rhys's emails, and the library, where I looked for books as if they were drugs, because any distraction was welcome. Plus Dean had been going out, having fun, and enjoying himself the whole time. That didn't bother me; it was more the feeling that I was left behind. The whole time we'd been together, I had focused on him and him alone; he had been the axis my world spun around, and without him, the ground was crumbling beneath my feet. Maybe that was what was hardest: losing all the things Dean held together probably meant more than losing him. But now I was finding myself...

"Let's go grab a drink," I said.

"Sure. Look, that dude over there has a keg of beer." We walked over to the group around him. "Hey, you don't happen to have two extra cups?"

He lifted his brows and his friends laughed.

"Yeah, in exchange for your names. And a joke."

"A joke?" Kate frowned.

"Which of you is up for it?" he asked.

I could barely talk with all those strangers staring at me, but then I forgot the whole thing and stopped worrying about if I looked stupid or if I was falling victim to some new prank popular among college students.

"So there's two grains of sand that are walking through the

desert. And one says to the other, 'Hey, you know what? I think they're following us…'"

It was silent as a grave. Then the guy with the beer started cracking up, covering his stomach with his hand, eyes half-closed. That reminded me of Rhys. The gesture. The wrinkles around his eyelids. He resembled him a bit, tall and blond, but this guy was muscly, with a broad back.

"Jesus, that's terrible! What's your name?"

"Ginger. Where's my beer?"

He smiled at me again and served two more beers while one of his friends chatted up Kate, asking what year we were in. I grabbed the plastic cup and walked off to look around. Everyone seemed to be having fun, and I liked being a part of it. I took a deep breath. Then I took a few sips and watched a group of girls dancing and fooling around in the middle of the living room. They didn't seem to care what anyone thought of them. And I envied them. And I wanted to join in. And…

"You want to dance? Come on!" Kate tugged at me.

I don't know how, but we ended up with those girls, and they accepted us without even knowing our names. I started laughing when I saw the faces Kate was making. And I just let myself go. I danced, I sang, I shouted, I got excited, I chanted along with that group of strangers when I heard the first notes of "The Time of My Life."

"Will you take a picture of us?" Kate asked a couple walking by. She handed them her phone, and we mugged for the camera. "Thanks."

"We look amazing!" I said when she showed it to me.

"It's great. You should send it to Rhys."

I hesitated. We hadn't sent each other any photos yet. We hadn't even exchanged numbers. I guess we had gotten used to our routine, doing things our way, and neither of us wanted to ruin it.

But that night I felt happy. I felt like myself.

"Why not?" I shrugged.

When Kate sent me the photo, I gave it one last look, then attached it to an email to him. No subject line, no text. Just an image.

Someone bumped my shoulder, and I almost dropped my phone. He raised his hands as if to say sorry, but then he saw me and smiled.

"Ginger! The girl with the bad jokes…"

"The beer guy." I put my phone in the back pocket of my black pants. "You still never told me your name. You've got one up on me."

"True." He reached out to shake my hand. "James Brooks."

"You the host?"

"I am indeed." He smiled.

10

Rhys

TOMORROW, I'D SEE MY MOTHER after a year's absence. And then I'd be catching a plane for Los Angeles. I'd leave behind another city, its people, its streets, its environment. But unlike the strange feeling that overtook me when I left Paris the month before, leaving now felt right. It meant that everything was following its course. That the world was moving. That I was moving with it, spinning round and round.

I didn't want to think about it much though.

I was on edge and needed to clear my head and put my thoughts to sleep. That's why I found myself at the club I had been working at. I laughed when the people around the table did, but I hadn't heard the joke, and I didn't care either.

I took a deep breath and a sip of my drink. I listened to the music, an EDM mix with a wild rhythm. I felt soft fingers stroking my hair, sinking into it. And Sarah's hot breath close to my mouth.

"Your head's somewhere else today," she whispered.

I nodded. I hadn't told her I was going to see my mother the next day. Or how strange I was feeling that night. I didn't tell her the drink in my hand was my fourth or that I was about to order a fifth in the hope of just blanking out, even if I had to wake up with a hangover and my mother would notice, because she knew me that well.

"What's up with you, Rhys?" she asked.

"Nothing. I'm great." I smiled.

I liked Sarah. I'd liked her since the first time we'd wound up in bed together two years ago, hanging out all night, having fun. But right now, I felt far away from her and from the rest of my friends there too. I wanted out of New York. To run away from myself.

Even if by then I knew you couldn't escape your own skin.

I closed my eyes when I felt her fingers caress my neck again, slipping downward, tickling. I laughed as I thought of what was coming.

"We should end this on a high note."

"I have to get up early tomorrow," I said.

I didn't pull away when her lips touched mine. It was almost a friendly gesture. Simple. I saw her beautiful green eyes and sighed.

"The other night left me wanting more."

"Me too." It had been a quickie, impersonal, and then we'd crashed, almost without talking. "But we'll see each other in LA. Aren't you filming there soon?"

"Yeah, next month."

Sarah was an actor. She did ads for all types of things: toothpaste, frozen meals, tires, lotions. Ninety percent of her work was in LA or New York, so she was always back and forth.

"You'll call me, right?" I smiled.

"I'll think about it, Rhys," she responded mirthfully.

I felt a vibration in my pocket just then that took my attention away. *Ginger.* Six letters that had unexpectedly become part of my life. I left my glass on the table. And I smiled like an idiot when I saw it was her. The message didn't have a subject line. I held my breath when I opened it and saw the picture.

It was her. She was with another girl, with a drink in her hand, and her eyes glowed as she looked at the camera. The photo was blurry, but I saw every detail: her transparent black shirt, the shadow of her bra beneath it, her hair messy, her happy expression; yep, *insanely sexy*, that was it.

"Who is it?" Sarah bent over to look at my screen.

"A good friend." I got up, downed what was left of my drink, and looked at the people seated around the table. "Guys, I've got to bounce."

"Come on, Rhys, stay for another round," Mason said.

"Next time. I'll call." I waved and bent over to say goodbye to Sarah with a kiss on the cheek. Then I left the club.

The spring nights in New York were cold. The wind was blowing hard as I walked down the street, hands in my jacket pockets. I felt my phone. I thought about her again. I sat on a bench at the playground in Hell's Kitchen Park, where I gazed up at the moon, thinking and enjoying the solitude, the feeling that tomorrow I'd be somewhere else, somewhere much warmer, and that I was still in control of my life. Because I didn't know then that the opposite was true: that life was pulling me along and I was stumbling after it, not even sure where I was going.

I don't know how long I was there before I took my phone out and looked a second time at the photo Ginger had sent me. I rubbed the screen with my fingers. Jeez. She always made me smile. It didn't matter if I'd had a shitty day; I could open my computer or look at my phone, and she always put me in a good mood. Always.

I started typing…

Picked my words carefully…

I felt her near me.

11

Ginger

I SAT ON THE PORCH swing with the flower pattern, cracking up at something James said. I don't remember what. After a few drinks, anything seemed funny to me, no matter how stupid. He sat down next to me, and I shouted as the swing jerked and I had to grab on to one of the creaky chains. I could hear the music and the partygoers in the background.

"Is that my drink?" I said, pointing at his hand.

"Not unless you tell me another joke."

"I'm not a circus clown."

"You are the funniest girl I've met today though." We'd been talking and dancing awhile inside and had finally decided to get a breath of fresh air.

"Let's see." I took a deep breath like I was getting ready for a big performance and turned toward him. He was staring at me. The swing started to move again. Our knees touched. "What did the banana say to the Jell-O? I haven't even undressed yet, and you're already trembling all over."

"Jesus, Ginger!" he laughed.

My phone buzzed just then.

I looked at it, distracted, a little overexcited. But everything froze when I saw his name. I smiled as I read the message. I've never seen such an insanely sexy cookie. Have fun. And remember: Us on the moon.

"It's weird we've never met before."

I looked at James. "Is it though? I never go to parties like this."

"Why, because you used to have a boyfriend?" he guessed. "And now you...don't?"

I saw him looking at my phone, which I stuffed in my pants pocket while I shook my head. "No. I'm not with anyone."

"Good to know."

"Why?"

"I don't want trouble."

A second later, he was kissing me, and I was frozen. It was slow, soft, almost delicate. Eventually I managed to react, wrapping my hands around his neck and laughing as I felt the swing rock. He laughed too. I kissed him back, but harder, enjoying that intoxicating feeling and wanting it to keep going on. After dancing and not thinking about anything, I felt happy, at ease.

I was Ginger Davies.

One insanely sexy cookie.

12

Rhys

I STOOD UP WHEN I saw my mother. My heart was pounding. My mind was a mess, and I couldn't think straight. She looked the same as always: neat in her light-colored suit, hair pulled back, her severe hair a contrast to her kind face and her huge sunglasses. I used to joke that she looked like a Hollywood actor in them.

I walked toward her, and a second later, she was in my arms, and I was hugging her and didn't know if I'd be able to let her go. She was wearing the same cloying perfume as always. She pulled back to look at me from head to toe. Her lower lip was trembling; she was about to cry. I prayed she wouldn't.

"You're... You look good," she managed to say.

"You too." I smiled, almost as a reflex.

"You're still a mama's boy. Come on, let's sit down."

We settled next to each other at the table. She took my hand in hers, and I knew she wouldn't let it go until our food arrived. We were on the glassed-in balcony of the Soho Grand, with views of the beautiful blue sky, broken by nothing but the vapor trails of airplanes flying over town. The waiter came to take our order, and when he left, I took a deep breath, finally starting to calm down.

"You need to cut your hair, Rhys."

"I just did," I said as she tugged at it, as if trying to gauge the length of every lock. "Don't be a pain."

She smiled, shook her head, and stopped.

Our food was served soon afterward. Two plates of spaghetti carbonara and water, which I hoped would dilute everything I'd drunk the night before.

"I think I'm a fucking pasta addict."

"Rhys, your mouth. You always have had a penchant for noodles: ramen, macaroni, all that. I don't care for it much, if you want to know my opinion."

"I remember that recipe you used to make with the shrimp sauce."

"You cleaned your plate every time."

I smiled. So did she. And that was enough. We ate, we caught up, and eighteen months of absence and sporadic phone calls went out the window. We were, once again, a mother and a son talking about whatever, with no tension. Before that fateful Christmas, we'd been close, and I'd liked hanging out with her: going out to eat, shopping for groceries, catching a flick. I remember it used to surprise me how distant my friends' relationships with their parents were, as if they were strangers living in the same home. Then everything changed, and the secrets and the harsh words destroyed the pleasant memories.

"Where are you headed now?" she asked.

"Los Angeles. I think. Yeah, Los Angeles."

"How do you not know?"

I shrugged, looking at her. "I'm still sort of turning it over."

I didn't tell her why. She already knew. Too many years. Too many conversations. Too many reproaches. Sometimes I couldn't even tell myself why I felt that strange satisfaction every time I reached an airport with no ticket and nothing but a bag on my back. That tickle when I didn't know what plane I'd get on. The hours waiting, drinking coffee, reading books, listening to music, and watching people go back and forth. It was addictive.

We shared a dessert.

"I'll come for a longer visit next time."

"Does that mean you'll come back home?"

"Home, no. Close."

"Rhys, honey…if only you'd tell me what happened."

"You already know, Mom. He didn't understand. He wanted me to follow in his footsteps, take over the investments, all that bullshit," I lied.

She hesitated, then nodded. "Does that mean you had to end up like this?"

"The argument got out of hand."

"You need to sit down and talk."

"I can't. Things have changed." I shrugged.

I pretended not to care. I pretended not to feel anything. I wanted to get up and walk out, but I held back, smiled, and feigned things I didn't feel just to make her happy. I wanted to ask about Dad, find out if he was okay, but as always, I didn't. We spent a few more hours walking around the shops and having coffee. Then it got late, and she ordered an Uber to her hotel.

We waited until it arrived.

"Will he pick you up at the airport when you get home tomorrow?" I asked.

"Yeah, don't worry about that."

"Okay." I nodded. "Mom, I…"

"See you soon, Rhys."

"Yeah. That's what I wanted to say."

"Good. Give me a kiss." I let her squeeze me tight. "Remember not to do anything you'll regret. And be careful. And Rhys, I know how you are, but if you need money, there's a checking account in your name…"

"I'll be fine, Mom," I assured her.

She nodded and looked at me with sorrow as she got into her Uber.

I stayed there until the car took off down the street. Then I slung my backpack on my back, grabbed my hand luggage, and an hour later I was at JFK Airport. I felt warm inside as I listened to the noise, the constant movement of people in the shops and cafés, the voices over the PA. I walked automatically until I reached one of those giant screens that showed the departing flights.

There were tons of flights headed to LA. I slid my finger over the bright letters. Then I saw it. London. The flight left in five hours. I wondered what the chances were that there was still a seat. I don't know. It was crazy. I must have been crazy. But it's not as if I had anywhere else to go, or anyone waiting for me in arrivals, or any commitment at all.

I looked at all the flights. All the options. For a few crazy moments, I thought about how fun it would be to show up in

London the next day, go to Ginger's dorm, surprise her. She'd shout like a banshee when she saw me. I tried to tell myself it wouldn't be weird. We talked every day, I was a rambler, and I had nowhere else to be.

So I decided. *To hell with it.* I'd make it up as I went along.

I got in line at one of the counters.

My phone buzzed. I took it out. I had a message. I don't think my heart ever beat so fast from reading an email. Or that I ever felt so many things. Joy and sorrow at the same time. Pride and frustration, all mixed up. I took a deep breath. Fuck.

"Can I help you with something?" the girl said.

"Yeah, sorry. A ticket for the next available flight to Los Angeles."

"Next flight available is at nine."

"Sure, that's fine."

13

From: Ginger Davies
To: Rhys Baker
Subject: You were right...

You're not going to believe it! Where do I start! I just woke up, so you can imagine how late we came back. I was puking until dawn. I guess I'll remember NEVER TO DRINK from now on. Anyway, Rhys, you were right about everything. I needed to get out of my comfort zone, meet people...

...kiss a man.

Because yep, that's what I did. I didn't plan it. It didn't even cross my mind when I agreed to go to the party with Kate. It just happened. With the guy who was pouring beer there. I spent all night telling him jokes. I didn't try to impress anyone (I danced like an idiot because I have no sense of rhythm, and I was too drunk to watch my mouth). I don't know. Then we went outside to clear our heads a little, and we sat on this swing that honestly was not relaxing at all, and to make matters worse, it kept creaking.

And he leaned over and kissed me.

I know, you're thinking right now that I'm acting (and writing) like a fifteen-year-old girl, and you know what? You're right. That's how I feel too. Don't blame me. This is the second person I've ever kissed. And I've realized two things: Dean was overrated, and I was right—all that saliva isn't normal. Don't get grossed out. I didn't know. I didn't have anyone to compare him to.

James kisses way better.

I don't know what else to tell you. My head feels like it's going to explode, and I'm still sick to my stomach, but I'm happy, and I want you to be the first to know about my progress. I know you're dying for me to develop my sex life and all.

But let's talk about you…

Have you seen your mom? I hope so.

Where are you? Still in New York?

From: Rhys Baker
To: Ginger Davies
Subject: RE: You were right…

I like the subject line of your email, but it was only a matter of time until you learned what I already know: I'm always right. That goes for your love/sex life too. (Can we call it that from now on? I like the sound of that.) Anyway, Ginger, I'm glad you had fun and you've kissed that second person. You deserve it. I'm also glad you're realizing there's a whole world out there beyond Dean and his excess slobber. (I can't get it out of my mind. Why did you tell me?) Talk to me about this James.

I just got to LA a few hours ago. I'm at a motel, but tomorrow I'll go stay with my good friend Logan. He'll have his guest room free then. This carpet looks like it might come alive. It's got stains on it from 1920, if not earlier. An archaeologist could make a study of it. And it smells weird. But apart from that, it's not bad.

Yeah, I saw my mother...

It wasn't as uncomfortable as I'd imagined. You know how you can recreate a situation in your head so many times, and then it happens, and you're surprised how it's way less of a big deal than you expected? Well, that's pretty much how it was. She showed up, I hugged her, we had lunch, we took a walk, and then she went back to her hotel. We barely talked about Dad. It was good, really good.

I hope your stomach's better.

Good luck with it. (Yeah, I'm laughing.)

From: Ginger Davies
To: Rhys Baker
Subject: RE: RE: You were right...

Is there something funny about my stomach being like a washing machine spinning round and round right now? Seriously, twenty-four hours have gone by, and it's still holding the night against me.

But let's get to the important thing: your mother.

You don't know how happy I am, Rhys. For you. And I hope you don't let so much time pass until you see her again. As for your dad…you never told me why you got so mad at each other. What happened? I'd prefer not to ask you directly like this, but I'll probably die of old age if I have to wait until you tell me on your own. You're like a snail, all curled up in your shell, and even when it's sunny, you don't stick your head out. (I'm trying to make a joke here.)

I'm so envious of you right now. I imagine you walking down one of those beaches in LA full of people playing volleyball and surfing, and you're wearing sunglasses and a sleeveless shirt and eating a burrito from a stand or something like that. In case you care, it's still cold here and—big surprise—the sky's gray. I'm wearing a sweater and two pairs of socks. (Laugh if you want, but I still think it's super romantic for someone to want to warm up my feet.) Anyway, it doesn't matter, because I've got finals next week, so it's not like I'd see the sunlight anyway.

From: Rhys Baker
To: Ginger Davies
Subject: Los Angeles

You've perfectly described what I was thinking of doing today.

I admit it—calling me a snail makes sense. I don't know, Ginger. The truth is, it's hard for me to talk sometimes, even to myself, let alone other people. And you're the person who knows the most about my day-to-day life now… It's just complicated. I mean, maybe *it's* not complicated; maybe *I'm* the one who's complicated. I think I started to realize at age sixteen that something wasn't right with me, that I like being with people, but at the same time it wigs me out and I need solitude, that opening myself up makes me feel empty afterward, and emptiness scares the shit out of me.

Good luck with your exams, Ginger.

From: Rhys Baker
To: Ginger Davies
Subject: [No subject]

I have no right to ask you to understand me, so I'm not going to. I think it's enough if you're just there on the other side of the screen, even if you don't like me as much as you used to.

From: Ginger Davies
To: Rhys Baker
Subject: Sorry

Shit. I'm sorry, Rhys. Last night I didn't respond because I was in the library super late, and I came back home so tired that I fell into bed and went straight to sleep. I hope you don't think I was mad because you didn't want to tell me the thing about your dad. I still like you as much as I used to! Snail and all. A snail's a fascinating—what is it? An insect? Anyway, the way they carry their home on their back, it's just like you, ha ha ha. (I know, I'm not funny; I've memorized so much stuff for my test tomorrow that my brain won't hold anything else.) I understand you, Rhys, even if I don't exactly. You know what I mean? I hope so, because I'm being serious. That's the feeling I had the night we were in Paris, that you understood me even if you didn't, and that you just listening to me was enough.

If someone read our emails, they'd think we were crazy. But like you said, we're up on the moon, right? So don't feel pressured to tell me anything. I'd rather just know what you want to tell me, even if I keep asking you questions nonstop. That's just how I am. And sorry if I'm kind of absent these days; I'm in the library living off of crackers and sandwiches from the machine. My life's pathetic right now, so you're the one whose job it is to say interesting stuff. How's everything in LA? Is it still all beautiful and sunny? (I'm sure it is, but be nice and don't make me jealous.) Did you find a job? Are you already at your friend Logan's place?

From: Rhys Baker
To: Ginger Davies
Subject: RE: Sorry

I had that same weird feeling when we met in Paris. It doesn't seem possible that it was five months ago. I remember it like it was yesterday, but at the same time like something far, far away. I know that doesn't make much sense…but I feel like you'd understand.

I like thinking that we share the same insanity, Ginger.

Don't worry, just study. You don't have to keep me entertained. But try and eat something better than crackers and sandwiches if you can. Remember, soon you'll be free. Do you have plans for the summer? I think I'll stick around here until September or October, but I'm not sure. I'm at Logan's. This morning we hit the waves for a bit. (I think I'm getting my groove back, and it's been years since I surfed.) I have an interview in three days at a club on the beach. The money's okay, and I get free drinks. So wish me luck.

From: Ginger Davies
To: Rhys Baker
Subject: Goooood luuuuuccck!

Just so you know, tomorrow I'll spend the whole day sending tons of positive energy your way from the other side of the world, and I'll keep my fingers crossed while I think about you.

   My laptop battery's about to die, so I'll go ahead and send this before it shuts off. Sorry for still being so absent! The torture (my exams) is almost over. I think I'll just lie down in bed and close my eyes without getting undressed, that's how tired I am. Tell me something fun, Rhys.

From: Rhys Baker
To: Ginger Davies
Subject: RE: Goooood luuuuuccck!

Well, your energy must have reached me, because I got the job. I'm happy. The place is sick. The mixing table's on a wooden stand in the middle of the beach, I can be up there DJing barefoot, watching people have fun, and when my shift's over, I can join the party. It's nice, the thought of working by the sea.

Something fun, something fun...?

Okay. I'm addicted to pasta, spaghetti, ramen, udon, whatever... When I was a kid, I thought it was neat how it was shaped. Don't ask me why I was such an idiot. Also, I used to be scared to get on a Ferris wheel. Let me rephrase that: it still scares the shit out of me. If you're laughing, stop. I'm also terrified of big grasshoppers; they're so ugly.

I hope these confessions make your night go by better.

I also hope you're not too tired.

And that you did well on your exams.

Get some rest, Ginger.

From: Ginger Davies
To: Rhys Baker
Subject: DONE!

I finished! I can hardly believe it, honestly. I don't know how I did on the rest of my exams (well, I think), but right now all I can think about is how I won't have to touch another boring textbook until next semester begins. I'm ready to spend the summer reading novels and wasting time.

Maybe I should warn you: this email's going to go on forever, because I have so much to tell you after so many days. So get comfortable and grab some popcorn.

First things first: I can't stop thinking about you liking pasta so much. I know it's silly, but I'm over here like, "Oh, that's so cute!" Plus it just doesn't seem like you. You don't strike me as someone who'd care about stuff like that. You made me remember that night in Paris in your attic (I still think of it as your home) when we were eating those cup noodles, sitting on the bed, and talking nonstop. You're right about time though; I feel the same way: sometimes it's like it was years ago; other times like it was last week. And sometimes—note the craziness here—it's like it never happened at all. I know, right?

I agree about the grasshoppers...

As for Ferris wheels though...are you for real? I can't believe it! It's not like it's supposed to be scary. That got me thinking (what doesn't?), and I was imagining you coming to London and me taking you to the London Eye. It's 450 feet tall; until 2006 it was the biggest one in the world. We could go up there together. I'd figure out a way for you not to be afraid so you could enjoy the views.

Sometimes I wonder if we'll ever see each other again. Don't pay attention to me; these are just dumb things I think about. All that studying has left me a little flighty, and my internal filter's turned off, and no one will take away my laptop and throw it out the window before I finish the longest email in all of history.

Let's talk about something more sensible though: you've got a job! Congratulations. It sounds amazing. I imagine you there with a mojito while you fill the whole area with music. I'm still waiting for you to send me one of your songs, BTW. No rush.

What else...? Oh, summer. I'm not thinking of doing anything special. I'll go home and spend a few days with my family before we take our vacation in Glastonbury. It's a small town in Somerset County. It's big with people into mysticism and stuff.

Like there's all these myths and legends around it. In case you were wondering, no, I'm lucky enough to have a family that doesn't believe in that stuff. That's a relief, but I still feel like I'll be writing you every ten minutes when they're around, because I've gotten used to being on my own and doing my own thing since college, and I'm not sure how well I'll handle the constant contact.

I hope after this gigantic email, you'll write me one that's at least half as long. I deserve it, I think. Tell me stuff, Rhys. And enjoy the sun for me.

From: Rhys Baker
To: Ginger Davies
Subject: Congratulations, Ginger Snap

I'm glad to know your period of seclusion in the library's come to an end. I'm getting used to my routine at work. My coworkers and my boss are great. So is the ambience here. I work in the afternoon and evening, but I like the afternoon better. Seeing the sun come down while the music seems to permeate every-thing...then enjoying myself with everybody the rest of the night, waking up on the beach in the morning and hearing the sea...

As far as seeing each other again...

I think about it too. Who knows?

Maybe we'll go on writing each other all our lives, but our paths will never cross. Or maybe we'll meet in some little corner of the world. I still don't know about your plan for getting on the

Ferris wheel. I think I'd have a panic attack, and you wouldn't find me attractive anymore. I can't risk that, Ginger.

I know what you mean about feeling like Paris never happened. But it did. I was lucky that day. BTW, can you get a ticket out of a machine yet? I've been wanting to ask you for months.

You haven't heard from Dean?

What about Mr. Second Kisser?

Enjoy the summer. I was thinking about all the things you were telling me, and you know, it's kind of nice that you're traveling as a family. Like in the movies when all kinds of dumb, funny things happen. Have a good time. And write me as much as you want. I won't get tired of reading your emails, Ginger.

From: Ginger Davies
To: Rhys Baker
Subject: I KNOW HOW TO BUY A TICKET

I guess you think you're funny…

Of course I know how to buy a ticket! But the thing was in French, and the button for English wasn't working. I don't know why I'm bothering to explain this to you though; you're probably cracking up laughing at me. If I ever convince you to come to London and get on the Ferris wheel, you can bet I'll get my revenge laughing at you and watching all your manly charm melt away.

I'm glad you like your job. I don't know about you sleeping on the beach though. You know the world is a dangerous place? So be careful. Don't drink too much. I don't want to act like your mother, especially since I was puking my guts up just a few weeks ago, but... I worry about you.

Yeah, I had to do that project with Dean. I told you about that, didn't I? It was uncomfortable at first, but in the end it was okay. I get the feeling he was trying harder than normal because he felt guilty. Great for me—I needed the A. We didn't talk about anything personal, but I feel like I'll see him again this summer. Probably he'll come over for dinner with his parents one day, plus, we live close, just ten minutes walking.

As for James... I'm seeing him this afternoon. I haven't been in touch with him since the party. As you know, I was basically living in the library, plus I don't really know what can happen between us since I'm leaving next week. It'll sound terrible what I'm about to say, but I don't even remember that well what he looks like. He was a good kisser, he was sweet, and I thought he resembled this other guy I know, but that's it. It's like all my memories from that night got shoved into a blender.

Kate still laughs when we talk about that.

From: Ginger Davies
To: Rhys Baker
Subject: My date

I guess you must be working, so you'll read this later or tomorrow. I just wanted to tell you that I got back from my date (?). I guess I'll call it that because I'm all excited.

We spent the afternoon in a well-known café here where they make the best hot chocolate in the world (with all kinds of flavors and sizes and all the toppings you can imagine. It's heaven on earth). We didn't do anything special, but it was nice. We caught up. Now that I think about it, you'd probably find our conversation ungodly boring. It was all that stuff you told me you hated in Paris: What are you studying? How old are you? Do you have siblings? Where do you see yourself in ten years? I guess that's normal in ninety-four percent of cases when two people meet. (I made that number up, in case you're googling it or whatever.) *The Little Prince*'s philosophy is utopian and hard to apply to real life. Anyway, I did learn some stuff about him: He lives in the house where the party was; it belongs to his parents, but they're at their other place in Scotland now (they moved there when they retired). He works at a law firm, and he's twenty-six, like you. He likes chocolate with strawberries. If you want to know my opinion, that's G-R-O-S-S. Lord Chocolate is a solitary man and has no interest whatsoever in dalliances with Lady Strawberry. At most, he might go for a fling with Miss Mint, but we're talking short-term. A quick fuck. (Yes, Rhys, I can write the word *fuck* without blushing.)

Later he walked me to the dorm. Yes, he kissed me at the door. But my head wasn't spinning this time, and neither was his. So that was nice. We agreed that we'd talk on the phone next semester, but you know how it goes; I don't have much faith. Still, it was nice to see him and feel those butterflies in my stomach when we said goodbye.

From: Rhys Baker
To: Ginger Davies
Subject: Butterflies

Butterflies? For real? Ha ha ha ha. I'll try to forget you wrote that. I do want to talk about the other thing, so you don't act like an idiot if he does call you in a few months: Would you honestly go out with someone willing to have Lord Chocolate sleep with Lady Strawberry? I know everybody's got their defects, but this is serious; it's the kind of thing that will ruin a relationship at some point.

I don't like what you were saying about the philosophy of *The Little Prince* not functioning in the real world. First of all, we live on the moon, and anything can happen there, right? If I'm honest with you though, I still haven't read the book, so I have no idea what I'm saying. Either way, I don't like to think anything's impossible.

I'm glad Dean worked hard on your thing.

Don't worry about me. I'm always good.

From: Ginger Davies
To: Rhys Baker
Subject: RE: Butterflies

Okay, I'll take your advice and pay attention to a person's taste in chocolate before committing to anything. I don't want to get a divorce and go around telling people it was "irreconcilable strawberry-related differences" the way movie stars do.

Read the book. I'll talk to you about it one day.

From: Ginger Davies
To: Rhys Baker
Subject: YESSSS!!!!!!

I aced all my subjects! I've never been so happy before.

And I'm ready to spend the summer forgetting everything I've learned.

Tonight I'm having dinner with Kate to say goodbye, because she's leaving a few days early. I'm already packing my bags. If I'm less reachable the next few days, that's why.

Take care. I don't care what you say. I worry about you.

From: Rhys Baker

To: Ginger Davies

Subject: RE: YESSSS!!!!!!

Congratulations, Ginger Snap. You deserve it.

Let me know when you're home.

14

—

Ginger

I SAW MY SISTER, DONNA, on the train platform and ran toward her like crazy, dragging my bags behind me. We hugged tight. I had the feeling that an eternity had passed since the last time we saw each other, even if really it was just a few months and we talked on the phone several times a week.

"You cut your hair!" I shouted.

"You like it?"

"I love it! But you didn't tell me!"

"Ginger, I can't tell you everything. You'd probably want to know how many times a day I go pee," she said, laughing, as she picked up one of my suitcases.

"Of course I do. You're my sister!"

"We need to go. Otherwise, we'll be late. Dad got a reservation at that restaurant you like so much, the one in Notting Hill. Look at me. Okay, phew. No visible tattoos or piercings."

"Why should there be?" I followed her.

"You've only got a year of college left, so I wanted to make sure you weren't in the do-something-crazy phase. Not that I'd have a problem with it, but if you had a ring in your nose, I'd want to have advance warning before Mom and Dad freaked out."

I touched my nose reflexively and sighed. I was as far as could be from the tingle Donna described when someone has a new experience, whether that be getting a tattoo or cutting their hair and dyeing it pink. Something inside me insisted I stay curled up in my nest, in the security of the familiar.

"No. I never even thought of doing that..."

Donna had come to pick me up in a taxi, and the driver helped us put the luggage into the trunk. We headed for the restaurant. My parents were probably already there waiting. It was a small place in Queensway where they made the best hamburgers with peppers I'd ever had in my life. There was a bowling alley there; it was nothing sophisticated, but the food was great. I thought about Rhys with his spaghetti and smiled.

I was right—my parents were already waiting for us.

Mom kissed me, hugged me, and embarrassed me in front of a young waitress who was looking at us with pursed lips as though trying not to laugh. My father rested a hand on my shoulder and told me he was *proud of me* for getting such good grades and not letting things with Dean affect me.

We sat at the table, which had a crazy black tablecloth with images of smiling forks and spoons on it. We didn't need to look at the menu before ordering.

"When are we going to Glastonbury?" I asked.

"Next Thursday. By the way, your father and I wanted to tell you something we were thinking about."

"You'll love it," my father said.

"What would you think about spending a few days at the office when we come back? We were thinking that since you'll join the company next year, it would do you good to get familiar with everything. Plus you'll get experience. We're obviously happy with what you're learning at school, but you should learn about the practical side of it as well."

"Uh, I mean…"

I knitted my brows and looked at Donna, and she looked down into her plate as if it, too, were taking part in the conversation. I wanted to say no. Worse still, I wanted to *shout* no, loud and clear. NO, NO, NO. But that simple two-letter word got stuck in my throat, even as my parents were gazing at me all excited.

"I guess I could do it…"

"How nice, Ginger!" My mother literally applauded. "Just imagine how proud your father will be going to work every day with his little girl."

"Pass the ketchup?" Donna interrupted her.

"Of course, honey, here. So, Ginger, tell us how things have been going lately. Have you talked to Dean? When I call you at night, you always seem distracted, like you want to hang up. More fries?"

"Yes, please." I grabbed one off her plate.

"That's because she's busy writing at night." Donna looked at me with a dumb smile, fork in hand. "I can't believe you don't know." She shook her head and kept eating.

"What are you writing?"

"A novel?" Dad asked.

"No…it's more like a diary…"

"But she sends it to another person."

I slid my hand under the table and pinched my sister's leg. She yelped and then laughed. Then she threw an arm over my shoulders and sighed.

"Come on, Ginger. This is important to you. I wasn't making fun. I'm just surprised you haven't told them. She has a pen pal. Not like in the old days with pen and paper; she sends him emails. It's great!"

"Why didn't you tell us?"

"What's his name?" Dad asked.

"Rhys. He's from America. And I didn't say anything because it's not important; he's just a friend. We talk, we tell each other things, that's all."

Obviously my parents knew nothing about the day I broke up with Dean, decided to catch a plane, and wound up in Paris with a backpack with panties, socks, and crackers in it. The only person in my family who knew was Donna. I was almost surprised she'd kept the secret, even if she hadn't managed to stay quiet about Rhys. I guess my relationship with him was so special I wanted to keep it to myself, like a possession a person likes so much they never use it because they're scared of breaking or damaging it. I wanted to preserve Rhys. And in a way, I liked it just being *our* thing. I wondered if he had told anyone about me. Knowing him, my guess would be no.

"What's he do?" my father asked.

I shook my head and took a deep breath. "He's a DJ. And a composer."

And he'd never let me hear his stuff, but I said nothing about that. I noticed Dad scowl and look down at his plate.

Donna smiled. "I think he's fascinating. Everything about him."

"Everything?"

"Everything she's told me."

"What's so fascinating?" Dad asked.

"Well, he travels all over the world, right, Ginger? All by himself. What a great way to get to know yourself." Donna read a million self-help books a year, and even though she'd studied fine arts, she had the soul of a psychologist, and my father hated it. "And he doesn't make spelling errors. That's always a plus."

"I guess so," Mom agreed.

Talking about Rhys with my family was the last thing in the world I felt like doing. Apart from spending half the summer going to work with Dad, I mean. And unfortunately, those two subjects took up our entire conversation during the meal. And so, when we got home to our residential neighborhood in East London, I was almost happy to have a little time to myself to unpack my bags.

My old room was just as I'd left it when I went off to college. It was so ordinary, it could have been a set for a cheesy teen movie. A corkboard full of pictures of my high school friends, friends I talked to less and less because we had taken different paths, and others with Dean and me posing like lovebirds. My sister was there too, clowning around when we were little. Then there was the desk at the wall with its pretty floral wallpaper, covered in pens, notebooks, and aromatic candles, right near the bookshelf and the closet.

I wanted to find a room to rent when I graduated next year. I would start working at the family firm and go out on my own at the same time. Lots of people I knew did that when they turned eighteen, but I'd been lucky enough to get room and board with my scholarship. Anyway, prices in London were so high that living on your own was like mission impossible.

Donna came in without knocking.

"Mom's asking if you want spinach and cheese quiche for dinner. Since we just ate, she's obviously already thinking about what to make next."

"Yeah, that's fine for me."

She sat down next to me on the bed. "Are you mad at me?"

"No, why do you ask?"

"You know. Because of Rhys."

"I'm not mad," I said.

"Ginger...it's okay if you are. You can even shout at me if you need to. It's your right. To tell the truth, I was surprised you hadn't mentioned him to Mom. I just assumed she knew, and... I don't know, I thought it was funny. But then I was thinking maybe you wanted to keep it to yourself, right?"

I nodded, but I didn't shout. I just couldn't. Still worse, I didn't know how. How can a person be incapable of expressing anger, rage, or fury? Maybe I was scared that people would stop loving me if I did. Maybe I thought it was best to be the other way, sweet little agreeable Ginger. I was scared to disappoint the people around me. I was afraid not to give my best to people.

I guess that's why I agreed to work that summer.

And that's why I still hadn't talked to Dean...

And that's why I couldn't scream at Donna...

And that's why...that's why...I had a knot in my throat most of the time, as if all the things I couldn't express had gotten stuck there inside me, hidden in some corner. But a little bit of that I could let out. With Rhys. With him, I was myself.

"You're right, the whole thing with Rhys doesn't matter…"

"It does matter," Donna insisted. Sometimes I had the feeling my sister was actively trying to stretch the bond between us tighter, that she was testing me.

"No. It's silly. I should unpack my bags."

"Ginger, look at me. Rhys isn't just whatever. I know he's not. I know you. He's special to you, isn't he? Nod if I'm right."

Despite myself, I ended up moving my head up and down slightly.

"Good. Now, let's get down to business. When can I see a photo of him?"

I laughed and got up, throwing my suitcase on the bed. "I don't have any. I told you. And I wasn't lying."

"He must have an Instagram or something."

"Nope. I already looked. But he's…gorgeous."

"Gorgeous!" My sister cracked up laughing.

"I'm serious! Don't make fun of me." I was laughing along with her. "The first time I saw him—which was the last time I saw him too—I thought he was like one of those rock stars that have seen and done it all and are tired of life, but at the same time, they're ready to just go crazy at the drop of a hat. You know what I mean?"

"Not as well as you do, obviously."

My sister moved on to other things, talking about her job while she helped me hang my more delicate dresses in the closet. She was waitressing at a pub on Carnaby Street in Soho. She ended up working there after telling her boss during the interview that she was an artist, and they offered to exhibit her work there for customers and anyone who might help further her career.

She hadn't had any luck. And obviously my parents were disappointed. What they really didn't like was her sharing an apartment with six other young people. Mom had tried to get her to listen to reason and take a job as a receptionist at their company, but my sister refused. I admired that. She didn't care if she didn't make everyone happy. She always did what she wanted. I hugged her, and she got up to leave.

"Are you spending the night here?" I asked.

"No, I'll leave after dinner." She smiled.

I sat on my bed and opened my laptop.

I didn't have any messages from Rhys.

I sighed, stretched out my hand, and grabbed his sweatshirt, which I had put aside when I was unpacking. I hadn't put it on since that day at the airport. And of course I hadn't washed it. There wasn't a trace of him left when I smelled it (and I did, especially those first weeks apart), but I still liked the idea of having a piece of him with me. It reminded me that he was real, even if he was thousands and thousands of miles away, on the other side of the world.

15

Rhys

THE WIND WAS COOL, AND the waves were licking the shore. I took a deep breath. I could feel my lungs fill with air and everything around me spinning. I was lying on the sand in my bathing suit in the wee hours of the morning. Now and then, the cold water reached my toes. I concentrated on that. On breathing. On breathing. On breathing. I don't know how much I'd drunk, just that I'd left the party, the crowd, that hot chick I didn't feel like talking to. And now I was here, staring into a dark sky full of stars that seemed to tremble up high.

And the moon bright and round amid shadows.

The moon, it always reminded me of her.

16

From: Ginger Davies
To: Rhys Baker
Subject: I'll never make it!

I've been home for two days, and I'm already thinking of suicide. Seriously, Rhys, it's awful. AWFUL. And I love my parents. But they just stress me out! They're so ridiculously perfect, and that means I have to be ridiculously perfect, especially since Donna isn't anymore. I have the feeling that all the family's hopes are vested in me, and it's just not fair. I'm going to take a deep breath.

From: Ginger Davies
To: Rhys Baker
Subject: I'll never make it! (Part 2)

Right, so my mom came into my bedroom while I was writing you, and I got so nervous I hit Send. And off she went. I think.

She comes in between five and ten times an hour. Sometimes she just knocks, opens up, and says, "I just wanted to make sure you were okay." And I look at her like, *Are you crazy?* I know, I'm a bad daughter and you're an angel fallen from heaven for being willing to listen to me. Thank you, Rhys. Thank you.

Anyway, this summer, when we get back from vacay, I'll have to go every day to work with my dad (plus Donna's only managed to get off three days in total to stay with us; then she'll have to take the train back). Conclusion: lying around and reading is over. I'm imagining you on the beach right now, and the envy's killing me. You must be super tan. I know you have a job, but I always have this feeling like your life is an eternal vacation.

I hope there's Wi-Fi in Glastonbury.

From: Rhys Baker
To: Ginger Davies
Subject: Be a tough cookie

Maybe it's because I've had a bit to drink, but I want to tell you what I think you should do right now. Open your closet, throw a bunch of summer clothes in your bag, go to the airport, and catch a flight straight to LA.

Spend the summer with me, Ginger. It'll be fun. We can get drunk together, and I'll teach you to surf, and we'll swim at night on the beach. Naked. If you want. You've probably never done anything like that, right? Leave your swimsuit on the shore and run out into the water? I'll be your accomplice. Think it over.

Fuck that job. It sounds boring.

From: Ginger Davies

To: Rhys Baker

Subject: RE: Be a tough cookie

My God, Rhys, you can't say something like that to me.

YOU CAN'T, OKAY? Because I can't stop thinking about how awesome it would be, and it's impossible. Don't write me again when you're drunk, because the stuff you come up with is too tempting, and I can't even allow myself to fantasize about it.

From: Ginger Davies

To: Rhys Baker

Subject: [No subject]

Are you mad at me? I don't expect you to understand, but in my world, there's such a thing as obligations, schedules, things to do.

From: Ginger Davies

To: Rhys Baker

Subject: ...

Okay, we're at the hotel and I have internet, but I guess you don't, because you still haven't written me back. Seriously, are you going to be mad at me forever? I didn't even do anything. I would like to be there, but I can't...

From: Rhys Baker

To: Ginger Davies

Subject: Sorry

I'm sorry!! Of course I'm not mad, Ginger. How could I get mad over a thing like that? I understand. It was just a crazy idea that popped into my head. I'll try not to write you again when I'm drunk and it's after 3:00 a.m. I've barely rested these days. Sarah showed up, and I've moved into an apartment with her for a few weeks until she has to leave again.

Enjoy your trip. Tell me how everything goes there.

From: Ginger Davies
To: Rhys Baker
Subject: Intrigued

Who is Sarah? I don't think I've ever heard you talk about her.

From: Rhys Baker
To: Ginger Davies
Subject: RE: Intrigued

She's a friend. Ish. You get it.

From: Ginger Davies
To: Rhys Baker
Subject: RE: RE: Intrigued

I don't know whether to be more offended by how quickly you've found a substitute to spend the days with in LA or by the fact that you had a "special friend" and didn't tell me. I'm kidding, but you could actually tell me about your life sometime.

Everything here's fine. It's pretty, the typical charming little town. My mother's taken so many photos that we had to buy another card for her camera. My father spends the whole day making plans for all the things we'll do in the office when we return to London. He's excited. Enjoy yourself, Rhys.

From: Rhys Baker
To: Ginger Davies
Subject: RE: RE: RE: Intrigued

You're right, Ginger. I've been thinking about your message all day, but I couldn't answer you until now, after Sarah's fallen asleep. It's true: you give me much more of yourself than I give to you, and it isn't fair. I'm... I'm trying. I want you to know, despite everything, that right now, you're the person who knows the most about me. If I'm honest with myself, I'd have to say you're my best friend. And that's after only—what, six months that we've known each other? Seven. Almost? Since the end of January... I feel like I've been talking to you for years. I don't even know why. I guess these things happen: you just meet a person and let them in for no reason.

Okay, so Sarah is a "special friend." We hang out sometimes in New York or Los Angeles. We have fun together, you know. She's an actor; she does commercials. She's nice; you'd like her. I met her one night years ago.

I don't know what else to tell you…

I hope you're well.

From: Ginger Davies

To: Rhys Baker

Subject: That was nice

Okay, what you said about me being your best friend was nice. I don't know how you get me to instantly go from being so pissed at you to wanting to hug you, Rhys. The truth is, you're my best friend now too, I think. At least the person who knows the most about me. Sometimes I feel like I tell you absolutely everything, and that's a little scary.

I'm glad you're having fun with Sarah.

Did you meet her one night the same way you met me one night? I want details!

BTW, I start work tomorrow.

I'll keep you informed. Kisses. (Why haven't we ever signed off that way? "Kisses" or "Hugs" or "Take care"? Is it because we send so many messages it would start to sound fake? Like when you give someone a hug or a kiss on the cheek to say hi, but you don't feel it.)

From: Rhys Baker

To: Ginger Davies

Subject: RE: That was nice

I guess I just have that effect on women. My charm, you know.

No, I didn't meet her one night like you, Ginger. I met her… I don't know, it was different. I met her at a bar, we had drinks, and we ended up in a hotel. That's what I mean when I say it was different.

Tell me about your first day at work.

Kisses, kisses, kisses. (I feel them!)

From: Ginger Davies
To: Rhys Baker
Subject: I wish someone would kidnap me

The subject line sums up my first day at work. Honestly, I feel kind of guilty because Dad was so proud and excited… He blushes at times like this. When he introduced me to the staff, he looked like he'd had a sunstroke. Fortunately it passed.

I felt good and bad at the same time.

Good because he was happy. Bad because I didn't want to be there.

I know what you mean now about that night being different. But that makes me wonder something. I'm just going to blurt it out and hit Send without rereading this message, okay? Otherwise I'll regret it. Do you think, if the circumstances were different, the same thing could have happened with us? I don't want to put you on the spot. You can be honest with me. I have my own ideas. I just want to know if you'd have noticed me if you saw me in a bar.

I'm going to send this before I stop myself.

Don't pay me any mind.

From: Rhys Baker
To: Ginger Davies
Subject: [No subject]

Ginger, Ginger, Ginger…

From: Ginger Davies
To: Rhys Baker
Subject: RE: [No subject]

What the hell does that mean?

From: Rhys Baker
To: Ginger Davies
Subject: What it means

It means there are some questions better left unanswered. But if you can't bear the intrigue, the answer's yes. If I'd met you in a bar and the circumstances were different, I'd have probably come over, we'd have had a drink, and we'd have talked. And then, I don't know, I'd have bent over and whispered in your ear. And I'd have stroked your knee under the table. We'd have wound up in my apartment, but instead of eating noodles sitting on the bed, I'd have kissed you all over until you moaned my name. And then I'd have taken my time memorizing every inch of your naked skin. Every freckle. Every mole. Every scar. Every curve.

But you know what? I'm glad that didn't happen. Because what we have is a thousand times better, and I don't have it with anyone else. This friendship of ours is special. Now it would be best if we pretend we've never talked about that parallel reality.

From: Rhys Baker
To: Ginger Davies
Subject: U okay?

Did you die of a heart attack, Ginger Snap?

From: Ginger Davies
To: Rhys Baker
Subject: I'm fine

You're an idiot. And yes, I'm fine. You honestly think I'm that impressionable? Ha. You'd have to do way better than that. But you're right, it would be best to forget it, because it doesn't matter anymore. I was just wondering…

Work sucks. Still. And Dad's still happy. I was about to try and strangle myself today with the printer cable, but then I remembered it's just a few more weeks till I'm free again. Or till I go back to the dorm. Same difference. You know, now that I'm about to start my last year of school, I've started asking myself if I'll even be able to work every day. If I'm honest with you, I don't want to think about it.

What about you? Is Sarah still with you?

From: Rhys Baker
To: Ginger Davies

Subject: RE: I'm fine

Ginger, I think you're more impressionable than you imagine. But I said let's forget it, and I'm going to try not to add anything else.

Did you ever wonder if you like what you're doing? I'm going to tell you something I don't think I ever have: I didn't just study first-year psychology. I did the same with law. And political science. That's right. The perfect son, you guessed it. Seriously, I wanted to like all that stuff, but it didn't fulfill me. Classes felt like they would never end, and I wound up skipping most of them. The only good thing about college was the frat parties. (I know, I know—but my Dad was a brother and so was my grandfather. Anyway, the line ended with me.)

That's where I met Logan, by the way—my friend I lived with in Los Angeles before Sarah got here. He did finish his law degree, and he has a small firm on the edge of town. Nothing fancy. Sometimes I look at him and think to myself that I could have had a life like that. But I don't know. There's something missing. Even now I don't know what it is. I think I still need more time to understand myself. I hope, as always, you'll be able to figure out what I mean here and see the logic in it.

What I'm trying to tell you, Ginger, is that you shouldn't do anything that makes you unhappy. That sounds like one of those motivational phrases they print on T-shirts or coffee cups, but really, life's too short not to take advantage of every second of it.

I'm not so sure what to do right now. I think I'll stay here a few more months and then maybe go to San Francisco. No reason to stray too far.

17

Rhys

I CLOSED MY LAPTOP AND looked out the window for a few seconds. It was hot out. The sun had just risen. I thought about my life there in Los Angeles. But then Sarah moved behind me. She was lying in bed naked, curled up with a bundle of white sheets.

I smiled as I walked over. She was groggy.

"What are you doing up at this hour?"

"Answering an email. Who gets to shower first?"

"You," she said quickly, closing her eyes.

I looked for some clean clothes to put on and walked into the bathroom. I turned on the cold water. That first burst of it made me shiver, but I stayed there, immobile, until I got used to it, and finally I started liking it. I heard someone say something once about how pain or an ice bath or vertigo woke a person up all at once, made them conscious of their skin, of the feeling of being alive. Because it was physical. Direct. Something that pulls them out of that comfort we instinctively seek.

When I came out, it smelled like freshly brewed coffee and Sarah was talking on the phone. I noticed the light coming in through the window, the effect of it, the way it curved slightly and resembled a small rainbow, reflecting off the kitchen table.

"What are you looking at?" Sarah hugged me from behind when she hung up.

"Nothing. Did they tell you if you're filming today?"

She nodded and kissed me on the cheek before going to pour herself a cup of coffee. I waited until she was done to serve myself, and the two of us had breakfast in silence while the clock ticked away up on the wall.

They say the silences are how someone knows if the person in front of them is the right one. I think that's a lie. Or that there's more to it. A silence can be comfortable but empty. Or a silence can be tense, electrifying; it can even mean everything. Like the one I shared with Ginger more than six months ago in that attic, when I felt her pulse in her wrist against my fingers and we were looking at the full moon's glow. I guess every instant is unique. That nothing can ever be repeated.

"I don't feel like leaving," she said.

"Did you get your tickets yet?"

"Yeah, last night. I used your computer."

She looked away, suddenly uncomfortable.

"And...?" I arched my eyebrows.

She set her coffee down on the table and took a deep breath, as if she needed a few seconds to know what to say. I could feel myself tense up. Not because she had seen those messages, but because she had decided to barge into that part of my life without even knocking on the door. I only let Ginger in. She could climb in through the open windows, the hidden cracks, the chimney...

"I'm sorry. I only saw the last couple of emails...but my battery was out, and when the screen turned on, the messages were just there, and... I don't know, Rhys. I feel like we met two years ago, and I still don't know anything about you."

"Sarah..."

"And that thing about how with her it was different..." She stood up, walked over to the window, and closed it. The light dimmed, disappeared. But I looked at the place where it had been.

"I wasn't going to say anything, okay? I woke up this morning and was like, *Okay, I'm going to just pretend everything's okay, and by the time we see each other in New York again I'll have forgotten it.* But then I asked you what you were thinking about, you said, 'Nothing,' and I knew you were lying."

"What are you getting at?"

"Just what you told her. That phrase."

"Which?" I got up.

"How sometimes you just meet a person and let them in for no reason. I don't think that's it. There needs to be an explanation. And I want to know what it is."

My stomach ached when I saw her like that, eyes damp, lip trembling, gaze hoping that I could give her something when I knew I couldn't. Maybe I'd been selfish with her. Maybe I hadn't paid enough attention to the signs.

I took a deep breath. Pensive. Uncomfortable.

"It's the truth, Sarah. There is no reason. I don't know why I can open up to her and not to you. I'm sorry."

She was quiet, and I stepped forward to hug her. She didn't pull away. I closed my eyes as I felt her lips on my jawline, her hands rising up my shirt, her skin against mine as I sat down in one of the kitchen chairs and pulled her on top of me. I hesitated. Not for me, but for Sarah. Because I wondered if I was hurting her worse then. But I let her keep going. I let her body move against mine, push her hands through my hair, and kiss me hard, with teeth, reclaiming me.

Then our panting filled everything. She came. We came.

She stood up. She had kept her T-shirt on as we did it. She looked at me with a mixture of anger, affection, and confusion. I took her hand and pulled her back into my lap, kissing her on the forehead.

"What are you doing, Sarah?"

"I don't know," she whispered.

"This was never a problem for us before, Sarah."

"Yeah…" She looked wounded. "But I thought that was just how you were, Rhys, the way I knew you. I thought you just didn't like to talk about yourself, that you couldn't relax with another person and tell stories about your childhood or worry about what another person was feeling. And now I find that. Another person. One I've never even seen. I accepted that I couldn't change you, but this…this ruins everything." She shook her head, walking away.

"You're giving it too much weight…"

"I'm spending tonight in a hotel."

"I don't get it. We have an open relationship. And she's a friend. You're acting like we've been going out for years and I just cheated on you."

"It's not that. It's that you've opened my eyes."

"Fine." I sighed as I buttoned my pants.

"See? That's exactly what I meant. Would you act that way if she was the one about to go sleep in a hotel? No. And we're both your friends. That makes it worse. You haven't even fucked her. Whatever. You're not going to understand. And I don't want things to end all ugly with you."

I was nervous, frustrated...a little bit of everything. Because I didn't want to think about it, basically. Sarah took a quick shower, came out dressed, grabbed her bag, and left. I assumed she'd return that afternoon, when filming was over. I stayed in the kitchen, tracing out the faint shadows on the table, pensive.

I don't know how long I stayed like that before I walked over to the synthesizer.

Then I lost all sense of time. Everything was that sound, the bass, pounding in my head, over and over, tirelessly, until I found the rhythm I wanted, the only one that would work. *Boom, boom, boom.* I closed my eyes, thinking about what was to come afterward, remembering feelings. *Boom, boom, boom.* It was almost midday when I saw my phone vibrate on the table and took off my headphones.

It was Logan. He'd been at my door for twenty minutes.

I opened up, and when he saw me, he shook his head. He had a bag from a nearby burger place. He headed straight to the dining room and took out everything.

"I assumed you hadn't eaten." He gave me a sidelong look before proceeding. "Sarah called me and asked if she could stay at my place tonight, so... I just assumed something had happened."

"She told me she was going to sleep in a hotel."

"Right. What happened exactly?"

"Nothing. I don't know." I grabbed a burger, unwrapped it, and fell back on the sofa, taking a bite and thinking. "I mean, yesterday everything was cool, and now all of a sudden she's acting like we're serious."

"So you're not?"

"Of course not. What's that question even supposed to mean?"

"I was just thinking like, you guys do see each other a lot, right? And you have for a while now. I don't see the difference between that and being *serious*."

That got to me. Logan showed no emotion as he devoured his burger, even though he must have known what he'd said was ridiculous. Very few people knew me as well as he did, even if there was lots he didn't know, lots I didn't tell him, like about the existence of Ginger. Or what had happened with my dad. Or how hard it was for me to talk to my mother week after week...

I realized in that moment that one of my best friends, a guy I'd met at college seven years before, barely knew anything about me. Just the things I let him see, the little trail of breadcrumbs I left behind.

"It's impossible for me to have a relationship with anyone."

"Why? Sarah's incredible."

"Of course she is. But I'm on the road all the time, remember? I don't see myself living two or three years in the same place. Or longer. My whole life. The same goes for getting a mortgage or having kids or anything like that."

Logan studied me a few seconds in silence. "What are you hoping to find, Rhys?"

"Find? Nothing. Why?"

He shook his head and shrugged. "I just have that feeling

sometimes, that you're looking for something. Forget it. I wouldn't marry anything except one of these burgers. And even then, I'd cheat on it with the cheese."

I tried to smile, but I couldn't.

And I couldn't ignore what he'd just said.

That feeling sometimes, that you're looking for something.

18

Ginger

THE WEEK DRAGGED ON FOREVER. Working with my father was emotionally exhausting, especially having to pretend the whole time that there was nothing in the world I liked better than being there. I found myself spending more and more time alone in the office imagining I was lying on the beach, not thinking, not doing anything, just feeling the warm sun and the salt breeze on my skin.

With Rhys. Showing up next to me.

I tried to take refuge in that illusion as the clock ticktocked slowly onward. I looked around Dad's office: piles of papers; printers shooting out the latest invoices I was responsible for; drawings of next season's cabinets hanging on a gigantic corkboard by the desk; smooth, boring walls I'd be staring at for weeks till summer ended...

And at last, it was coming to an end.

The next day I'd catch a train and go back to the dorms. My sense of relief was palpable. I smiled as I remembered I'd gotten permission to move to a larger room I'd share with Kate. I wanted to *live* that last year, and for a second, sitting there in that office, I hoped it would go on forever. I didn't want to confront *adult life* or work or have any responsibilities at all.

"Are you done with the invoices?"

"Yeah." I got up when my father came in. I turned off the printer, grabbed the papers, and pointed at the table. "Should I leave them here?"

"Yeah. I'll take a look at them tomorrow."

"Okay." I walked around the desk.

My father wrapped an arm around my shoulders and pulled me into him. He smelled like rolling tobacco (he'd tried and failed to quit a few times) and the fabric softener Mom had used since I was a kid. I took a deep breath, feeling surrounded by a sense of the familiar. I didn't know what we were doing there, really, until he looked around and sighed with satisfaction.

"Someday, little Ginger, all this will be yours."

I swallowed and noticed the knot in my throat. Dad turned off the lights, and we walked out. I said nothing on the way home.

"Are you all right, Ginger? You said you were all right with it…"

I needed a moment to realize he was worried about lunch. Dean's parents and mine were seeing us off, like in the old days. I shook my head.

"I don't mind. Really."

"All right. But if you change your mind, just say you don't feel good and go to your room. Ginger, I know maybe I wasn't as tactful as I should have been when you and Dean split up. I've been thinking about it a lot lately…"

"Dad, for real. Forget about it. It doesn't matter."

"I just thought he was a good guy…"

"And he is. But not for me. That's no reason not to like him."

"Fine." He took a deep breath, a bit more relaxed.

I appreciated his thoughts, but I didn't want my father to change the way he was with Dean. He'd always treated him like the son he never had, and he expected him to take a role at the top of his company. There was no way I was going to wedge my way into the relationship they'd been building for so long just because we were no longer boyfriend and girlfriend. It was fine. More than fine, even.

I didn't mind not getting an explanation...

Or that we hadn't even talked about it...

I kept repeating that, trying to convince myself. When we entered the house, the scent of meat pie was in the air and the whole Wilson family was in the living room. Dean's parents hugged me so tightly, I was afraid they'd break a rib. We hadn't seen each other all summer, and it was weird, to say the least. Maybe they didn't realize I'd been avoiding them, because the past few weeks had been depressing enough without initiating an uncomfortable conversation I wasn't ready for.

Dean stared at me with his hands in his pockets. He looked nervous. I nodded at him and went to the kitchen with the excuse of helping Mom take dinner out of the oven and put it on the plates.

Donna was last to come in, when we were already sitting down at the table. She took a generous portion and sat down beside me, thank God. I looked down at my plate and listened, chewing, paying attention only to the display cabinet full of old knickknacks Mom had never wanted to throw out: gifts from when we were baptized, old decorations long out of fashion. After a few bites, I felt the food getting stuck in my throat. I took a drink of water, trying to figure

out why I was so upset. Finally I dared to look up at Dean, and...
I didn't feel anything. Not a trace of longing when I saw his brown
curly hair, the movement of his Adam's apple, or his dark eyes.

We were close not too long ago, working together in class, but
funny enough, there in my home was the first time I felt differently
about him. I think it was because I hadn't realized till then what
a constant presence Dean had been in my life ever since I was in
diapers. I got that nasty scar on my knee when I tripped and fell
running after him down the street behind my house when I was
seven. He was the only boy I'd made love with. The first in everything. The one who took me to prom. The one I applied to college
with. So many moments. So many memories...

And now he was there in front of me like a stranger.

My stomach started turning and I stood, wiping my mouth
with a napkin. Everyone stopped talking and looked at me, not
understanding.

"I don't feel very good. If you'll excuse me..."

I walked up to the second floor, stumbling on the carpet. Once
I was in the bathroom, I washed my face with cool water and tried
to calm down. I didn't know what all that was about. It didn't
make sense. Or maybe it did. Maybe it made complete sense at the
moment.

I heard knocking at the door.

"Ginger...can you open up?"

It was Dean. I took a deep breath, slid open the lock, and let him
in. We looked at each other in the bathroom mirror.

"I think... I think we should talk."

"It's about time," I murmured.

"What?"

"Nothing."

He followed me to my room. Inside, he looked at the corkboard still full of photos of him. The silence was uncomfortable. Dean looked too big and too strange in that room, as if he didn't fit there, however little sense that made.

"I don't know where to start."

"Me neither," I said.

"I guess we should have had this talk months ago. I've been thinking about it since then…" He walked over, and I felt the mattress sink as he sat close to me, still nervous. "I don't know, Ginger, you've always been in my life, and I… I guess I had a breakdown and didn't stop to think about your feelings. I'm sorry."

I took a breath, surprised. Mainly because I knew him so well and he wasn't someone used to saying he was sorry. In his eyes, I saw he was waiting for a response, and I was trying to work out if I was angry, if I had a right to be, or if I should *be understanding*, and if that meant I'd be turning back into the Ginger I didn't want to be. I shook my head.

"I should scream at you. I should…"

"That's not you though."

"Yeah. But I want to."

"I'd like us to try to be friends. I'm not asking for us to see each other often or anything like that, but we could see each other one afternoon for a coffee or something. I don't know."

My nose tingled. And it wasn't because of Dean; it was because of me. I looked down at the comforter, at a loose thread that seemed to hang there, unwanted. *What a life*, I thought. Being there, lost, unable to move, unable to be a part of the fabric around me, stuck. That was how I felt in that moment. Two parts of me were fighting against each other. One of them wanted to forgive Dean, be his friend, get back something of the relationship that had brought us together for so many years. The other wanted to get up, suck in a deep breath, and start screaming. But I didn't even know what to scream. I didn't hate him. He'd hurt me, the way he'd done things, but I'd also hurt myself, for just taking it when I should have reacted. Not for him, but for me. I felt that ship had sailed now, and there was no point in trying to catch it. And the Ginger I was now didn't even want to in her heart.

I remembered that swallowing that pain had, in a way, brought me into contact with Rhys. How ironic. I guess every action, every detail, every decision takes us toward a different destination, and sometimes your fate can change when you least expect it.

"If you want to be left alone..."

I shook my head. "I forgive you."

Dean smiled, and before I could prepare myself, he leaned over and hugged me. I couldn't get my arms around his back, but I didn't pull away. I was still a little uncomfortable until he let me go.

"You know... I miss you."

I couldn't tell him I missed him too. Those months away from him had helped me get to know myself better, even if I was still lost, and I had a new friend, had kissed another guy, and had gone out on a date...

"I'll need some time to learn to be comfortable with you again. I'm not saying no to a coffee sometime in the future, but it'll need to be later. And I think... I think I at least deserve an explanation of what happened. Why all of a sudden you wanted to live and experience new things and all."

That was hard for him at first. He opened and closed his mouth, looked down at his hands, let the seconds pass. Then his shell cracked, and he told me how he'd been feeling, how the monotony had worn him down, how he felt he was missing something, even if he wasn't sure what. It hurt a little, because I was part of that routine that wasn't enough for him, but I could also understand.

"Are you better now?" I asked.

"Yeah. I think so. It depends." Dean cocked his head, looking curious. "How about you? You seem different, Ginger."

"I'll take that as a compliment."

I smiled. So did he.

19

From: Ginger Davies
To: Rhys Baker
Subject: Home sweet home

I'm back at the dorm. Isn't it weird that this kind of feels more like home than home? I guess it was a process, so I didn't really realize it. But one day I woke up, and the place in the city had changed from "home" to "my parents' house," and it was as simple as that. It was less mine, even if I have a room and all my things there. It's almost like a museum.

Do you still have your old room, Rhys?

I don't know why, but that's hard for me to imagine.

I haven't heard from you much lately. Are you okay? I hope so. I don't have much to tell. I'm excited and terrified for the school year. On the one hand, it's great to be sharing a room with Kate and to know that next summer will mark the end of a major phase in my life, but I'm also scared of what will come afterward. I think I'll feel like a tennis ball getting struck, bouncing back and forth, and getting lost. And I'll have to deal with things I'm not even thinking about right now, but whatever, I'm also excited to start my *adult life* (you probably hate that expression).

I forgot to tell you I talked to Dean. He came with his parents to eat at my house. I thought it wouldn't affect me, because we see each other at school and all, but I think it was different, seeing him in that environment, because I couldn't stop remembering all that we had shared. Weird, right? How complex emotions are. I felt like I'd been keeping mine down too long, and when I finally let them out, they were...faint, like they'd lost intensity. The heat in them was gone.

I have to go. I'm taking a walk with Kate.

Kisses. Waiting for signs of life.

From: Rhys Baker
To: Ginger Davies
Subject: Signs of life

Sorry for being a little absent; things have been complicated these days. Yeah, I hate the expression *adult life*. It should just be *life*, nothing else. My favorite story used to be *Peter Pan*, so don't pay me any mind.

You know it's been a while since I've been home, but the last time I was there, my room was just your typical teenage guy's bedroom. There were fewer posters and less junk, but the shelves were still full of models I used to make with my dad, and a baseball signed by one of my favorite players was on the desk and… I don't know, I can't remember anything else. Books, photos, stuff.

I've been thinking about the thing with Dean for a while now… I think I get it. How the setting made it feel different. What did he say to you?

From: Ginger Davies
To: Rhys Baker
Subject: RE: Signs of life

I won't go into my conversation with Dean until you tell me what's up with you. You seem…glummer than usual? If that's possible. Come on, Rhys, you can trust me. I'm a good listener (reader).

Kisses (for real).

From: Rhys Baker
To: Ginger Davies
Subject: RE: RE: Signs of life

That's the problem, I don't know what's up with me. This has been a weird summer. I've had fun, I've had sex, I've laughed, I've hung out on the beach, I've written songs, I've spent time with friends, but at the same time… I don't know, I have this feeling I'm looking for something and it's not there. And maybe… maybe it just doesn't exist.

I like your kisses (for real).

From: Ginger Davies

To: Rhys Baker
Subject: RE: RE: RE: Signs of life

I get it, Rhys. I think we all feel that way sometimes, even if we don't all look for *it* as intensely as you. But we are all aspiring for that *something more*, right? Has it occurred to you that maybe you're looking for what they call happiness? Also, some people are able to just accept their surroundings, and some aren't. I don't know. Maybe it's sad, but that's just how it is…

From: Rhys Baker
To: Ginger Davies
Subject: Life

I don't like to think about you just accepting things, Ginger.

Especially not if you think it's fucking sad.

I know you think you need to, but you don't have to hold on to a nine-to-five, buy a car, get a mortgage, get married, have a honeymoon in the Caribbean. Don't get me wrong. All that's perfect if you're into it, but you can't see it as an obligation or something that's written in stone.

You can be whatever you want, Ginger.

From: Ginger Davies
To: Rhys Baker
Subject: RE: Life

Everything you're saying is brilliant in theory, but it's hard to make happen in practice. But who cares? I don't want to talk about that. What would change? You didn't conform, and you still can't find whatever you're looking for. Isn't this why the conversation started?

From: Ginger Davies
To: Rhys Baker
Subject: RE: Life

Rhys, are you mad?

From: Ginger Davies
To: Rhys Baker
Subject: RE: Life

If you're mad, you might as well know I think you're acting like a five-year-old. Six, maybe. If you're lucky. This is class-idiot behavior.

From: Rhys Baker
To: Ginger Davies
Subject: RE: RE: Life

Whatever. I've got the brain of a six-year-old.
    (Better than being an eighty-two-year-old.)

From: Ginger Davies
To: Rhys Baker
Subject: RE: RE: RE: Life

Ha ha ha. I can't believe it.

You know what, you may act all independent and depressed and like you're just over life, but you remind me sometimes of the typical spoiled little kid who was a football star in high school and got to be prom king like in the movies. Admit it's true, and maybe I'd be willing to sign a truce.

From: Rhys Baker
To: Ginger Davies
Subject: RE: RE: RE: RE: Life

Maybe you just hit the nail on the head, Ginger Snap.

So fine, I'll sign the truce.

From: Ginger Davies
To: Rhys Baker
Subject: I HIT THE NAIL ON THE HEAD?

What does that mean? Rhys, Rhys, RHYS.

Answer me. Seriously. Don't let the curiosity kill me.

From: Rhys Baker
To: Ginger Davies
Subject: Let's negotiate

You first. You still haven't told me about your fascinating emotional conversation with Dean before you went back to the dorm. Don't make me beg.

From: Ginger Davies

To: Rhys Baker

Subject: RE: Let's negotiate

If I tell you, will you explain what you meant by hitting the nail on the head and give me a brief report on what your former life was like? I hate how we always get lost in other subjects.

From: Rhys Baker

To: Ginger Davies

Subject: RE: RE: Let's negotiate

Deal. You tell me about Dean, I'll tell you what you want to know.

20

From: Ginger Davies
To: Rhys Baker
Subject: My part of the deal

Okay, it was a gray morning—it always is—and I had been in the office with Dad (I'm trying to make this read like a novel so it will be more intense). I felt weird there, thinking about how I'd be there next year, watching the hands of the clock move on the wall. I don't know. It was probably a little bit of everything, now that I think about it. Plus my period had just started. I don't know if you care, but I'm including that because I think it's a good explanation for why I was so sensitive. It got worse when I got home and I saw Dean's parents were already there. I never told you this, I don't think, but they're great. We hugged, *blahblahblah*, and we sat and ate at the table together. My sister showed up a little later. All of a sudden, I looked at him and I felt…something. Grief. I remembered everything we'd been through together, afternoons playing, all these moments from when we were growing up…

Don't you think it's sad how sometimes you lose touch with a person who at one time meant everything to you? It's weird. I know they say life takes turns, people come and go, and whatever, but maybe we shouldn't pretend that's just normal. It scares me to think human beings can up and change like that.

Anyway, my eyes started stinging (I'm not the type to just cry like that; usually it's gradual, I try to avoid it, but eventually it overwhelms me), and I got up and went to the bathroom. He came not long afterward and asked if we could talk. We wound up in my room sitting on the bed. It's weird to think how things change sometimes, you know? That was the same place where he kissed me one afternoon five years before, when we were doing our science homework. And now we were there talking about our breakup. It's crazy. Ironic. How little you can predict things.

I guess I understood him. And I forgave him. Especially because I realized what hurt wasn't so much losing him as a boyfriend, but just giving up all those years of friendship and the trust we had. That hit me, seeing him there, at home. I remembered all the important things Dean had walked all over just because he didn't have the courage to give me the explanations I needed, you know?

But it was strange… I didn't feel sad…

I even thought how, if things hadn't happened in exactly the way they did, you and I would never have met. Fate is funny like that. I mean, imagine if Dean had wanted to talk to me, and it had dragged on for two or three hours. I'd never have caught that plane. I'd never have felt so lost, because at least I'd have had the answers I didn't get at the time. You wouldn't have seen me struggling with the ticket machine. Even if a traffic light had turned red and I'd gone down to the station a minute later, we wouldn't have seen each other. Don't you realize how fragile it all is? The thread is so thin, it's almost scary to touch it.

So to sum things up: it was better than I expected. I blew off some steam, he explained himself, he told me I seemed different (I liked that), I realized bad things sometimes bring good things with them, and before I left home, after packing everything in my suitcase, I took down basically all the photos of Dean that were still up on the corkboard in my room. Don't ask me why I left them there all summer. All I know is that until I brought that stage to some kind of close, I wasn't ready to stuff them into a box. I left just one, from the day we graduated from high school, because I still had good memories of that moment, and he was a part of it, after all.

We've decided we'll have coffee one day. Who knows? I'm not saying I'll do it tomorrow, but maybe a time will come when I'm in the mood for it.

I'll bet you regret saying you wanted to know all the details. Well, too late, Rhys. And now you owe me a big, long email revealing your deepest, darkest secrets. Don't be stingy with the deets.

From: Rhys Baker
To: Ginger Davies

Subject: RE: My part of the deal

Right, I think I get what you mean about Dean. And honestly, when I thought he was an idiot who didn't deserve you, I hadn't considered that he was your friend. Or all the stuff you experienced with him. I know what you mean about people forgetting things quickly, but didn't you ever think maybe that was a survival mechanism?

Because some things…just hurt too much.

PS: Don't freak out. I'll send you another email soon and keep up my side of the bargain. And I promise I'll try to put it all out there, as much as I'm able to, even if I suck at it. You're lucky—I can't fall asleep tonight.

From: Rhys Baker
To: Ginger Davies
Subject: Second try

Honestly, Ginger, I don't know where to start. For half an hour, I've been looking at the computer screen, and I've started this email a million times, but then I keep erasing everything I write. I think that's why I sent you the other one earlier, because I wasn't sure how long it would take me to write this one. It's morning here, so I guess you're already at school. Ginger, Ginger. You know what I like most about you? How you let me see you from the word go, without asking for anything in exchange, without hiding. You made me want to do the same, to give you…

something. I don't know why it's so hard for me to talk about myself. I'm not anyone special. I haven't had a traumatic life. In theory I'm no different from you, but…look at us. Me writing and erasing and rewriting while you're probably banging on the keyboard nonstop.

From: Rhys Baker
To: Ginger Davies
Subject: A part of me

Okay, it all comes down to that time I told you that you'd hit the nail on the head. It's true: I grew up in a big house in one of the nicest parts of the state. We had a maid and a gardener. I had a happy childhood. I adored my father. I adored my mother. We looked like the perfect family.

And yes, Ginger, I was captain of the football team, the guy who got invited to all the parties and went out with the hottest chick in class. And—right again—I was prom king. So what do you think? Impressed? I never pushed to make these things happen; they just did. I didn't even try. I had everything a person could want in arm's reach. For a long time. My life was idyllic.

From: Ginger Davies
To: Rhys Baker
Subject: RE: A part of me

Rhys, I don't know what to say. I didn't imagine… Honestly I was joking when I said all that stuff. I never thought a person like you...the person I met... I don't know, I mean, I can't even imagine you like that as a kid. Just forget it. Don't tell me anything you don't want me to know, my snail boy. I'll be your friend no matter what.

From: Rhys Baker
To: Ginger Davies
Subject: The other part of me

So the other side of the coin is that I had never felt emptier than I did at that time in my life. Or more alone. Is there any solitude that's sadder, Ginger, than being surrounded by people but feeling like there's no one there?

Remember what you told me that night in Paris about how you were scared you'd killed and buried the true Ginger? Honestly, you don't have to kill the real you; you can just throw a muzzle on and forget yourself day after day. I feel like that's what a lot of us do. We convince ourselves we want to be a certain way that doesn't come naturally from within us, and we don't even really like it. It doesn't fulfill us; it doesn't move us. But we force it. And we keep trying. And the years pass. And you start doing this thing and that thing, and you convince yourself that you can be happy since everyone else is (or looks like they are). But you know what? It's not true. And one day, I realized that.

I realized I just had one life, and I didn't want to throw it in the trash.

I realized the time had come to change things.

And here we are, Ginger, talking about what life means...

From: Ginger Davies
To: Rhys Baker
Subject: RE: The other part of me

For the first time ever, you've made an effort to really open up. You're doing great. For real. See? Nothing bad happened; the world's still going on its merry way. I'm proud I can inspire you to open up and be more expressive. I admit I didn't expect what you told me about your past, and it surprised me, but... I like it, Rhys. I think you're the most contradictory, unpredictable person I know. I wonder if that should scare me.

From: Rhys Baker
To: Ginger Davies
Subject: RE: RE: The other part of me

Why should it scare you, Ginger?

From: Ginger Davies
To: Rhys Baker
Subject: Reasons

My sister says you're interesting. Not just that, but "addictive." Like one of those series where the writers manage to make you always want to watch the next episode. Why? Because things happen that you can't predict. Surprises. And you want to know more. People don't get hooked on something if they know how it ends. At least, not as intensely.

From: Rhys Baker
To: Ginger Davies
Subject: RE: Reasons

You're losing me, Ginger Snap.

But I like that thing about me being addictive.

From: Ginger Davies
To: Rhys Baker
Subject: Relax

Don't let it go to your head. What I mean is, what would happen if you suddenly got tired of me and stopped writing? It'd be like not knowing the ending.

From: Rhys Baker
To: Ginger Davies
Subject: RE: Relax

I'll never get tired of you.

From: Ginger Davies
To: Rhys Baker

Subject: RE: RE: Relax

I see you've run out of words to tell me about your past. Get some rest. Your fingers must be rubbed raw. (I'm being sarcastic, in case you can't tell.)

PS: I'll never get tired of you either.

21

Rhys

WHEN I WAS LITTLE, I thought Sundays were the best day of the week. I can almost still feel the happiness I felt upon waking. I'd open my eyes and realize I didn't have school and my dad would be at home all day. I remember the light that would come through the kitchen window in spring, the sound of branches swaying in the garden, the birds chirping, how happy I was as I ate my cereal and Dad read the newspaper across from me, drinking his coffee. Sometimes he'd frown, displeased. Or maybe laugh. Sometimes he'd read a story aloud, especially as I started getting older. I'd try to respond appropriately. Years later, we started arguing, and my mother would grin on the other side of the table; then finally she'd leave. Probably she got bored of listening to us.

It wasn't just being with family that made Sundays special. It was rather…a feeling. A warm, agreeable, lazy feeling, but lazy in the good sense of the term. I never felt that again, and with the passage of years, it vanished.

22

From: Rhys Baker
To: Ginger Davies
Subject: Los Angeles

I've decided to stay a while longer in LA. They've said they'll keep me on another two months, until December, and I've agreed. I don't feel like going to San Fran. Probably having Logan here is part of it. I haven't told you much about him, but I've known him since college, and that makes me feel at home. It's hard to explain, because we barely have anything in common, but I guess sometimes that doesn't matter.

What are your plans for the week? Lots of stuff to study?

From: Ginger Davies
To: Rhys Baker
Subject: RE: Los Angeles

Good, I like the idea of you staying in one place for a while. I don't know how it doesn't drive you crazy going back and forth all the time. How long ago was it we met? Eight months? And you've already lived in three cities. I couldn't do it. I'd miss stuff. Like opening my drawer and seeing all my socks matched and folded together.

Yeah, I've got tons of work. I guess that's how it is being a senior. I'm thinking about my final project, but I don't really know...

From: Rhys Baker
To: Ginger Davies
Subject: For real?

That's the best thing you can think of, Ginger, a well-organized sock drawer? You think I don't have socks of my own? Maybe not thirty pairs like you, but I've got a week's worth, and I know how to wash them.

I'm sure you'll come up with something for your project.

From: Ginger Davies
To: Rhys Baker
Subject: RE: For real?

Okay, so the socks were a dumb example, but you get the idea. Routine. Stability. Thousands of things go into that. Traveling back and forth between cities makes it impossible to have any normal relationships.

From: Rhys Baker
To: Ginger Davies
Subject: Wrong

I've got a sock drawer.
    And I have a relationship with you.
    Find another excuse.

From: Ginger Davies
To: Rhys Baker
Subject: Patience

You're an idiot.
    I was talking about romantic relationships.

From: Rhys Baker
To: Ginger Davies
Subject: RE: Patience

Those types of relationships aren't my thing, so maybe there's
something positive in my present situation. Otherwise I might run
the risk of fucking things up with someone who matters to me.

From: Ginger Davies
To: Rhys Baker
Subject: Curiosity

Why aren't they your "thing"?

So I was right from the beginning. You're a one-night stand kind of guy. So predictable, Rhys. You've let me down.

From: Rhys Baker
To: Ginger Davies
Subject: Expectations

What did you expect, Ginger?

From: Ginger Davies
To: Rhys Baker
Subject: RE: Expectations

Nothing and everything. I didn't expect you to be one of those guys who's allergic to commitment, who hides behind that to amuse himself with spending the night with girls. Not that there's something wrong with that—don't misunderstand me. I'm not looking for anything serious either, but that's not a rule or a principle; it's just what I'm into right now.

What I do know is, a true relationship requires effort and sacrifice. Whereas a random fuck means not thinking and just letting yourself go. And those two things aren't compatible.

From: Rhys Baker
To: Ginger Davies
Subject: ...

Did you ever stop to think that something that requires "effort and sacrifice" is already a problem? I don't understand why we should impose things on ourselves that don't make us happy. Life would be way easier if we just felt and lived day to day without pressure, without having to follow the herd down this or that road.

From: Ginger Davies
To: Rhys Baker
Subject: RE: ...

Are you calling me a sheep?

From: Rhys Baker
To: Ginger Davies
Subject: RE: RE: ...

I've painted myself into a corner, right? Whatever I say, you're going to get mad. So to hell with it, I'm risking it all. Maybe I am sometimes kind of a "snail," but you're a little bit of a "sheep" too.

From: Rhys Baker
To: Ginger Davies
Subject: Confirmation

I guess it's official: you're pissed.

From: Rhys Baker
To: Ginger Davies
Subject: Clarification

I didn't mean that as an insult. I was just saying you tend to follow the script in life. And if that's what you want to do, it's fine. But maybe you could try to respect people who don't too. So I'm not looking for the kind of relationship you described. Who knows though? Maybe when we're forty and we're still talking, you'll find me living in a ranch in the Midwest with twenty kids and my second wife, and you'll laugh when you think of this moment. But right now...at this very instant...I just can't see it. It's not a part of my plans.

Come on, Ginger. I miss you.

Help me start November on the right foot.

From: Ginger Davies
To: Rhys Baker
Subject: Note

I want to make one thing clear. First of all, you can't have twenty kids when you're forty. You've only got fourteen years left. That means it would be impossible.

From: Rhys Baker
To: Ginger Davies
Subject: Smart cookie

I mentioned living with my second wife. Who's to say I didn't get my first wife, who used to be my lover, and my second wife pregnant at the same time? Do the math. Ten kids each for two women is totally doable.

From: Ginger Davies
To: Rhys Baker
Subject: I'm getting bored

You can't see me, but I'm rolling my eyes. And eating a chocolate donut and writing with one hand and thinking that sometimes you piss me off so much, I wouldn't even give you a bite if you were here. Hear me? Zilch. Not a nibble. Not even a lick.

From: Rhys Baker
To: Ginger Davies
Subject: Mmmm

Jeez, Ginger, do you have some kind of sexual fetish with donuts? Relax, I think I'll survive without running my tongue across your snack. Unless, of course, *donut* is a code word.

From: Ginger Davies
To: Rhys Baker
Subject: RE: Mmmm

Pig.

From: Rhys Baker
To: Ginger Davies
Subject: RE: RE: Mmmm

You're the little piglet, eating in bed with one hand at your

laptop, probably licking your fingers while you write, Ginger
Snap.

From: Ginger Davies
To: Rhys Baker
Subject: RE: RE: RE: Mmmm

SAUIHFSAF QWAUFHB QWJFBSC

From: Rhys Baker
To: Ginger Davies
Subject: RE: RE: RE: RE: Mmmm

Does that mean you're pounding on the computer?

From: Ginger Davies
To: Rhys Baker
Subject: RE: RE: RE: RE: RE: Mmmm

While I think of you, yes.
    Good night, Rhys.

From: Rhys Baker
To: Ginger Davies
Subject: RE: RE: RE: RE: RE: RE: Mmmm

Ha ha ha ha ha ha ha ha. Ha ha ha ha ha ha ha ha.
    Good night, Ginger Snap. Get some rest.

23

From: Rhys Baker

To: Ginger Davies

Subject: The Little Prince

I can't sleep. So I've spent the last hour rereading our messages, and I've realized you've never told me really about that book you like so much. So maybe now's a good time. That way I'll have something to do tonight besides stare at the ceiling until dawn.

From: Ginger Davies

To: Rhys Baker

Subject: RE: The Little Prince

You know what would help you sleep? Reading the book yourself. There must be a bookstore or library nearby where you can find it.

From: Rhys Baker

To: Ginger Davies

Subject: RE: RE: The Little Prince

Right now, I'd rather you tell me. Things are always better from your perspective, Ginger. Didn't I ever tell you that? Well, they are.

From: Ginger Davies
To: Rhys Baker
Subject: RE: RE: RE: The Little Prince

Fine, but in exchange, you have to promise me you'll read it one day. It's a sweet parable about friendship and the meaning of life, like one of those magical stories from childhood, except this one is for adults. The first time I read it, I actually was a little girl, and I didn't understand any of it. I found my copy in Skoob Books, a secondhand shop in Bloomsbury. It was a very old copy, and I've held on to it like a treasure, obviously. I bought it despite my mother's protests. She wanted me to pick something else; she didn't like that it had pictures. Imagine my disappointment when I started it and realized it was for grown-ups. But luckily, I got bored years later and decided to grab it off the shelf and take a look. I must have been fourteen. And it fascinated me, and I had no idea it would keep on surprising me when I reread it. That's one of the secrets of *The Little Prince*: you can reread it a dozen times, and you'll always learn something new.

If you're still reading this message and haven't died of boredom, I'll tell you this: It's the story of a man who ends up in the desert in the Sahara when his plane goes off course. There, he meets the Little Prince, who's left Asteroid B612 looking for answers to his questions and for a friend. When they meet, the first thing he asks is for a picture of a lamb inside a box. For the protagonist, who's a grown-up with grown-up values, the Little Prince signifies purity, innocence, a return to his own essence.

From: Rhys Baker
To: Ginger Davies
Subject: RE: RE: RE: RE: The Little Prince

I admit it: It sounds nice. What happens next?

From: Ginger Davies
To: Rhys Baker
Subject: RE: RE: RE: RE: RE: The Little Prince

If you read the book, you'll find out. There's a bunch more characters that symbolize different archetypes, like the fox the Little Prince manages to tame and become friends with, and the rose. I mean, the rose deserves its own whole chapter, but just so you understand, it lives on Asteroid B612, and the prince watched it grow up, watered it, took care of it, obeyed all its demands, because it's a needy flower, but still, for him, it's the only flower in the world. But then he comes to earth, and he discovers an entire rosebush...

From: Rhys Baker
To: Ginger Davies

Subject: RE: RE: RE: RE: RE: RE: The Little Prince

Aren't you going to tell me more? Come on, Ginger, give me your whole version of it.

From: Ginger Davies
To: Rhys Baker
Subject: RE: RE: RE: RE: RE: RE: RE: The Little Prince

Sorry, but no. Good night, Rhys.

24

From: Rhys Baker
To: Ginger Davies
Subject: Mental note

Don't ever let me go out partying with Logan again. Seriously, if I ever end up telling you I'm going to go hang out with him, remind me of the November 14 when we wound up high and sitting in the police station.

My head hurts. I think I need some sleep.

From: Ginger Davies
To: Rhys Baker
Subject: RE: Mental note

RHYS, YOU GOT ARRESTED?

From: Rhys Baker
To: Ginger Davies

Subject: Good morning

I don't know how many hours I've slept. Yeah, we got arrested. Yesterday my boss's boss told me if I was willing to move, he could give me a job for a year at one of his other clubs. So we went out to celebrate, but it was supposed to be chill; the plan was to just grab a drink. It turns out, though, that we met a couple of girls there who were on vacation. A couple of girls who happened to have weed. A couple of girls we wound up at the beach with at the crack of dawn. You can imagine the rest.

I don't remember most of it. Just that at some point I was out by the sea, the cops stopped us on the boardwalk, and Logan threw up in the car that was taking us to the station.

What did you do over the weekend?

My head still hurts.

From: Ginger Davies
To: Rhys Baker
Subject: Bad morning

Thanks for going to bed yesterday without responding; I was freaking out. I kept asking myself what you might have done, and I was about to try and find out if they had computers at the jail so I could keep emailing you or whether we'd have to switch to pen and paper.

That reminds me: we've never exchanged numbers. I'm not saying we have to, but it is kind of weird, right? You're my best friend, and I can't call you if I ever feel like talking to you or if something happens. Whatever, forget it.

My weekend was way more normal than yours, obviously. I went out with Kate and some girls from our class who are really cool. I had a beer, played some snooker, and got to my dorm without getting arrested. Congratulate me.

This week I have a few exams.

I envy you so much sometimes, Rhys...

From: Rhys Baker
To: Ginger Davies
Subject: RE: Bad morning

My phone number? Do you have a hidden agenda, Ginger? J/K. I'll give it to you if you'll give me your address. Your birthday's next month, right? I want to send you a present.

From: Ginger Davies
To: Rhys Baker
Subject: [No subject]

Sounds a little like a mail bomb.

From: Rhys Baker
To: Ginger Davies
Subject: RE: [No subject]

HA HA HA. You're fucking nuts, Ginger.

From: Ginger Davies
To: Rhys Baker
Subject: Nerves

I was kidding! Sorry I didn't answer yesterday. I'm basically living in the library again. My address is at the end of this email. But you should know… I'm really nervous! I don't know if I ever told you, but getting presents drives me up the wall. UP THE WALL. Like I want to know what it is that reminds you of me or that you think is right for me, and I'm scared you'll get it just right, and I'm scared you'll screw it up completely. No pressure though. When I was little, I used to always scour the house trying to find my Christmas gifts. Sometimes I'd make Donna and Dean help me find them. So my parents ended up hiding them at the company's office because they were always afraid I'd open them early. (I was young when I learned Santa didn't exist, because my birthday's three days before Christmas, and I only got one set of presents. I know, it's horrible, and no child deserves to go through that.)

But let's get back to what matters.

Your job. Where to now, Rhys? If it's Europe, maybe we could meet somewhere. There are more and more cheap flights all the time. I don't want to seem like a stalker though. I'm not going to call you, BTW, even if I do have your number; I just like to know that you'll be there for me if I ever do need you.

From: Rhys Baker
To: Ginger Davies
Subject: RE: Nerves

Okay, here's my number then. You can call me if you want, but I like these emails. It's the best thing when I get home, you know? Like right now: I came home, cracked open a beer, plopped down in an easy chair by the window, and opened my computer to read your message and write back. I like that this is something only the two of us share.

Oh, and I'll hit the mark with my present. You don't realize it, but I know you better than you think. Peeking in every corner of the house like a crazy person trying to find your presents—yeah, that sounds like you.

Will you spend your birthday at home or in the dorms?

Sorry, I won't be coming to Europe this time. Maybe in the summer. I'm going to the other side of the world. To Australia. I needed a change...

From: Ginger Davies
To: Rhys Baker
Subject: The end of the earth

AUSTRALIA? That's the literal end of the earth. I hope there's Wi-Fi there. And that you'll send me photos of koalas. They're so cute. I don't know what it is about them, but they're fascinating, the way they evolved to hug things. Plus they're super furry.

You're so lucky, Rhys. Take me with you. Put me in your suitcase.

I've got a plan: Kidnap me. We'll enjoy a month of vacation on a heavenly beach of white sand. Then you can ask for a ransom. My parents love me; I'm ninety-nine percent certain they'd give a good amount of money for me. (Remember, I'm supposed to take over the family business.) With that, we can record an album, and you'll get famous. I'll bribe my professors so they'll let me make up my exams, and I'll graduate summa cum laude. Plus I'll be in the papers because of the kidnapping. What do you think? It's an airtight plan IMO.

Shit. I don't want to take my exams. I don't want to spend the winter in London. It's cold all the time. It doesn't matter how I dress; I always feel like an ice cube. And the sky's always gray. And you just keep traveling back and forth from one hot, fun place to another. I hate you. A little bit.

Don't act like you know me soooo well. I'm a mysterious girl, enigmatic. Ha ha. By the way, I'll spend my birthday half here and half there. I'll spend the morning here packing my bag, and then I'll catch the train to have lunch at home. I'll stay there for Christmas.

From: Rhys Baker
To: Ginger Davies
Subject: You say when

Come with me. What's stopping you?

From: Ginger Davies
To: Rhys Baker
Subject: RE: You say when

Very funny, Rhys. I don't know, maybe I have a degree to finish?

For example. Not that it matters. It's just a minor thing. Also, I need to start my job after. Just that.

From: Rhys Baker
To: Ginger Davies
Subject: Life is long

True, you have to finish school. But when you do, there are still lots of summers left. Who knows, maybe one day you'll catch a plane for Australia or somewhere else? You did do it once, remember?

From: Ginger Davies
To: Rhys Baker
Subject: RE: Life is long

Yes, I remember how I was lost until some dude looking bored with the world came up and rescued me. Rhys, let's admit it, I'm not one of those adventurous chicks destined to take on the world. Probably the opposite. Probably I'm just waiting for the world to crush me. But it's fine, I've got lots of other things going on. Not all of us have to be brave and independent and all that. I don't know, I see you and I think, I just couldn't live like that: grabbing a bag and taking off on my own. I'd probably lose my shit, break down in tears, and run for the first embassy I could find.

From: Ginger Davies
To: Rhys Baker

Subject: Routine

I feel weird when we go for more than a day without writing. Turning on the computer and not finding one of your emails makes me sleep badly, just so you know.

I told you already. I'm addicted to your emails.

25

Ginger

I WAS NERVOUS. I ALWAYS am on my birthday, plus I was expecting a package from Rhys. That's why I'd woken up at 6:00 a.m. and hadn't managed to get back to sleep despite hours of tossing and turning. I finally got up, trying not to make noise because I didn't want to bother Kate, and I had a weird feeling in my chest as I reread our last couple of emails.

I felt like something wasn't right.

Like I was backsliding.

That first semester, I'd been so busy thinking of my final project, my classes, and my future plans that I hadn't devoted much time to myself. I was just someone who would settle as soon as I found a warm, comfortable nest, and that was what the nest I had built with Kate bit by bit over the past few months was: safe, stable. And so once again, I was turning in on myself.

And once again, there he was, reminding me of all the things that were out there. Other places, other countries. An entire world.

Part of me was bothered by it.

Another part of me liked that he was trying to shake me up.

Kate awoke sometime after nine and tackled me into bed, singing the happy birthday song while we laughed. Then she hopped in the shower, and I ate an energy bar and looked out the window at the leaden sky. It looked like snow. For a moment, I thought about how nice it would have been to celebrate my twenty-second birthday somewhere warm and far away, where there was no such thing as routine.

"You coming to breakfast?" Kate asked on her way out.

"No. I had an energy bar."

"Are you really going to wait here for your present?"

"Don't look at me like that, Kate. If I leave, and the mailman comes and I'm not here, I won't get it till after Christmas vacation. I can't wait that long."

"Fine. Tell me if you change your mind. I'm going to have a coffee with the girls, and then we're going to the same pub we were at the other night. Claire left her keys there."

When I was alone, I grabbed two textbooks I hadn't packed yet and looked back over some notes, trying to do something useful. I kept getting distracted though, looking out the window, watching some students laughing against the wall of the dorm building while they smoked. First-year kids, second-year, maybe. I had to remind myself that I was nearly done here. I still couldn't accept it. Worst of all, I wasn't especially excited.

Someone rang the doorbell.

I got up so quickly, I hit my knee on the corner of the table and cursed. I took a deep breath and didn't bother putting on my shoes, thinking the mailman wouldn't really mind if he saw me in my reindeer pajamas and a different-colored sock on each foot.

But when I opened up, it wasn't the mailman.

There was a young man with messy hair and a lazy smile leaning on the doorframe like he owned the place, as if he knew it like the back of his hand. I felt butterflies in my stomach. He looked at me. I looked at him.

"Happy birthday, Ginger Snap."

"Rhys…" I could barely speak.

"Try to be a little more enthusiastic."

"No, dammit, it's just that… I just didn't see it coming! Rhys! You're here!" I reached out and touched him without thinking. I rested my hands on his chest, and he laughed just as I remembered him doing, with crow's feet in the corners of his eyes. "Rhys!"

I hugged him so tight I was almost hanging off his neck.

And we remained there, breathing, silent, together.

He still smelled like mint. And also like him. Which meant like no one else.

"That's more like it," he whispered in my ear, and he pulled away, following me into my room and closing the door. I felt him there, in every corner, between walls I thought would never hold him.

"You caught me by surprise. I mean, I was hoping your gift would come today, and I just assumed it was the mailman when I heard the doorbell ring. If I'd known it was you, I would have combed my hair and gotten dressed. I mean, this is the second time we've ever seen each other, and I'm wearing pajamas. With reindeer on them. Donna gave them to me for Christmas a couple of years ago, and… I'm talking too much again. Rhys, please, do something to shut me up. I'm nervous!"

He just smiled, standing in the middle of my room, stroking his chin, and looking at me with his eyes intense, warm, gleaming. "I'm not going to stop you. I missed hearing you talk."

"You're...you're..." I took a deep breath, still confused.

"The best friend in the world, I know."

He didn't ask permission as he walked over to what he immediately knew was my side of the room. He could just tell. My heart was pounding as he bent over the desk and looked at everything, curious, calm. Since he wasn't talking, I watched him, focused on his blond hair, a little longer with a few curls touching his ears; his sun-toasted skin; his gray eyes, looking more intense now that his face was a deeper color. He was wearing pale jeans and a black sweater under his leather jacket. And he had two braided bracelets on his right wrist.

"Let me know when you stop staring at me," he said.

Then he lay down on the bed. My mini bed. Unmade. On top of the pile of blankets, he laid an arm behind his head, and his sweater climbed up, revealing a few inches of tan skin. He raised an eyebrow as he looked at me.

"You weren't so arrogant the last time I saw you," I replied.

"You were just as sexy. Nice pajamas."

I sat on the bed and observed him. He stopped smiling. I guess it was because he could see how serious I looked after those first few minutes of confusion. I'd only seen him once in my life. Once. Fewer than twenty-four hours. And yet, he knew me better than anyone. He knew everything about my day, my routine, my fears, my worries, my weirdest thoughts. It was crazy. I reached a hand out toward him.

His eyes held my stare.

I touched his cheek.

"I can't believe you're here."

26

Rhys

IT WAS HARD FOR ME to believe I was there too. That I'd decided to change routes and make a stop in London on my way to Australia. But I'd done it. The day before, I was standing by the ocean saying goodbye to the city that had welcomed me for months. And now I was there, in her room, in front of the girl who had wound up in my life for reasons I couldn't fathom. By chance. Over something stupid.

I took a deep breath when I felt her fingertips rub my cheek. Softly. As if she were scared to dare to touch me. I wanted her to keep doing it. I wanted to grab her wrist and pull her close. I wanted to kiss her. Hard. With lust.

"What are you thinking about?" she asked.

"Nothing. Everything. This moment."

Ginger laughed and pulled her hand back. The bed smelled like her. That entire damned place smelled like her. And all I'd needed was a second to know which side of the room was hers. She stood up with a furrowed brow as she looked in the full-length mirror beside her closet.

"I should clean up a bit..."

"You look good to me."

"Rhys."

"When do you need to be home?"

"I told them I'd be there by lunchtime."

"And then...?"

"I... I'm sorry, I can't look at you without laughing."

"Ginger." I suppressed a smile.

"I'm just nervous! And when I get nervous, I laugh. What made you just come here without warning me? I get it, birthday surprise, but still... I want to hug you, but at the same time, it's so weird that you're even here."

I tried not to show how funny I found the whole thing. How funny I always found her. I stood up, walked over, and rested my hands on her shoulders. I bowed my head to look directly into her eyes.

"Calm down. My flight leaves at nine. So once again, we have less than twenty-four hours ahead of us. Now go shower and get your suitcase, and we'll go to the train station. You'll have lunch with your parents, and we'll spend the afternoon together. In the city. You'll be my guide this time. That's only fair."

"Rhys... I'm so happy!"

"I'm glad."

"Where are you going to sleep?"

"I got a hotel room. I'm not as crazy as someone I know." I dodged the hair clip she threw at me. "Someone whose aim is as bad as her ability to buy a subway ticket."

I laughed as she cursed to herself, gathering her clean clothes and walking into the bathroom. Then I sighed. I tried not to show it, but I was nervous. Alert. It made me uncomfortable having to hold my breath when I got too close to her and felt that little jolt inside. And all that order: her neat desk, organized even if it was full of colorful junk (pens, notepads, candles, candy). It all defined her so well. And I couldn't stop imagining her there in that bed, computer open, eating a donut with one hand as she wrote me.

There was a lot I couldn't stop imagining.

I looked at the sky through the window when the sound of the water in the shower ended. I memorized its color, that gray that surrounded us and that she always complained about in her emails to me.

Ginger came out soon after. I smiled when I saw her.

She was wearing jeans and a sweatshirt. Her hair was pulled back in a simple ponytail.

"I'm ready. Sorry about my appearance. I'm not a miracle worker."

"You don't need to be. Where's your suitcase?"

A minute later, we were leaving in the direction of the train station while she called Kate, letting her know she was leaving early. I tried to memorize that walk, those walls, that small portion of her everyday world that I was finally seeing.

27

Ginger

"YOU STARING AT ME SO much is starting to make me uncomfortable."

"I can't stop doing it though. I need to keep doing it to convince myself you're still there. Anyway, I like looking at you, Rhys. Whatever. Forget I said that. I just... I'm not being weird, okay? Stop laughing."

He shook his head, still smiling, as the train kept roaring ahead. We were sitting next to each other. The tips of his shoes were rubbing mine. His bronzed arm was resting against the window, and he kept looking out, as if he wanted to preserve that constant movement.

"Tell me again why you decided to come."

"I already told you back at the station."

"Tell me again. Please. Pretty please."

"I wanted to see you, Ginger."

"That's so sweet." I cut him off.

He rolled his eyes, and I grinned.

"So you used to be captain of the football team."

"That matters now because...?"

"Because it's so hard to believe after getting to know you. I don't know. The way you move. The way you act. Your tough-guy attitude."

"I told you, it was a phase."

"I still think it means something."

"You're going to torture me forever, aren't you?"

"Yeah. That's the plan," I admitted, laughing. "By the way, you never did tell me what happened with the girl you were dating when you were prom king."

"We broke up," he said, looking away.

"Obviously. I meant why…"

I stopped talking when the train rocked, and Rhys grabbed my thigh and smiled, looking down at the little pineapples on my shoes.

"That's awful summery for London."

"I like contrasts," I said.

"As long as you can control them…"

"What do you mean by that?"

"Don't we have to get off here?"

"Shit! Yes!" I jumped up, and Rhys grabbed my suitcase from the overhead compartment before running for the doors, which were about to close. Once out, we looked at each other, grinning, as the train took off.

"Is your house close to here?"

"More or less. Let's take a walk."

We walked away from Victoria Station and into the chill wind of the city. Rhys looked around.

"I could sit and wait for you in one of these cafés."

"Wait for me?" I narrowed my eyes.

"While you have lunch with your family."

"What?" I shook my head. "No, of course not. You're coming with me. You can eat with us. My mother will be pleased to meet you, and there will be plenty of food."

Rhys stopped in the middle of the sidewalk as the people kept walking past. I could sense the tension in his shoulders, the doubt in his eyes.

"Does your mother know I exist?"

"Yeah. My sister blurted it out."

"Did you tell your whole family about me?"

"Eh. Yeah. It just came up. What's wrong, Rhys?" I laughed. "It's not like it's some secret that can never be confessed. Come on, it's my birthday, stop dawdling."

I grabbed the sleeve of his jacket and pulled him until he started walking again. We passed through St. James's Park. Rhys was quiet but attentive as we crossed streets and I shared stories with him about my life and my childhood. *I fell down on that corner. I used to meet up with my old friends at that café, people I don't really see anymore. That's Donna's favorite restaurant, but really it's nothing special.*

I saw him take a deep breath when we stopped in front of a two-story building that looked almost identical to its neighbors. I rang the doorbell.

"Ginger!" My mother was wiping her hands on her apron as she looked over at Rhys. He seemed nervous. But at the same time, curious. "Oh, hello."

"Can we do the introductions inside?" I asked, pointing to my heavy suitcase. My mother stepped aside and let us through. The central heating surrounded us, and I took off my gloves and scarf as I explained who Rhys was in fits and starts and he greeted her timidly. "He's going to stay for lunch. Then I'm going to show him around town."

"Around town? How many days are you staying, Rhys?"

"I'm leaving tomorrow," he replied.

"Oh, London is a place you can spend a lifetime exploring; a few days just doesn't work. Do you like shepherd's pie? I hope so. Ginger didn't tell me you were coming, but I'm sure I can whip something up with what I have in the fridge if you prefer something else. Are you more of a meat or fish person?"

"I'm fine with what you're serving." He smiled, a little tense.

"Great. Go relax in the dining room. Your father will be right back. Donna's coming late. By the way, Ginger, I invited the Wilsons; I hope that's not a problem. I can tell them something came up and have them over for tea tomorrow..."

"No, Mom, it's fine. We're going to put up our things."

We climbed the carpeted stairs to my room. Rhys left his backpack at the foot of the bed and took a look around. It was the second time in just a few hours that I felt as if he were rooting around inside me, looking for *something*, for details...

"Who are the Wilsons?" he asked.

"Dean's parents. This is him."

I pointed to the photo I'd pinned to the corkboard the summer before, when I hadn't yet moved back to the dorm, which showed us together on graduation day. Rhys stared at it a moment, and I wondered what he was thinking.

"Why are you so nervous?" I asked.

"Me?" He looked at me, amused. "I'm not."

"You look like a lion about to pounce. Tense. Away from your natural habitat. Dropped in the middle of some hostile territory you don't recognize."

"I guess it's been a long time since I was in a real home."

I was surprised he was so sincere, that he'd spoken so viscerally like that, when normally he always avoided hard questions or turned the conversation elsewhere. We looked at each other in silence; then he turned back to the photos. I held my breath as I watched him. It was still hard to believe he was here, just a few inches away. I could smell him. All I had to do to touch him was reach out my hand...

We heard my father's voice downstairs. He had arrived with the Wilsons, and it wasn't hard to see how uncomfortable Rhys was, even if he was making an effort. I tried to get him to feel as comfortable as possible, introducing him quickly and walking him to the table, giving him the chair beside me, ignoring Dean's curious look as he settled down across from us.

Fortunately, the conversation revolved around the new cabinets coming out next season. My father said they were going to set the market on fire. He'd signed an agreement with several department stores to carry them.

My sister showed up just before dessert and greeted Rhys familiarly, as if they'd already met. She sighed loudly as she flopped into her chair, and smiled when Mom walked through the doorway holding a cheesecake with a few lit candles.

"Happy birthday to you, happy birthday to you..."

I felt weird. I was twenty-two years old, and I felt like a one-year-old child. As the voices around me enveloped me, my mother set the cake in the middle of the table. I turned to Rhys for a second. Just one. His eyes met mine, and he smiled.

Then I made a wish.

And blew out the candles.

"Ginger told us you travel a lot," my father said as he served himself the biggest piece of cheesecake and got ready to attack it with his fork.

"Yeah, I'm headed to Australia for a while."

"How come?" Dean asked.

I think that was the first time he spoke to him. Rhys chewed the piece of cake he'd just put in his mouth and looked at him pensively, as if he were really thinking.

"I don't know. Work. Other stuff."

"So if you had to choose a place you liked best out of all those you've been to?" Donna asked. As Donna looked at him expectantly, I could feel his leg moving, brushing mine slightly as he leaned forward.

"I guess Paris has something special about it."

"Sure. You think that too, don't you, Ginger?"

I scowled at my sister. "I don't know. I'll find out one day when I go."

"I'd be happy to show you around," Rhys said.

I wanted to kill him. And my sister. They both looked at each other with a knowing grin as we finished our desserts. Then, after deciding against tea with the Wilsons, we helped clear the plates and I said goodbye to them as quickly as I could.

It was my birthday, and I loved being with them, but I only had a few hours with Rhys, and I didn't know when we'd see each other again. Maybe in a few months. Or in a year. Or never.

28

Rhys

THE COLD BUFFETED US AGAIN as we stepped outside. The color of the sky foretold nothing good, but all I had to do to warm up inside was look at her. It had been worth coming here, crazy as it was. Ginger was happy. A smile crossed her face as we walked to the bus stop. She was determined to have us get on one of those red double-decker buses. On the upper floor, we settled down in the very front, enjoying our views of the city.

"You're serious about giving me a tour?"

"I certainly am. Have you ever been here before?"

"Once, but it was a long time ago; I can barely remember it," I replied, dredging up a couple of memories. "I was seven or eight, and I came on a trip with my parents. All I remember is the hotel we were in had all these old paintings and furnishings and it scared me. I don't think I slept one night the whole way through."

"Oh, poor little Rhys," she joked.

I got lost in her eyes for a few seconds. They were big and clear, and her smile, graceful but mischievous, made me laugh.

"Where are you taking me?" My curiosity was getting the better of me.

"We're going to Camden. I think you'll like it there. The neighborhood, the feeling there. I know a place where they make the best arepas in the world. We can walk around there, then come back on the Tube, and..."

She bit her lower lip. Watching her made me feel faint.

"And...?" I asked.

"We can get on the Ferris wheel. The London Eye."

"No fucking way."

"Come on, Rhys! It'll be fun!"

"*No* giant Ferris wheels."

"Are you really that scared?"

"Ginger..."

"Okay, fine," she said.

"I'm not scared. I have vertigo."

"Same thing."

"It's not."

"You're scared because of your vertigo."

"Let's just leave out the word *scared*."

"We'll save this argument for later. This is our stop."

I followed her down the narrow stairway and we got off at Camden Road. We were greeted by garish colors and buildings with crazy statues on their facades. There was a funky atmosphere in the cafés, the shops, and the tattoo studios lining the street. I stood in front of a display window for a second while people milled around me, then I felt her fingers touch mine briefly before grabbing my hand tight.

"You're not trying to lose me, are you?" She pulled me away.

I held my breath as we crossed the bridge over the canal and entered a narrow street full of food stalls. She was still clasping my hand. Her steps were resolute but calm, as if we walked around there every afternoon. And that made me wonder. What it would be like in an alternate reality where we lived here, sharing a routine, a life...

29

Ginger

I KNEW I SHOULD LET go of him, but I didn't want to. It was bitter cold, but his hand was warm, his skin soft. And big. And it fit perfectly in mine. I had never imagined something so simple could be so comforting. I could feel my nerves in my stomach, but at the same time, it was all familiarity and closeness.

A contrast. He was full of contrasts.

We barely talked as we walked through Camden, enjoying the sights, enjoying being together on our own. Rhys flipped through some albums in a huge shop full of records and old tapes. I peeked in the window of a tattoo studio as I chewed on one of the arepas we'd purchased.

"You like anything in there?" He leaned close beside me.

I looked at the designs and shook my head. "No. Anyway, what do yours mean?"

"How do you know I have tattoos?"

"I saw you. With your shirt off. In Paris."

Rhys smiled. Slowly. "And you couldn't forget about it..." he joked.

"Idiot. I'm not blind."

We continued walking. I ignored my desire to take his hand again, instead sticking mine into the pocket of my chocolate-brown coat.

"Which one are you asking about?"

"I think… Didn't you have one of a little bee?"

He smiled, stopped, and lifted his sweater, revealing a small bee just above his hipline.

"Why?" I asked again, looking up.

"That's my first one. I was basically a kid, but I saw it as, like, an homage to life. Don't you remember what Einstein supposedly said? 'If the bee disappeared off the surface of the globe, then man would only have four years of life left.' If there's no pollination, there's no seeds; if there's no seeds, there's no plants, and without plants, there's no life. Plus, I like bees."

"You never cease to amaze me…"

"I assume that's a good thing."

"So you won't see your family for Christmas?"

"No. I haven't been back home. What will you do?"

"You know, same as every year. We'll have lunch, give each other presents and cards, put up the mistletoe. Dad will make the same old jokes…"

"Your parents seem like good people," he said distractedly.

"They are, more or less. I don't have any complaints. Don't you miss your folks, Rhys? I mean, if you hadn't had a fight with them, would you still be living this way…?"

"I don't know. I always liked traveling."

"Did you travel much before?"

"No, I was home more."

I looked down at the sidewalk as we headed toward the Tube station. I remembered when we'd done something similar in Paris almost a year before. Sitting together. Our legs rubbing every time we took a sharp turn. Him pensive. Me nervous.

It was already getting dark when we were out again and walking across side streets on our way to see Big Ben. Rhys stood there looking around, leaning on the wall in front of the bridge across the Thames.

He glanced over at me. The wind shook his hair. "You never asked me about your gift..."

"I thought this was it," I replied.

He turned and rested his hip against the wall. "This?" He looked confused.

"You. Being here with me."

He smirked. "I know that's every girl's dream, but..."

"You're about to make me scream."

"Sorry. I won't make you wait anymore." He reached into his jacket pocket and brought out his cell phone and earbuds. He untangled the cable, slightly frustrated. Nervous. I could tell then that this moment was important to him. He looked up. "It's a song."

"For real?" I came closer to him, excited.

"Yeah. 'Ginger' is the title."

"You wrote a song for me?"

Rhys nodded and pushed my hair out of my face, putting one earbud in my right ear while I slipped the other into my left. I got lost in his eyes as the first notes sounded. It was bass. Just bass. A rhythmic thumping, constant and clean, and then more sounds, more notes joined it. It sounded sad and happy at the same time. Like a vine climbing some solitary forgotten place, covered in flowers, but also in thorns.

No one had ever given me such a beautiful gift.

When it was over, I asked him softly to play it again. He laughed and pulled out the earbuds.

"It's yours. Forever."

"What do you mean?"

"When I was in LA, someone offered to buy it, but I decided not to sell. You can listen to it till you get tired of it. I'll send it to you. Promise."

"You really turned down an offer for it?"

He shrugged. "There are famous DJs out there who buy other people's compositions. They've got the reputation; other people have good material. Who knows? Maybe one day I'll put it out on my own."

"Why this song?" I asked.

"It's based on your heartbeat. Your pulse."

I remembered it then, his fingers on my wrist on that long-ago night, searching for my pulse, memorizing it in the darkness.

We stared at each other in silence.

He was so close...and, at the same time, impossible to reach.

Mist was blowing from his lips, mingling with the mist from my own. He stepped toward me and gave me his hand. I accepted it, not quite knowing what I was doing. He walked on, across the bridge, toward the Ferris wheel further off. I memorized him, his long steps, the oval shape of his nails, which I ran my fingertips over, his height, his square shoulders...

Then I realized something.

"Are we going where I think we're going?"

"Didn't you want to go up in that damned Ferris wheel?"

"Didn't you say it gave you vertigo?"

"Yeah, but no one calls me a coward."

He had a curious look on his face. I laughed. The trees around us were decorated with white and blue Christmas lights. Rhys seemed nervous as we waited in line. The cold was intense that night, and there were fewer people than usual. I looked up in the sky as the first snowflakes fell, small and ephemeral, vanishing once they'd touched the ground.

He didn't let me go as we got into one of the compartments along with two other couples, all four of them tourists. Rhys kept one hand on the railing and his eyes focused on the glass until we reached the top. Then he closed his eyes and clenched his teeth.

"You're missing everything, Rhys!"

"I fucking hate heights," he grunted.

"Come on, do it for me. Just for a second."

He took a deep breath and blinked. He saw the river twinkling beneath us, the glimmering lights, the starless sky.

"Shit." He looked down.

"Why'd you come up here?"

"For real, Ginger?" His eyes were daggers, and I giggled, which did nothing to improve the situation. Fortunately the tourists were on the other side of the capsule. "I just can't take the way it keeps turning. Distract me. Tell me something."

He turned to me, still gripping the railing, his chest rising and falling as he panted, his eyes staring into me and trying to ignore everything around him.

"When I was little, I used to have silkworms…"

"That's not working. I need out."

"Rhys, relax." I grabbed his hand.

"Fuck. Do you not get vertigo?"

"I do," I whispered.

"Really?" He took a deep breath.

"There are many different types of vertigo."

That got his attention. "What kind are you talking about?"

"There's kind that makes you shiver right before you do something crazy."

"Ginger…"

I didn't let him say anything else.

I stood on my tiptoes. And I kissed him.

I felt his lips against mine.

His hands creeping down my waist.

His rapid breathing…the taste of him.

I felt all of it in that instant.

30

Rhys

I SLID MY TONGUE ALONG her lower lip before sinking it into her mouth and looking for more. More. As I kissed her, I forgot I was four hundred feet in the air, I forgot my fear of heights, and I forgot that this wasn't supposed to happen. All I could think about was her, how good she smelled, how good she tasted, her body pressed against mine, how I needed more of her, much more, how I never wanted to let her go. Impossible things.

I groaned against her lips. Closed my eyes.

She came in for more. Slow. Soft.

And I let her. Vertigo: that kiss, something I'd never felt before. Vertigo: that was her. Looking at her and knowing that *we* no longer existed.

I don't know how long we were there...

Lost in that moment...

So close to the moon...

31

Ginger

I DIDN'T KNOW WHAT I was thinking when I decided to kiss him. It was one of the few times I'd ever let an impulse, a whim, what I really wanted, carry me away. And I knew if I had it to do over again, I wouldn't change a thing. Despite everything that started on top of that Ferris wheel late in the evening. Despite all that changed. Despite all that broke and was born in that moment. Because sometimes, a small act is destined to mark your whole life, to set you on a path that wasn't even there a moment before. Even if we're not aware of it at the time.

But I did know. And I knew it would hurt when we got out and I saw his face, the tension in his jaw and shoulders. And I knew it had been worth it to chase the memory. Sometimes you just know, even when knowing stings.

We walked through a nearby park in silence. The snow was falling harder and starting to stick, covering the ground with a fine layer of white that shone under the orange of the streetlamps. Rhys sighed as I tried to catch up with him.

"Could you stop running?" I asked.

He was taking long, quick steps, almost leaving me behind. He turned. His face was cloaked in shadow. "That shouldn't have happened, Ginger. I'm sorry."

"Why not?" I finally reached him. "Rhys…"

"It's ruined everything."

"That's not true. It hasn't."

"I have nothing to give you."

I crossed my arms. I was wounded, angry. "Did it ever occur to you that maybe I don't want anything from you? I know how things are, Rhys. I know it may be years until we see each other again. Or maybe we never will. But I wanted that. I wanted to kiss you tonight…"

"Dammit, Ginger…"

"And you did too."

"You're going to make everything complicated."

"We just have a few hours."

"Shit," he grunted between clenched teeth, running a hand through his hair.

From his expression, it was impossible to tell what he was thinking. He just shook his head again, barely, as if to himself, then stepped forward, and I felt his body against mine, one of his hands on my neck, and he pushed my chin up softly and covered my lips with his in a kiss so deep, so different from any other, that it seemed unfair to call it just a kiss. After all, there were many kinds of kisses. Rhys's were intense and warm, full of all the things we had suppressed up to then. I hadn't dared to admit that I needed him. I was addicted to him, to everything he had given me through those words we exchanged every day. I wanted to know more about the

Rhys from years ago, who had run off in search of something he still hadn't found, and the Rhys from tonight, who had made this the most special birthday I'd ever known.

I don't remember how long it took us to reach the hotel.

I just know I couldn't stop smiling as I looked at him.

We stopped every minute to kiss.

"Jesus, Ginger." He held my chin.

"I think it's just one more street."

Rhys's look was serious. Firm. Decided. He didn't hesitate. "If you come up, nothing's going to happen, understand?"

"Why not?" I unwound my hands from behind his neck.

"Because I need it that way, Ginger. I... I don't know what I'm doing tonight, but I don't want to regret it tomorrow. I don't want to lose what we have."

"You're not going to lose me," I whispered.

He observed me a few seconds, still doubting, still stiff. His hair and his dark jacket were covered in snow. Mist was streaming from his lips. The cold had made them red; my kisses had made them redder. I reached up and caressed them slowly. Rhys caught my wrist and stared into me, and I could hardly breathe.

He wove his fingers into mine and continued down the street that led to the hotel, saying nothing when he took out his key card and slid it into the back door. We went inside. The warmth embraced us. The carpeted floor silenced our footsteps as we climbed the narrow stairway to the third floor, where he had a room. I trembled when we got inside. It was so small, just room enough for a bed, two nightstands, and a little en suite bathroom.

The windowsill was low enough to sit on. I drew the curtains and leaned against it while Rhys took off his jacket. I could feel him behind me, and I leaned into his chest. I was nervous. Happy. Sad. Everything all at once. His arms wrapped around me, and I could feel his breath on my neck. The snow was falling harder now, covering the streets with white, and the balconies, the tops of the streetlamps and traffic lights, and London's Victorian roofs...

32

Rhys

SHE SMELLED DELICIOUS. CREAM CAKE or sweet caramel. I took a deep breath, resting my chin on her shoulder and my hands on her waist.

"You didn't take off your coat," I whispered.

She shook her head and started unbuttoning the big buttons on the front. I helped her. She turned into me. Her legs touched mine; our eyes looked for each other's in the shadows. I held my breath as she ran her fingers through my hair and then down, drawing a soft line on my face, my lips, my chin.

"Why can't we…?" she asked softly.

"Ginger…don't make this harder than it is."

"We'd have the memory to hold on to."

"Memories are much more than they seem."

"It doesn't have to mean anything. It's just you and me. For a night."

"Come here, Ginger." I sighed, sat back, and pulled her onto my lap. I stretched my feet out until they touched the other side of the windowsill. We sat there like that for hours, just watching the snow, letting time slip past. Sometimes our lips joined. Sometimes we listened to each other's breathing. Sometimes I wanted so bad to say to hell with it and take off all her clothes that my fingers trembled as I ran them across the hem of her shirt, and the temptation grew stronger and her kisses more intense until it almost hurt to look at her.

"What if we never see each other again, Rhys?"

"What do you mean?" I stretched out a bit.

"What if we don't see each other for years and years? What if you have a girlfriend, kids? What if I've met someone and gotten married? What if…?"

"Ginger…" I sighed.

"Don't look at me like that. Answer me."

"What do you want me to say?"

"Won't you regret not doing more tonight? Not knowing what it might be like for us to be together? Not letting something happen when you know you want it…?"

"Dammit…" I stood up and walked to the other end of the small room. "Of course I'll regret it. I already regret it now."

Still by the window, she listened as I continued. "This is just how it has to be. I'd be happy if you wrote me in a few years and told me you were going to marry someone and they were going to make you happy. I want you to be happy."

I leaned against the wall and slid downward until I was resting on the gray carpet. We just stared at each other for what felt like an eternity. She was scowling, angry, unable to understand my words, my way of loving her. She was moving her foot rhythmically. Her hands were folded in her lap.

"I don't know if I would be happy if you had a girlfriend…"

She said it so low, so softly…that it made me laugh. At that, and at her, for how visceral it was, because she didn't care if it was wrong; she was ready to confess her fears aloud. To me, at least. And that made it even more special, knowing she was letting me see her that way, letting me see through her…

"I wouldn't hold it against you. But you shouldn't worry about that…"

"Why? Because you don't believe in love? Because it scares you?"

"It doesn't scare me. It's not that. I do believe in it. Sometimes."

"You can't believe in something *sometimes*. Either you do or you don't."

I stroked my jaw, took a deep breath, and tried to be honest with her for once—for a night—because Ginger was willing to be honest with me.

"What I believe in is moments. I believe you can fall in love many times in your life, with the same person, with different ones, with yourself, or just with a period of time."

She looked out the window.

"I don't know if I could invite you to my wedding," she said.

I laughed. Ginger did too.

And I got up and walked toward her again. It was still snowing, but the outline of the moon was visible, just barely, in the midst of the darkness, a slender, waning sickle.

"I see it too," she said, guessing at my thoughts.

"Us on the moon," I whispered.

I don't know how much time passed before she fell asleep with her head resting on my chest. I watched her in silence, memorizing the lines on her face and convincing myself that I preferred to regret all those what-ifs over the risk that I might lose her forever. I thought of Paris; even there I had asked myself what would have happened if I'd dared to kiss her in the airport. Where it would have led to if we'd tugged on that thread, if we could have woven something new or only pulled what was already there apart. I thought about the detours we take and those we leave behind because we're too scared of where we might end up.

She murmured something incomprehensible when I picked her up and laid her in bed. I lay beside her and took her hand. I searched for her pulse, the constant rhythm of the song that accompanied me as I closed my eyes.

33

Ginger

I SWALLOWED, TRYING TO DISSOLVE the knot in my throat. But no luck. Because he was leaving. Because I knew the memory of last night would soon feel distant. And it wouldn't be enough. And I couldn't stop looking at him, every inch of him, as he dragged his two suitcases. His firm steps. How little he hesitated. His hair uncombed, exactly as it had been this morning, when I kissed him on the neck as he slept and he smiled before opening his eyes...

He stopped as he reached security. He turned back to look at me, sighed, and seemed a little sad. His eyes were bright and were staring straight into mine...

"I guess this is goodbye," he managed to say. Then he smiled and bit his lower lip.

"You said that to me before. Almost a year ago."

"I know. I'm super original..."

"Come here."

He pulled me close and hugged me.

What would it be like to stay there forever, sheltered in his arms? I asked myself that, pressing my face into his chest until he pushed me away softly. For a moment, I thought I'd burst into tears if I looked at him again. And there was no reason to. I didn't even expect this visit. I didn't expect anything. And yet he'd come...

He grabbed my chin and lifted my face.

"Hey, Ginger Snap, what is it? Come on, look at me."

"It makes me sad that you're going. I know it shouldn't..."

The words were silenced as his lips crashed into mine. The kiss tasted like something. I don't know what. Like goodbyes. But also like something sweet and pretty. Like one of the many paragraph breaks in our lives, the ones we hadn't even started to count yet.

I held my breath when we separated.

I saw his expression. His desire. His doubts.

He bent over. His mouth touched my lips.

"Don't wait for me, Ginger."

Five words. Five words that pierced me. That hurt. But I understood. That was the last thing Rhys said to me that cold morning before turning around and walking away. I stayed there a few seconds watching him as he waited at the back of the line. Then I turned around too and walked off without looking back.

Part 2

—

TRUST. PAUSE. ABYSS.

"Straight ahead of him, nobody can go very far..."

The Little Prince

Part 2

34

From: Rhys Baker
To: Ginger Davies
Subject: I'm still alive

My flight got delayed, and then arriving was this huge ordeal. It took me almost half a day to get the car keys I needed because of some bullshit with my license. Anyway... I'm here, I'm alive. I don't know if I told you, but I rented a house by the sea. It's a little old, and it needs some urgent repairs, it's almost falling apart, but the place... I wish you could see the sunset with your own eyes, Ginger...

From: Rhys Baker
To: Ginger Davies
Subject: I'm still alive

Is everything okay, Ginger?

I haven't heard anything from you...

From: Ginger Davies
To: Rhys Baker
Subject: Me too!

Sorry, these days have been a little chaotic with last-minute Christmas shopping, holiday meals, enough cards to paper a bedroom, and family stuff in general. You know how it goes. I'm glad you made it in okay, Rhys.

By the way, don't forget to send my song.

I want to hear it again...

From: Rhys Baker
To: Ginger Davies
Subject: Ginger's song

Wish your parents and your sister a Merry Christmas from me. When I was there, I got so distracted with everything else, I forgot to say it. They were really nice. I hope you enjoy the holidays, Ginger. Here's the song.

I start my new job tomorrow.

From: Ginger Davies
To: Rhys Baker
Subject: RE: Ginger's song

How was it? Your coworkers cool?

From: Rhys Baker

To: Ginger Davies
Subject: RE: RE: Ginger's song

Yeah, all good. It's summer here, so there's a lot going on. The place isn't that big. It's close to the beach. It's called Byron Bay. It's touristy and full of people at this time of year. Can you believe there are people who go to the supermarket and walk down the street barefoot? It's different from anything you and I are familiar with. I don't know, I've got this feeling I'll end up staying here longer than I thought.

From: Rhys Baker
To: Ginger Davies
Subject: A new beginning

Happy New Year, Ginger Snap. I don't remember if you told me what plans you have today, but I hope you have fun. Here, we're the first people to wish everyone a happy New Year. I like starting it off knowing you're there on the other end of the ocean and the screen, on the other end of everything, basically, although that doesn't mean you feel far away. Sometimes I think it's the opposite. Maybe miles aren't what really separates people or brings them together.

I didn't do much, honestly. Just worked late and drank a little with some guys who were at the bar and live nearby. I walked home looking at the moon. Asking myself what this new beginning will bring us.

Maybe nothing will change.

Or maybe this year will be very different.

35

Rhys

"THE NUMBER YOU ARE DIALING cannot be reached at this time. Leave a message when you hear the beep." *Beeeeeeep*.

"Hey, Mom. Happy New Year. I just wanted…you know, to tell you that and see how you were doing. I remember you told me you were going on a cruise with Dad for Christmas. I guess you still can't get a signal out there. Be careful, okay? And enjoy the trip as much as you can. Tell me all about it when you get back. Love you."

36

From: Ginger Davies
To: Rhys Baker
Subject: Happy New Yeeeeear!

Happy New Year, Rhys! I'm so happy you're enjoying yourself there. I looked for the place on Google, obviously, and you're right, it looks like one of those dreamlands that don't exist anymore. Have you met lots of people? My guess is yes. I don't know how you can hang out with so many people being all closed up and reserved the way you are. How do you do it, Rhys? I don't think I ever asked.

I didn't do anything that special last night. After dinner I went to the bar where Donna works, drank a few glasses of wine, and hung out with some friends of hers till her shift ended. Then we went somewhere else. I had a good time, but it also felt weird.

Tomorrow it's back to the dorms.

From: Rhys Baker

To: Ginger Davies
Subject: Why?

I don't do anything special. I just hang out with people. But I get what you're saying. I guess I offer every person what they expect of me. It's easy.

Why did you feel weird the other night?

From: Ginger Davies
To: Rhys Baker
Subject: RE: Why?

Do you also give me what you think I expect of you?

From: Rhys Baker
To: Ginger Davies
Subject: RE: RE: Why?

No. That's why you're my only real friend.

You didn't answer my question.

From: Ginger Davies
To: Rhys Baker
Subject: Weirdness

I don't know, I don't want to make this complicated, but I keep thinking about what happened between us. It almost doesn't seem real, you know? And I'm sorry that things have been different or weird since then, but they have been, right? Am I crazy? Or have you noticed too? I guess it's normal, but at the same time, I don't want anything to change. I don't even really know what I'm writing...

It's just, Rhys, I've never felt this way about anyone before.

From: Rhys Baker
To: Ginger Davies
Subject: RE: Weirdness

It was real. It was perfect. But you said it...don't let anything change. We're good like this, right, Ginger? Someday you'll meet someone else, someone special, and you'll think just that: *I've never felt this way about anyone before.* Listen to me.

From: Ginger Davies
To: Rhys Baker
Subject: RE: RE: Weirdness

Okay. I get it. You're right.

From: Rhys Baker
To: Ginger Davies
Subject: RE: RE: RE: Weirdness

Ginger...don't listen to me.

That's just what I was scared of.

From: Ginger Davies
To: Rhys Baker
Subject: Forget it

I know, Rhys. I'm sorry. These weeks have just been so up and down, between Christmas, going back to the dorms, realizing that I barely have a few days to present my work proposal for graduation...

I'm freaking out. I don't know what to do.

From: Rhys Baker
To: Ginger Davies
Subject: RE: Forget it

Imagine yourself leading a company. What do you see?

From: Ginger Davies
To: Rhys Baker
Subject: The reality is...

I see a warehouse full of wooden samples and sawdust. Further off, to the right, I see a long gray hallway that leads to the offices where the managers meet with the PR people, the board, and the designers. That's what I see, Rhys. I guess I could focus on the job differently, somehow, examining the company as it exists, looking at the weak points or possible areas of improvement. But if my father reads it, he'll probably have a heart attack. And I'm afraid my professor will fall asleep during my evaluation. Let's be honest, no one gets excited about cabinets. Kate is doing an amazing project (she started a month ago) about an electric car company that rents to tourists. I wish I could just steal it from her.

From: Rhys Baker
To: Ginger Davies
Subject: Change reality

The cabinet doesn't have to be the be-all and end-all of your future, does it? Forget cabinets for a second, and imagine what kind of company you'd like to run if you had the means to do so. You told me that when we met, right, that you loved the idea of running something? Creating. So think of it like that. What would your dream be? (It doesn't matter if it's just that, a dream.)

From: Ginger Davies
To: Rhys Baker
Subject: RE: Change reality

I've been thinking about it all day…

And I think… I don't know… I imagined a publisher. A little one, right? Nothing too pretentious. I've never been tempted by the idea of writing, but every time I read a book, I wonder not just about the writer, but about the person who decided to pub-lish the book when it hit their desk—who got excited, looked at the letters and words, and saw potential, something interesting that needed to be shared with people. Isn't that something? I mean, almost everything in life is like a chain. Like dominoes, one falls, and the rest just go along with it, but there's always got to be something that starts it, a spark, even if we don't think about it much of the time. Things are so weird... I'm going to stop rambling.

From: Rhys Baker
To: Ginger Davies
Subject: RE: RE: Change reality

I love it when you ramble. And I like your ideas even more. Tell me, what would your publisher be like? How would you focus your work?

From: Ginger Davies
To: Rhys Baker
Subject: Okay, let's ramble then...

The project is to develop a business plan with hard numbers and strong proposals, just like if I was putting it together for investors, understand? There are many different aspects, and I have to take a global approach, looking at the economic and social aspects, anticipating possible roadblocks, looking at my location, the competition, the market as it exists, strategy...

I don't want to bore you. I probably am though...

I think I avoided thinking about it until now because what's the point? I always knew what I was going to do when I graduate... I knew it even before I started college. Don't get me wrong; I'm not dying from excitement, but I'm grateful. Not everyone has a family business. I'm lucky.

I guess I can dream though, right?

From: Rhys Baker
To: Ginger Davies
Subject: RE: Okay, let's ramble then...

You can always dream, okay? Before and after leaving college. Who knows? It's impossible to predict what we'll be doing in ten years. Or are you really so sure?

I think I get the idea behind the project...

I wish you'd tell me how you imagine it. Your publisher, I mean, if it existed. What would it be like? The décor, the mood, going in every morning.

Come on, take a walk on the moon once in a while. It's not so bad up here.

From: Ginger Davies
To: Rhys Baker
Subject: Ten years

Okay, look, however tempted I am to take a mental trip to the moon and let my fantasies of outer space carry me away, in another, parallel life, if I did decide to start an independent publisher, I couldn't afford an office in a good area of downtown, not even a little one, so I'd locate my offices somewhere in West London, for example. Somewhere calm but easy to get to.

I imagine a small but nice office. With light and plants (even if we both know finding light is almost impossible in this city). The walls: white or some warm color, soft ocher maybe. The furnishings should be in different styles and different colors, I don't want the place to look like a hospital. And shelves, obviously. Lots of white shelves lining the (wide) hallways and the meeting room.

The working environment should be optimal, of course. I'd be a flexible boss and really nice; every morning I'd bring in coffee and cakes. My employees would never criticize me. The only things they'd ever say behind my back would be stuff like, *Did you see what a cute blouse Ginger's wearing? She looks amazing in that color.* In the midst of all that positive energy, we'd publish one or two books a month, maybe less. I like the idea of carefully choosing each project, taking good care of it, giving it space, making it shine as much as possible.

Maybe I'm getting ahead of myself...

As far as your question, yes, Rhys, I do pretty much know what my life will be like in ten years. I'll be working at my family's company, I'll be happy when I take the reins and make improvements, I'll be married, maybe, or be close to getting married. I'll be living in a two-story home with an attic, and I'll have a dog. Or a cat. I haven't decided, but I've got time to figure it out.

How do you see yourself in ten years?

From: Rhys Baker
To: Ginger Davies
Subject: RE: Ten years

For someone who supposedly doesn't want to walk around all the time on the moon, I'd say you've spent a lot of time up there lately. I like that, Ginger. I like that little fantasy of yours, and I can almost imagine you between the shelves, listening to your employees' murmurs as they compliment that T-shirt that fits you so well. (Is it low-cut? I need details.)

For right now, your biggest question then is whether you'll have a cat or a dog. I don't know if it makes sense, but I haven't stopped laughing since I read that. It's no surprise that I'm aimless by comparison. And you know what? You were right, I don't know where I'll be in ten years. It scares me to think about it. I'll be thirty-seven. What are people that age supposed to do?

From: Ginger Davies
To: Rhys Baker
Subject: I'm going to kill you!

Oh God. Oh God. OH GOD.

I'm going to kill you, Rhys. How could you? Today is exactly one year since we met. It's our friendiversary. AND I JUST REALIZED YOU HAD A BIRTHDAY AND YOU NEVER TOLD ME. SO OBVIOUS. I don't know how I never realized it. Oh wait, yes, I do. BECAUSE YOU NEVER TOLD ME.

When was your birthday, Rhys?

CONFESS.

From: Rhys Baker

To: Ginger Davies

Subject: RE: I'm going to kill you!

It's not that big a deal, Ginger. It's just a birthday. I didn't even think about it. But if you're so interested, it's August 13. I don't like celebrating it though.

So today's our friendiversary. (I'll try not to repeat that outside this email to keep my pride intact.) So tonight, one year ago, you and I were walking through the streets of Paris. And dancing to *"Je T'aime…Moi Non Plus."* And eating cup noodles. And looking at that moon you sometimes avoid…

From: Ginger Davies

To: Rhys Baker

Subject: You're the worst

I know your tactics, Rhys. You get (me) all sentimental to try to make me forget about your birthday, when we both know it was an out-and-out betrayal. We're going to celebrate our friendiversary. (It's a cool expression; I don't know what you're so embarrassed about. I want to throw open the windows and scream it to the world.) You visit me for my birthday, and I don't even get to visit you for yours?!

Give me your address. I'll send you a present.

From: Rhys Baker

To: Ginger Davies

Subject: I'm the best

You're the funniest girl I know. Did I ever tell you that? Seriously, I can't read your messages without smiling, and I don't mind admitting smiling isn't my thing. But you're blowing everything out of proportion. I just don't like getting older. I already told you my favorite story when I was little was *Peter Pan*. And thinking about what I'll be doing in ten years—screw that. Same for presents. Presents get on my damn nerves. Not the way you do—I like that—but in the bad way. So, Ginger Snap, let's forget all this and stick with the original thing: I'm twenty-seven, got it?

Would you really have visited me anyway? We both know the answer's no. I was in LA, and I remember you turned me down when I extended an invite.

PS: I love you getting sentimental over me.

From: Ginger Davies
To: Rhys Baker
Subject: You're not the best

Rhys, let's be serious. You invited me to visit one night when you were drunk, and I barely had time to respond before you had a so-called friend named Sarah at your place. She and I probably would have walked past each other through the front door. I don't know if you realize that.

From: Rhys Baker
To: Ginger Davies

Subject: I sure am

Do I notice a bit of anger?

From: Ginger Davies
To: Rhys Baker
Subject: Come down to earth

No, Rhys, I'm not angry. I just wanted to say that what you offered me was anything but an invitation. This whole thing is because of you not telling me about your birthday. And your fear of getting old. Give me your address, and let's stop worrying about it.

BTW, I started my project. I like it so much, I was up late mapping it out. I thought about interviewing the heads of some small publishers in town and maybe even including that as an appendix. Obviously my focus would be on the business side.

From: Rhys Baker
To: Ginger Davies
Subject: RE: Come down to earth

Fine, address below, but I don't know how the mail system works here. My mother sent me a package a couple of weeks ago, and it still hasn't arrived. I live outside of town in a house that looks like it's about to collapse. I'll send you a photo later on, but it's getting dark out, and I'm writing from the porch. The sky's red. Not pink or orange, intense red like a ripe cherry. I wish you could see all this, Ginger...

I like the idea of those interviews.

And I like hearing you're excited.

But what you said is wrong. I'm not afraid of getting old. I just like (but am also freaked out by) living with uncertainty. Not knowing what I'll be doing, not having a plan. It's addictive. I don't think you can understand, Ginger, but there's something freeing about it. Thinking that maybe I'll be in India next year or New York or here. And the bad part…well, I guess that implies certain things. You know. Solitude. Or the feeling that I'm just treading water sometimes. But I like that. I don't think I would know how to live otherwise now. And I don't feel like stopping to think about what I should do or my future plans or what my life will be like in ten years. Maybe I'll be dead. That's how hard to predict it all is.

From: Ginger Davies
To: Rhys Baker
Subject: RE: RE: Come down to earth

Dammit, Rhys, don't say that. If you were here, I'd hit you. I know it's true, that the possibility exists that we won't be in this world in ten years, but it doesn't even cross my mind. And it shouldn't cross yours.

You want to know how I imagine you?

Victorious. I think you're going to end up putting out a song, probably while you're working in some bar, and hundreds or thousands of people will hear it. Millions. You'll get famous, you'll be walking around looking all tough and melancholy, and it will drive your fans (or do you prefer the term *groupies*?) wild. Probably you'll have a kid with some Russian model with an impossible-to-pronounce last name.

And you'll still be free and off traveling.

What do you say? Is that tempting?

From: Rhys Baker
To: Ginger Davies
Subject: [No subject]

First off, yeah, I like *groupies* way better. Thanks. And second, if I had a kid with some Russian model with an impossible-to-pronounce last name, I wouldn't still be off traveling. I mean, maybe, if I got custody or whatever. I don't even know why we're wasting our time imagining this nonsense. Anyway, I wanted you to know I wouldn't let my kid grow up far away from me. I don't know why you'd think that.

From: Ginger Davies
To: Rhys Baker
Subject: RE: [No subject]

I don't know, I guess you just don't seem like someone who would enjoy having a schedule and responsibilities and all that. I was just joking, Rhys. Just being silly.

From: Rhys Baker
To: Ginger Davies

Subject: RE: RE: [No subject]

Anyway, I know how to use a condom, so you can discard that theory. I'm working a double tonight, so I'm going to try and get some sleep. XXX

37

From: Ginger Davies

To: Rhys Baker

Subject: What do I do?

You know who called me? You'll never guess. Remember James, the guy I drank beer with at a party at the end of last semester? We had sort of a date after? Remember, he was the one who thought it was a good idea for Lord Chocolate to mingle with Lady Strawberry. Anyway, we caught up, just talking about whatever, and he asked me if I wanted to go out Saturday.

   I don't know, Rhys. What should I do?

From: Rhys Baker

To: Ginger Davies

Subject: RE: What do I do?

What do you want me to say…?

   Go out with him, Ginger. He seems like a nice guy, right?

(Ignoring the chocolate, which is unforgivable.) You can always just take a car home if you get bored.

From: Rhys Baker
To: Ginger Davies
Subject: RE: What do I do?

So what did you end up doing? You have a date this Saturday? I barely slept. I went out with people from work when we were done. You can imagine how late that was. We wound up laid out on the beach with a couple of bottles of rum. It was fun, but I had to pull Tracy out of the water; she almost drowned. She's completely nuts. My boss said he was going to give me a raise. Don't know if he'll remember today…

From: Ginger Davies
To: Rhys Baker
Subject: My date

I decided to meet with James on Saturday. I'm crossing my fingers for everything to go well so I don't end up booking a car before dessert.

Who's Tracy? You never mentioned her.

And nuts…? Like me?

From: Rhys Baker
To: Ginger Davies
Subject: RE: My date

Yeah, I haven't given you the rundown on my coworkers. There aren't too many of us. There's Garrick, the boss (or rather, my boss, because the big boss is usually at his club in LA). There's Josh, a server who makes these amazing vegetable sandwiches before night falls and they close the kitchen. There's Tracy, who works the night shift with me. She's a bartender. No, she's not nuts the way you're thinking; she's actually crazy. She'll do anything that pops into her head.

I guess you'll tell me how your date went...

From: Ginger Davies
To: Rhys Baker
Subject: Arrrrgh

I know I've still got another whole day, but I've gone through my whole closet, and I don't know what to wear tomorrow. I don't have ANYTHING that looks good on me. All I want to do is cry, curl up in bed like a cat, and stay there forever. But Kate said we just have to go have a beer with some classmates at this place nearby, so I'll make an effort.

Help me, Rhys.

From: Rhys Baker
To: Ginger Davies
Subject: RE: Arrrrgh

Simple: put on something revealing.

From: Ginger Davies

To: Rhys Baker

Subject: RE: RE: Arrrrgh

You're such a pig. Anyway, I finally found something decent, and now I'm waiting for James to come pick me up. I'll tell you how it went.

From: Ginger Davies

To: Rhys Baker

Subject: Up late

I'm back. And since I can't sleep, I ended up turning on my computer to write you. Everything went well. It turns out he was going out with a girl this whole time, and that's why he didn't call me after the summer. It was an ugly breakup, so I guess he's not looking for anything serious. Me neither. It doesn't make sense if I'm going to finish college in a few months and move away. It's not so far away, but I'm also not into the idea. We went to a restaurant I hadn't been to. It was fun. At least he's not one of those guys with whom the conversation doesn't flow. He works at a law firm, I think I told you that. I talked to him about my senior project, and he loved it. He doesn't think it's idealistic at all, can you believe it? Before I knew it, we had already had dessert and the place was about to close, so we took a walk and had a drink nearby. Then he walked me to the dorm.

I think I'm getting tired now...

Good night, Rhys.

From: Rhys Baker
To: Ginger Davies
Subject: You sure this isn't a movie?

For real? People actually go on that kind of date? I thought you were just going to hang out for a bit. I guess I thought the classic "date" went extinct decades ago. Did he kiss you on the doorstep? I think that's the one cliché you're missing. It makes sense for you though.

You can't imagine the ordeal at work yesterday.

Tracy lost it. She got up on the bar and started dancing. I don't know when the rest of us decided that was a good idea too (we were drunk and about to close). Anyway, the bar broke. *Craaack*—the end. We're all going to chip in to replace it before the big boss comes back. Luckily, he's still in LA.

From: Ginger Davies
To: Rhys Baker
Subject: RE: You sure this isn't a movie?

Yes, Rhys. There was a kiss on the doorstep. It was perfect.

From: Rhys Baker
To: Ginger Davies
Subject: [No subject]

Did I make you mad? I was just kidding…

I'm glad you had fun, Ginger. This James guy sounds all

right. I wasn't making fun of you, I promise. And what if I was—that's okay, right? You like classic things. I don't see anything wrong with that.

From: Ginger Davies
To: Rhys Baker
Subject: RE: [No subject]

I didn't let it bother me, but you made it sound boring. Or bad. Or out of style. I'm sorry I'm not fun or crazy or wild like Tracy. But look, there are simple girls like me who are happy to just have a nice evening out, normal, peaceful, talking with someone and getting to know them. And instead of going skydiving on the third date or getting up on a bar and dancing (is that supposed to be cool? It sounds dumb to me), we're happy to choose a nice dessert, like chocolate mousse with orange.

From: Rhys Baker
To: Ginger Davies
Subject: RE: RE: [No subject]

I don't get it, Ginger. I never said you were simple. You're the opposite of simple. That's why I like you. For how complicated you are.

So what? Are you going to keep going out with James? Even though he allowed Lord Chocolate to have a dalliance with Miss Orange? I wonder what Lady Strawberry thinks of all this. I doubt she likes it one bit.

PS: You'd have thought the dancing on the bar was funny if you'd seen it in person. It's one of those things that isn't funny unless you're there.

From: Ginger Davies
To: Rhys Baker
Subject: RE: RE: RE: [No subject]

We're going to the movies tomorrow.

I know it's predictable, but don't say anything. You know what the temperature is here? We don't have an idyllic beach or anything like that. Plus, he let me pick the movie. That's sweet and adorable, don't deny it.

I'll tell you how it went later. And sorry if I've been a little defensive these days, but I thought you were making fun of me. I don't know, Rhys, with emails it's hard to grasp the tone behind a person's words. That's probably it.

I hope you fixed the thing with the bar.

Tell me how everything's going there.

From: Rhys Baker
To: Ginger Davies
Subject: No options

You're not giving me many options, Ginger. But let me just say I'm happy that you're happy. And that you're not going to freeze tonight. You're right, I remember the cold in London... I was in the snow there with a complicated girl a few months ago...

Everything's cool here. I like it.

We fixed the bar.

From: Ginger Davies

To: Rhys Baker

Subject: RE: No options

Sorry I didn't write much this week. Between my final project, my exams, and going out with James and the girls, I can hardly remember my name. I got an interview with the founder of the publisher Bday. Her name's Lilian Everden and she's…amazing. I don't know, I hope I don't start shaking in front of her. She started from nothing, and she's done amazing things without help from anyone.

I'm seeing her tomorrow. And then I'm going to have dinner with James at his place. I'm not stupid, I know what that means. I'm kind of excited. I haven't slept with anyone in more than a year. At the same time, I'm scared I've forgotten how the hell it's done. I mean it. I'm afraid I'll mess up. Fall off the bed. Say something stupid at the wrong time. We'll see. I don't want to imagine it.

Tomorrow I'll tell all. I'm crazy nervous.

38

Rhys

MY EYES FLEW OPEN. MY phone was ringing. My phone…it should have been on the nightstand, but I couldn't find it. I got out of bed and crouched down to pick it up off the floor. I must have unintentionally thrown it down on the first ring. I squinted and saw it was Ginger.

Ginger…calling me…

My heart sped up.

"Hey?" she whispered. "Hey," she repeated. "I'm sorry… I'm sorry for calling… Oh, Rhys, I just realized the time difference. I don't know why I didn't think of it. It was just…an impulse. I woke you up, didn't I? Sorry."

"It's fine. Is everything okay?"

I looked over my shoulder at the girl sleeping in my bed and slipped away, barefoot and shirtless. I started walking. First down the porch's wooden steps, then onto the warm sand and toward the sea.

"Yeah, everything's okay. Sorry, I can't talk very loud. James is asleep. I'm just nervous. I don't know why, I felt like calling you."

"Did he do something to you? What is it, Ginger?"

"No, no. It's nothing like that. It's just, I don't really know what to do now. I mean, I can't sleep. Not with him. It's impossible. Believe me, I tried. It's not just that he snores; it's that I keep tossing and turning and I feel weird here."

I sat on the sand. The sun had just started coming up. Soft light was swelling on the horizon, but the sky was dark. Cloudless. I took a deep breath and concentrated on the sound of her voice, the way she pronounced her words in the English accent that I loved, even though it made her sound stiff. I tried to think of anything but touching her, kissing her, sinking inside her...

"You want to go, right?" I guessed.

"Yeah," she confessed. And she whispered, "I just felt so many things all at once. I need to be alone to process everything, you know? And I need my bed."

I remembered how she fell asleep in my arms at the end of December...

"Well, you should do it then."

"But I don't want him to get mad."

"I see..."

"He was really...considerate."

"What does *considerate* mean?"

"You know. With everything."

I could almost see her blushing. "Leave him a note. That's the best option."

"Yeah, that sounds good, right? Like *Thanks for last night, James. Call you tomorrow.* No one would get mad at that, would they?"

"No, and if he does, he's an idiot. So that way you'll know."

"Okay. I think I have a piece of paper in my purse."

"Do you have your clothes nearby?"

"Almost all of them."

I could barely hear her. "What does that mean?" I held my breath.

"Don't make me say it out loud…"

"No fucking way. You lost your panties?"

"Rhys! Dammit! You're going to make me wake him up."

I couldn't help but laugh. I did it loudly, amused, and fell back in the sand, sighing as I gripped the phone to my ear, staring up at the slowly brightening sky. I could hear her mumbling protests.

"I've looked everywhere, and they're not here. I took my dress and my tights off downstairs when we were on the sofa after dinner, but the rest of the stuff is in his bedroom, where he is now. It's totally dark in there; I can't see a thing. I've run my hands all over the floor, and there's nothing there. What do I do?"

"I don't really see the problem. You've got tights and a dress. It's fine."

"Very funny, Rhys. I wish I could cry."

I tried not to laugh. I wanted to hug her just then. "Let's focus on what to do now. Put on what you have. Look in your purse for a piece of paper, and write him a note. I'd leave it in the kitchen by the coffee machine. That never fails."

"I see you're an expert."

"Been there, done that, Ginger Snap."

"Rhys, that sounds so…"

"Like a pro, right? Are you dressed yet?"

"Not like a pro, like a dirtbag, that's what I meant. Yes. I'm dressed."

"Okay. Where are you now?"

"In the bathroom on the second floor. I haven't moved from here since I called. So I'm going to go downstairs and pray the steps don't creak. I didn't notice when we were coming up. Here I go."

I heard her take a breath and start moving.

"All good?" I asked.

"Yeah, I'm in the kitchen now. Writing."

"Add a little kiss mark."

She clicked her tongue, but I think she listened to me. Then I heard steps again, and she didn't say anything as she walked out the door. I think that's what she was doing—I heard it close.

"There it is! I'm out, Rhys!"

"Now's the part where he sees you from the window…"

She screeched and I laughed again. She was so…her.

"I'm going to see if I can find a taxi stand."

"Be careful. It must be getting late there."

"Yeah." All I could hear was the echo of steps on the sidewalk. "Thanks for this, Rhys. I was getting a little nervous in there. I mean, I get that it shouldn't be that hard to leave a note and go, but I felt… blocked. Trapped or something."

I took a deep breath, feeling my chest rise and fall.

The murmur of the waves, her voice like a song…

"Was the night as good as you'd hoped?"

"I think so. I mean, yeah. Right, so I see a taxi stand, but there's no one here. I don't want to keep you on any longer, Rhys. You've done enough. I'll write you tomorrow, okay?"

"No. Don't hang up. I'll wait with you."

"There's no need," Ginger replied.

"It'll make me feel better."

"As you wish…" she sighed.

"So it was as good as you'd hoped."

"I guess. Different from Dean. I mean, James is more…intense."

"Intense…" I squeezed the phone.

"I guess he has more experience. But…" She lowered her voice. "Taking off my clothes in front of another person was weird. You know what it's like when you've gone out with a person so long that you don't look at them or touch them the way you did in the beginning when everything was new? I mean, probably you don't, because you've never been in a serious relationship, but it's a bit like that. Routine. Doing something from inertia."

"What do you mean?"

"Just that everything was different. The way his skin felt. How we kissed. How he touched me. Is that what it always feels like for you, Rhys? Meeting one person and then another…"

"I never stopped to think about it."

"Well, try and imagine it. You've been going out with someone for years, and you've memorized every detail of them, every freckle, every mark. I don't know. It's weird to touch a body you know nothing about and still enjoy it. Like you're flying blind. Whatever, forget it."

"I think I understand. Pretty much."

We said nothing else until I heard her get up.

"There's my taxi. I'm hanging up. Thanks, Rhys."

"No worries. Good night, Ginger."

A car door closed, and she hung up. I sighed, lying on the sand, thinking of everything...of the night Ginger had had, the night I'd had, as if it was a parallel reality... The times I'd imagined what fucking her would be like, making her laugh, making her be a different person. One who understood herself and let others understand her. Someone different. Better.

I sat up slightly and watched a couple surfing in the distance, as though welcoming the new day. Then I got up. I turned my back to the dawn and returned home without looking up. Thinking of her the whole time. At least until I got to the room and saw Tracy sleeping in the sheets. I put my phone on the nightstand and lay down beside her. I closed my eyes. I felt her arm wrap around my waist, and I squeezed into her, seeking the warmth of a body I barely knew but made me feel less alone, gave me the fleeting sensation that I was close to someone, that I had an anchor, if only for the moment.

39

From: Ginger Davies
To: Rhys Baker
Subject: Hey!

I got up in a good mood today, don't ask me why; there's no reason. And since I know what you're going to say, no, it's not because I'm sleeping with James sometimes. I can't stand the way guys say that: *What you need is a good fucking*. Honestly, I think what most guys need is a chastity belt. Anyway, where was I going with this…? Right, happiness. I woke up, I grabbed my project (I had already printed everything I did the other day), and since Kate was still asleep, I went to a café for breakfast. I hadn't done that in ages. Sometimes something as simple as getting up on a Saturday, taking a walk, and sitting alone at a table is enough. I ordered toast and coffee. It's still a little chilly here, but I sat outside. I've been looking over the interview I did with Lilian Everden a few weeks ago. The waitress probably thought I was insane when she saw me there smiling by myself, but it was so inspiring…

I'm really happy with the outcome.

I realize I have everything I need. I don't know why we sometimes get lost in complications instead of just looking around and seeing how fortunate we are. Think about it. I've made new friends. I have a good relationship with my ex (whenever we see each other in class, he always says *How are you, Ginger?*, and we've sat together once or twice, though I can't say we talk much). Then there's my family: they've got their good and bad points, but they're there and I love them. I have a friend with benefits. In a wink, I'll be done with school, and I'm lucky enough to be able to jump right into a job. That's huge, right? Did you ever look at things that way?

From: Rhys Baker
To: Ginger Davies
Subject: Save some for me

The one thing I'm asking myself is where you bought those magic mushrooms that are making you feel so good. If you want to send me some, I won't say no. BTW, my birthday present still hasn't gotten here. What did arrive was a package my mom sent me a million years ago. Inside was a bunch of canned food (she must think I live in the middle of the jungle) and new socks (why do mothers always think, wherever you are, you can buy anything you need except socks?). I also asked her to send a picture from when I was in high school to show you. You're going to laugh. It's me with the football team after winning the championship that year.

Ready...it's attached. Don't be mean.

I do think you owe me something in return.

From: Ginger Davies
To: Rhys Baker
Subject: [No subject]

Can you hear me laughing from here? Because I am. I can't believe THAT BOY is you. Your hair is layered, Rhys. LAYERED. Like in an eighties movie. You look so preppy in that uniform and that pose... Who's the cheerleader leaning on your shoulder? Your ex-girlfriend? The prom queen?

Why should I give you something in exchange?

That's coercion. I'm still laughing.

From: Rhys Baker
To: Ginger Davies
Subject: Fine, it's coercion

Yeah, that's my old girlfriend. What do you think? She was a little superficial. But she wasn't a bad person. I think. To tell the truth, we didn't talk much. We basically just hooked up in the back seat of my car every time we had a free moment.

I made an effort, before you start chewing me out.

I absolutely hate photos.

From: Ginger Davies
To: Rhys Baker

Subject: Deal

I can see you two connected on a very deep level.

Okay, let's make a deal. Tell me why you hate photos so much, and I'll share something pathetic about my childhood. That seems fair.

From: Rhys Baker
To: Ginger Davies
Subject: RE: Deal

I don't know, I don't like the idea of freezing a moment. It doesn't mean anything. A stranger could look at a photo from a family reunion and not feel anything. Just seeing faces or smiles, noticing a haircut or clothes, is nothing. I like keeping memories for myself, because I know what color and scent they had, you know? An image can't convey that. It's just flat. A piece of paper. I prefer taking mental photographs.

From: Ginger Davies
To: Rhys Baker
Subject: RE: RE: Deal

"Mental photographs"? How modern, Rhys.

Look, I know what you mean, but I don't agree. I know a photograph can't convey the sensation of a real memory, that tingle you feel when you look back, all those subtleties...but it's also nice in its own way. For me, it's like the prologue to a real memory. Sometimes I look at the pictures I have hanging on the corkboard. I just realized I don't have any pictures of you. Worse, I don't have any of us together. I don't know if we'll see each other again, but if we do, you better be sure I'll take a bunch of photos, even if you complain and scowl at me.

I'm sending you my part of the deal.

Don't laugh too much, okay?

From: Rhys Baker
To: Ginger Davies
Subject: Little Ginger...

Is that you? For real? It doesn't look like you. It's funny, I didn't see any pictures like that on the corkboard in your room when I was at your house. You should know, you're a serious cutie with those round little cheeks... And those huge braces! I felt the urge to tug on the ponytails of that studious little girl.

Of course we'll see each other again.

But no photos, Ginger.

From: Ginger Davies
To: Rhys Baker
Subject: RE: Little Ginger...

I know, my braces were horrible. It didn't help that I smiled like a horse. If I think about it, I'd have to say that if we were in the same class, you probably wouldn't have spoken to me. You'd have been busy being prom king, and I... I was always invisible.

I lucked out having Dean as a neighbor and son of my parents' friends, because relationships just weren't my thing. Not that they necessarily are now, but at least I don't blush every time someone talks to me. *Studious* is right—I was a total nerd.

From: Rhys Baker
To: Ginger Davies
Subject: RE: RE: Little Ginger...

Why do you feel that way? I think we would have been friends.

From: Ginger Davies
To: Rhys Baker
Subject: You know we wouldn't

That's not true, Rhys. You'd have been too busy staring at those giant round perfect breasts that your girlfriend seemed to be trying to stuff in your face in that photo from the football championship.

From: Rhys Baker
To: Ginger Davies
Subject: RE: You know we wouldn't

So? The one thing has nothing to do with the other. I could stare at her boobs and be your friend at the same time.

From: Ginger Davies

To: Rhys Baker

Subject: RE: RE: You know we wouldn't

I doubt it. Teenage guys have exactly one neuron. And that neuron is usually busy with things that are stupid or gross. It doesn't matter, Rhys. We're just theorizing about things that never happened. I wasn't even being serious.

I need to let you go. I'm seeing James tonight.

From: Rhys Baker

To: Ginger Davies

Subject: Speaking of realities...

Maybe we don't need to overthink it when we talk about who would leave whom. Look at who doesn't have time to write lately because she's busy with something that back in the day would have taken up my one neuron. (Also, I've always had more than one neuron. Surprise: I'm not one of those guys who can only focus on one thing at a time.)

From: Ginger Davies

To: Rhys Baker

Subject: RE: Speaking of realities...

Are you jealous, Rhys? Don't make me laugh.

From: Rhys Baker

To: Ginger Davies

Subject: [No subject]

So what? I can be jealous.

From: Ginger Davies
To: Rhys Baker
Subject: RE: [No subject]

Okay, I'm guessing you got home drunk a few hours ago after having fun with your friends (and banging some chick), and now you've opened one last beer and turned on your computer. Probably you thought it would be fun to mess with me because I'm the type of girl who blushes when she says the word *fuck*. Let's not talk about that stuff. I'm over the attitude, Rhys. I'm writing you less because I'm busy with James, my exams, and my final project. But don't pretend I've abandoned you.

From: Rhys Baker
To: Ginger Davies
Subject: RE: RE: [No subject]

Yeah, I got home drunk. Yeah, I banged Tracy in the bathroom at the bar. Yeah, I cracked open a beer when I got here. Am I that predictable, Ginger? I wasn't trying to tease you though. I think we usually understand each other through email. I guess you thought I was making fun of you for sleeping with James, but for me, it was just a remark. We'll work it out.

I understand you're busy…

But tell me, Ginger, what other words make you blush? Don't leave me hanging. I've been wondering since yesterday.

From: Ginger Davies
To: Rhys Baker
Subject: RE: RE: RE: [No subject]

You're not predictable; it's just that I know you better than you think. And I get your jokes. They're just not funny.

Stop trying to get on my nerves.

From: Rhys Baker
To: Ginger Davies
Subject: RE: RE: RE: RE: [No subject]

Come on, fess up.

From: Ginger Davies
To: Rhys Baker
Subject: RE: RE: RE: RE: RE: [No subject]

What do you want me to say? Yes, there are words and expressions that make me uncomfortable. So what? I don't know what they are when you put me on the spot; it's not like they're something I think about. Can we change the subject?

From: Rhys Baker

To: Ginger Davies

Subject: Assumptions

So I'm supposed to believe neither Dean nor James is the kind of guy to whisper dirty talk in your ear in bed. Weird. I have the feeling that's exactly what you'd like. That it would turn you on. Obviously you won't admit it.

From: Ginger Davies

To: Rhys Baker

Subject: RE: Assumptions

Since you can't drop it, I'm going to start sending you long emails with reflections about life, what we're going to be doing in ten years, pure romantic love that lasts forever, having kids…

From: Rhys Baker

To: Ginger Davies

Subject: RE: RE: Assumptions

Fine, Ginger, you win. I give up.

40

From: Rhys Baker
To: Ginger Davies
Subject: New project

You can't begin to imagine the hangover I have. For real. My fucking head is spinning. It was a wild night. My boss came (my real boss, the one who's usually in LA). His name's Owen. And he wants me to be a part of a project, producing a single. I'm supposed to do the music, and his sister's going to sing. So like a song, just by the two of us. To be honest, I had my doubts. But after five drinks, I forgot them and said yes.

I don't know. I guess it's weird not to have much ambition when I really do like composing, but I'm worried something might change.

Tell me how you are.

Studying, I imagine.

Good luck. You're almost there.

From: Rhys Baker
To: Ginger Davies
Subject: I'll entertain you

Since I know you're hiding away in the library now that you've made it to the final stretch, I'll entertain you a little. Everything here is the same. Owen left. He'll be back in a few weeks with his sister, I'm supposed to play her some stuff, and we'll see how it works out. He wants to do the song in Brisbane because it's cheaper. At least at first. I'll keep you informed.

Between that and work, I've been busy lately. I was off last night. You can't imagine how wild Tracy was being. We ended up swimming naked at the beach, the tide dragged us out, and we took forever to find the clothes we'd left on the shore. It was fun.

Break a leg on your exams, Ginger.

From: Ginger Davies
To: Rhys Baker
Subject: Soooorry!!

I know, I'm the worst friend in the world, Rhys. Really sorry. You guessed right, I'm in the library 24/7 on a steady diet of crackers. But I'm happy for you! The song thing sounds amazing! For real. I don't know, I have a good feeling about it. And obviously I want to be the first person to hear it. You're talented, Rhys. You need to take advantage of that. Not that you don't do so when you're working, and I know that's what you like, but you could get more out of it.

You can't imagine all the nights I fall asleep listening to "Ginger." It's the best birthday present anyone's ever given me.

When you tell me stories about crazy nights that end with naked swimming in the ocean, I have this feeling like we're living on two different planets. As if you are on Mars and I am on Saturn. I envy you a little sometimes.

Kisses (for real).

From: Rhys Baker
To: Ginger Davies
Subject: Us on the moon

What's this about Mars and Saturn? We're on the moon, Ginger. Don't wander off through the galaxy without warning me. I might send you some material I'm working on, because sometimes it sounds like shit to me, and then a second later, I think it's genius.

Keep eating crackers.

From: Ginger Davies
To: Rhys Baker
Subject: RE: Us on the moon

You're right. I'll stay on the moon.

Please send! I want to hear it. I'm sure what you've done is amazing.

From: Rhys Baker
To: Ginger Davies

Subject: RE: RE: Us on the moon

I'm attaching three different mixes. And the lyrics in a separate file. It's just a rough cut, okay? Lots of details need to change, but you'll get the idea. I want to know which one conveys more... just more, okày? More of whatever.

From: Ginger Davies
To: Rhys Baker
Subject: I love them!

I like the first two. And the lyrics are...perfect. Did you write them? I had no idea you could write like that. I especially like the chorus: "I still don't know what I feel / after all that time inside myself / until I got to the edge of the mountain / and I found you in the fog."

It's funny you'd say that about the mountain though, keeping in mind you've got a terrible fear of heights.

I don't know which I'd pick. The first one, maybe.

But don't make me choose.

From: Rhys Baker
To: Ginger Davies
Subject: RE: I love them!

I repeat: I'm not scared of heights. It's a physical reaction. That's different. Plus I think I showed you on the Ferris wheel I'm basically over it.

I like the first one best too, Ginger.

Thanks.

From: Ginger Davies
To: Rhys Baker
Subject: Get real

You're honestly going to use what happened on the Ferris wheel to convince me you're better? Rhys, you were losing it. You literally said, "I hate fucking heights." You told me you needed to get down. Judge for yourself. I had to kiss you to keep you from bursting into tears.

From: Rhys Baker
To: Ginger Davies
Subject: RE: Get real

If I could get my hands on you...

You're so funny, Ginger. You kissed me to keep me from crying, not because you were crazy about me from the first moment you laid eyes on me. Sure.

From: Ginger Davies
To: Rhys Baker
Subject: RE: RE: Get real

Exactly. It was exactly how you just said it.

From: Rhys Baker

To: Ginger Davies
Subject: RE: RE: RE: Get real

A bit of advice. Don't ever have an affair. You're such a bad liar, you'll get caught before you even know you're into the other person.

From: Ginger Davies
To: Rhys Baker
Subject: Who do you think I am?

Great. Because I'm never going to have an affair.

I know this must be incomprehensible to you, but I believe in fidelity.

From: Rhys Baker
To: Ginger Davies
Subject: RE: Who do you think I am?

Why do you think I don't get that? No one believes in fidelity and loyalty more than me. That's why I give them to so few people. I don't run the risk of not keeping my word. I would never betray a promise. And I would never let down someone who mattered to me. What else do you think of me? I'm almost scared to ask.

From: Ginger Davies
To: Rhys Baker
Subject: About you

Sorry. You're right. I think sometimes I say the wrong thing when we talk about that stuff because a) I idealize you too much, and b) it helps me avoid disappointment if my fears turn out to be true. Let's be real, you're not the most open person I know when it comes to talking about things like…fatherhood, the future, love, or commitment. You don't even like to talk about your family. And I'm scared to ask.

From: Ginger Davies
To: Rhys Baker
Subject: About you (part 2)

But I think you're incredible, Rhys.

You're brilliant. Independent. An adventurer. Brave. Sincere. Reserved (that's not bad). Handsome (I'll never repeat that again). Smart. You can spell (predictably, that matters to me). You're tender sometimes (you were the night you found me lost in Paris). You're sincere. Direct. Fun. A little gross (you probably think that's a virtue, that's why I'm putting it in). Creative. Contradictory. Melancholic. Aloof (that will be sexy for your future fans). Authentic.

From: Rhys Baker
To: Ginger Davies
Subject: Mmmm

I see you're doing well in my absence, Ginger. Very good. I especially like you calling me brilliant, authentic, and gross.

Now I know what to put on my CV. And…you're right (I'm not especially stubborn, am I?), it is hard for me to talk about certain things, but I think a lot of people are that way. Try and ask James about kids, and pray he doesn't take off running. I'll wait for the results of the experiment.

From: Ginger Davies
To: Rhys Baker
Subject: RE: Mmmm

I'm sorry to tell you that I did talk to him about it, and it went fine, normal. He wants to be a father and hopes he can get married someday, even if he doesn't know when. He's not so weird. If everyone was like you, the human race would go extinct. No one would ever go out with anyone longer than a couple of months. I guess every person is a world.

From: Ginger Davies
To: Rhys Baker
Subject: DONE!

It's over, Rhys! I'm SO happy! I'm speechless. A little dizzy too. These days have been chaos, that's why I haven't written you (but you haven't written me either, I guess you're busy swimming naked or having some other wild adventure). I passed all my classes, two with the highest grade, and I got an A on my final project. I don't think I've ever felt so proud. I'm terrified too, because starting a new life like this all of a sudden is scary. But

I'm also excited. This week, I'm moving. For now, I'm living in my sister's apartment. She has roommates, Michael and Tina, but it turns out Tina's moving in with this boyfriend she's only known for a few weeks, and that works out great for me.

What else…? The worst thing was saying goodbye to Kate. She's staying with her parents in Manchester for a while; then when November comes, she'll look for a job in London.

I feel like a bottle of champagne full of bubbles and the cork has just shot out. I'm going to finish packing my bags. Then I'll say goodbye to every wall, every corner, every patch of grass I've walked on all these years…

I know, I'm getting sentimental.

I'm done. I hope you're well. Kisses.

41

Rhys

I WAS GOING TO MEET with Owen at the club I worked at
every night. But it was daytime, and it wasn't open yet. When I got
there, I waved. A woman walked over and smiled before giving me
a kiss on the cheek. Her name was Alexa. She had long blond hair
and legs that wouldn't quit. Everything about her was long. I could
easily look her in the eye. I remembered how with Ginger, I always
had to bend down to do that. And I thought of the impression she
made on me when I first saw her in front of the ticket machine, a
year and a half ago or more. So short. So funny. So pissed... She
reminded me of a child's cartoon.

Alexa was the total opposite.

We sat down at a table, and Owen brought over a few beers
while we started talking. At first, all I did was listen, getting the lay
of the land. I still wasn't sure this was a good idea. Why did I want
anything else? I was happy with what I had, right? My job was
perfect, simple, with no obligations and no goals. So what was I
hoping for from this? Fame? I'd never been interested. Money? I had
tons in savings, and I'd never even felt tempted to touch it. Personal

satisfaction? Maybe. Feeling like I was *doing something* besides just getting drunk and wandering around.

"The lyrics are perfect!" Alexa beamed at her brother before resting a hand on her heart and looking at me. "So deep. Just… I just want to change the gender, obviously. I'd like to give it a run-through. I just need to get the harmony."

Of course. I'd written it from a guy's point of view.

"Sure, we can change that up."

For the next half hour, I played the song several times while Alexa tried to match the lyrics with the music. She sang the chorus a couple of times, making her brother smile. He seemed to think it was going well for a first meeting. She could sing. Her voice was sweet but strong. Her version was more straightforward and sadder until it peaked, then the change was brusque, potent.

"Where can we meet to rehearse?"

"I don't know. Here. Or my place. Wherever you like."

Alexa nodded, and her brother got up to take a call. I took a sip of my beer, and she hummed the chorus again. She'd gotten it down fast. And she hadn't argued or given me any headaches. I'd been worried about that when I took on the project. We looked at each other with satisfaction.

"I think it's going to be brilliant," she said.

"I hope so." I rubbed my jaw. "As for rehearsal…"

"Just trust yourself." She rested a hand on my arm. Not hesitantly, the way Ginger would. Just like that. Unafraid. "You've done amazing work, really. My brother tried this a few months ago with a guy he knew who worked in a different club, but between you and me, it was so horrible I just told him I can't sing that. I'm not going to do something I'm not certain about. This song, though, these lyrics…it's gorgeous. It's exactly what we've been looking for forever."

I liked that. I liked her, her voice, the way she said that.

"So when do you want to get started?"

"If it was up to me, I'd say tomorrow." She withdrew her hand.

"How much longer are you staying here?"

"Just a few weeks, till the song's done. Then I'll go back to Los Angeles for the launch and the PR. My brother and I have tons of contacts there. Who knows? This could be the next big hit."

I nodded, not knowing what to say.

Owen came back from his phone call with another round of beers and a smile on his face and settled down in his chair while his sister talked about plans, ideas for our project, and marketing. I became distracted at some point.

"Rhys, are you listening to me?"

"Sorry, what were you saying?"

"That I heard good things about an illustrator here in Byron Bay. His name's Axel Nguyen. Everyone knows him. I'm certain he's our guy. Go see him one of these days, tell him what we're doing, and let him know he should get in touch with me when he's done." Owen took a card from his wallet and handed it to me.

"Sure. Perfect."

"Great. Everything's settled then."

I returned home at midafternoon. The sun was shining bright in the pale-blue sky. The wind shook the vegetation on the road home. Then I saw it. A package on the top step. I grabbed it. It was from Ginger. I took a deep breath and set the keys down on the counter.

I took an apple from the fridge and walked out to the back porch, kicking off my shoes and sitting on the wood surface covered in sand from the beach, which the wind brought in every day. I took a couple of bites, looking at the box, wrapped in red-and-gold paper with a big bow, which was slightly damaged after all those weeks it took to reach its destination. I finished my apple, tried to calm my pulse, and opened the package slowly, imagining how Ginger would have folded the paper, cut the little pieces of tape, and placed them on the seams, concentrating (with wrinkles at the top of her little nose) then sighing with satisfaction.

It was a tiny old book. *The Little Prince.*

There was a note on the first page.

For Rhys, the boy I share my apartment on the moon with because "he was only a fox like a hundred thousand other foxes. But I have made him my friend, and now he is unique in all the world."

I smiled and took a look. I found a list of dates on the back of the cover. It must have been all the times she'd reread it. The pages were full of underlines in different colors, notes in the margins, and goofy little drawings. I realized, surprised, that this was the copy Ginger had bought at that bookstore in Bloomsbury and told me she held on to like a treasure. I felt something warm pressing down on my chest as I read one of the notes she'd scribbled:

He fell in love with the flower and not with its roots, and in autumn, he didn't know what to do.

I read it and read it again. I spent half the afternoon thinking it over, digesting the words, turning them over. Thinking about what happened when petals fell and only roots were left. Still worse, what if there were no roots, nothing at all to tie me to the earth?

42

Ginger

"HOW WAS THE DAY? DO you feel like an exec?"

"Eh…no. Unless *feeling like an exec* means nearly falling over from exhaustion, thinking about taking a vacation my third week of work, and what I can do between invoices so everything isn't so goddamn boring."

My sister's smile vanished as I tossed my bag onto the sofa and settled down next to her. She wrapped an arm around my shoulders and pulled me close. A quiz show was on TV. I'd been working at the family business for three weeks. It wasn't much different from my internship the summer before, even if my dad kept saying I was his "right-hand woman" and future CEO. I could feel the angry stares of coworkers who thought (and maybe they were right) that I was a daddy's girl and hadn't had to work hard to get where I was. But no one looked at Dean like that. For some incomprehensible reason, he'd managed to butter up half the staff in his first couple of days, with his charming smile, his jokes at lunchtime, and his gentle, open attitude.

"Is it so bad?" Donna looked worried.

"I wouldn't say *bad* exactly, but I feel out of place. Every day at the office, I tell myself this will finally be the day things start to go better. But every hour is an eternity. It doesn't help seeing Dean like a fish in water. What is it about me?"

"It's nothing about you, Ginger. You're just different."

"Sure. But, like... I'm supposed to have been familiar with this company since I was a kid... For years I've assumed this would be my future, and I'm not sure I can do it."

"Yeah, but like, you don't have to do it, obvs."

"*Obvs*? Where'd you get that from?"

"It's something Amanda says. Don't worry about it. Stick to the subject."

Amanda was my sister's girlfriend. That was something else my parents hadn't expected from Donna: for her to be gay. Just as they didn't expect she'd never care a jot for the cabinet business. Or that she'd study fine arts. Or that she'd decide to shave her head not long after starting at the bar where she still worked. Me, on the other hand—I struggled to do all they expected of me, even when they never asked for it.

Why do you do it, Ginger? That question crept into my mind sometimes. It was obviously dying for an answer, but as soon as I sensed it, I always whisked it away again instead of taking it seriously.

"What I'm trying to say," Donna continued, "is you're not obliged to do things you don't want to. You know that, right? You can change your mind, Ginger. I did."

"But I've been preparing for this for years."

"Yeah, but sometimes things don't work out the way we like."

"And Dean...he's doing an amazing job there."

"You are too. He's just different."

"No, you don't understand. Remember last week when I stayed up so late three or four nights in a row? I wasn't talking with Rhys; I was writing a report with some proposals I wanted to send to Dad. That's another thing. Calling my boss *Dad* is weird as shit. Anyway, I was breaking my back trying to give everything the right focus; you know how resistant he is to change. And for what? For nothing. The other day, I go into his office, I see the report under a pile of papers in the corner, I ask if he's read it, and he's like, 'I haven't had time, honey, but I'm sure it's wonderful.'"

"I know. He treats you like his daughter, not like a colleague. That's what you mean, right? It's complicated, Ginger. Dad adores you. You're the apple of his eye."

"He adores me, but every time I tell him something, even if it's just a minor suggestion, he scowls and frowns like one of those pugs with the little squished-up face."

"You're right, that is what he looks like."

Donna started laughing, and I couldn't resist doing the same.

"I guess I'll get used to it..."

"Yeah." She sighed. "By the way, how is Rhys?"

"Ah, great. Really great. Brilliant."

"Are you mad at him or something?"

"No, not at all. It's just his life is so marvelous..." I got up, walked around the bar that separated the kitchen from the living room, and opened a carton of juice. Donna watched me from the sofa. "He's recording a song with Alexa Goldberg. As you can imagine, I googled her. She's amazing. She can sing like you wouldn't believe. I saw some videos of her on her Insta. There's a photo of her with Rhys. You know who doesn't have a photo with him? Me."

"Are you jealous?" She looked amused.

"Yeah. A little. I just saw it. I'll get over it. But he told me he hated photos. Maybe all he means is he hates them if I'm in them."

"Ginger, you act like an idiot when you talk about him."

I went back to the living room with my pineapple juice in hand. I tried not to pay attention to what she'd said. I knew I acted like a little girl when it came to him, but I couldn't help how I felt. He was THE GUY. I'd never thought so much about anyone else, not even when I broke up with Dean, not even when I said goodbye to James a month before leaving the dorm and we did it on the carpet in his room. With Rhys, it was different. Not like a fleeting thought that appeared and vanished. In some weird way, he was always in my life, in my head, in the emails I read and wrote every night. When something dumb happened or something major, I smiled, knowing I'd be telling him about it a few hours later. Like the week before, when the alarm at Harrods went off as I was walking out, and two security guards ran after me like I was a hardened criminal. I was so tired after staying up the night before working on that report, which was now gathering dust, that all I could think of to shout was, "I'm innocent, don't hurt me!" And then, with tears in my eyes, I looked at the ground while they were going through my bag.

"Sometimes I don't understand why he still talks to me."

"What's that supposed to mean?"

"I'm boring, Donna."

"Don't be silly! Anyway, Rhys adores you. I still remember how he looked at you during our Christmas lunch. Not to mention what happened after."

"I'm the one who kissed him," I repeated.

"So? You or him, what does it matter?"

"He'd never have done it."

"Ginger, you need to get out more."

"I'm serious. If it had been up to Rhys, that kiss would never have happened. I think he just felt sorry for me. He's a sweetie, even if he doesn't look like it. So he just went along." I shrugged. "Anyway, I have a long, boring summer ahead of me. Again. You working tonight?"

"No. So pick a movie, get the chocolate ice cream out of the freezer, and stop whining, okay? Don't make me start playing the big sister. Besides, Michael's out of town all weekend."

Michael was our roommate. He wasn't a bad guy, but he didn't talk much (or at all), and he hardly came out of his room when he was around (apart from raiding the fridge or taking an hour-long shower). He was an IT guy. He had a shaved head, tattoos, and piercings in his eyebrow and tongue. When she came to visit, my mother would purse her lips every time she saw him. She didn't like his "inelegant" appearance, as she called it, and she never understood why we wouldn't let her pay his part of the rent so the two of us could live alone. "It would do wonders for your quality of life," she'd said.

"Why don't you invite Amanda over?" I asked.

"Maybe tomorrow. Today's a Davies girls night."

I smiled. I liked how that sounded. I got the ice cream from the freezer and flopped down next to her with two spoons in hand while she turned on the TV.

43

Rhys

AXEL NGUYEN LIVED LESS THAN a half mile from my house. I was almost certain I'd seen him out surfing by the beach. I took a look around when he invited me in and felt uncomfortable somehow when I realized this was a home and not just four walls. He was nothing like what he'd seemed when I first met him weeks before at the club. And I wanted to leave there right away, turn around and not look back.

"Sorry, it's a fucking wreck in here. My kids, you know…" He shook his head. "I mean, why lie? It's my fault too. I must have my newest portfolio here somewhere…"

I watched him dig through the papers, paints, and junk on top of his desk. The house was in complete disorder. But that chaos so full of life was stimulating. There were paintings on the doorframes, on the chair legs, and in some of the corners, as if they'd wanted to mark every single space, making the place unique. The living room was full of toys, and there were storybooks on the ground. While he went on opening and closing drawers, I crouched down and picked up a piece of paper.

"Wow, look at these colors," I said.

"My kids, they're super artistic. And of course, Leah's the best painter in town. Actually, though, I'm the one responsible for the craziness." He looked up at the ceiling beams with their drawings and symbols. Then he went on looking around his desk. "Ah, here it is. It was in this folder."

I came closer and looked at the cover design for the single. All I'd told him during our informal meeting was the specifications Alexa had given me. I still hadn't seen the final result. Axel had been in touch with Owen since then, and Owen was the one to give him the thumbs-up. It was when I saw Axel in a café that morning that he asked me if I wanted to see it. And it was every bit as good as I'd imagined.

A cliff surrounded by smoke and shadows. A red sky. The title we'd chosen, "Edges and Scars," was at the top, and underneath, *Rhys Baker feat. Alexa Goldberg.* I looked at it a long time, almost surprised, as if those weeks of recordings, meetings, and rehearsals with Alexa hadn't been real until now.

"Bro, it's not that bad…"

"Fuck no, it isn't. It's perfect."

"You were starting to scare me," he said.

"I was just trying to take it in. It's incredible."

"Cool. Well, that's that. You want a smoke?"

I told him I didn't smoke, but that I'd go with him. We went out onto the porch, and Axel lit his cigarette. We remained quiet as we observed the stretch of the sea further off.

"Where'd you tell me you were from again?" Axel asked, expelling smoke.

"Tennessee. In the U.S."

"What takes you so far from home?"

"Just life," I sighed.

"Don't you miss it?"

"Sometimes. You from here?"

"Yeah. I moved here with my family when I was little and grew up here. Then I went to college and came back. I spent a few months in Paris years back, but it wasn't the same. I'm anchored here, to this stretch of sea," he said proudly.

"What do you mean?"

"Just that. It's my anchor. We all need one, don't we?"

"I don't know what you mean…" I murmured.

"I mean something to sustain us."

"Sustain us…" I closed my eyes.

"Cities, circumstances, decisions all change us as we go through life, don't you think? We're malleable, like the clay my kids play with. I wanted to keep being the person I was here… I think that's what it is."

I blew out a breath of air.

"Not all of us have an anchor," I said.

"Sometimes it's not a place. Sometimes it's a person, a dream… Who knows? There are so many variables. Listen, I won't keep you any longer." He gave me a look that was indecipherable. I don't know if it was curiosity, or if he saw something in me. But it made me uncomfortable. "Good luck with the song."

I thanked him and repeated that the image was perfect before walking down the steps of the porch so similar to mine and onto the sand of the beach. I took off my shoes and kept going slowly, breathing deeply, savoring the scent of the sea. An anchor. That's what mattered. Anchors, roots, nests.

It was so simple and painful at the same time...

44

From: Ginger Davies
To: Rhys Baker
Subject: I hate my life

When I think of college, I see all those memories through a rainbow with little stars twinkling around them. I don't know how I could have ever complained. My "adult life" is so much worse. (I don't care if you hate that expression, because that's what it is.) I get up at six, wolf down breakfast, grab a train packed with people, then walk for a long time, to reach a place where everyone seems to treat me differently because I'm the boss's daughter. It's not fair. I mean, Dean got hooked up there too, but people ignore it because he's not directly related and because he just knows how to win them over. Yesterday he brought everyone donuts. Why didn't I ever think of that? It's something people in the movies do all the time.

I'd go on torturing you with all the details of my day, but a) I don't want you to stop being my friend, and b) I have a *super-fun* meeting about new handle models.

From: Rhys Baker
To: Ginger Davies
Subject: RE: I hate my life

Come on, Ginger Snap, it can't be that bad. I wish I could do or say something do encourage you. I suppose adapting is always hard. And you've hardly had time for yourself since finishing school. Why don't you ask your father for a few weeks' vacation? You didn't take any time off last summer either. Maybe you need to relax a bit, and then you'll feel more ready to face things.

I don't know, Ginger. I'm trying to cheer you up, but I'm terrible giving the kind of advice that you see in fortune cookies. I'm not a mood-lifter. You just blow off all the steam you need, okay? You know I'm always here.

From: Ginger Davies
To: Rhys Baker
Subject: RE: RE: I hate my life

Yeah, I guess you're right, but I didn't dare ask for time off when I found out Dean was about to come on board. It would have looked bad, right? Lazy. I know I'm not in a competition with him, but I want to show that I can handle it. I've been studying and preparing myself for years.

Almost the whole staff left to have coffee together during

their twenty-minute break, but no one told me. When I walked out of my office, no one was there, just Dad, who was happy to have the time alone with me to go on talking about the new handles we're putting on the white cabinets. They used to be bronze; now they're silver. Imagine that.

From: Rhys Baker
To: Ginger Davies
Subject: I don't understand

Why didn't you go with them during your break?

From: Ginger Davies
To: Rhys Baker
Subject: RE: I don't understand

Because it's obvious they didn't want me to. Rhys, it's horrible. I feel just like I did when I was little and I had braces and everyone at school ignored me. But back then, at least Dean helped me; now it seems like he's forgotten I exist.

From: Rhys Baker
To: Ginger Davies
Subject: RE: RE: I don't understand

Dean's an imbecile. I can't stand you feeling like that, Ginger. I wish I could be there to help you out or tell you some jokes or make your life easier.

From: Ginger Davies
To: Rhys Baker
Subject: I admit it

I imagine that, you know? A parallel reality where you live in London. Your apartment's close to mine, we get together every Friday night for dinner, and we catch up in person instead of sending emails. You're working in some popular club, and I go there to see you sometimes, when you're hosting a big event. Obviously this fantasy doesn't include going to the office every day; instead I have my own independent publishing company. And I'm an elegant, self-assured woman living in the big city who is capable of saying no when she doesn't want to do something.

From: Rhys Baker
To: Ginger Davies
Subject: RE: I admit it

Well, on paper it doesn't sound bad, right, Ginger? Who knows? Maybe one day. I don't know if I could hold up for too long in London. And I couldn't see you just once a week. Two or three times would be better. The publishing company, though, that sounds real to me; that doesn't sound like a fantasy at all.

From: Ginger Davies
To: Rhys Baker
Subject: I'll get used to it

Whatever, it's fine, I'll adapt and figure it out. At least things are good at home. I love living with Donna. And Michael's a good guy, even if he doesn't talk much and my mom's scared of him. The other day, he was asking about your song; I was lying in bed screaming out the lyrics to "Ginger" because I didn't think anyone was home, and he knocked on the door and asked me who the song was by. I was all over the place when I tried to answer him, but I think he realized it was an as-yet-unknown artist (and you are that, Rhys) who was on the verge of breaking out.

How's the project going? When will it see the light of day?

Everything will be amazing, you'll see.

From: Rhys Baker
To: Ginger Davies
Subject: Dates and stuff

It launches in a week, but I guess promotion has already started. I'm glad I'm here and don't have to be exposed to it. It's for the best. Alexa tried to get me to go to LA with her, but I don't know, I don't feel like going anywhere now. I'm doing well here; it's relaxing. I think you'd like it.

From: Ginger Davies
To: Rhys Baker
Subject: It's not fair

By the way, I didn't tell you when I saw it a few weeks ago, but Alexa put a photo of the two of you on her Instagram. (Yeah, I was stalking you, whatever, don't laugh or roll your eyes.) What kind of nonsense is this? You're my best friend, and I can't take a photo with you, but she can? It's not fair. Sometimes I forget what exactly your face is like. Not the main outline, obviously, but the little details. I'd like to have you on my corkboard of happy memories. Because you're one of them, Rhys.

From: Rhys Baker
To: Ginger Davies
Subject: RE: I hate my life

Alexa pushed me, and I couldn't say no. She's stubborn.

But if it really bothers you, I'll send a photo. I just took it. The beach is the same one you can see from my back porch. I hope it keeps you from forgetting the little details, and you can hang it up on your corkboard.

From: Ginger Davies
To: Rhys Baker
Subject: CONGRATULATIONS

Congratulations, Rhys! Today's the big day! I can't believe I logged on to Spotify, and there was your name. And the song... it's perfect. Brilliant. You're brilliant. You must be so proud. Does your whole family know? I hope so, because they'll be just as happy as I am.

Tell me how everything goes, Rhys.

Best of luck.

Part 3

—

SUCCESS. INDEPENDENCE.
SEARCHING.

"Well, I must endure the presence of two or three caterpillars if I
wish to become acquainted with the butterflies."

The Little Prince

45

From: Ginger Davies
To: Rhys Baker
Subject: Happy Birthday!

Happy birthday, Rhys! I can't believe how fast time is passing. Twenty-eight. You're so old. It's just been a month or two since last year's present reached you, and I'm already wrapping the next one. (I'm trying to be funny. Next time you'll keep me informed of major dates.) I bought you something I hope you'll like. Have a good day. Spend it surrounded by friends.

Lots of kisses (real ones, with feeling).

From: Ginger Davies
To: Rhys Baker
Subject: How are things?

I guess you must be crazy busy. The song's a hit! How many streams have you gotten? All the times I've listened to it on Spotify must have boosted your numbers a lot. Seriously though, it's so amazing to search for you on Google and see you pop up like that. I'm so proud! Everywhere I go, I tell people Rhys Baker is my best friend. When I go through the checkout lane at the supermarket I'm like, "Give me a discount, because I'm friends with Rhys Baker. That's right, the one with the song." Sorry, I'm rambling. I just want you to know how happy I am that everything's going so well, and I hope I hear from you soon. I miss your daily messages, even if I get that you're super busy now.

Take care, okay? More kisses.

From: Rhys Baker
To: Ginger Davies
Subject: Stress

Sorry, Ginger. Seriously, I feel so bad for being absent these past few weeks. Everything's been complicated, Owen and Alexa have more contacts in LA than I thought, and I don't know how, but they've gotten the song streamed more than three hundred thousand times. It's pretty incredible when you keep in mind that no one even knows who we are. It's cool and all, but at the same time, I didn't expect this, and I'm sort of freaking out. They want me to go there and do promo with Alexa, but I'm not sure if it's a good idea.

You know what I really want to do?

This. Go out on the porch with my laptop and a beer, read your messages, and write back to you. Watch the night fall. Look at the moon and imagine the impossible. Look at this book you gave me, which I've reread probably more times than you have...

But let's stop talking about me. Tell me how things are going with you. How's work? Better? Have you adapted after those first few months?

From: Ginger Davies
To: Rhys Baker
Subject: RE: Stress

I get you, Rhys. I love imagining you there on the beach relaxing. It's very you. But I also get that the Goldbergs want to squeeze everything they can out of this moment. The song's amazing. And I'm not surprised so many people like it. If you released "Ginger," it would be every bit as successful or more, even if, obviously, you'd have to change the title. Anyway, don't do anything you don't want to. I'm telling you this from experience. Sometimes I think if I could turn back time, I'd do everything differently...

But this is my reality now, right?

Things are fine at work. No real changes. The good thing is I don't care anymore if all my coworkers blow me off because I'm the boss. At least this girl Sue has been talking to me a lot lately.

Dean continues to knock everybody out, of course. Can you believe my father listened to his suggestion about how to package the drawers? It was stupid (it's just that the corners get scuffed sometimes), and I've proposed way more interesting things he hasn't even paid attention to. I don't know, Rhys, I feel like I'm just posing here. I do the billing and other basic stuff, and it goes without saying, this isn't why I spent four years in college.

I don't want to bore you though.

Your life is so interesting…

I will tell you one funny thing. The other day I opened the bathroom door without knocking, and you know what I saw? Michael, our roommate, masturbating. It was so…embarrassing. First because I couldn't not look. I'm human, you know? And he's…um…big. XXL, as my sister put it. Second, I spent days avoiding him at home. I'm still doing that, actually. I'm scared he's going to come talk to me, and then I'll get nervous and say something stupid. Like if he said, "Hey, are you the one who finished the milk?" I'd probably just respond, "Dick, dick, dick, DICK," like a crazy person. I don't know how long I can live with him without crossing paths. If only I could get that image out of my head, aargh.

From: Rhys Baker
To: Ginger Davies
Subject: Bad girl

Come on, admit it. You liked it. You noticed how big he was, right? That must mean something. I'm cracking up right now. I've told you that you're the funniest chick I know, right? And a bad girl to boot…opening the bathroom door without knocking… Remind me never to be your roommate.

As far as work—you're not just posing.

I hate you feeling that way, I really do. I hate it.

I'm going to have to go to Los Angeles after all. I guess I can deal with it for a while. I'll do the promo, and I'll spend Christmas with my mom before returning. Moving is the last thing I've felt like doing these past few months, and now look at the irony. It must be karma or something.

Even if I did release "Ginger," I'd never change the title. Why should I? I could never call it anything else. But I feel... I don't know, I think it would make me feel weird to share something of mine, you know? Something of yours, actually. Or maybe it's something of ours.

From: Ginger Davies
To: Rhys Baker
Subject: It must be karma

I like the sound of that, *something of ours*.

I'm sorry you have to go to Los Angeles. When do you leave? I noticed you keep getting more and more streams. Amazing. I'm so, so proud of you.

From: Ginger Davies
To: Rhys Baker
Subject: Just what I needed!

You won't believe it! Like it wasn't enough that everyone thinks I got a leg up when Dean and I got our jobs the exact same way— thanks to my dad—now it turns out Dean is going out with our director of marketing. They told everyone last Friday at the end of the workday, when we were all gathered in the boardroom. Since then, they've spent the whole week clinging to each other like leeches. How sweet. So not only does he get treated better because of his fake smile and because he isn't actually related to the boss; he's also found true love. I know I sound hateful, frustrated, and jealous, but I am, sort of. It's terrible to admit these things out loud, but… I guess that's what we human beings are like. In theory, I know I'm being unfair. But in practice…that's just it. Practice is a whole different story. I spend the day shut up in my cubicle eating sandwiches from the machine. (They're awful and I've put on five or six pounds from that nasty sauce they have on them.) Then I go home and I'm exhausted. And I take it out on Donna. That's the worst thing. Or on Michael. (We did run into each other; I told him to lock the door, even though I know it's partly my fault for not knocking.)

I hate myself a little these days.

Tell me what's up with you. Kisses.

From: Ginger Davies
To: Rhys Baker
Subject: You still there?

Hello! Rhys! Are you alive?

I'm starting to worry…

From: Rhys Baker
To: Ginger Davies
Subject: [No subject]

Sorry. Dammit. It's just been chaos these days…

I'm in Los Angeles, and I haven't had a minute free since I got here between meetings and parties where I keep getting introduced to people with weird names I've never heard before. I think I need time to absorb all this. I don't know, I just didn't see it coming. That's the bad thing. I miss the slow life I had in Australia, the ease, the sea, not having to get dressed in anything but a bathing suit and a T-shirt to go outside (if that); it's almost like time's stopped there sometimes. The good thing… I guess I can't say I'm bored. That's the least applicable word to my situation. Here I have something to do every day. Big things. I barely have time to think before I'm thrown into some new situation. Tomorrow, for example, I have a radio interview at eight in the evening, on a channel called Xdem, I don't know what time that is in London or whether you'll be able to listen to it.

As for Dean…it's normal for you to feel that way, isn't it? Who wouldn't? You spent your whole life getting ready for something, then he seems to be doing better at it than you. Don't take that the wrong way. All I want to say is, maybe your place is somewhere else. Didn't that ever occur to you, Ginger? I know it scares you even to think about, but it is a possibility. Who knows? Look at me. Never in a million years did I imagine I'd be here, getting dressed to go to dinner with some pop singer.

46

Ginger

WHEN I FINALLY GOT THE radio station's webpage to load, I put on my headphones. Right away, I heard the presenter. The interview had already started. I tried to rewind it, but I couldn't, so I just listened.

"So you didn't see this success coming?"

"Not at all," Rhys said.

"But…" Alexa added.

"Were things different for you, Alexa?"

"Why lie? It did occur to me. Rhys's song is amazing. The lyrics are deep; the chorus is catchy. Why wouldn't it be a success?"

"Well, before, nobody even knew who you were."

"True, true," she giggled. "But a girl can dream."

"Exactly. Of course she can. So, Rhys, tell us, when did you first want to become a professional DJ? Was it a hard road?"

"Honestly, no. It was almost by chance."

"What do you mean?"

"I never even considered it. Can I be totally honest?" He sighed, and I could almost see him smiling from thousands of miles away.

"My boss, who's now my producer, brought it up one night at the club. I thought he was crazy. I was going to say no, but after five drinks, I forgot to."

You could hear Alexa and the presenter laugh.

"You weren't so uncertain, right, Alexa?"

"Not at all. I knew when I heard the material, I had something big. Rhys is modest, but he obviously has talent, and this is just the beginning. There's much more to come."

"How do you guys get along?"

"Great, great." Alexa's enthusiasm kept striking me as excessive. Everything for her seemed to be *fascinating, amazing, incredible,* and she always drew her words out to give them more emphasis. "Working with him is so easy. And we had a connection right away, didn't we, Rhys? Now we're basically inseparable."

"She's kidnapped me," Rhys joked, and she laughed.

"You're clearly very close. What are your future plans?"

"Right now, we're just focused on promotion. Next Saturday, we have a show at Club Havana. After that..." Alexa lowered her voice to sound more interesting. "Let's just say it's a secret, right, Rhys?" Another stupid giggle. "But most likely we'll soon be confirming our dates at a very well-known festival. That's all I can say for now."

"You're clearly keeping busy!"

"We sure are," Alexa replied.

"One last thing. Before we say goodbye with "Edges and Scars" one more time, I'd like to ask you both one question: What is success for you?"

"Success is fulfilling your dreams, reaching your goals."

"What about for you, Rhys?"

"Success…" I could hear the uncertainty in his voice. "I guess it comes when you learn who you are and you can be faithful to that."

There was a brief silence before the presenter spoke again, overdoing it with the enthusiasm, telling his listeners goodbye and putting on the track. I listened to the first chords, but then I turned it off. I was thinking about what Rhys had said. In his words were secrets, pain, longing. No matter how relaxed he seemed, I knew he'd had to drag those words up from the depths.

47

From: **Rhys Baker**

To: **Ginger Davies**

Subject: **Congratulations!**

Happy birthday, Ginger Snap! Sorry I've been away so much lately. I've been busy. How are things? What are you up to today? Sorry I couldn't give you the present you deserved this year. I finally decided to go home. I'll spend Christmas Day with my mom since my dad won't be around; he's got an important business trip. I hope I don't feel weird just dropping in after three years away.

Tell me about you, Ginger. How does twenty-three feel? How are things at work? Is Dean still going out with that chick?

Kisses (lots of them, for real).

48

Rhys

THERE ARE PLACES THAT HAVE a certain kind of light. This occurred to me as I parked in front of the home where I grew up. The winter sun struggled to pierce the sky in Tennessee, and when I looked up, I had to squint. It was cold. I knew that cold. It seeped into my bones.

I walked slowly up the sidewalk. I had a knot in my throat. My mind was a blank as my feet led me up the front stairs and I rang the doorbell. My mother opened up. Her sweet aroma enveloped me, her trembling arms; she seemed to think I'd vanish if she let me go. Her voice whispered in my ear: "I'm so, so happy to see you…"

She trembled as she stood back to look at me. "Rhys… You're so handsome. You've lost some weight. But still handsome." The words seemed to stick in her throat, and she made me follow her to the kitchen, which was huge with flawless white cabinets and our breakfast table set with a bowl of fruit and flowers from the garden.

"You look good," I said. "Pretty."

My mother managed a thin smile before turning around and

glancing at the oven, which was giving off a delicious scent of something. I came close and looked through the glass.

"Spaghetti?" I asked, surprised.

"Yeah. The cheese is melting on it right now."

"Spaghetti for Christmas?"

"I know it's your favorite. I thought you'd be happy."

I blinked, almost uncomfortable. Tense.

"Thanks, Mom." I wrapped an arm around her shoulders and kissed her quickly on the head. "I'm going to take my things upstairs, okay?"

"Sure. There's still ten minutes."

I climbed the spiral staircase slowly to the second floor. The family photos were hanging on the wall in chronological order. First came those of her and Dad before I came along. Young, good-looking, with clothes from long ago, and then on their wedding day. Soon after that, I appeared. Barely a year old, in my father's arms, while he looked at the camera with a cigarette between his slightly downturned lips. Me on a bike, a little older; I could still remember how they taught me to ride it on the streets of that subdivision. I took a deep breath. Birthdays: seven, ten, and twelve, always with a smile when the button on the camera clicked to immortalize that moment in front of a cake covered in candles. My mother standing next to me on graduation day. Dad with an arm around me in front of the car they gave me for my twentieth birthday.

I rested my shoulder against the doorframe, unable to walk inside my room. It looked exactly as Ginger had guessed it would in her email more than a year ago.

Ginger... I didn't want to think about her either.

Lately, I hadn't wanted to think about anything.

I noticed on the shelves the models that Dad and I had put together when I was still a kid. They were still keeping my room clean, that was obvious; there wasn't a single grain of dust to be seen. Ships, monuments, an airplane. Models frozen in time. All those hours invested. What a waste.

I heard my mother calling me down for lunch. I left my bags on the floor and walked back to the kitchen. On the big table, which used to be full of friends, family, and neighbors on every holiday, there were now just two glasses and two plates of steaming spaghetti. But after three Christmases alone, it was perfect.

"Delicious," I said after taking a bite.

"I still remember how you like it with the onions crunchy."

"It hasn't been so long, has it?"

"I mean…three years is pretty long, Rhys."

I looked across the table at her. Closely. Her cheeks were more sunken than they had been the last time, in New York. And she had more wrinkles. Were her eyes a little shrunken, maybe? I wasn't sure. Can eyes shrink? Around her neck was the gold chain I helped my father pick out as a birthday present years ago; she never took it off. It was thin and had a blue teardrop mother-of-pearl pendant she fidgeted with when she was nervous.

Just as she used to, she looked at me nervously. "When are you going to finally sit down and talk with him?"

"Mom, don't ruin the meal," I responded.

"I'm serious, Rhys. The years are passing…"

"I know. And they'll keep passing. I have nothing to say to him."

I swallowed, but that didn't make the knot in my throat disappear, so I grabbed my glass of water and took a sip. "Don't look at me like that. I promised you I'd call you every week, and I have."

"Yeah, great. That doesn't mean…"

"Mom…" I shook my head and sighed.

I didn't want to talk about him. Let alone with her. I was keeping my part of the deal, even if I didn't know why. Maybe because I was scared. Maybe because it was easier that way. Maybe because I didn't want to think about the wick that one day caught fire and made everything explode. I'd fucked up, I knew. I'd acted like a spoiled brat, an idiot, running away when my parents needed me most. But he…he had broken me.

He had cut me adrift.

And I was still lost in that sea.

And there was the issue of pride.

Pride. His, mine.

Pride that blinds a person, that sends them into a rage, that makes them stay away for years waiting for an *I'm sorry*, for some words from the other person that will bring them relief, not realizing that they want the same. And time passes. Time buries us. And underneath it, buried in some deep, dark pit, we forget how to return to the surface.

There was only one point of connection for us. Her. My mother. I thought of this as I looked at her, memorizing her aging face, the way she cut her spaghetti because she couldn't stand to get tomato sauce on the corners of her lips. She had always been the nexus between Dad and me. The center that held us together.

"Fine, we won't talk about it if you don't want." She gave in. "But at least tell me how things are going, honestly, with details, not just by saying *cool* and *great* the way you do over the phone. I want to know what's happening with that song."

"We didn't expect it would be so big."

"I'll bet. Are you happy?"

"I guess." I shrugged.

"You don't seem like it."

"I don't know." I spun my fork in the noodles. "I guess I was fine, you know? In Australia. It was chill there, and I was living by the ocean, and I thought... I thought I'd stay longer. I wanted to. I think it weirded me out having to go somewhere for the first time without deciding it on my own, you know?"

"Yeah." She smiled. "You and obligations."

"And life in LA is the total opposite. Fast. You almost don't even notice it passing. You should come out sometime for a few days. Or a week. As long as you'd like. It would be fun."

"Is there a girl in the picture?"

She looked amused. I laughed.

"Sort of."

"Ginger, wasn't that her name? Are you still talking with her?"

"It's not Ginger, Mom."

She was the only person I'd spoken to about Ginger. About how important she was to me. About how we'd been talking for almost two years, even if our conversations had thinned out in recent months. I thought it was my fault, because I was always busy, but it was her too; she was busy with work, her new schedule, her life in London...

I missed her when I had a free second not surrounded by people or when I was having fun and doing something crazy. In those moments, Ginger would creep once again into my mind, as if she were there to fill my empty spaces. I thought of her and the gift she'd sent me for my last birthday, which had never reached me, because I had left before it arrived. I imagined the box at the door of my house on the beach, carefully, painstakingly wrapped. I imagined that and I had the feeling that not everything was well.

"Who's the girl then?"

"Alexa. The one who sings with me."

"You're going out with her? Is it serious?"

"Not exactly…"

"It's one of those hookups you kids are into."

I couldn't really call myself a kid anymore at twenty-eight years old, but yeah, I guess that's what it was. A kind of closeness. A relationship, but different. Because unlike the girls I'd been with those past few years, with Alexa it wasn't just sex. We spent every day together between promotional work, shows at night, plus the trips to festivals we had coming up…

"I guess everything's going great then."

"I suppose," I whispered.

But I couldn't escape a feeling of heaviness, apathy, the idea that something about all that wasn't right, as much as I wanted to just give in, go with the current, stop fighting against myself.

49

From: Rhys Baker

To: Ginger Davies

Subject: The Little Prince

I read the book again. It's fascinating. When I think about the
dedication, I keep asking myself: Am I your domesticated fox?

From: Ginger Davies

To: Rhys Baker

Subject: RE: The Little Prince

If *domesticating* means creating bonds, then yes.

From: Rhys Baker

To: Ginger Davies

Subject: RE: RE: The Little Prince

Does that mean you're the Little Prince then? In a way, that would make sense. You're a good person, Ginger Davies. And you believe in friendship. Shit! You believe in everything in general; you're one of those people who still has faith in humanity. That's something most of us lost long ago. You probably still want to leave cookies out for Santa Claus at Christmastime. There's a phrase in the book, "Only the children are flattening their noses against the windowpanes." I'll bet you do that every time you pass a pastry shop.

I've been lucky. No one could have done a better job "domesticating" me, Ginger.

From: Ginger Davies
To: Rhys Baker
Subject: RE: RE: RE: The Little Prince

You're an idiot. I leave him milk. Cookies are too high in sugar and saturated fats; I don't want to give the old man a heart attack. Jokes aside, when I met you, I thought you'd like this book, because I saw you as a big kid, and I still do, someone who refuses to be an adult and looks at the world with a longing to play, make mischief, and discover new things.

From: Rhys Baker
To: Ginger Davies
Subject: RE: RE: RE: RE: The Little Prince

You think too much of me. But I wish what you said were true.

From: Ginger Davies
To: Rhys Baker
Subject: RE: RE: RE: RE: RE: The Little Prince

It is. You do have one of the fox's traits: loyalty. And you're like the narrator, because you can look inside yourself but also listen to others. And the Prince too: that's the little boy who still lives inside you. You've even kept your pride, like the rose. And you're the only person I know who'd be happy living alone on an asteroid.

From: Rhys Baker
To: Ginger Davies
Subject: RE: RE: RE: RE: RE: RE: The Little Prince

Thanks, Ginger.

50

Ginger

CHRISTMAS. INSTEAD OF *HOME SWEET home,* the first thing I thought when I sat at that table surrounded by people was, *God, make this torture end as soon as possible.* Because my father was there talking, all proud about my work at the company as if he'd even let me do anything at all that past year and a half except staple papers, check invoices, and stare at the clock. Donna was there too, having to deal with the Wilsons' questions about whether being a lesbian meant she didn't want to have kids. And the icing on the cake was Dean sitting with his wonderful girlfriend. She had skin like a model in a cosmetics ad and a smile that made it impossible to hate her even a little (I had tried), and she was also smart, intelligent, and classily dressed.

"Would you pass me the mashed potatoes, Ginger?"

"Sure. Here, Stella." I handed them over.

"Next year's going to be amazing, now that we've got two geniuses on staff," Dad said with a smile. "Sorry, Stella, I mean three."

"I won't hold it against you, since I started just two years ago," she said, and we all laughed.

Dean looked at her adoringly. Like a planet revolving around his girlfriend, his sun. It was stupid, but I couldn't help thinking he'd never looked at me that way before, and that should have told me things weren't going right.

I held out as best I could, answering the Wilsons every time they asked me something about work. "Yeah, I'm happy there." "Of course it was worth all that time in school." "Yeah, we're lucky; my old roommate Kate still hasn't found a decent job. It's tough."

When dessert came, I was surprised to see Dean getting up to open a bottle of champagne he had put in the fridge to chill. He poured it into glasses my mother kept in a glass cabinet with the special crystal and plateware, the stuff we only used on special occasions. Strangely, Dean didn't sit down with us.

"Everyone, I have an announcement to make."

He grabbed Stella's hand, and she got up too. She seemed nervous, and her cheeks were flushed, even though the heat wasn't up that high. I looked at Dean and knew what he was going to say. I thought of Rhys. How I wished he was there. How the year before, a few days before my birthday, he had sat at that same table and I had spent the whole meal with a knot in my stomach while we glanced at each other and his knee rubbed mine. And now I was there again, and everything was so different. I didn't feel better. I didn't feel more like an adult or more fulfilled. I wasn't happy.

"Stella and I...we're going to get married."

"Oh my God, Dean!" My mother got up, excited, came around the table, and hugged him so tight I was afraid the poor guy's head would pop off. Then she kissed Stella loudly on the cheek. "I'm so happy for you both! You make a wonderful couple!"

"Congratulations, champ!" Dad squeezed his shoulder.

I congratulated them both, too, once Donna was finished. They talked about wedding preparations while we ate dessert and toasted the good news. They were going to do it in May. It would be a simple ceremony, intimate...

"I'll clear the table, Mom; don't bother getting up," I said, stacking the dirty plates and taking them to the kitchen. She thanked me and looked back at Stella, who was now talking about what kind of dress she wanted to wear.

I left the dining room and put the plates in the sink. I decided to wash them by hand since the dishwasher was full. I had just rolled up my sleeves when Dean came in and stood next to me. He grabbed the soap.

"What are you...?"

"I'm helping out."

"There's no need."

"Just let me."

"Fine."

Elbow to elbow, we started scrubbing. The silence was uncomfortable, but I didn't completely understand why. I was happy for him. I wasn't jealous. It was something else. Maybe...I just wanted the same for myself. Or something like it. I don't know. I was having a hard time; I was disappointed in everything. I hoped it would pass.

"Aren't you going to say anything?" he asked.

"About what? I already told you..."

"You're happy for me. Right. Are you sure?"

"Dammit, Dean, of course I am."

"Okay. I just... I was worried. I didn't want to hurt you, Ginger.

I know it's been two years since we broke up, but I also know I told you I needed time…but with Stella, everything happened overnight. I guess it was love at first sight. These things happen, don't they? When you least expect it."

I dried my hands with a rag and turned to him.

"Dean, it's great, honestly. I'm telling the truth. Stella seems amazing, and you basically drool every time you look at her. I'm sure you'll be super happy together."

"Then…why are you like this?"

"Like what?"

"You know. Mad at me."

"That has nothing to do with the wedding. It's just that at work… I don't know, Dean, you acted like you didn't know me. I understand that our relationship was basically that way in our last year at college too, but you could have recognized I was having a tough time. You could have invited me to have coffee with everyone on morning break, you know. I'm not saying it's your fault, but…"

"You're right." He cut me off.

"Am I?"

"I've been selfish."

"That's not what I meant. Not exactly."

"It's true though. When I started at the company, you know, I guess I was on a roll, and I wasn't really thinking about anyone else. Can we do a reset?"

"Sure." I smiled and sighed.

51

From: Rhys Baker

To: Ginger Davies

Subject: Happy New Year, Ginger Snap

Here we go again. I celebrated it with a bunch of people, but you're the person I was thinking of. I don't know why. Don't ask. I know I shouldn't write you when I've been drinking, but I keep thinking about you… You feel so far away…and finally I decided to leave the party and come back to the hotel… Alexa still isn't here.

The moon is round tonight. You know something? It's not actually a perfect sphere; it's oval or egg-shaped. The moon's an egg, what do you think of that, Ginger? Funny, right? Speaking of, I hope that whatever you're doing right now, you're having a blast…maybe going a little crazy.

If we lived in the same city, we'd do a different crazy thing together every day. I wouldn't let you wimp out, no matter what kind of faces you made. I don't know what I'm getting at; it's just that I miss you, Ginger. Can you miss a person you've only ever seen twice in your life? I guess it's that those two nights with you were the best ones I remember. Do you do that ever? Remember them?

Maybe I should stop writing now. I just wanted you to know I'm a shitty friend for being so absent lately and that I miss you, but I think I already said that, and despite everything, you're one of the most important people in my life…

I found a little bottle of gin in the minibar, so…to your health, Ginger! I don't know when or how, but I think we should see each other this year.

From: Ginger Davies
To: Rhys Baker
Subject: Happy New Year, Rhys

I was surprised by your email. Sometimes I like drunk Rhys better than sober Rhys. He cuts loose easier. Takes more risks. Anyway… you're really important to me too, and I don't like there being distance between us. But sometimes… I do have this feeling like our worlds have pulled apart, you know? I don't know, your song just blew up so fast, and now your life… Like everything I tell you about my days seems so boring and stupid and routine compared to what you're up to. Don't get me wrong, I'm happy for you. Really. A bunch. You've got talent. But just don't get lost. Okay?

From: Rhys Baker
To: Ginger Davies
Subject: I wouldn't

Sorry. I reread my message from the other night, and I promised myself I wouldn't write you again when I was drinking, but now it seems I'm having trouble sticking to it. You know what it is? I'm one of those people who gets nostalgic and sentimental when I'm drunk. Don't laugh, it's true.

I won't get lost, Ginger. I've had some weird days, but I think I needed them to remember some stuff. I went to see my mom for Christmas, I didn't tell you that. Actually, I haven't told you anything about what's been going on the past few weeks, but yeah, I saw her. We had spaghetti with melted cheese. And we talked. And I remembered why I love her so much. But at the same time, it scared me because of all that implied.

Sometimes I wish I just didn't feel anything... That would be easier...

The whole house is still full of photographs. You were right. I think I don't like them because they're the prologue to a story that only the people there know about. Like a door. You open it up, and you go inside...and then it's hard to come back out. Not to mention just the memories themselves... Don't you think we distort them sometimes? Memories...they're moldable; they change, depending on the perspective and mind of the person they belong to. I just keep wondering if many of the things I remember might not be true, if there are things in them I couldn't see because I didn't have the right information.

Crazy, isn't it? Anyway...

Don't ever say again that you think you'll bore me. It's not true. I never get bored with you, Ginger. And I like knowing everything about your days, even if it's just routine stuff. It's definitely more interesting than all the bullshit and stupid little stories I hear every time someone gets introduced to me, and lately that's all the time.

From: Ginger Davies
To: Rhys Baker
Subject: RE: I wouldn't

You don't know how happy I am that you went to see your mom and you spent the day together. Are you ever going to tell me what happened with your father? I guess your relationship must have taken a turn when you were a teenager. It happens to all of us, right? On different levels, obviously. But we think our parents are superheroes and the best people in the world, and then we grow up and start noticing their weaknesses, the fact that they, too, make mistakes, all these things no one can understand when they're little…

I know you don't like to talk about this. And yes, I think what you say about memories is true. They're not always true to reality. I guess it depends on the prism you see them through. Why are we getting so philosophical, Rhys? I'd like to tell you something funny, but I can't think of anything… I'm going through a weird moment, you've probably noticed. It's not just your fault that we're not in touch as much. Sometimes when I get home at night, I sit in front of the computer and…for the first time ever, I don't want to tell you about my day. It's not you; it's that my day is always garbage.

I guess time will make that better.

From: Rhys Baker
To: Ginger Davies
Subject: I remembered!

Happy friendiversary, Ginger Snap.

That word still makes my skin crawl… But it's two years ago today that we met, so I guess I'll try and get past it again. Things sure have changed in that short time, haven't they? You were in college, you'd just broken up with Dean, and I was in Paris with no idea what was coming…

And now here we are. Being all philosophical.

I need to go because my plane's leaving in a few hours, but I promise I'll get back in touch as soon as I'm at the hotel.

From: Ginger Davies
To: Rhys Baker
Subject: Friendiversary

It's true! It makes me shiver when I think back on it. What times those were, right? Honestly, I miss how easy it was, living at the dorm, eating in the cafeteria, my whole life revolving around what happened on campus. I knew you'd end up making it and would have fans. Maybe you're not super well-known yet, but everything takes time.

Where are you going? A festival in Nevada?

From: Rhys Baker
To: Ginger Davies

Subject: RE: Friendiversary

Yeah, I'm spinning tomorrow night.

Okay, I'm ready to tell you about my father... We got along fine when I was a teenager. Well, actually, I was the typical spoiled brat from a wealthy family, remember? My grades weren't stellar, but I got by, and I was good at sports. The problems came later. For a long time, everything was great. When I was a kid, I adored my dad. You're right. For me, he was invincible, like a superhero. I loved having breakfast with him on Sundays, and sometimes, on the weekdays, I'd wait for him, playing outside the front door just to see him get home with his suitcase and his jacket and tie on.

From: Ginger Davies
To: Rhys Baker
Subject: RE: RE: Friendiversary

It's so sweet, all this you're telling me, Rhys.

So when did everything change?

From: Rhys Baker
To: Ginger Davies
Subject: RE: RE: RE: Friendiversary

I guess I veered off the straight and narrow. If that even exists. I tried three different majors. I dropped out of all of them. I was lost. I didn't like anything; nothing made me happy or fulfilled me. My parents were more or less understanding, but naturally, they pressured me a little. What parent wouldn't? Plus, my dad had always hoped I'd work for his practice. And then...my mom got sick.

I've never talked about that, I don't think.

She had cancer. It was really bad. It's still hard for me to think back on. Seeing her like that, I mean. Just eaten up by illness. Struggling to survive. I know it's fucking selfish, but it hurt me to see her every day. It was like... I don't know, like someone cut open a hole in my chest. I can't even explain it in words. I've never been good at communicating, you know that, Ginger; it's not my strong point, though you're maybe the one exception. I held on as best I could, swallowing all those emotions.

But then something happened. And I abandoned her.

I left. I did it when she was at her worst point. The doctors didn't even know if she'd survive. But I left. I couldn't... I just couldn't stay...

That was the first trip I took. I didn't know then I'd just keep traveling. I was a bad son, I know. I don't know what I was thinking. How I could do it? I don't know why she forgave me when I never told her what I was feeling. She didn't need to. But I came back, and she hugged me. With Dad, though...that was where everything fell apart.

I fucked up. And he destroyed me.

I guess it was only fair.

From: Ginger Davies
To: Rhys Baker

Subject: I'm so sorry

My God, Rhys, that's terrible. I won't tell you that you did the right thing, but you were young and sometimes we don't know how to manage our emotions. We all have the right to regret things and to say we're sorry. The situation was too much for you, and you made a mistake. You just shouldn't pay for it forever. It's so sad that you and your father haven't talked…

From: Rhys Baker
To: Ginger Davies
Subject: Everything's fine

Believe me, it's best like this. Let's change the subject. We're getting dark, aren't we, Ginger Snap? What happened to the times when we used to joke around in all our emails and talk about your marvelous dates or other bullshit? I miss that.

By the way, in mid-March I'll be at a festival in Germany. It's not exactly next door, but you could always catch a plane and come see me. Be crazy. The way you did one night when you met a boy in the subway in Paris.

What do you say? It could be fun.

From: Ginger Davies
To: Rhys Baker
Subject: In case you forgot

Maybe you don't remember I'm presently enslaved. I work from

Monday to Friday, and when the weekend comes, I'm exhausted (and I often still have to go with Dad on visits to our purveyors and things like that, but it's best not to go into it, because you'll die of boredom).

Anyway, I'm not interested in being a third wheel. I nose around on Alexa's Instagram sometimes, and two days ago she posted a photo of her sitting on your knees in the VIP at some club as she was giving you mouth-to-mouth. (I hope you survived. I'm praying for you, but just so you know, I think her technique's off.) You didn't tell me you were together. I know she goes almost everywhere with you, so it would be...very uncomfortable.

I don't think I told you this, but Dean's getting married.

From: Rhys Baker
To: Ginger Davies
Subject: Come on, Ginger

Seriously? He's getting married? That was a turbo courtship.

I was still breathing, but thanks for worrying about me. And I'm not with her. Not exactly. What's it matter, anyway? I want to see you.

From: Ginger Davies
To: Rhys Baker
Subject: RE: Come on, Ginger

"Not exactly" is very ambiguous.

And yeah: Dean said, "Love at first sight."

From: Rhys Baker
To: Ginger Davies
Subject: How it is

I just don't know, okay? I don't know if we're together. Should I? Sometimes I don't understand myself.

From: Ginger Davies
To: Rhys Baker
Subject: It's easy

Are you in love with her?

From: Rhys Baker
To: Ginger Davies
Subject: RE: It's easy

Shit, Ginger. Where do these questions come from? I don't know. I have no fucking idea.

From: Ginger Davies
To: Rhys Baker
Subject: RE: RE: It's easy

Maybe you don't know, but you should.

From: Rhys Baker
To: Ginger Davies

Subject: [No subject]

So let's just accept that I'm an emotional disaster, and I don't even know what being in love is. Are you so certain about it, Ginger? If it means fucking someone and spending a lot of time with them, then yes, I am.

From: Ginger Davies
To: Rhys Baker
Subject: Being in love

No, Rhys, it's not just fucking someone and hanging out because you happen to be on tour with them. I'm not an expert, but I think being in love is more than that. It's feeling a tingle in your stomach when you see them. Not being able to stop looking at them. Missing them even though they're right there. Wanting to touch them at all hours, talking about any- and everything, feeling like you lose all sense of time when you're together. Noticing the details. Wanting to know everything about them, even the stupid stuff. You know what, Rhys? I think it's actually like being on the moon permanently. With a smile on your face. Without fear.

From: Rhys Baker
To: Ginger Davies
Subject: RE: Being in love

Then no, I'm not in love. Not with her.

52

Rhys

LOOKS. WORDS. MOMENTS.

Three things that can change everything.

There are moments that should disappear, that you regret so much, you wish you could go back in time and change them, erase the looks full of bitterness, drown out the cutting words, the ones that wound you, that tear into you at the roots.

Who would we be without roots? How would we remain grounded on the earth? What would happen when the wind blew and shook us and there was nothing familiar to grab on to?

53

Ginger

SHE WAS SO PRETTY...

Her hair was pulled up on top of her head with a few curls falling loose. Her makeup looked natural, her lipstick was dark, her eyes were full of happiness. Her dress was white, the bodice tight—it fit her like a glove. When she reached the altar, Dean extended his hand, and she took it, smiling nervously.

I could hear people in the audience sighing.

Years ago, I thought I'd be standing where Stella was. Across from Dean, looking into his eyes in front of our families, waiting for the moment when we'd exchange our vows and celebrate at the banquet.

It's funny how life changes. I think I'm on a straight path, and suddenly the ground crumbles, cracks open up, and I can't keep going. I make decisions, and they move me from one place to another. I guess in the end, it's just circumstances that pile up. And that was why Stella was there in a wedding dress instead of me, and a part of me felt happy, because there was no sense in trying to imagine things could have gone differently. But another...a darker part of me, harder to grasp, kept crying about all the plans I'd made as a girl, a teenager, that had progressively fallen apart, and I could do nothing about it.

No matter how hard I had tried, even if things had gotten a little better, I still hadn't been happy. I'd thought everything would be different. I'd finish school, be happy at the family company, feel fulfilled, marry Dean...all that. All that stuff I had just taken as a matter of course.

But instead I was standing there in a pale-yellow dress that made me look like an ugly piece of lemon pie. The wedding ceremony was sweet, simple, nice. I clapped when it was over, and they walked out of the church. Things between Dean and me had gotten better in the past few months, after that uncomfortable conversation in the kitchen at Christmas. The same went for my relationship with my coworkers. They included me in their plans. I went out with them for coffee. I even felt like I fit in once they stopped seeing me as a weirdo who was also the boss's daughter. The funny thing, though, is that feeling more comfortable didn't make me any happier with the job.

Maybe that was the real problem.

The one I was too scared to think about.

"Langoustines for the second course. Nice," Donna said, smiling when we sat down at the table in the banquet hall. She passed me the menu. "And mint mousse."

"You'd think you haven't eaten in years."

"Look, there's the bride and groom." She cut me off.

Everyone around were all smiles as the bride and groom made their appearance, walking toward the table in the center. We were sitting nearby, with my parents and some cousins of the Wilsons. We enjoyed the menu while we chatted. Donna was especially animated. My mind, though, was elsewhere.

On Rhys, to be exact.

On him, and on the message I'd read that morning when I woke, where he was giving me encouragement to face the day, because he knew, even if I didn't feel anything for Dean anymore, the moment meant something for me. In a weird way. Complicated. Like a revelation, realizing I no longer held the reins to my life.

He had made me smile a lot before I put on the yellow lemon-pie dress. Rhys had that gift. It didn't matter if we drifted apart or there was tension between us because we didn't agree on something; in the end, the waters always calmed, we reconnected, and we understood each other. All it took was a few emails.

At the moment, we were talking more than ever. About everything. The month before, he had ended whatever it was he had with Alexa and taken a unique opportunity to work the upcoming summer in Ibiza. He'd rented an apartment on the island to be able to settle in before the summer came and was spending his days composing music and writing to me. He seemed so happy that I wondered if he really liked that creative, solitary part better than the performances that came afterward and that were supposedly the point.

"Earth to Ginger," my mother said.

"Sorry, I was…"

"On the moon, as always," she said, not aware that she was right, that I was more on the moon than ever. "We were just saying Stella's dress is simply precious."

"It really is." I ate half my sorbet in one bite.

"It would look terrific on you."

"On me?"

"Yeah, when you get married. Which I hope will be soon. You're not a spring chicken anymore. I think the way it's cut would flatter you."

"Honestly, I don't think it will be soon."

"I could get married too," Donna said.

"Oh, sweetie, I know, but your sister…"

"To Amanda, I mean. We've talked about it."

"Have you?" My father seemed surprised.

"Yeah, why wouldn't we?"

"You haven't been together long."

"I don't even have a boyfriend," I reminded my parents.

"What about that boy…? The one who came for your birthday that one year. Rhys, I think his name was."

"We're just friends, Mom."

"He was handsome," she sighed in resignation.

"Not especially classy," Dad said.

"Why do you judge people like that?" Donna rolled her eyes. "You should get with the times. I feel like you're stuck in the Middle Ages."

"You're forgetting a few things. Your father and I are very happy with each other. What matters to us is your stability. Look at Dean: so young and so focused on the important things. What's wrong with knowing what you're doing? If you really want to marry Amanda, that's wonderful. As for you, Ginger, stop drinking. Your cheeks are turning red."

"I'm trying to anesthetize myself," I said. Donna laughed.

I still was a while later. After the meal came the dancing and the cocktail service. I had my fair share with Donna, sitting at a table with younger people we knew from work, laughing softly every time one of us said something stupid and analyzing the dance moves of the guys further off, who were trying to add their flair to the celebration. I don't know how much time had passed or how many drinks I'd consumed when I heard my name. I knitted my brows, finished what was left in my glass, and turned around.

"Ginger, I think it's your turn," Mrs. Wilson said.

"My turn?" I babbled, a little woozy.

"You were supposed to give a speech," Donna reminded me.

Shit, shit, shit. I wasn't in any shape to give a speech, but there, in the silent room, I stood up with all the dignity I could muster and waddled like a dizzy duck in my high heels to the center of the crowd. I started sweating in front of the microphone. From my handbag, I withdrew a couple of wrinkled pieces of paper. In theory, I was going to talk about what wonderful friends I had been with Dean ever since we were little, what a beautiful couple he and Stella made, and how proud I was of him. But all I saw was a bunch of blurry letters in no order whatsoever. So I put my so-called speech away.

"Well, I, this…" I cleared my throat. "All I'd like to say is, I've known Dean since…I mean, since we were pooping in our diapers. And peeing. Peeing too, obviously. We're human beings." I heard some chuckles, but I didn't know why. "We grew up together, then we started going out, and then he left me." Deep silence. "And the moral of all that is, it had to happen, because he had to meet Stella, right?! Stella, by the way, the most gorgeous girl I've ever seen. Stella, I want your hair and eyelashes!" More laughter. She smiled from her table, and that encouraged me. "You make an incredible couple! Like Brad Pitt and Jennifer Aniston! Before the cheating and the divorce, I mean. Anyway, I'm happy for you, and I was thinking today about decisions and crossing paths and how some changes are worth it. I'm happy you met. It was destiny."

I heard applause, and I took a deep breath, trying to keep my balance.

"I also want to add that I'm going to give you a very special gift, Dean. Besides just the high-powered blender for making smoothies and stuff. Shit! I ruined the surprise. Whatever. The other gift is…my job! That's right, I'm giving you my job. And my office. It's horrible. I hate it so, so much…"

This time, there was no applause. Just murmurs.

Donna started walking over.

"I think… I think you'll do an incredible job at the company," I went on. I couldn't stop myself; it was as if all of a sudden I was vomiting everything up. "And that's only to be expected. You're an incredible guy. So smart. Just so you know, the desk wobbles a little, but…"

"Ginger, that's enough. Wrap it up."

"Goodbye! Thanks everyone! Long live the bride and groom!"

Another round of applause, whistling, hurrahs.

I don't know why, but I couldn't stop smiling.

54

From: **Ginger Davies**
To: **Rhys Baker**
Subject: **It's a nightmare**

I want to die, Rhys. Seriously. It's awful. Everything. I don't even know where to start. Remember the Saturday of Dean's wedding? Well, I had to give a dumb speech, and I spent days preparing it, but... I didn't think about the possibility that I'd be drunk. You can't imagine how delicious the cocktails were there. So I wound up making a complete ass of myself in front of all the guests. I wouldn't be surprised if it went viral on YouTube. But most importantly: I quit my job.

Yep. At my ex's wedding.

I told him he could have it.

I don't know what my deal was; I guess I just lost control. Donna said in one minute I let out all the things I'd been repressing for years. I spent all yesterday vomiting and lying on the sofa crying, full of regret. I didn't even have the strength to write and tell you. You know what's worse? Today, Monday, I went into the office. Dad wanted me to see him, and he told me it was fine, everyone can have a bad day, and even if he didn't like being embarrassed in front of all our colleagues at the wedding, we could just pretend nothing happened, and I could go back to work and handle the pending invoices.

So...I told him no.

I didn't even think about it beforehand. It just came out. I don't want to work there. I don't want to get up and go there every morning. That's it. And it's the truth. At the end of the day, I put all my stuff in a cardboard box and carried it out, and I left my family's company, right there before my father's eyes. (He's not picking up the phone, but Mom says he'll get over it.)

I'm lost, Rhys. Lost and depressed.

My future looks very dark right now.

From: Rhys Baker
To: Ginger Davies
Subject: It's not a nightmare

Congratulations, Ginger! It was about time. I'm proud of you. Not proud that you got hammered at Dean's wedding, but proud of all the other things. I have to tell you though, I looked on YouTube for "speech by drunken ex-girlfriend at London wedding," and nothing showed up. For real though, it doesn't matter where or when you did it. You were brave. I've been hoping this would happen ever since I met you. I always knew that wasn't where you belonged, even if I never came out and told you. I didn't want you to be mad at me, and I think there are things people need to figure out and decide for themselves.

Your future's not dark, Ginger. It's immense. A big blank page in front of you. And you can write whatever you want there.

From: Ginger Davies
To: Rhys Baker
Subject: You really think?

I had the feeling you wanted me to do it.

But are you serious? A blank page? I guess… The problem is, I don't know what to write on it. I spend all day watching TV and eating crackers. I think I've got issues. That's what Donna says.

From: Rhys Baker
To: Ginger Davies
Subject: I really do

Look, Ginger, what do you want? Probably lots of things. Make a list: What you long for. What you dream of. Crazy things that go through your mind. Let yourself go for once. No limits.

From: Ginger Davies
To: Rhys Baker
Subject: My list of things to do

I just got home and it's one in the morning. No, two. Whatever.

I spent the whole night in the bar where Donna works because according to her, I "need to get out and get a breath of fresh air." While I was drinking beer—I've realized alcohol does wonderful things for me (irony intended)—I wrote some stuff on this piece of paper.

I'm attaching it. I think I should go to bed.

· Go somewhere.
· Have a kid. Or two. Or three.
· Do something totally crazy.
· Sunbathe without thinking about anything at all.
· Have a fling. ~~Or a three-way.~~
· Dance with my eyes closed.
· Cut my hair. Or dye it pink.
· Start a small publisher.
· Have a cat (that loves me).
· Fall in love for real.

I'm so tired, Rhys…

I thought everything was going to be easier when I finished college, and all I feel is my room spinning round and round… like a Ferris wheel… Remember? The kiss we shared up there. I lied when I told you I did it so you wouldn't burst into tears, but you must know I just wanted to kiss you.

You tasted so nice…like mint ice cream…

From: Rhys Baker
To: Ginger Davies

Subject: How naughty...

Well, well, who'd have ever guessed, Ginger?

A three-way, huh? I don't know why you crossed it out; it sounds amazing to me. In general, I find the list very reasonable and interesting. Except for the thing about the three kids. That's a little scary. But I have something very important to tell you: I know how you can fulfill all those wishes. Ready? Here goes:

Spend the summer with me, Ginger Snap.

I'm being one hundred percent serious. I have a free room in the apartment I don't really use. Put whatever you need in a backpack—just summer clothes and a bathing suit; the rest you can buy here—catch a plane, and that's that. Don't think twice. Don't look for a million excuses the way you always do. What do you say?

From: Ginger Davies
To: Rhys Baker
Subject: Shit

Shit. I guess acting like a moron is just what I do now. I can't stand being shut up in this house with nothing to do and no goals on the horizon. But still, spend the summer with you? Have you lost your mind? I can't do that, Rhys.

And the thing about the three-way was a lie. I was just bull-shitting.

From: Rhys Baker

To: Ginger Davies
Subject: I won't take no for an answer

Ginger, Ginger...why are you so predictable? I knew you'd say that: *Have you lost your mind?* It's the same thing you say every time I propose something totally reasonable to you. So tell me what's stopping you, and I'll let it go. What is it? Does the idea of spending the summer alone in the city really appeal to you that much? Come on, Ginger Snap, you haven't had a real vacation since I met you. That can't be healthy. I looked at tickets. Next Wednesday there's a cheap flight that departs in the morning. Don't overthink it. It'll be fun. You and me. The island. The sun. No worries.

From: Ginger Davies
To: Rhys Baker
Subject: Madness

Maybe I'll regret it in five minutes, but I think you're right. I deserve that vacation. And it's not that crazy, is it? We are friends. It's a good excuse to see each other, and I've saved some money these past few months, so screw it, Rhys! I'm going!

Part 4

—

LOVE. MADNESS. SKIN.

"It is only with the heart that one can see rightly;
what is essential is invisible to the eye."

The Little Prince

55

Rhys

I FELT IT WHEN I saw her emerge from arrivals. That tickle. Goose bumps. The desire to bridge the distance that separated us. She was wearing a huge backpack on her back, her hair was sticking out in all directions, and her clothes were too heavy for the weather in Ibiza at this time of year. I walked slowly toward her, enjoying the feeling of seeing her before she could see me. When she did, her lips curved upward, and she took off running. It was less a hug than a collision, a blow to the chest.

I laughed and held her a few seconds.

She smelled just as I remembered...so fucking good...

"You...you haven't changed a bit," she said, taking a step back to look at me. "You're so tan. I look like a ghost standing next to you. I've been eating carrots to activate my melanin, but if I'm never in the sun... I don't know. I'm nervous, Rhys."

"I can tell." I smiled and draped an arm over her shoulders before guiding her toward the exit. "Take it easy; you've got plenty of time to lie on the beach in the sun. How long has it been since we last saw each other?"

"A year and a half. Why?"

"Nothing. You're just improving with time."

"Come on! Don't suck up to me."

She nudged me with her elbow. It tickled. We walked to the parking lot, and she talked the whole time. Her voice was still comforting to me. Her saying the first thing that came into her mind and combining topics that had nothing to do with each other. Her dark hair rubbed against my arm.

I stopped and let her go, and she furrowed her brows.

"Come on... You didn't tell me you had a motorcycle."

"I rented it. It's practical. Let's go."

I got on and waited as she hopped on the back and adjusted the straps of her backpack. I could feel her getting tense as I started up and we headed out. Her hands felt weak, holding sometimes on to the seat and sometimes on to my T-shirt. When I stopped at the first red light, I took a deep breath.

"Unless you want to fall off and die, Ginger..."

I grabbed her hands and wrapped them around my waist.

"I didn't know..."

"Hold on tight," I said before speeding up.

56

Ginger

I FELT A TINGLING ALL over my body as we traveled across the island and I observed the countryside: greens, blues full of light, all passing by at top speed. It was so different from London...so full of light and color...and then there was him. Rhys. His back against my chest, his shoulders firm as he drove, his blond hair blowing wild in the breeze. I held on tighter. His stomach was tense, hard. I held my breath.

I didn't want to think about why I felt that way.

About why everything in him awakened everything in me...

I put aside those feelings and just enjoyed the view, and twenty minutes later, he slowed down as a row of short houses and taller buildings appeared in the distance. He parked and took my backpack before helping me down.

"It's here? Are you serious?"

"Yeah. It's calm here. Or as calm as this place can be in the summertime. You like?"

I was already walking toward a sign that read Portinatx. Not far off was a small cove, curved, with water the color of turquoise.

It made me want to dive in headfirst. There were boats swaying at a distance from the rocky coast. The sun was reflected in the water, which shone as if it were full of crystals. It smelled of summer. I couldn't help but smile.

"It's paradise," I said.

"I'll show you the apartment."

We walked a few streets inland from the sea into a kind of subdivision. Rhys took out his keys when we reached a three-story building, and we climbed the stairs to the top floor. I shouted with excitement when I went inside. It was simple, comfortable, decorated in the same blue and white I'd seen everywhere on the island, and a purple bougainvillea rested against the sliding glass door in the living room, which opened onto a balcony with a wood table and a few chairs with gray cushions.

"Follow me, I'll show you the rest. The kitchen's not huge, but I don't use it that much anyway. The bathroom's here. Here's my studio." It was little, with a table full of electronic gadgets. "My room..." There was an unmade bed, with wrinkled white sheets and some clothes tossed on a chair to the side. "And yours, right next door."

"It's perfect."

I walked across the room to open the wood-framed window and let in some fresh air, leaning out a little. I could see bits of blue water between the trees surrounding us. I sighed, happy.

"Do you regret coming? You know you can't just escape out the window," he joked.

"No." I turned around. "I was thinking this is probably the best decision I've ever made in my life. I want to go down to the water now! I want to… I don't know, I want to go out and see everything! Are you working today? Tonight?"

"No. I'm all yours today." He smiled.

"Then what are we still doing here?"

It took me ten minutes to throw the clothing in my bag onto the bed and put on my bathing suit. It was dark red, with a dumb frill around the neckline, but it had been years since I'd been to the beach, and I'd just assumed I'd buy a nicer one once I got here. I put on a white summer dress on top of it and walked out of my room. Rhys was there waiting for me on the sofa, shirtless, in swim trunks. He looked up at me and smiled. I tried not to admire his naked torso more than I should, and we went to the beach with two towels wrapped around our necks and a backpack with fruit and water inside.

We walked down the wooden stairs, and I screeched with joy when I took off my sandals and sank my toes into the sand. How could something so simple be so pleasurable? I asked him, and he laughed. But it was true. And I thought to myself that I should have done that a long time ago. Get away for a week at least. Or a few days. Take a vacation. I hadn't done anything like this in years. How ironic that I was feeling so happy right when I'd just lost everything. For the first time I could remember, I had no goals in front of me. I was living in the now.

A now in which I took off my dress and blushed as I saw Rhys looking at me, amused, grinning, with a glimmer in his eyes.

"What?" I stretched my towel out on the sand.

"Nothing." He laid his next to mine.

We lay down. Something about his expression got to me. I tried to ignore it. Even though it was midafternoon, the sun was burning hot.

"Come on. Say what you were thinking," I demanded.

Rhys looked at me from the corner of his eyes, turning on his towel.

"Nothing, just…your bathing suit surprised me."

"Why?"

"Because it's from the nineties."

"That's not funny, Rhys."

"I'm serious. When did you buy it?"

"Uh…let me think." I tried to remember, and I bit my lower lip when I realized. "I was sixteen. Some friends of my parents had invited us to a barbecue; they had a place in the suburbs with a pool…" I took a deep breath and shook my head. "It's not that bad, is it? It could be vintage, right?"

Rhys laughed and reached over, and I held my breath as he ran a finger along the frill of my neckline. I shivered. That gesture alone made me shiver. It was so small and would have meant nothing if anyone else had done it.

"On you, it's not so bad, that's true."

I rolled my eyes to try to distract him from my blush and walked off to take my first dip in the sea in ages. Rhys followed me. The water was transparent, delightful, and…freezing! I shouted when I stuck a foot in.

"Come on, don't be chicken. It's easier to do it all at once."

He had gone in headfirst and was already several yards away, with the sun gleaming on his body and his eyes focused on me, waiting.

"Are you sure this is good for your circulation? I'm not…"

"Ginger, either get in, or I'm going to come back and throw you in. Ten, nine, eight, seven…"

"Hey! I've spent years living in the gray and damp…"

"Six, five, four…"

"I need to acclimate myself!"

He was close now. Very close.

"Three, two, one…"

"Rhys, wait!"

He jumped at me. I turned around and ran off to the shore as quickly as I could, laughing, panting, unable to make it more than a few feet before I felt his hands around my waist. Then he hurled me into the salty water. He fell in with me, his body clinging to mine. I took a quick breath when my head rose to the surface a few seconds later. Rhys laughed, holding on to one of my hands. I splashed around indignantly, but eventually his laughter drew me in, and the water stopped feeling so cold.

It was in that moment, with the sun on his face, his bright eyes half-shut but staring into mine, that I realized that Rhys glimmered. That was it. He was a star. Unlike him, I had always known that. As we rocked in the water, looking at each other as though it were the first time, I remembered that the only stars I knew how to draw had sharp points with a bright center; they were beautiful, but they were hard to touch.

"What's going on?" he asked.

"Nothing. I'm happy. I feel good."

It was true, despite the premonition I'd just had. I tried not to think of it anymore. I looked at the water droplets hanging from his eyelashes, the almost imperceptible freckles around his nose, his wet lips, slightly open…

"I'm going to go get some rays."

"Sure. I'll be right there," he said.

I took a deep breath, swam off, and climbed back on my towel. I opened my backpack and took out a slice of watermelon, watching him paddle around lazily. Then I lay back and smiled as I felt the sun's caresses.

"You'll get burned if you don't put on sunscreen."

I opened one eye. Rhys was lying down beside me.

"The sun'll go down in no time."

"It's just my advice; you can take it or leave it. But you're... whatever. You'll see."

"I'm what?" I sat up.

"You're white, Ginger. Very, very white."

"I'm not that white!"

"You're virtually see-through."

"Dumbass."

"Are you going to put on sunscreen or not?"

"No, thanks."

I grabbed the sunglasses he'd just taken from the backpack and put them on. They were aviators. I didn't want to think about how good they must look on him. I let the sea's murmurs envelop me, breathed in the scent of summer and peace, and when I opened my eyes, the sun had almost vanished beneath the horizon, and the sky was an orange tone reflected in the water. I yawned and looked at Rhys, who had his earbuds on and was watching the sunset. He smiled when he saw I'd woken up.

"How long have I been asleep?"

"A while. You must have been tired from the trip."

"Yeah. What are you listening to?"

"Some studio sessions."

"May I?" I asked doubtfully.

"Sure." He passed me one of his earbuds. "Maybe you won't like it as much as the last one. There are no lyrics, it's all electronic."

"Haven't you ever thought about singing yourself?"

He shrugged. "I don't know. I could try. We'll see."

"Hit Play."

The sounds were strong, potent. Animated too. Something to dance to. I imagined listening to it at full blast in a club full of lights, with people jumping all around...

"When can I watch you work?"

"Tomorrow night. But are you sure? You can stay home if you don't want to be out that late..."

"Of course I'm sure! I can't wait."

"Okay." He smiled, looking at the horizon.

"How many nights do you work?"

"Three. Tuesday, Thursday, and Sunday."

"What about the rest of the nights?"

"That's when other guys work. Fridays and Saturdays are for the bigger-name DJs; a lot of them don't have set schedules. Here, listen to this."

He skipped ahead to a harder, darker track.

We stayed there until the sun set completely and decided to go back to the apartment and shower before going out to eat. Rhys got in the shower, and I hung up what little clothing I had in my bag. Apart from those garments, I just had a tiny makeup case and a pocket-sized book I'd bought at the airport before leaving. That was it. It was as if, for the first time in my life, all I needed was myself.

When I was done showering, I put on some comfortable shorts and a tank top. I wasn't sure whether to wear a bra. My breasts weren't really big enough to need one. But in the end, I put one on, the way I always did.

"Ready?" Rhys asked when I came out.

"Ready," I answered with a smile.

57

Rhys

THE NIGHT WAS WARM AND pleasant. We walked to a restaurant near the beach and sat on the patio. The menu was in English, so I didn't need to translate anything before the waiter came to take our order.

I looked at Ginger. She was precious, even if she'd taken a beating from the sun. Her hair was still wet from showering, and even without being combed or dried, it curled a little at the tips. She got embarrassed and nudged me under the table with her leg when she noticed I couldn't take my eyes off her.

They served us a pitcher of sangria with fruit.

"Are you trying to make me uncomfortable?" she asked.

"What am I supposed to do? You're hot."

"Is that how you hook up with all the girls?"

"Why are you saying that?" I laughed as I poured two glasses.

"I was just thinking about that when we were on the beach."

"You were thinking about what? You've got to be more specific, Ginger."

"That. All the girls you must have shared the same moment with through the years. Lying on the beach, watching the sunset. Also, you never did tell me what happened with Alexa."

"You already know. I wasn't in love with her."

"You've never been in love with anyone," she responded.

"Yeah." I took a sip of sangria and looked at her.

Too much, maybe. Too closely.

Because I understood then that there was nothing I liked more than that, looking at her and memorizing every little gesture, every frown, every detail of her face. She was wearing earrings that looked like small strawberries. Her lips were soft, juicy. I remembered kissing them. Licking them. Biting them. I sighed. Then I drank a little more.

We had dinner, and she told me her relationship with her father was still tense, even though they had talked a few times after she'd decided to leave the family business. Ginger picked at some fries while we ordered a second pitcher of sangria. Her cheeks were pink, her eyes bright and aware.

"Let's talk about the list," I blurted out.

"The list? Please, Rhys, I was drinking..."

"You're drinking now, and you seem to be thinking perfectly clearly."

"Let me clear that up: I was drinking, and I was lonely and sad."

"Come on, Ginger. It's your list of wishes."

"A list of wishes I wrote on a napkin."

"Who cares? Point one, travel somewhere, you've gotten that done. As for point two, having kids...are you sure? One, two, three? Like they were...I don't know, artichokes?"

"Artichokes..." Ginger laughed.

"Or whatever. You're twenty-three years old."

"So? I've always wanted to be a mother."

"Really?" I was astonished.

"Yeah. You should think about having kids. You're about to turn, what...twenty-nine? You're not that young anymore. It's not just kids; what I mean is maybe you should think about finding some stability."

After a pause, during which I could only hear the word *stability* echoing over and over, she said, "Forget it, let's move on to the third thing."

"Do something crazy," I said.

"We've got plenty of time to think it over."

"Four: sunbathe and not think about anything."

"I think I took care of that today, but just in case, I'll keep it up every day until I leave." She drank what was left in her glass, and I took out my card when the waiter approached to take our pitcher away.

Once I'd paid, we got up and walked awhile on the boardwalk, slowly, slightly drunk, her hand grazing mine now and again unintentionally. Or maybe it wasn't unintentional. I don't know. Her dark hair was now wavy down her back. I reached up and touched it once or twice.

"Are you ready for point five?"

"God, no, Rhys!" She covered her face with her hands.

"Have a fling. Or a three-way."

"That's not right!" She stopped, crossed her arms, and looked at me, and the wrinkle in her nose and her sun-reddened face made me laugh. "I nixed the three-way."

"I could still read it, Ginger. Now answer me a question…"

"No. I don't want to talk about it." But she was giggling as she said it.

"A three-way with another girl or another guy?"

"Mmm…a guy. So two guys."

"Well, now. Very interesting."

"It's just an idea; really it was more to do something out of the ordinary than have a three-way per se. It doesn't matter. You've probably had tons of them."

"Yeah." I noticed that made her uncomfortable, and asked why.

"It's just that I've never done anything unexpected in my whole life. Look at you: all these countries, all these girls, all these experiences… You're probably even bored of sex now, and I've hardly tried anything except missionary."

"Jesus, Ginger."

"What?"

I held my breath, leaned down to look her in the eye, and bit my lower lip. My heart was pounding. I had promised myself that I'd avoid this kind of situation this time, keep my hands to myself, maintain my distance…and already, I was failing, and it hadn't even been twenty-four hours since I picked her up from the airport.

My lips touched her neck.

She shook in response. Tense.

"You don't just get bored of sex. In different circumstances, in a different life, maybe we'd already be doing it, right here, right now, leaning against this car," I whispered in her ear. "But what happened last time made things weird between us. So we're going to try to stick to the rules…"

Ginger looked at me, confused. "Look, I think I can keep my hands off you without following any rules. But thanks for being so considerate and thinking of everything."

"You sure?" I raised my eyebrows.

"Your success has gone to your head."

I laughed, and she gave me a playful slap as we took off walking again down the wooden steps we had taken that afternoon to go to the beach. We walked on the sand in the darkness. The murmur of waves was audible in the distance. I don't know when exactly, but we found ourselves laughing again about something stupid and lying in the sand without thinking about anything else. The moon was shining in the starry sky.

"Next one: dancing with your eyes closed."

"That's easy. But I want to dance for real. With my mind a blank. Not caring if I look stupid or people think I'm crazy."

"I like that. Seven: cut your hair or dye it pink."

"Yeah, but not right now. I'd like to do that at some important moment, you know. So the physical change represents an internal one. I've always wanted one of those haircuts French girls have, with the straight lines."

"You'd look good like that. Now for the important one."

"I don't even want you to say it out loud."

"Eight: start a small publisher."

"Could we drop it for a minute? Seriously, I promise I'm not avoiding the subject, but I'm drunk right now, I'm happy, and look—I can make an angel in the sand just like when it snows!" She started moving her arms up and down.

I laughed. I wanted to tell her I'd spent lots of nights with lots of girls on the beach, but never one like her. Never with a person I could just be with, without hiding, without putting on that quiet-guy act everyone else knew so well.

Because Ginger brought out the best in me.

She made me not want anything more.

"What about the next one?"

"Have a cat that loves me?"

"Are you worried about getting one that hates you?"

"Of course. I'll get one from a shelter if I ever have a stable job and my own place and all that. Do you realize, it's as though I've never done anything worthwhile in my entire life? I feel like I'm starting from zero."

"Is that bad?" I turned to her.

"I guess not, given the situation…"

"Last one."

"That sangria was delicious."

"Don't change the subject. Falling in love for real."

"Look at you, talking about falling in love!"

I sat up and looked at her. She was so relaxed…so happy…at the foot of the moon. Her clothes wrinkled, her hair mussed, just a few inches away…too close. Way too close… I sank my fingers into the sand, trying to suppress my desire for her.

"I don't get it," I said.

"What don't you get?"

"The last part. *For real.* What does that mean? You've never actually been in love?" I heard her breathe deeply, her eyes still staring into the heavens.

"Maybe. Maybe love and being in love aren't the same thing.

What I want is to be crazy about someone. I want it to hurt not to touch them. I want to feel a tingle in my stomach, and I want to do it two or three times a day, and I want to have eyes for him alone. You know, the intensity of those first months, before your emotions calm down and routine sets in..."

I gulped. My heart was shouting at me.

My fingers sank deeper into the sand.

A kiss that never happened got lost among those words.

58

Rhys

"FUCK, GINGER. I TOLD YOU that you were going to get burned."

"The sun was almost down though."

"I'll go to the pharmacy to look for something."

"I want to cry. It hurts," she moaned.

I bent down, kissed her on the head, and went to look for my keys. It was three in the afternoon, and we'd just woken up. Ginger was so red, I was shocked when I saw her. The outline of my glasses around her eyes was white, making her look like a raccoon. I could hardly keep from laughing when I saw her walk into the kitchen for coffee looking like that.

I returned after buying cream to soothe the burn and told her to lie on the sofa so I could rub it into her back after she'd done her face, arms, and legs. She obeyed and I slowly lifted her shirt.

"Careful."

"I know. Relax."

"I promise I'll listen to you next time," she said as I spread the cream on her. I took a deep breath as I touched her waist. "How can

I even go outside? I'm supposed to go to your work tonight. You won't be able to introduce me to your friends..."

"Don't be stupid."

"They'll think I'm a lobster."

"I'm going to unfasten your bra, okay?"

"What? No, leave it. It hurts."

I held her down softly when I saw she was trying to get up, and I undid the clasp. She took a deep breath as that torture device was removed, and I rubbed the cream on slowly. Then I pulled her T-shirt back down and stood, my mouth dry.

"Don't act stupid, and try to stay comfortable for the next few days."

"I need to buy clothes," she complained.

"Fine. We'll go tomorrow afternoon."

59

Ginger

I DON'T KNOW WHAT I imagined when Rhys told me about his job in Ibiza, but this wasn't it. I never thought the place would be so big, with all the people going wild inside, jumping and drinking to the rhythm of the music. I was amazed to see the spectacle as I was dragged up to the VIP lounge on the second floor, which looked down on the whole area. The floor seemed to be vibrating to the music.

I looked around and saw two guys and three girls, young, good-looking, and dressed for the occasion, not at all like me in my beach clothes with my face burned by the sun.

"Bro, you disappeared," one of the guys said. He had an English accent and uncombed, dark curly hair.

"We thought you died," a young blond added.

"Alec, this is Ginger, the girl I told you about."

"What's up, precious? Come here." He motioned toward the empty seat next to him. "Don't worry. I'll stay with her till you're done."

"Cool. So this is Bean, Emily"—he pointed at the blond girl—"and her friends…"

"Helen and Gina." They introduced themselves when they realized Rhys couldn't remember their names.

"Right. Sorry. I gotta go…" He looked at me hesitantly.

"Relax, bro, I'll take good care of her." Alec wrapped his arm around my shoulders and lit a cigarette. I guess smoking was permitted in the VIP. Among many other things, as I had discovered. "Get out of here, Rhys."

He looked back at me one more time and disappeared into the crowd. He had spoken to me already that afternoon about his friends. Or rather, his acquaintances. He'd been hanging out with them since he'd gotten here. He was closest to Alec, the nephew of the club's owner.

"Where are you from?" he asked me.

I caught a bit of secondhand smoke and coughed. "London. You?"

"Me too," he smiled. "So you're Rhys's best friend? Or so he told me. How'd you meet?" He took another drag of his cigarette, not letting me go.

"Long story."

"I love long stories!" Emily shouted.

"Yeah, okay…well… I'd just broken up with my boyfriend, and I wanted to do something crazy, so I caught a plane to Paris. And I was trying to get a ticket for the subway, and… Rhys just appeared."

"So then what happened?" I noticed Emily wasn't wearing underwear when she crossed her legs in that tight fuchsia miniskirt.

"Mmm… We spent the whole night walking around Paris…"

"Who'd have ever guessed Rhys was so romantic?"

Alec laughed and everyone else went along.

"That's not what I meant. We just became friends."

"You look tense." Alec massaged my right shoulder. "What do you want to drink? Bean, go find a server. I don't know what the deal is, but we haven't seen him over here for ten minutes," he growled, looking at the empty glasses on the table.

"Look, Rhys just started," Gina said.

I could feel a thumping in my chest, and I stood up and walked toward the railing with a smile on my face as I looked at the booth across from me. He was inside wearing his headphones, staring down at his mixing table, as the first notes blasted, slow, subtle, rising.

It was magical. Addictive. Absorbing. The way he moved his hands, the way he concentrated on what he was doing, isolated from the rest of the world, even if he was surrounded by hundreds of dancing people. I don't know why, but as I watched him, I wanted to cry. From emotion. But also from something else...

Something deep, without a name...

"Fascinating, right?"

I flinched as I heard Emily's voice next to me. I nodded, distracted, and accepted a drink from her, taking a sip. It was a little strong.

"He's good," I said.

"He's better than good. This is just the beginning."

"What do you mean?"

"He's going to be big. Trust me. Soon he'll be swimming in cash, he'll be at all the big festivals, and people will stop him in the street to ask for his autograph."

I was about to ask aloud the question that was swimming

through my mind, but in the end, I kept it to myself. *What does* big *mean?* How could someone describe their goals and dreams with words like that? My eyes were fixed on Rhys, on how absent he seemed, or lost in himself, as the colored lights flashed around him.

Not that I didn't want something *big* for him... But I couldn't stop thinking about all the *little* things that might be lost on the way. The things that shaped a person's life. Things that glimmered less, but were full of smiles and love, emotions that added color to everyday life...

I don't know how long I stood there entranced by him, trying to soak him in. When he was done, I was still standing there, my hair on end, a knot in my throat. I turned and saw Alec cutting lines of cocaine with the edge of his credit card on the table.

He looked up at me with a devilish grin.

"Save you one, babe?" he asked.

"No, thanks." I sat down.

Uncomfortable. Nervous. Feeling out of place after my feelings had carried me away when I'd seen Rhys in the booth. Emily bent over one of the lines, holding a tiny tube, and inhaled.

Alec looked back at me when she was done. "You sure? It's good stuff."

Rhys appeared in the doorway before I could say no again. He looked first at me, then at the table, then narrowed his eyes.

"What are you doing offering her that stuff?" he shouted.

"Relax, bud. I was just trying to be a good host."

"Shit." Rhys ran a hand through his hair, then reached out for me. Something about him, a fragile look, made me take his hand. "We're going, Ginger," he said.

"Already?" Emily asked.

"Yeah, man, stay awhile. Give this a try. This is your shit," Alec said, passing him the tube. Rhys shook his head, said goodbye, and dragged me out behind him. I blinked, confused, looking at his back, the tension in his shoulders, the sweat on the blond tips of his hair. The music enveloped us...

And I tried to fit my image of him into what I had just seen. Tried to make all the Rhyses come together as one, but I couldn't. And he felt further away from me than ever.

60

Rhys

WE WERE ON THE PATIO, each of us with a Coke in our hand. I could smell the sea breeze, which was blowing on us lightly. There were no sounds but crickets from far away. Ginger had barely said a word since we left the club. I sighed. I stretched my legs out and rested them on the edge of her chair, grazing her. For almost the first time since we'd met, I didn't know what her expression meant, what was going through her head.

"Ginger..." I whispered.

"You never told me."

"Yeah. Because it doesn't matter."

"It does. You do drugs."

"Everyone does. It's..."

"It's what?" she asked.

"It's normal, Ginger. It is."

"Rhys, please..."

She got up, but I caught her before she could leave and pulled her into my lap. I pushed her hair out of her face, nervous, hating to see her scowl, hating the disappointment on her face.

"I'm sorry. You're right. I shouldn't do it, but in this environment...this world..." I shook my head. "I won't make excuses. I didn't want you to ever find out, because I didn't want...this. I didn't want you to look at me the way you are now."

Ginger wrapped her arms around my neck. "For a moment, Rhys, I felt like I didn't know you."

"Shit. Don't say that. Because if you don't know me, then who does?"

She didn't answer. She didn't say anything. And that silence, that sudden emptiness, scared me.

61

Ginger

THE NEXT FEW DAYS WERE relaxed, pleasant. On Friday afternoon, we went to Ibiza Town, and I bought a couple of new bikinis, some clothes for the beach, and then, in a fancy shop, I looked for something to wear out at night. I tried on three outfits in all. Rhys waited patiently outside the door of the fitting room. The first outfit I decided against before even showing it to him. The second made my boobs look weird. And the third...even I had to stand there looking at myself in the mirror. It was a simple strapless dress, snug, short, cherry red.

I walked out. He looked up from his phone, looked down, then looked back up as though he hadn't seen me the first time. His gray eyes slid slowly down my body, and I suppressed the impulse to run back into the fitting room.

"It's too short," I said, "plus..."

"Are you kidding? You're taking it."

I smiled, still a little timid. "It'll do for Sunday."

"You can wear it around the house too."

"Rhys, you're an idiot."

I rolled my eyes before shutting the door and undressing. When we were done shopping, we walked around for the rest of the afternoon, passing through steep stone streets surrounded by low white houses, until we reached the foot of the fortress. There were markets, craft tents, and tons of places to eat. We wound up having dinner here in the yellow light of the streetlamps over the patio where we sat. With him in front of me, I thought. *Everything's perfect.* Even if there was a barrier that seemed to be slowly rising between us. Even if our differences were pushing us apart.

I didn't bring up the drugs again. Over the next couple of days, I just tried to enjoy his company, actually telling him the first thing that came into my head instead of looking for my laptop to write him an email. The hours flew by like this; we spent the evenings watching the sunset and the mornings enjoying an unrushed breakfast before planning to travel the island or explore some of the more remote beaches.

When Sunday came, I started to get nervous.

I fixed myself up a bit, put on my red dress, and said less than normal on our way to his work. When we got there, Rhys walked toward the back door to avoid the line. Inside, he pulled me close. "Wait. I'll go up with you."

"What do you mean?"

"I mean I have to spin in the booth. While I do, you can hang out in the VIP with Alec and everyone from the other day. They're not bad people; it's just…"

"No, I'm staying here," I said.

"Here, where?"

"With the people. Dancing. Having fun."

"Are you sure? Ginger…"

He looked down into the top of my dress for a second, and I saw him take a deep breath. I nodded. He smiled. I didn't want him to be nervous while he was working, or to think about me and whether I was okay. I would be okay. I definitely would. Tonight I was going to live in the moment like the rest of the people here; screw sitting in a VIP booth. I wanted to get out there and dance, laugh, and not think about anything. Even if I had to do it alone.

"Look for me afterward. I'll be near the booth."

I stood on tiptoe to kiss his cheek and turned around, heading for the bar, trying to make my way through the crowd to order a piña colada. I closed my eyes when I took my first sip. It was delicious.

One song transitioned into the next, and I knew Rhys was now in the booth. I could tell when it was his music; it always started slow, gradual, as if he needed a few seconds to get ready. I looked up at him, like everyone else who was dancing, and I smiled with pride. He was so handsome…so serious… His blond bangs bounced against his forehead while he grimaced, timid. He didn't look often at the audience. It seemed to embarrass him.

He was elusive, as always. Hermetic. And very much himself.

At some point, I stopped looking at him so much and let the music suck me in—the music, the feeling here, the second drink I ordered, and the very nice girls who tried their best to speak to me in English as we danced and laughed together. At two in the morning, the real party started, and the whole place was filled with soap bubbles. I think it was one of the most fun nights of my life. There. Alone. Surrounded by a bunch of strangers jumping and shouting.

I didn't even realize Rhys's session was over until I looked up at the booth and saw another guy standing there with headphones around his neck.

"There you are, Ginger Snap," I heard whispered in my ear.

I turned, slipped, and held on to Rhys's shoulders. He was covered from head to toe in foam, and I couldn't stop laughing. He smiled at me.

"Did you have fun?" he asked.

"Tons. It was amazing. Come on, let's get a drink."

We ordered two mojitos at the bar. Rhys was wearing a baseball cap. No one seemed to notice us as we walked around, squeezed together tight, caught up in the atmosphere of lights and colors that brightened his face in the shadows. Then I did it. I stopped thinking, closed my eyes, and just danced. With him. With myself. Not caring if I looked like an idiot or if everyone was watching me. Just... following the music. Just feeling Rhys next to me. So dangerously close. With the ground shaking beneath our feet. His pupils were fixed on my lips, which I licked when I opened my eyes.

"Ginger, fucking hell..." he grunted. His hand was on my waist, moving downward.

"What are you thinking about?"

"You already know."

I could see him wavering. Tense. Anxious. Then I stepped back, putting distance between us. I wasn't going to be the one to take the risk. I wasn't going to force it if it wasn't supposed to happen. I turned, ready to head back to the bar, and felt his arms around my waist, his chest pressed into my back, his lips on my neck, kissing me softly.

I took a deep breath and trembled. Rhys came back around in front of me, his fingers toying with the edge of my red dress.

"See how we should have made rules?" he said.

"I told you I'd keep my hands to myself."

"We never talked about whether I'd be able to though…"

His lips pushed into mine then, with longing, with hunger, and I wrapped my arms around him to keep from slipping and falling on the foam-covered floor. I panted as our tongues touched, kissing as if the world was about to end and our time was running out. We moved through the room, eyes closed, without separating, without paying attention to anything around us. Just him. Me. The two of us lost in kisses, in lights, in the dense air inside. I wanted more. I wanted all of him.

Rhys was the one to pull away. He was breathing hard as he took my face in his hands and stared me straight in the eye. He looked lost, but more alive than ever. Scared and euphoric. Hungry, disoriented. I looked at his red lips.

"Let's get out of here." He kissed me again.

And again. And again. And every kiss was an invisible trace of him.

62

—

Rhys

I KNEW I'D FALL VICTIM to temptation as soon as I saw her in the airport terminal. And even though I knew, I hadn't done anything to avoid it. She was making me crazy. How good she smelled. Her smile. Her voice. Every detail. The thought that I could be by her side. And tonight...seeing her dance that way, without thinking about anything, her head not crowded with a million worries and obligations, in the red dress that rose inch by inch up her thighs every time she shifted her hips...

I was doomed.

And now we were on the shore, as far as we could go, walking, kissing, and finally falling down together onto the sand. If I'd ever had any doubts, they vanished when I felt her body pressed against mine, every curve making me delirious, every kiss lighting a fire inside me...

"If we don't stop, I'm going to fuck you right here."

"Rhys..." She laughed, and I took a deep breath.

"I'm serious, Ginger..."

"There are people here. They might see us."

"They're far away," I murmured.

She softly arched her hips, seeking me. I pushed her hair from her face and bit her lip. She panted. I felt something come loose in my chest and pushed a hand down between her legs slowly, leaving behind the fabric of her dress. She shivered. I went higher, unable to stop looking at her as I pushed her underwear aside and she chewed her already red lower lip.

"Rhys, they're going to see us."

There weren't that many people around. Just some groups of young people and one or two couples, none of them paying us much attention. It was a dark night, and the moon was waning. Our moon.

I rubbed her between her legs. She moaned.

"Tell me, what should I do…? Ginger, look at me."

Her eyes were cloudy, full of desire.

"Keep going," she whispered, arching her back.

So I did. Slowly. Memorizing every detail of her. Sinking my fingers into her. Holding on to the moment. Savoring it. Smiling every time she got impatient and tried to make me go faster. Until she decided she wanted to play too and slipped a hand between our bodies, looking for me. I mumbled something, I don't know what; I hadn't expected that. She unbuttoned my pants and took me to the limit. I groaned, shuddered, because…I was losing control. We were panting, caressing each other, lying on the sand. The rest of the world blurred around us. Time seemed to slow down. I sought her lips. Licked them. Bit them. Stroked them as if this was the first time we'd ever kissed, because the flavor of her tongue was the sweetest thing I'd ever known. I rubbed her harder now, and she tensed up, trembled.

I reached up toward her throat, let my thumb touch her neck, rising to the edges of her lips, never taking my eyes off her.

Her breathing kept getting harder.

My heart was about to explode. And she let herself go. We let ourselves go. Pleasure embracing us both. Her moans drowned by kisses I could no longer suppress and the murmuring of the waves. When I managed to stop shaking, we took off our shoes, I lifted her up, and we went out into the sea fully dressed. The water was warm. Far off, we could hear voices. Neither of us said anything. I don't know how long we were there, holding each other, swaying, her legs around my waist, her face resting on my shoulder. What I remember is, when we emerged, I had sobered up, and when we got on the bike, we were still soaked. Ginger spent the entire time leaning her head on my back, and when we returned to the apartment, we flopped down on the couch, still dressed, still wet, legs wrapped around each other, weary, with words caught in our throats that neither of us dared yet to utter.

63

Ginger

THE SUNLIGHT WAS WARMING THE living room when I opened my eyes. I didn't know what time it was, but I had the feeling it was past midday. I stared a moment at the dust specks floating through the air, absent-minded, still confused about what had happened in the past few hours. I remembered spending the night with Rhys on the sofa, waking at dawn, curling up tighter against him, and falling back to sleep.

When I got up, I saw he was gone.

Anxious, I took off my dress and showered. My hair was a disaster, knotty and full of sand. When I got out a half hour later, the apartment smelled of coffee and Rhys was in the kitchen, his back to the door. I watched him a moment, cleared my throat, and walked in. He looked at me askance and dumped a few teaspoons of sugar into his cup.

"You were gone when I got up." I couldn't think of anything else to say.

"I went to get coffee. We were out."

"Thanks. I think I need it."

He stood back from the counter when I came to serve myself. But I couldn't. I was still trying to decide what cup to use when I felt his eyes on me, his chest swelling before he spoke, his hands putting down the cup he'd picked up.

"What happened last night..." he began.

"I know. It shouldn't have happened." I didn't bother looking at him. I didn't want to.

"It's too risky."

"Yeah," I agreed. "A terrible idea."

"You. Me. It could be a catastrophe."

"Yeah. Best to avoid it."

"Okay." He stepped closer to me.

"Okay." I held my breath.

And a few seconds later, he was grasping my chin in his fingers and our gazes intertwined just before he gave me a quick, savage, nervous kiss. I moaned, surprised. He lifted me up and sat me on the white kitchen table. I wrapped my legs around his hips, pulling him into me, breathing hard. It was just like that with him. We went from zero to infinity in a matter of a second, losing control, our minds going blank. I'd never wanted anyone so bad. I'd never had another person so close to me and yet needed them to be even closer, impossible as it was. I sank my hands in his hair and pulled softly as his lips got lost in the neckline of my loose dress.

"Rhys..."

"What?"

"What does this mean?"

"I don't know." His pupils were dilated, his gray eyes unusually dark, his hands already under my dress. "It means my desire is stronger than my fear of losing you." He pulled at my underwear. "And yet I'm terrified of losing you. Of something...breaking between us. But when I look at you..."

I untied the knot in the drawstring of his sweatpants, and he groaned and sank his tongue into my mouth.

"We won't let anything break."

"Promise me." He stroked my cheek.

"I promise, Rhys. I do."

He let out the breath he'd been holding and lifted my dress, and his body molded itself to mine: deep, wild, and yet tender when he held me close. I was breathless, and I bit his shoulder, clutched him tighter, still sitting on the table. His back was straight, his body tense, his heart pounding. I felt full of him, full of something so intense that I didn't want to name it while the pleasure absorbed me. Rhys moved quicker now. Later, I would still feel a tickle when I thought of this moment: our muffled cries, his face as he sank inside me, the strength of him as he pushed in, my nails digging into his back. We barely kissed. We bit each other, stared into each other, felt each other. We let ourselves go.

And I guess something did change...

Because we got lost.

64

Rhys

GINGER GRINNED SLOWLY AS I proposed we strike the item *Do something crazy* off her list. We went that afternoon to a tattoo shop. And we got the same thing. Something little, but ours. A crescent moon on each of our wrists.

She was the first person I'd ever gotten a matching tattoo with.

And even then, I knew she'd be the last.

I couldn't imagine doing that with anyone else. I couldn't imagine gawking like that at any other girl while someone engraved in her skin the desire we both felt to have our feet on the ground, look up high, and try to touch the moon.

I thought of how much she'd changed since I met her that night in Paris. Maybe she had stumbled once or twice, maybe she hadn't yet found her place, but she was braver, stronger, more beautiful. Everything I wasn't. I could almost imagine her in the future, slowly watering her roots, feeding them, watching them grow. That was it: I was watching her grow. I could see how she was feeling better, more stable, with well-defined limits, even if she still had decisions to make. Unlike me. That was the problem. I didn't see myself. I didn't have roots. I was...vague. I was smoke. I wasn't anything.

65

Ginger

UNTIL THEN, I DIDN'T REALIZE you could get to know a person through his skin. Or that nakedness was much more than just taking off your clothes. That sex, pleasure, hours between the sheets…could be fun, exciting, tender, and endless. Like this morning, after hours of caresses with our mouths, our hands, our eyes…

"What time is it?" I asked, distracted.

"Two a.m." Rhys kissed me and ran the palm of his hand over my naked breasts, provoking a shiver. We were sweating, satiated, a little tipsy after a bottle of wine shared over dinner on the patio. "We should probably shower before going to sleep. Actually, let's take a bath."

"Sure." I smiled as he stood up.

The water was warm. I leaned my back into his chest as I submerged myself, and he hugged me from behind. I stretched out my feet over the tub's lip. There was no sound. Just the soft dripping of the tap and Rhys breathing into my ear. I closed my eyes. I didn't want to wake up. I didn't want to change anything about this moment, and I didn't want to tell him aloud that I was scared what we were living was just an interlude with a before and an after. How could I ever forget this? How could I meet another man and not compare it with what I was experiencing with Rhys? How could I keep going without looking back...?

"What are you thinking about?"

I felt a tickle on the back of my neck. "Nothing. This. Us. Now."

"Mmmm..." He hugged me tighter.

"What about you? You're a little quiet today."

"Yeah. I was thinking about what you want..."

"What?"

"You know. Your list of wishes."

I turned, confused, trying to catch his eye, splashing water around us. My legs moved atop his, our bellies touched...

"You mean number five?"

"Yeah. Do you want that?"

I wanted to laugh. No, I wasn't interested in a three-way. We'd been getting to know each other for weeks, discovering each other... and all I wanted was for it never to end.

"If you need it, if you're curious... I don't know. I could try."

"Try? You think you might not be able to?"

He took a deep breath and looked away. "I don't know. When you said it the first time, I swear, I thought it was the hottest thing in the world. Like a dream come true." His hands were rubbing my legs, climbing up to my knees. "But now... I don't think I could take it."

"I have zero interest," I whispered.

"Good. Because you're making me greedy."

I rubbed my fingers across his chest, touching the little bee he had tattooed lower down. *Life*. That's what it meant to him. I smiled, thinking about all the little parts of him I had left to decipher. Then I thought of the future, how to keep us above water, how to save what we had, and I became depressed.

"What's going to happen when I leave?"

"I don't understand." He was still caressing me.

"You know. When I go, we'll just stick to the script, right? Each of us with our own lives, meeting other people…" Something got stuck in my throat. "I don't know if everything can be like it was. I don't know if I want to know. I don't know if we can just talk about whatever, about those things…"

"Ginger…" His voice was hoarse, cracking.

"We should change our arrangement, right?"

"Like setting boundaries? I don't know…"

"Just at the beginning, okay? When I leave, at least for a while, I'd rather not know what you're doing or with whom. And then…" Without realizing it, I brought my hand to my chest, nervous. "Then everything will go back to normal, I'm sure of it. After the first few months. We'll forget this…"

"What if I don't want you to forget it?"

I stood up. Rhys let me go, and I walked out of the bathroom. I grabbed a towel and looked at him, thinking, while I covered myself up, asking myself if I could cover up other things too: my heart, my mind, my true nakedness. I realized I knew better than him the danger we were in. Or else we didn't feel it the same way. Or we didn't feel the same, period.

"I'm going to need it though, Rhys, because it's the one way to move forward. We talked about that, right? We're making this up as we go along. And then we'll be friends again."

"I don't understand why you're angry."

"I'm not. It's not that…" I hesitated, nervous. "It's just… I think I should buy my return ticket, not because I'm planning on leaving yet, but just to have a date, you know? So we'll know how much time we have left. It'll be easier that way. More practical."

He fixed me in his gray-eyed stare. His eyes were intense. Deep. Wounded.

"Do what you want."

I bought my ticket on his laptop in his room. He spent a while longer in the tub, and when he came out, I heard him pour himself a glass of whiskey and walk out to the patio. I thought of the date: the day after his birthday. Just two more weeks. Did I make a mistake? I got in bed and rolled around.

A while later, I felt his weight on the mattress. The smell of alcohol. His hand around my waist pulling me into him. But I knew he was still angry. The problem was that we felt the same, but we still couldn't understand each other. We weren't aware yet that we were two mirrors.

66

Ginger

THE DAYS RAN TOGETHER: LONG drives on the motorcycle to watch the sun set in Benirrás, walks down to the beach, which was surrounded by trees and paths and hills, letting the serenity envelop us as we listened for the faint sound of nearby drums or the murmurs of the people. When we sat on the sand, Rhys would grab my hand and draw spirals on it with his fingers. I'd smile, close my eyes, and take deep breaths of sea air, feeling the breeze blow through the light T-shirts and dresses I'd bought at the markets on the island. I'd stopped wearing a bra one morning, when I went to the beach alone because Rhys was still asleep. I had splashed around, taken off my bikini top, and laid on the sunny shore, arms extended, listening to the seagulls coming close over the coast. Maybe it was stupid, but I'd felt freer than ever, lighter, happier. Leaving behind my life in London, the life that had tied me down and kept me from thinking about what I really wanted, was like tearing away a veil and finally seeing the light. Opening my eyes, but differently, seeing everything from a new perspective.

And Rhys had been the ideal companion on that voyage. He'd

never told me directly that I had to break free, but he had always been there waiting for me in case I ever did.

One afternoon, when the sky was red like a pomegranate that had exploded and shed its color over everything, I looked at him, squinting.

"What?" he murmured.

"Thank you, Rhys. Seriously."

"What's this all about?"

"Nothing. I was just thinking how good I feel, how lucky I am to be here right now, watching this sunset with you. Come here and kiss me."

Rhys bent over and trapped my lips tenderly. When we separated, I rested my head on his shoulder and looked at the gathering clouds.

"I don't want this summer to ever end."

Me neither, I thought. But I didn't say it aloud.

67

Rhys

THREE DAYS, EIGHT HOURS. THAT was exactly how much time we had left until Ginger caught her plane back to London. I was starting to hate that city. *London.* And I hated the feeling pressing down on my chest. This had been the best summer of my life, but I kept noticing the bittersweet taste in my mouth every time I kissed her. It was our impending goodbye: a thorn in my side, a rock in my shoe, a stomachache, anger, selfishness...

"Stop scowling like that." Ginger reached out and smoothed my forehead with her thumb, smiling under the light of the patio where we were having dinner. "You haven't asked me again what I've been up to these past few days."

Recently, when I'd been working, she'd stayed behind at the apartment, sitting at the table on the balcony and writing nonstop in a little notebook she carried everywhere she went. She was also looking up things on my computer. I knew what she was doing. Of course I did. My curiosity had made me look at her search history, but I didn't want to pressure her or even bring the subject up until she'd decided.

"You want to tell me?"

"Yeah." She smiled, excited, eyes shining. "I think I'm going to do it, Rhys. I think... I want to start a publisher. A small one. Independent. Just like in my graduation project, remember? I sent you endless boring emails about it..."

"They weren't boring."

"Whatever. The point is, I've looked at the numbers, and it's doable. It's risky, and I don't know if the bank will lend me the money I need, but..."

"I've got money. Lots."

"Are you kidding? I could never accept something like that."

"Why not? I don't want it."

"I don't understand..." She looked confused.

"It's from my parents. They opened an account for me when I was little, and it's stayed there, growing every month. I haven't touched it for four years."

"Since your argument with him."

"Don't get off the subject. I could give you whatever you need. Or lend it to you. At least it would go toward something worthwhile."

"We'll see. First, I want to try to get a loan. And then... I've been thinking over all the things I'd need to do: rent an office, find a distributor, look for a major project to launch with..."

"Would you need to hire staff?"

"One person, at least. It's a lot of work. To keep from going broke, I might need to take on freelancers, for the typesetting, editing, maybe translating in the future. But I'll start with books in English."

We smiled.

"So you're finally going to do it."

"Am I...? Rhys..."

"Don't hyperventilate, Ginger."

"It's just, at one moment I think it's my life's dream and it's all wonderful, and the next moment I'm so scared I want to call Dad and ask if there's still room for me at the company, even if it's just sweeping up sawdust."

I bent toward her and reached up to tuck a lock of hair behind her ear, looking at the rest of her face, the little wrinkles in the corners of her eyes, her button nose. I stroked her cheeks with my knuckles.

"I trust you. You'll make it."

Ginger smiled. All the worry disappeared at once as she got up from her chair and sat on my lap right there, not worrying about who might see us or the woman at the next table over pursing her lips in disapproval. I wrapped my arms around her neck and gave her a long, soft, deep kiss.

68

Ginger

IT WAS ALL I COULD think or talk about: the future I imagined for myself when I returned to London, the excitement, the anticipation, all those ideas going through my mind, even if I forgot half of them right away. I was...euphoric. And Rhys would listen to me and smile, even if sometimes he seemed far away from me and even himself, as if he were fading out.

"Rhys, are you seeing the same thing as me?"

"A street full of people?"

"No! A photo booth!"

"No, Ginger Snap..."

"Come on. Please."

I pulled him along, and he only resisted slightly before following me into the little square cell. I closed the blue curtain to be sure no one could see us and slipped my money in. I was sitting on him, one arm over his shoulders, our faces together, and I laughed when he put a hand under my dress. I kissed him, and the whole moment was immortalized: the magic of feeling his lips on mine.

Rhys looked at the strip of photos when it came out, and the hot night wind surrounded us. I saw his expression change. He tore off a couple of the pictures, one of us smiling, one of us kissing with his hand buried in my hair. He slipped them into the back pocket of his jeans.

"I thought you didn't like photos…"

"I like these," he responded softly.

69

Ginger

ONE DAY, I FOUND THE copy of *The Little Prince* that I'd given him in his nightstand. It was more ragged than I remembered, with yellowed edges, dogeared pages. There were new underlines and notes in the margin in his handwriting. Inside the back cover, he had written the dates when he'd reread it, just like I used to do in the front. And underneath, in a corner, he'd written a quote from the book: *The baobabs start out by being little.*

70

Rhys

I DIDN'T WANT TO FUCK it up. I couldn't stand the thought of leaving behind a bitter memory when this was our last night together, but I still had that same feeling I'd had in my chest for days now. Crushing. Asphyxiating. I took a deep breath. We'd gone to a Mexican restaurant near the apartment, five minutes away at a slow walk. We had fajitas and nachos for dinner before the time came to blow out the candles stuck in a ball of chocolate ice cream while Ginger sang "Happy Birthday," making me laugh. I had turned twenty-nine by her side. Like a crazy person, she kept shouting, "Make a wish! Make a wish!" And I realized the one thing I wanted was impossible. An exit off the road of my life, which was full of potholes.

We were on our second Coco Loco and our third shot of tequila. Ginger was wearing a white dress that made her tan stand out. She'd struggled to achieve it, and she liked showing it off. Her hair was loose, her eyes were shining, her hands were stretched out on the table over mine, and she was tracing circles with her thumb. I was bewitched, watching her skin stroke my own, sometimes grazing the edge of the quarter moon that she, too, had tattooed on her wrist.

"Rhys, are you okay?"

"Yeah. Why?" I looked up.

"You seem absent. More than normal, I mean," she joked, but then she turned serious, her brow furrowed. "What we've been through together this summer..."

"We don't have to talk about it."

"I just want you to know I've had the best time of my life. I wouldn't change anything. Not a single day. Every hour has been perfect. With you. Here. And you were right when you said a few weeks ago that neither of us should ever forget it. I just was scared. I thought it would hurt too much."

I took a deep breath. Uncomfortable. Angry. Sick. "So it doesn't hurt?"

"What do you mean?"

"I don't know, you just seem..." I shook my head. "Forget about it."

I got up. We had already paid, so all I had to do before leaving was finish the last sip of my drink. Ginger followed me down the street. I wanted to disappear. I could feel the darkness infiltrating those parts of me I didn't like and that I didn't want her to see. Selfishness. Insecurity. Fear.

"Rhys! Where are you going?" she asked, agitated, trying not to be left behind. She ran past me and came around in front of me. Her small hands against my chest. Her eyes full of reproach. "What do you think you're doing?"

"I don't know..." I rubbed my face.

"Okay. It's okay. We've been drinking."

"Goddammit. I knew you'd make everything complicated."

"How can you say that to me?" she asked in a thin voice.

I wanted to let out all the things that were making my throat close up, but I couldn't. Instead, I felt it closing tighter and tighter...

Ginger was standing in the middle of the street, eyes welling with tears, lower lip trembling, arms crossed, as if protecting herself from me. I hated it. Seeing her this way. The guilt. Feeling I always ended up hurting the people I loved most, the way I was doing with her. I sucked in a breath.

"I don't want you to go."

"Rhys..." She stepped toward me.

"Goddammit, Ginger. It didn't have to be like this."

"How else could it have been?"

We looked at each other in the darkness of the summer night. We were just a few inches apart. And I could make those inches disappear if I wanted to.

"Easy. Simple. Just fun and nothing else."

"Fuck you, Rhys!" she hissed.

I grabbed her wrist before she could turn around. "Wait. I didn't mean that. I didn't want..."

"You said it. Imbecile."

"I know, okay? But this is killing me, just watching the time run down, not knowing when we'll see each other again, you acting as if you don't even care."

"I can't believe this."

I let her go. Anxious. Nervous. Angry.

"I was trying not to ruin our last few weeks together! What did you want me to do? You didn't exactly seem moved when we were talking that day in the tub. *Do what you want*! That's what you told me! So I decided I'd just be like you, follow your philosophy, and try to think in the present, just enjoy myself, and leave it at that."

"Well, congratulations. You did it," I grunted.

"Yeah. And I'm almost happy about it, seeing that all you wanted out of this was another hookup, the kind you forget before it's even over. I know you, Rhys. I know what you're like."

"If that's what you think, then you don't know me at all."

I stared daggers at her. She was sobbing.

"You're right." She wiped away her tears. "But I wanted to hurt you. I wanted to because I can't stand you being so blind. You always seem so far away, impossible to even reach…"

"Do I seem that way now?"

"No." She stepped toward me.

I felt a knot growing. In my stomach. In my throat. My heart was pounding so hard, I brought a hand to my chest to try and still it. I looked at her. So brave. So whole. So different from me. I was getting smaller and smaller, more and more cowardly…

"You still don't understand, do you?" she whispered.

She hugged me. I felt her hot breath on my neck and her voice surrounding me, entering every hollow in my body, filling the void.

"I'm in love with you, Rhys. I have been for a long time. I think it started that night when I met you in Paris."

I trembled, holding her tighter against me.

"There are days when I almost hate you, because you shine so bright I can't see you, and you make it impossible to even look at any other guy…"

I kissed her hard, trapped her against the wall, groaned against her mouth, and she gripped my T-shirt before sliding her hands beneath it. I should have told her then. I should have grabbed the back of her neck so she couldn't avoid my stare and told her I was in love with her too. But I didn't. Again. I didn't kiss her in the airport in Paris before she left. I didn't dare take the next step in London. And here, tonight, I wasn't up to her level, I couldn't squeeze the words out.

I was confused. Stagnant. In a daze.

So lost in my own feelings that I couldn't tell what was her and what was me. I don't even remember exactly how we got home. Just that we stopped at every street to kiss. At every crosswalk, at every stoplight. I was anxious. Impatient. Unable to let her go. I didn't when I opened the door. I didn't when I took off her clothes in the hall, leaving a trail of clothing behind us.

We fell into bed. Her legs wrapped around my hips, I held her hands over her head, and I stared into her eyes. She was so beautiful. Her body locked beneath mine, skin to skin.

"But you said…"

"Rhys, just do it," she moaned.

"That thing about making it impossible to…"

"Please," she whispered.

"I want you to be happy and not just make me happy. But I'm fucking selfish, and I like thinking I'm special to you, even if, when I look in the mirror, I don't understand why you think I am." I split her legs wider with my knee and sank into her. "I feel you, Ginger. Too much. I feel you all over."

As if she were my roots.

And for the first time in my life, I realized I wasn't just fucking someone; I was making love to her. With her. With Ginger. I was…

loving her with my hands, with my skin, with my eyes, clouded by desire, with our bodies united, rocking.

I understood so much now.

And I remembered her words. The ones I read one day months before that made me slam my laptop shut in a rage.

What is it to be in love?

It's feeling a tingle in your stomach when you see them. Not being able to stop looking at them. Missing them even though they're right there. Wanting to touch them at all hours, talking about any- and everything, feeling like you lose all sense of time when you're together. Noticing the details. Wanting to know everything about them, even the stupid stuff. You know what, Rhys? I think it's actually like being on the moon permanently. With a smile on your face. Without fear.

71

—

Ginger

WE WERE TIRED, SATIATED, LOST on the moon.

We'd made love all night, almost without speaking. Or not speaking in words, anyway. Just with looks, touches, and sighs. My head on his chest, following his muscles down to his belly button with my fingertip, touching the tattoo of that little bee that symbolized life for him. I saw goose bumps appear on his flesh.

"You could stay."

It was just a murmur.

I sat up and looked at him. "Are you serious?"

"Why not, Ginger?"

"What would I do here?"

He wavered, doubted. "I don't know. We'll figure it out."

"Do you realize what you're asking me to do?" I started putting on my clothes, but he stopped me.

"I just mean, like, for now, dammit."

"Why don't you come with me?"

"Because we're already here. And I have a job."

"Seriously? For years, you've been going from place to place, laying your head wherever, and it never entered your mind that you could stay in London for a while? And now you're asking me to stay here. Far from my family. Far from everything, when you know I want to try to make my publishing career happen. And I will. You can't do this to me."

I was crying again. The whole day had been a roller coaster, down and up and back down again. Full of vertigo. Sad every time I looked at him. But also angry, disappointed, tender, unsure, yearning.

"You're right." He shook his head.

"Of course I'm right," I whispered, but I wasn't sure.

"Plus, we don't even know if it would work."

"Yeah. I guess."

"We should get some sleep. It's late."

Night after night, we'd stayed up late talking, laughing, getting drunk, burning the midnight oil in the bed that the sun shone on in the morning, but now, because I had to fly out the next morning, it was *late*.

Rhys turned off the light, and I lay beside him. His body was close to mine, hugging me. I couldn't stop thinking of how he said I could stay. And I couldn't breathe. Why did he have to say that? Why, why, why? That wasn't supposed to be an option. I shouldn't have been thinking about it.

"Ginger."

"What?"

I could feel him tense up.

"I don't talk to my father because...he's not my father. And she's not my mother either. Neither of them are my parents. I found out by accident that I'd been adopted. They never told me. And then stuff happened. Stuff that can't be undone. Words that can't be unspoken. That still hurt."

"Rhys, I'm so sorry."

"I just wanted to tell you because you're my best friend. And you always will be. It doesn't matter what happens. Ever. It's us on the moon."

I turned and looked for his face in the darkness. I stroked it with my fingers until I reached his lips and traced their perfect curves. "Always. I promise you that."

I kissed him slowly and sweetly. A kiss that tasted of goodbye.

72

Rhys

THE LIGHT WAS TRYING TO sneak in past the curtain. I turned around in bed and frowned when I saw what time it was on the clock on the nightstand. The first thing I thought was that Ginger was going to miss her flight. The second was that Ginger wasn't even there. I got up, anxious, and noticed her suitcase was gone. There was just a note on the kitchen counter.

I'm sorry, Rhys. I'm sorry I left like this. But I couldn't do it any other way, because I knew if I did, you'd ask me to stay again, and I knew that I'd say yes. And it isn't fair, okay? Not to me. Not to us, actually. But we'll get through this, okay? You'll see, everything will be perfect.

I'm fine. Don't worry, I called a taxi to pick me up. I'll write you soon. Take care. Seriously. Don't get lost.

Thank you for this summer.

Thank you for giving me so much.

73

Ginger

I HAD ALWAYS KNOWN RHYS would break my heart.

I don't know how or why. It was just that sometimes people know things instinctively. In the depths of my soul, I knew it the day I met him years ago, I knew it every time I read one of his emails, I knew it on the Ferris wheel in London when I first kissed him, and above all, I knew it when I agreed to live with him that summer without thinking about the consequences, without promises, pretending when our skin touched that it wouldn't shatter what we had.

Well, it didn't. Nothing shattered. But maybe it made it worse. Because we couldn't stop the cracks from opening up. And the problem with cracks is that they don't lead to instant destruction. They're not enough to make the building collapse on their own. But they're there. Threatening. And when it rains...the water starts pouring in from all sides.

Part 5

———

DREAMS. FORKS IN THE
ROAD. BEGINNINGS.

"Flowers are weak creatures. They are naive.
They reassure themselves as best they can.
They believe that their thorns are terrible weapons."

The Little Prince

74

From: Ginger Davies
To: Rhys Baker
Subject: All good

I made it, Rhys.

How are you? I never thought it would feel weird to be emailing you, but after the past few months, it's hard. Funny, right? How quickly we get used to the good things. By the way, Donna says I'm so brown, I almost scared her. She didn't recognize me! Can you believe it? Anyway, no more Amanda and Donna having the apartment to themselves. Don't know if I told you, but Michael, the guy I caught jerking off, left a few weeks ago. We have to talk about it, but maybe we won't get another roommate. We'll see. Honestly being by ourselves would rule.

I don't know what else to tell you. I'm still kind of out of it...

I have the feeling that if I open the curtains, I'll see the blue sea in the distance, but nope—back to reality; all I see is the street out front. It was nice, Rhys, as you know. I don't think anything could ever top what we lived together.

From: Ginger Davies
To: Rhys Baker
Subject: Come on...

Are you mad? Rhys, come on.

I miss you...

From: Ginger Davies
To: Rhys Baker
Subject: [No subject]

It's been two weeks. How long are you going to go without talking to me? What happened to "friends forever"? Rhys, I get it that you are mad that I left without saying goodbye, but it was better for both of us. For me especially. Can't you understand that?

From: Ginger Davies
To: Rhys Baker
Subject: [No subject]

At least pick up the phone. You're turning this month into hell for me. But whatever. You do you. I won't bother you again.

When you stop acting like a whiny little boy, you know where I am.

From: Rhys Baker
To: Ginger Davies
Subject: Busy

Ginger… I needed to catch my breath. I'm just having fun and getting through what's left of the summer. Remember when we were talking about having a three-way? Yeah, so I was wrong. I didn't remember how fucking great it was. Ending up at home with two chicks and enjoying myself like it was nothing. No complications. So easy…those are the things that are really worth it in life. Easy. Maybe I can show you next time.

From: Rhys Baker
To: Ginger Davies
Subject: I'm sorry

Fuck. I'm sorry. I'm sorry.
    I don't know what I was thinking…
    Ginger, pick up the phone. Please.

From: Rhys Baker
To: Ginger Davies
Subject: I'm sorry

Dammit, Ginger, I wish I could erase that message. I was

high. I'd spent the whole week drinking. I barely remember what I was doing. I'm a fool. And I'm sorry. I regret telling you that and hurting you. It didn't even mean anything. It was empty.

I miss you, Ginger.

From: Rhys Baker
To: Ginger Davies
Subject: I'm sorry

I know it's not an excuse, but the way you left fucked me up. When I woke up and didn't see you, I hated you for the way you decided for both of us. But I've been thinking these past few weeks, and I finally understand you. I swear I do. Because I know some things hurt so much, it's better to avoid them. Ginger, please, say something, okay? If you need time, ask for it, but please…let me know you're alive.

From: Rhys Baker
To: Ginger Davies
Subject: I'm sorry

You know what? I started this email four times, and each time I told myself that when I sent you that message, I wasn't myself. But then I erased it because I realized that at the moment, I was more myself than ever. I was the worst version of me, Ginger, the one that I sometimes wish you'd never met. The one that always reacts when I feel hurt by hurting someone in return because it's the only way to heal the wound. I hate myself, too, when I feel my emotions overwhelming me and I can't stop them. I wish I could organize them in my head like books placed alphabetically on a shelf. I never managed that, but I admit you're one of the few reasons why I would, why I want to keep trying.

From: Rhys Baker
To: Ginger Davies
Subject: I'm sorry

Ginger, you're killing me.

From: Ginger Davies
To: Rhys Baker
Subject: Signs of life

You're the biggest idiot I know.

From: Rhys Baker
To: Ginger Davies
Subject: RE: Signs of life

Fine, that works. I have never been so happy to be called an idiot. How did I ever get so lucky, Ginger, managing to meet you that night?

From: Rhys Baker
To: Ginger Davies

Subject: RE: Signs of life

I guess I fucked up again, and that's why you didn't respond, but I meant what I said. You make me feel lucky. What can I do to make things go back to the way they were before? I can't take this, not after all we've been through.

From: Ginger Davies
To: Rhys Baker
Subject: RE: RE: Signs of Life

If you hadn't actually been completely honest with me, I think I would have gone on ignoring you a few more weeks. You did this, Rhys. You hit me where it hurt. It's not fair, attacking me on purpose like that. Don't ever do it again.

You know what's the worst thing of all? Knowing all this about you. Knowing the worst version of you, as you said, and still loving you and looking at my email every night.

From: Rhys Baker
To: Ginger Davies
Subject: I know

You're right about everything.
Please forgive me.

From: Rhys Baker
To: Ginger Davies

Subject: [No subject]

Rhys, you're forgiven.

From: Rhys Baker
To: Ginger Davies
Subject: Thank you

I don't deserve you, Ginger.

75

Rhys

I MISSED HER SO MUCH some nights that I felt I couldn't breathe in the apartment we had shared. The truth of her absence grabbed me around the throat, and finally, when I couldn't take it anymore, I'd go out on the balcony with a drink; then I'd remember the hours we'd spent out there, while she touched the purple leaves of the bougainvillea that climbed the walls. Her shadow pursued me if I went down to the beach to take a walk as far as the lighthouse. Ginger was still there in every corner. Until I lost myself in the crowds, in the music.

There were good days, days when I thought I was getting past the memory of her body rubbing against mine. The feeling, growing more and more distant, of waking up in the morning and sensing the weight of her next to me, turning my head, seeing her sleeping with her mouth open and her arms stretched out like there was nothing to hide.

There were bad days too though. Days when I'd come back from a party and throw myself down on the couch with a beer in my hand, rereading old emails and trying to find something. A clue, maybe? A sign? Because sometimes, I thought we were making a mistake. In moments like that, I thought the only sensible thing I could do with my life was catch a plane and take off for London. And I'd ask myself what someone like me, so unstable, so far from the idea of what she wanted, could offer her...

And I'd get up and go for another beer.

Or whatever else there was in the fridge.

And I'd drink and stare out the window.

Contemplating an impossible moon.

76

From: Ginger Davies

To: Rhys Baker

Subject: News

They gave me the loan! I can hardly believe it after so many weeks of filling out forms and jumping through hoops. Did I tell you I hate banks? They're horrible places, with those cold marble floors, the greedy looks on the faces of the tellers, the way they size you up depending on how much money you have in your account...

The important thing is, it's done. It's real! I'm going to start a publishing company, Rhys! I'm floating on air. I owe it all to my father; he ended up cosigning for me.

What are you up to? How's everything?

From: Rhys Baker

To: Ginger Davies

Subject: RE: News

Congratulations, Ginger Snap!

I'm so happy for you. It's going to be brilliant, even if it's hard at first. Everything is, isn't it? You'll get used to it little by little. If you need more money, you know I'm here for you. As for your father, was he happy about it? I'm glad he finally came around…

I'm the same as always. They've offered me the same gig next summer with more perks. I guess I'll say yes.

From: Ginger Davies
To: Rhys Baker
Subject: RE: RE: News

I can't say Dad took it well exactly, but he's accepted it. We met for lunch, just the two of us. I showed him the business plan, told him all my ideas, and I guess he realized the project actually matters to me. He spent a long time looking it over with his reading glasses—he only puts them on when it's important. Then he put it back down on the table, took a deep breath, and asked me what I needed to start. It was nice, nothing sappy. I know it was a disappointment to him that neither of his daughters wanted to take over the company he loves so much, but I guess he'll get used to it. He wasn't exactly overjoyed about me spending the whole summer with you either.

So are you going to take the job?

From: Rhys Baker
To: Ginger Davies
Subject: Why?

What's your dad's issue with me? He barely even knows me; why should he care? He just met me that one time at Christmas, and we barely exchanged a word.

Yeah, I took the deal. Contract signed. I'll stay here.

From: Ginger Davies
To: Rhys Baker
Subject: RE: Why?

It's not personal, Rhys. He's always been leery like that. I think he liked Dean because he's known him since he was in diapers and there was no dirty laundry to air out. By the way, I didn't tell you yet, but Stella's pregnant. I'm going to be some kind of substitute aunt for my ex-boyfriend's baby. It's great. I'm actually excited for it to be born. I love how babies smell. I must be crazy, right? It's true though. Nothing else smells like that. It just makes you want to cuddle them.

From: Rhys Baker
To: Ginger Davies
Subject: A little...

Yeah, you do sound a little crazy...

Honestly, I have no idea what a baby smells like. I don't remember the last time I was even around a baby. It must be years. I think there's a mutual repulsion there. Or else they're just not part of my environment. I don't know. Anyway, I'm happy for them. I guess Dean is becoming the typical good guy from the movies, following the plan from A to B to C. I think about that sometimes. How easy it would have been to do the same.

From: Ginger Davies
To: Rhys Baker
Subject: RE: A little...

What are you talking about, Rhys?

Tomorrow I'll give you an update on everything with the publishing company. I've barely slept all week, I've been working without stopping, but it's been worth it! I'm about to go to dinner with Donna—and with my new coworker! (I love keeping you in the dark.) My sister said we had to do it up, so we're going to Pizza Pilgrims in Kingly Court. I swear they make the best pizzas in all of London. I'll take you if you ever come back some day. Also, Donna says hi. She just told me if I don't shut my computer, she's going to take it away and throw it out the window. Kisses and more kisses, Rhys. I'll give you more details if you do the same.

From: Rhys Baker
To: Ginger Davies
Subject: No good

Your new coworker? You just say that and leave me hanging? Whatever, I'll get my revenge at some point. But I want details, so I'll try to do a better job saying what I mean.

What I was talking about in my last email was Dean and the life he's living. You know, college, job, girlfriend, marriage, children. He must have bought a house too, right? So there you go. We talked about this a while back. I could have had a life like that probably. On paper it looks easy. But then, maybe it's not. Anyway, it's not for me. But when I see everyone else doing it, it makes me ask myself questions. Stupid shit. Like whether or not I'm wrong. Or still worse, if I'll even think the same way in a few years.

I wonder sometimes. What's going to happen. What I'll be doing with my life in the future. I can't see it. That's the problem. Everything's blurry.

I envy you sometimes, Ginger. You know what you want. You did even before you finished college, before you left the cabinet company; it was just that you didn't have the courage yet. I guess it scares me too, just in a different way. Because of my vertigo…and it's hard for me to jump when I don't know what's waiting for me at the bottom. It may not look that way, but it is. We should be born with an instruction manual under our arm, right? Everything would be easier that way. I've never understood people who say life's easy. How so? I find it complicated. Decisions, feelings. Then there are the questions we all have to ask ourselves: *Who am I? Where did I come from? What am I doing here? Why am I in this world?* Whatever, don't pay any attention to me.

Tell me how everything's going at the publisher.

Hopefully we can share a pizza there one day. Remember the one we had in Ibiza at the restaurant on the beach?

From: Ginger Davies
To: Rhys Baker
Subject: RE: No good

I didn't expect this when I told you to open up to me. Jeez, Rhys, I don't know where to start. I'm answering you now, and tonight I'll write you another email when I'm more relaxed, okay? So...let's see... Sometimes I don't know how to respond to you. I hate that. But I'm not sure if you'll like what I have to say. And it's this: I don't think everyone asks themselves those questions. Can you really imagine Dean having an existential crisis? Asking himself who he is, where he comes from, or what he's doing here? No. It's way simpler than that, even if you can't see it. But I like that about you. You're different.

I also understand that it confuses you.

And I understand...that until you find certain answers, you can't move forward, and the future looks blurry. And I hope you do find those answers, Rhys.

PS: It's impossible to forget that pizza. Mmmm. You can't see me, but I'm licking my lips as I think back on it.

From: Rhys Baker
To: Ginger Davies
Subject: What an idiot

I overdid it yesterday, right? I'm an idiot. I didn't think you'd take my words so much to heart. I'm fine, Ginger. I'm happy. We don't all want the same thing, that's it.

I'm dying to know more about the publisher.

From: Ginger Davies
To: Rhys Baker
Subject: Moving ahead

Okay, are you ready? Yes? No? I'm going to be working with Kate! Remember her? My roommate my last year of college? I don't think you met her when you came to visit me, but anyway, it stressed me out so much to think about having to spend so many hours with a stranger, coming to agreements, always being on the same page...so I thought, *Wait, Kate is amazing with business, she always has tons of incredible ideas, and she's working in a damn burger place!* So I decided to call her. We hadn't talked in ages. The last time was when I told her Dean was getting married. (I nearly die from embarrassment every time I think of it.) Then we kind of lost touch. You know, the summer with you and all that.

Conclusion: she said yes! She loves my idea. She still remembered my final project, and she's excited to move to London, especially because Donna and I agreed to rent her Michael's old room in the apartment. So everything's flowing smoothly. I'm so happy, Rhys! We're looking for the perfect office, and Kate will handle negotiations with the distributors and interview our freelancers. She can be serious, even intimidating if she needs to be. And let's be honest, that's not really me. I'd probably want to start peeing as soon as the meeting started, and I'd cry if the person said no or we couldn't make a good deal. Or maybe not, but either way, I'd prefer to deal more with the actual publishing like...finding THE PROJECT!

For now, I don't have anything special in mind. I've looked at a few authors I like, some self-published, others who have been around awhile, but they don't feel like the ones I want to launch with; they're more for something long-term, you know? What I want now is something different. Something striking.

But that's enough about me. Tell me how things are in your world. I assume Ibiza's calmer in October, right?

From: Rhys Baker
To: Ginger Davies
Subject: So happy about your progress

Brilliant, Ginger. I really mean it. Way better than starting off with someone you barely know. It'll be easier this way, even when you disagree about something. You'll know how to deal with the problems better. I'm so happy everything's coming together.

As far as your launch...you'll definitely come up with something. And you're right, it needs to be striking. You need to get the attention of booksellers and the media. It's not easy. But you can start slow; that's fine, right?

Yeah, things are calmer here now that the summer season is over. But I got invited to a festival in November, and I'm also working out some details for a New Year's Eve gig. I'll keep you informed.

77

From: Ginger Davies
To: Rhys Baker
Subject: Late

I know I shouldn't be writing this message or even sitting here in front of the computer so late at night when I'm tired and can't stop listening to your songs and remembering, but...this feels so weird, Rhys. Talking as if nothing had happened between us. As if all we experienced over the summer was just nothing. I know it doesn't make sense. I know I shouldn't hit Send, because we made a deal. But I need to tell you. Tomorrow I'll go back to pretending that everything's okay and that I never think about it. I'll talk to you the same as before.

I just wish it was easier to forget you, Rhys.

To forget the rest, everything I left behind.

From: Rhys Baker
To: Ginger Davies

Subject: RE: Late

I know, Ginger. I guess it'll pass, right? And we're not so bad at pretending! I've been thinking about the same stuff since then. Sorry I asked you to stay. You were right; it wasn't fair. And sorry for what I did afterward.

Get some sleep, Ginger Snap.

78

From: Ginger Davies

To: Rhys Baker

Subject: We found it!

We got an office, Rhys! We got it! Amazing, right? Kate's the one who found it. It's in Clapham. It's a nice area; it's not far from central London. I'm so happy! You've got to see it; I'll send photos. For now, I'm leaving the address below so you can look it up on Google Maps. It's the redbrick four-story building. We're on the top floor, but it's almost better, because Kate can go out on the balcony and smoke whenever she feels like it. My father's going to hook us up with free cabinets! He actually seems excited about the project. I mean, we all are. I hope I don't get disappointed.

I think you are already at the festival, right?

Did it go well? Were there lots of people?

From: Rhys Baker

To: Ginger Davies

Subject: [No subject]

Amazing, amazing, amazing…
    Just so great… Cool, Ginger!

From: Ginger Davies
To: Rhys Baker
Subject: RE: [No subject]

Wow. Thanks for the enthusiasm.
    Are you drunk, Rhys?

From: Rhys Baker
To: Ginger Davies
Subject: RE: RE: [No subject]

Sorry. Yeah, I was a little drunk when I wrote you last night. I got to the hotel in the morning after spinning and having a little fun afterward. Alec and some friends came with me, and it was…intense. But good. There were tons of people. All shouting my name. Can you believe it? I'm still trying to process it. I can't get used to it.

I'm so happy about the office. I looked at it online. The building looks great, and so does the area and the café downstairs. Congratulations, Ginger. You're living your dreams… So nice about your dad too. Just great.

I'm going to stay here a few more days.

I'll write you when I'm back on the island.

Kisses. Kisses.

From: Ginger Davies

To: Rhys Baker

Subject: Mommying you

I know you're going to roll your eyes when you read this, but I'm not sure Alec and the rest are good company for you. Don't get offended, but they seem like they're wasting their lives, and I don't want them to drag you down too.

From: Rhys Baker

To: Ginger Davies

Subject: Moms are boring

Wasting their lives? They're just having fun.

From: Ginger Davies

To: Rhys Baker

Subject: Fun?

I'm sorry, I didn't know having fun meant sticking whatever up your nose so you could stop being yourself. I'm just naive. I'll tell Donna right now to go buy a couple of grams for tonight so we can celebrate getting two desks for the office.

From: Rhys Baker

To: Ginger Davies

Subject: RE: Fun?

Do you realize how old you sound?

From: Ginger Davies
To: Rhys Baker
Subject: RE: RE: Fun?

I don't sound old, Rhys; I'm worried about you. I avoided this subject on purpose, just like all the others I avoid with you, because I didn't want to argue. But I worry about something happening to you. I think sometimes you're not aware enough of things.

From: Rhys Baker
To: Ginger Davies
Subject: Relax

Ginger, I'm fine. Better than ever.
   And I'm not going to let anyone drag me anywhere.

From: Ginger Davies
To: Rhys Baker
Subject: RE: Relax

Does that mean you didn't take anything?

From: Rhys Baker
To: Ginger Davies
Subject: RE: RE: Relax

Ginger…best not to talk about that. Just trust me, okay? Can you do that? And let's catch up on more pleasant things. Like your pretty little office. Will it take much longer till it's ready? Whatever happened with the distributor?

From: Ginger Davies
To: Rhys Baker
Subject: Routine

Whatever happened to that friend of yours you went to college with? The one who lived in LA and was a lawyer. His name was Logan, right? Don't you talk to him anymore?

Yeah, all our plans are keeping us busy; that's why I've had less time to write you. And when I get home, my sister and Kate suck up all the time I used to have for myself, either convincing me to make a real dinner instead of something premade or else watch a movie. Lately the days are just flying by. Especially now, with Christmas right around the corner. I still haven't bought any presents. Every year I tell myself I'll give myself extra days to do it, and every year I find myself with a week to go and it still hanging over my head.

I do trust you, Rhys. But that doesn't make me worry any less.

From: Rhys Baker
To: Ginger Davies
Subject: Congratulations, Ginger Snap!

Happy birthday! How does twenty-four feel? Especially now

that you're a businesswoman…is it very different from twenty-three? I hope so. Last year around this time, you were so down, remember? You hated getting up every day and going to work, and you wanted to kill Dean half the time.

Now, let's hope every year is better than the last.

And that you go on living your dreams.

From: Ginger Davies
To: Rhys Baker
Subject: I'm happy 😊

Thanks, Rhys. You're right, things have changed a lot in just a year, haven't they? I remember perfectly everything you're describing. It was at Christmas dinner last year that Dean announced he was marrying Stella, and I…all I could think about was you and how I wished you were there. I don't think I ever told you that. Maybe because you were busy with Alexa. Yeah.

Anyway, I'm much happier now.

From: Rhys Baker
To: Ginger Davies
Subject: RE: I'm happy 😊

Do I detect a hint of jealousy?

From: Ginger Davies
To: Rhys Baker
Subject: I admit it

I *was* jealous. Past tense. Guilty as charged. Alexa made me a little jealous. But I also just didn't believe her. I heard your interview on the radio, and she didn't seem like a bad chick, but she was too enthusiastic, like she was exaggerating. Just too much, you know? I don't think she was a fit for you.

From: Rhys Baker
To: Ginger Davies
Subject: Interesting...

So what's a fit for me?

From: Ginger Davies
To: Rhys Baker
Subject: RE: Interesting...

I don't know, Rhys. I have no idea.

  If I'm going to be honest with you, I don't even see you in a serious relationship. But that must be because I've never heard of you being in one. I mean, it's hard to imagine things you've never seen before, right? That's all.

From: Ginger Davies
To: Rhys Baker
Subject: Good luck!

I just wanted to wish you good luck (or is it "break a leg" for musicians?) at the NYE party tonight. I hope it's amazing, Rhys. I suppose you've been busy between the trip and getting ready for everything. Hopefully next year is full of good things for you. For both of us. Another thing: thanks for my birthday present! It came yesterday, and it's perfect! Pajamas with smiling spaghetti on them! I'll never take them off. Plus they're so warm...

79

Ginger

KATE, DONNA, AND I CLINKED glasses. My sister had just finished her shift and had shown up pretty tipsy. She'd just broken up with Amanda and spent the whole night behind the bar taking one shot after the other and ignoring her boss's looks, even though her boss was, honestly, really sweet and understanding. She was still letting Donna hang her pictures up on the walls of the bar, but lately Donna had hardly touched her paints.

"To us!" she shouted.

Kate's eyebrows rose, and she started laughing. "Didn't we already say a toast to us?"

"Who cares? To us! Again!"

"And to the office furniture!" Kate added.

"And to the plant in the kitchen that died yesterday!"

"And for ex-boyfriends who make us be godmothers, don't forget that!" Donna added, looking at me. I covered my hands with my face and laughed. I couldn't say no when Stella asked me, because I really did like her, and she barely had any family, and because their baby was so cute, I wanted to kiss him all over every time I saw him. "More!"

"I think you've had enough," I objected.

"Oh come on, Ginger, don't be a wet blanket."

They ignored me and ordered another round. At that moment, I felt my phone buzz and took it out of my pocket. I was dressed casually. I hadn't bothered putting on anything fancy for New Year's Eve, just tight jeans and a sweater. I held my breath when I read the name on the screen. Rhys.

"Who was it?" Kate asked.

"Rhys, but he hung up."

She and Donna looked at each other and laughed.

"What's so funny?"

"After all this time, you're still hung up on a guy you liked in college. Remember? You got so nervous every time you opened your laptop. It was adorable."

"I hate you sometimes," I growled.

I got up and walked out as the two of them continued to laugh. It was biting cold out, and I started to shiver. It was raining. They yellow lights of the cars were reflected in the puddles on the road. I walked away from the door down a narrow street in Carnaby and took refuge under the cornice of a building nearby. I dialed Rhys's number. He didn't pick up. Not on the first ring, not on the second, not on the third...

I almost hung up, but then he answered.

"The tastiest little cookie in the world!"

"I saw you called..." I began.

"Called? Nah..." He sounded blissful but strange, not much like the reserved, melancholy boy I thought I knew so well, the one who tried so hard to convince me he was something different by digging up the most unpleasant parts of himself and putting them on display.

"You did. A minute ago…"

"Weird… I don't remember…"

"Is your session starting?"

"No. At like three. Or four."

"Rhys." I clutched the telephone tight. "Are you high?"

Silence. Laughter and voices in the background.

"What do you want me to say?"

"No. Tell me no."

"No, I'm not."

"Don't lie to me, Rhys."

"Come on, Ginger! Don't be so lame. I'm trying to do things right, I swear, but sometimes it's like you buzz around me like a fucking fly…"

"Fuck you, Rhys. I'm hanging up."

I heard a girl's voice nearby and imagined unknown lips on his neck while he held the phone against his ear, pupils dilated…

"That's for the best. I'm a little busy right now."

It was all I could do not to throw the phone. I clenched my teeth, panted, watched the rain fall, feeling a million miles away from the festivities inside and not wanting to join in. Far from all the people there who were laughing, chatting, having fun. Far from everything. Even Rhys. For the first time in forever, I felt completely alone. Before, I had him at least, on the other side of the screen. The distance never kept me from feeling he was close. But tonight was different. Tonight he wasn't there. Many times lately he hadn't been. And I missed him. I wanted the boy I liked to come back: the one from those summer nights, the one with the lazy smile, the one who danced with me on the streets of Paris, and could write songs from a heartbeat, make me laugh effortlessly, talk about whatever, and turn my world upside down until I asked myself what I really believed...

80

From: Rhys Baker
To: Ginger Davies
Subject: Truce

How long are we going to go without talking, Ginger? We need a truce. Three weeks is too long. I miss you. And I know you miss me. Don't make me beg. Besides, I've got stuff to tell you.

From: Rhys Baker
To: Ginger Davies
Subject: Hurray!

Happy friendiversary! Even if right now I don't know whether you want to be my friend. Come on, Ginger. I might have been a jerk on New Year's Eve, but you and I need to patch things up. Dragging it on will just make things worse. Say something.

From: Ginger Davies
To: Rhys Baker
Subject: Truth

You say you *might* have been an idiot. Because you can't even remember, right? Of course I miss you, Rhys. You already know that. The same way you knew mentioning our friendiversary would make me go soft. But I can't pretend it doesn't hurt me to see where your life is leading you. I don't get it. You have everything you need to be happy.

From: Rhys Baker
To: Ginger Davies
Subject: RE: Truth

Ginger, don't be like that. This has nothing to do with happiness. What happened was just a moment, like lots of others. Let's forget about it, okay? If it makes you less angry, I should let you know I haven't gone out partying in weeks and haven't hooked up with anyone at all. I'm busy with something way more important. I've been talking to Logan again. You were right. When you asked me about him last month, I realized he was a good guy and I'd just left him hanging. So it turns out he's going to come see me for a few days in a couple of weeks. He says he needs to clear his head, and this way we can spend some time together.

Are you happy? I hope so.

Because I have this feeling I keep fucking things up. And I

feel like shit, Ginger, but when I'm doing it, I don't know, it's like I don't realize it. Or maybe I do. But not in the moment. In the moment, I don't feel anything. Then all at once, it comes up on me. The guilt. And I can barely breathe.

What's happening to us? Why can't we stop arguing?

From: Ginger Davies
To: Rhys Baker
Subject: Okay...

Fine, Rhys. I'm tired of us being mad all the time lately too, but you know, you matter to me, and I can't just keep my mouth shut when I feel like you're running in the wrong direction.

I'm glad Logan's going to see you; it's always good to catch up with old friends. Don't leave me hanging. I want to know what you're busy with right now. I have a lot to tell you too. A lot. But you first.

From: Rhys Baker
To: Ginger Davies
Subject: Here goes

Fine, I won't beat around the bush.

I'm going to record an album!

That's right. I got an offer, and I think it's a good idea. Something that's all mine. I wasn't sure at first, but then I thought, *Why not?* I've got tons of material, and plus, what I like best is creating, composing, mixing...

I'm psyched, but I want to stay calm about it. I don't like the idea of just putting whatever out, so I asked them for time. I'm excited, though, to shut myself up in my studio at the apartment for hours and hours, forgetting I've missed lunch and just boiling some cup noodles. I like how I feel when I'm deep in a project; it's like my brain reactivates after being asleep a long time. Or dazed, if not asleep. You get me.

What do you think? I was feeling weird about you not knowing, can you believe that? Saying yes without checking with you first. So crazy, Ginger.

From: Ginger Davies
To: Rhys Baker
Subject: RE: Here goes

What do you mean, what do I think? My God, Rhys! I'm jumping for joy! It's amazing! Huge! Just imagine! I'll be able to go online and download your album with your name right there on the front. I'm so happy. Especially because I know working on things like this is what you really like most. Creating, communicating, giving form to something.

It's the same for me though. We're idiots!

When the THING to do with my launch first occurred to me, my first instinct was: *Shit! I can't tell Rhys because I'm so pissed at him for being an idiot, and allegedly we're not talking now!* So I get what you're saying.

Anyway, it's time to talk about the THING. I don't know why I'm calling it that, so don't ask. I'm going to try to sum it up, okay?

Does the name Anne Cabot ring a bell to you by any chance? My guess is no, but she's the wife of one of the most influential men in England. Or better said, *was* the wife, because their divorce was finalized this week. So Cameron Reed is a well-known finance guy involved in all kinds of feminist causes, pro-equality etc., plus he has a ton of political contacts. You're probably asking yourself, *So what?* but the thing is, he was abusing his wife. It's a major scandal, and he doesn't want it to get out. He was also frequenting high-class hookers. A real peach.

Anne didn't say anything for years. She was scared of a scandal and of people not believing her because of how famous he is. But after the most recent beating, she left home and filed for divorce. She's smart, she's an incredible woman, but for years she's been running scared. She studied literature and graduated with honors, but she stopped being a teacher to follow him on all his trips. You get it. She gave up everything for him.

So now the rumor is she's writing her memoir. I wrote it off as impossible, assuming she already had a contract with a huge publisher, but one night, after thinking it over and talking to Donna and Kate, I found myself unable to sleep, and I decided to do something crazy.

I'm embarrassed to tell you, but here goes:

I showed up on her doorstep. In Notting Hill. I didn't knock, obviously. I stood there in the freezing cold until she came out midmorning. Then I pounced on her like a textbook stalker, just went for it. But I was tongue-tied, and I'm not even sure what I said. I did manage to tell her I was starting a small publisher and we were in contact with a number of authors but were looking for something big to debut with. She just looked at me, barely even blinking. I got my card out of my bag. I was shaking as I gave it to her. I told her I figured she'd already signed a contract with someone else, but just in case, I didn't want to let the opportunity go by. I was about to turn and run before she called the cops, when she asked me if I wanted to have coffee with her.

Yep. Just like that. Obviously, I said yes. We went to a place close by and talked a long time. I told her a little about my story: spending my whole life getting ready to work in the family business and then dropping everything to start the publisher. She seemed interested, and the conversation just flowed; it was like we'd known each other for ages. She was charming, honestly. So way after we'd both finished our coffees, she told me she was finishing her first draft, that she already had several offers from publishers I obviously couldn't compete with, and that she still hadn't decided anything.

I congratulated her. I realized I didn't have a chance. But then she asked me what the advantages of working with me would be. I was honest: as for money, there wouldn't be much, at least not until the book came out, but she'd be totally free to publish her book unedited. I'd be transparent with her, always available, and she wouldn't have to deal with a bunch of middlemen. I told her the truth, that I'd always wanted to publish something that mattered, get good books into people's hands, cherish them, polish them, work to make other people's writings shine. Be their champion.

So then...she smiled.

She said goodbye and told me she'd think it over, and two days later she called me to say YES.

Can you believe it, Rhys? I can't! Not yet! I'm on a cloud, I can't get used to it, and we've already signed the contract. I don't know. It's amazing. Powerful. It's just what I was looking for. Anne told me that after her divorce, she had more money than she could spend in several lifetimes and that what mattered to her most when she published her memoir was that it shouldn't be empty, just one more product on a shelf.

Jeez, I've been writing forever, I don't want to bore you to death, but I wanted you to know the situation. Hopefully everything will go well. And then in a few months, you'll be recording your album. And the publisher will start making money. I hope, I hope, I hope…

From: Rhys Baker
To: Ginger Davies
Subject: I'm proud of you

Damn, Ginger. That's incredible. I can almost imagine you outside the door of her house trembling from head to toe. But you did it! That's what I like the most about you. You're scared of so many things and sometimes you need your time to do them, but you always make them happen! Do you realize that? Just like I said the day I met you, you're complicated. But those complications are lovely; they're part of what makes you who you are. You grow and grow and get stronger and better all the time.

I can't wait to have that book in my hands.

From: Ginger Davies
To: Rhys Baker
Subject: Surprise!

I didn't tell you something important that I think you're really going to like...

We've filed the documents for the publisher. We spent days trying to think of a name, but Kate stressed that it had to be my decision, because she's technically not a co-owner, and besides, it was my life's dream. She wanted to let me have that.

So I'm calling it Moon Books.

Because if you think about it, Rhys, reading a book is almost like being on the moon. As you engross yourself in its pages, your feet leave the ground, and you travel, to other places, other worlds, other lives...

Plus, it reminded me of you. Of us.

From: Rhys Baker
To: Ginger Davies
Subject: RE: Surprise!

I don't know what to say... It's perfect.

And thanks for saying it reminds you of me.

81

Rhys

LOGAN'S PLANE LANDED IN THE afternoon, just as it was starting to get dark. I could hardly recognize him after a year and a half. I hadn't seen him since I was in LA with Alexa to launch the track we made together. Now, Logan was getting gray hairs, and his clothing was more…formal, elegant. He looked like a real-life lawyer, not the laid-back guy I used to know.

We gave each other each a hug.

"Sunny out here, huh?" he said, smiling.

"Not as much in wintertime as you'd think. Let's go."

He dropped his suitcase at the apartment, and we went out to have a drink and catch up. He was only supposed to stay for three days, enough for just a bit of R and R. All that work was getting to him. He'd gone from a tiny office in LA to a big firm in New York, and now he was a partner at another one. He looked tired, a little scattered, but still…there was something different in his eyes, something I didn't recognize from before. A glimmer.

"What about you? You haven't changed a bit."

I didn't like that. What did it mean? That I was stagnant,

comfortable, stuck in a routine? I shifted in my seat, uncomfortable, and took a sip of my second beer. Logan glanced at his phone before putting it back into the pocket of his khakis. He was wearing a designer belt. I'd never known him to be into things like that.

"There are some changes. I'm about to record an album. I think I told you that over the phone. I've got a gig set up for next summer. So everything's moving along."

"No more life on the road then?"

"What do you mean?"

"You know. You always used to be going from one place to the next. But it wears a person out. I don't know how you kept it up. Anyway, this place is great. It's not even spring yet, and the temperature's amazing."

I tore the label off my beer. "I've just let life guide me. I'd have been perfectly happy to go if they'd offered me a job somewhere else."

"It's cool, Rhys. I get it."

"Get what?" I asked.

"You're not a spring chicken, bud." He laughed, drank, and sighed. "Twenty's not the same as thirty, you know? Things inevitably change with time."

I shrugged and looked at him. "Why'd you change?"

"That's exactly what I wanted to talk to you about..." Logan rested his arms on the table.

"What's up? Something wrong?"

"Nah. The opposite. I'm getting married, Rhys."

I stared at him, pensive. "Wow. Congrats. Good job."

"Yeah. So another thing: you know the bride."

"For real? Is it someone from Tennessee?"

"No. You remember Sarah?" Logan sighed, uncomfortable, took a sip of beer, and drew a breath. "You used to have a thing with her on and off. Y'all shared an apartment in LA for a while. Years back. One day she got mad when she saw some emails from another chick and asked me if she could stay at my place. We saw more and more of each other, especially once I moved to New York..."

"I remember," I cut him off. "Sarah. Yeah."

"I don't want this to be weird."

"Why would it be?"

"You know. She was in love with you."

"Yeah, but shit, that was years ago."

"I know. But..." He gave me an uncertain look, then glanced away. "I wanted to tell you in person, because we decided not to invite you to the wedding. I'm sorry. I just think it would be uncomfortable. For me, especially. I can't help it..."

It took me a few seconds to manage a response. "You don't have to explain anything to me."

"Sure. I just didn't want to hurt you."

"I wouldn't have gone anyway."

"Are you serious?" He laughed.

"You know I hate weddings."

Logan nodded and ordered another round of beers. I tried to stay in the moment the rest of the evening, but I didn't do well at it. He talked about his firm, his life, the wedding, which would be at the end of summer, how he had immediately connected with Sarah, and I... I tried not to think of how I'd just lied to him, because I *would* have made an effort to go to the wedding of one of the few friends I'd ever really had, even if I wasn't tempted by the song and dance, especially since the ceremony was going to take place in some pompous, stuffy place in New York.

I tried not to think of other things too.

Like that feeling that I was getting left behind. Getting lost in shadows while everyone else had managed to finally see the light. I thought about roots that didn't exist. Anchors I couldn't find. About how I had more and more contacts in my phone, but with every new one, my solitude grew. I thought about Ginger, about how she was climbing like a vine that wouldn't stop growing, about how proud I felt of her and how disappointed she was in me. I could sense it. I could feel it. And I could tell I was also starting to rethink some of those paths I'd abandoned.

Like Sarah. What would my life have been like if we'd gone further and I hadn't pushed her away? I imagined us married by now, living in the big city with a kid, maybe with a second one on the way. Who knew? My entire existence was loose threads, possibilities I'd never let turn into something more.

Except for Ginger. That was one thread that was still there, still growing. And I knew I'd never be able to let it go. The same went for my mother. That was a thin connection, but a stable one.

And that was about it. And yet, funny enough, I was the one who'd cut people off, as though a part of myself had been fleeing company, friendship, love, everything good about existence. Maybe I had been looking for sorrow, solitude, unhappiness. Maybe I was even chasing them.

82

From: Ginger Davies
To: Rhys Baker
Subject: Drama

You won't believe what's happening! We got a letter from a big law office, and guess what, there's a "friendly warning" that we shouldn't publish Anne Cabot's book. Obviously, we knew her ex-husband would do whatever he could to sink the project, but I assumed he would just preempt us by giving interviews saying it was all lies and slander. I had no idea he'd actually try to keep the book off the market.

Worst of all, I have no idea how to proceed. So I got in touch with James. Remember him? The guy I had a beer with at the party and hung out with later. I called you that night because I was freaking out and I wanted to leave. (I'm so embarrassed when I think of it now.) Anyway, I remembered he was a lawyer, and I didn't want to ask my father for his lawyer's number because I knew he'd worry, so I have an appointment at the end of this week.

I'm a little worried, Rhys.

Hopefully it's not a big deal…

From: Rhys Baker
To: Ginger Davies
Subject: RE: Drama

Relax, Ginger Snap.

It's a smart move, putting it all in a lawyer's hands. And yeah, I remember James—the guy who thought it was a good idea to marry Lady Strawberry to Lord Chocolate, right? Wait and see what he thinks before you panic.

And tell me what happens, okay?

From: Ginger Davies
To: Rhys Baker
Subject: RE: RE: Drama

Okay then, here's the situation: Cameron Reed has enough money to pay the full-time salary of every lawyer in London; I'm a loser who up and decided to start a publisher and saddle myself with this bullshit. But the good thing is, James thinks there's a way to get Cameron to pull back before he sues for damages and something or other about privacy because of his role in the book. We've been thinking it over all week, and maybe if we go ahead, announce publication, and invest some cash in the publicity (my dad helped me out with the money; hopefully I can pay him back soon), we can draw the media's attention.

Our goal is to get the word out that Anne Cabot is about to publish her memoir of her years living in hell, and that there will be such an uproar that Cameron will decide to just tell his side of the story and leave it at that. He knows the more noise he makes, the more publicity he'll give us. Every move he makes could work in our favor; that's how James phrased it.

I'm worried, I won't lie to you. Anne, on the other hand, seems relaxed. I think she could already see all this coming. As far as any defamation or libel accusations in the future or whatever, Anne says she has medical proof that she was abused right before she left their shared home. James asked to see the documentation and is looking it over to prepare for whatever may come.

This means we have to push forward the publication date. The book will be out in three weeks. It's crazy. Kate says I'm going to give her a heart attack. What do you think, Rhys?

From: Rhys Baker
To: Ginger Davies
Subject: RE: RE: RE: Drama

Honestly? I think this is free publicity for you all. I never doubted it would be a success; now I'd bet my life on it. Think about it. People like scandal and dirty details. Whether he wants to or not, Cameron has to deny the charges. Silence will only make him look guilty. He's hanging by a thread because at the same time, if he talks too much, he'll make a bigger deal out of it. And this always attracts readers. Did Anne never call the cops on him?

ONLY AFTER WE MET 437

From: Ginger Davies
To: Rhys Baker
Subject: Steps forward

Anne is in the process of suing him. Or rather, her lawyers are. But that's a totally separate issue from the publisher. James is taking care of it. He's honestly been great. I didn't tell you this, because I was kind of nervous about everything that was going on, but when I went to his office in London and told him I'd started the publisher that I'd talked about being my dream years before, he was so proud that I burst into tears. I guess I was already feeling a little raw.

It's nice, right? I basically live in my office, and I can hardly catch my breath, but still. A year ago I was just getting ready to leave my father's company and go spend the summer with you, and now look. It scares me sometimes to look back and see how everything's changed. But listen: I keep sucking up the whole conversation with my BS, and it's been forever since you've told me anything about your album. Even worse, I forgot to ask you how everything was with your visit with Logan last summer. I'm officially the worst friend in the world.

From: Rhys Baker
To: Ginger Davies
Subject: RE: Steps forward

Relax. With all that's been going on, you've got an excuse. I was looking for news about your thing yesterday, and I found it on a bunch of newspaper websites. Amazing, Ginger. You publish in three days, right? Knowing you, you must be hysterical, so let me catch you up so you can relax your mind for a while.

Yeah, Logan was here. It was good. More or less. Chill. I think he forgot what it means to have fun when he started wearing pleated pants, but what can you do? No one's perfect. For real though, I realized that if we had little in common before, now it's turned into basically nothing. Friendships must be like that; you don't always follow the same road, one day you look at a person you've known for more than a decade, and you realize nothing binds you to them. Yeah. So he's getting married. To Sarah, the girl I was with years back. Amazing how life changes, right? It's best not to think about it.

Everything's good with the album. I met with the people from the label in Barcelona last week. They have big plans, but I've still got a lot of work to do. I've been backed up lately. I guess it'll pass.

I see it doesn't affect you as much when I tell you I'm proud of you. Joking aside, it's nice to look back and know I was there with you through these changes. You deserve success. Keep me informed about how the book launch goes.

From: Ginger Davies
To: Rhys Baker
Subject: Soooooo happy

You can't imagine how happy I am! The launch was amazing. Everyone came to the office: Donna, James, Anne, my parents;

even Dean got away from work for a while. Kate uncorked a bottle of champagne, and we sprayed it all over the floor in the hallway, but who cares? The booksellers have been amazing. Never in my wildest dreams did I imagine things could start off like this.

I have to let you go because we have more celebrations tonight. We have a reservation at a new restaurant nearby.

We'll talk tomorrow. Kisses.

From: Rhys Baker
To: Ginger Davies
Subject: RE: Soooooo happy

I'm so happy for you, Ginger. Enjoy this moment. Maybe soon we can celebrate together. Who knows? I hope you feel proud. I still remember sometimes that girl I met who was lost in Paris and laughed when people talked about their dreams.

Sometimes the turns life takes are okay.

83

Ginger

I REREAD THE SENTENCE FOR the fifth time, making sure it was perfect and that each word expressed exactly what I wanted to say. Then I looked up when I heard a knock at my door and saw Kate peeking in. She looked nervous.

"You've got a visitor, Ginger."

"Let them in."

"Okay…" She looked a little unsure. Turning her head, she stuck her head back in through the crack in the door. "I'll be smoking on the balcony."

"Sure. No worries." I got up.

Then I saw him. I watched him walk like a hurricane through the door of my office, a lazy smile on his face, his blond hair uncombed, in worn jeans that slid off his hips as he took step after step toward me. He stretched out his arms. For a few seconds, I froze, paralyzed, knees on the verge of giving out. It had been almost a year since I'd seen him, and… I still wasn't ready. Especially not now. This was the moment when I was least ready.

"What's up, Ginger Snap? Aren't you happy to see me?"

"I…" I brought a hand to my chest. "Rhys…"

Finally, I reacted. I ran toward him and hugged him. I felt his hand on my head, my cheek on his hard chest, his minty aroma enveloping us amid a rush of memories and shared secrets, moments frozen in time, nights in front of the keyboard.

I pulled away and looked at him. He was thinner, he had bags under his eyes, but he was still every bit as handsome as I remembered, eyes glimmering, with that special way of leaning down to bridge the distance that always separated us. I don't know…he was just him. Darkness and light at the same time. Dazzling and also the opaquest person I'd ever known.

"Have I changed that much? You're looking at me weird."

"No. Not at all. You're the same as always. You're…fantastic."

"You, on the other hand…" He stepped back and examined me. "You look different in that suit. You cut your hair. You never told me."

"I just haven't had any time lately…"

"I know. It looks good. You look great."

"Thanks." I gulped. I was nervous.

Rhys reached up to touch the tips of my hair. Then he stroked my chin and cheek, and we looked each other in the eye. We were both full of longing, memories, desires. I closed my eyes and felt his fingers rubbing my lips, tracing their outline, making me tremble.

He groaned.

And kissed me. Kissed me intensely.

Our mouths united in a kind of fury. Starved. Something quivered in my chest, something good and bad at the same time. All I still felt for him, all I'd always felt, fighting against what had to be.

I shook from pleasure and sorrow. Rhys picked me up and sat me on the desk. His hands were wild as they sought me out, grasping my legs, trying to unbutton my blouse.

I held my breath. Not even two minutes had passed since he entered my office after a year's absence, and already he'd turned my world upside down, making my skin burn as it touched his. Worse: before we had even touched.

I laid my quivering hands on his chest.

"Ginger... Ginger..." He kissed me again.

"Wait, Rhys. I can't. Not now."

He stepped back. I could see the incomprehension in the gray of his eyes as I tried to quickly button the blouse he had almost torn open. I slid off my desk and stood there leaning against it, hands clutching its edge, not wanting him to see me shaking.

"What's up, Ginger?"

"This isn't how it works." I glared at him now. I was furious— furious at him, furious at myself. "You can't just barge in and do this! You can't just assume that summer two years ago was something you can pick up and leave off at your whim."

Rhys took a deep breath as his brow furrowed. "Sorry. I wasn't thinking. I just... I saw you, and you know you do that to me; you know I can't get over you, don't you, Ginger? I can't keep my hands off you..."

He approached me again. Seductive, but without forcing himself, so certain in his every movement, so fascinating I couldn't take my eyes off of him.

"You don't understand..."

"What don't I understand?"

I told him softly: "I'm going out with someone."

He blinked. Confused. Then looked down and looked back up. I don't know what I saw in his eyes just then. There was...so much. Things mingled, tangled. I couldn't tell what it all meant. Maybe he couldn't either.

He ran a hand through his hair and paced through the office, hands on his hips, then stared at me. "Who is he? You never told me anything..."

"But...we agreed we wouldn't talk about that. You know, when we were together two summers ago. I didn't know if I should until I saw where things were going. Neither of us has talked about that stuff. You either. Unless you want to hurt me, I mean. Jesus, Rhys. I hate this. I hate it..."

"Ginger," he interrupted me, impatient.

"James. We're giving it a real try."

"James? Again? Are you kidding?"

"You say that as if I haven't been crashing into the same wall for years," I replied, not realizing my voice had started rising.

"What fucking wall?" he shouted.

"You, Rhys. You're my wall."

I blinked as I tried to stop myself from crying as I saw how upset he was. My eyes itched. I was starting to fall apart. I don't know what we were trying to do there staring at each other; in the silence, we were telling each other something, but I couldn't say what. I was almost relieved when Kate knocked again after finishing her cigarette on the balcony.

"I just wanted to remind you that you have a lunch date," she said, then, to Rhys, smiling: "A pleasure meeting you, Rhys."

I closed my eyes and sighed, trying to stay calm as she departed. He was still there, leaning against the windowsill and staring out into the gray sky, which looked as if it was about to spill its fury over us.

"Fuck…" I turned and grabbed my phone out of my bag.

"What is it now? You're getting married tomorrow, and you forgot to order the flowers?"

"Fuck you, Rhys," I hissed.

"What's the problem? It wouldn't surprise me if you forgot to tell me."

For a moment, I forgot I was supposed to have lunch with James. I forgot I was looking for my phone to try and cancel, even if, punctual as he was, he was probably almost there. I forgot everything that wasn't this moment. And I let my anger out. The rage I'd suppressed. The indignation.

"How can you be so goddamn selfish?! How can you throw it in my face that I didn't tell you about James when for years you've been fucking whoever you feel like, and I never even dared ask you for an explanation? What is it with you, Rhys? Has it ever occurred to you to think about someone else?"

I didn't realize until then that I was crying so hard, my vision was getting blurred. He came close, breaking the inches of safety that lay between us. He tried to hug me, but I pushed him away. I heard his labored breathing. But then I gave in, let him have his way, let his arms wrap around me as I sobbed into his chest. His hot breath in my ear made me tremble.

"I know I'm an idiot, Ginger. But I never felt anything for those girls. I always knew you were the one, that you were my rock…"

The buzzer downstairs rang.

Confused, in a situation I could never have predicted, I walked away from my desk and took a few Kleenex out of my bag to wipe my face and blow my nose.

"It's James. I'm supposed to have lunch with him."

"Give me a fucking break." Rhys closed his eyes.

"Please, if I matter to you at all, even just a little bit, try to act like a normal friend, Rhys. Are you listening to me? I know all this is difficult for both of us, but I don't want to hurt James. He doesn't deserve that. I didn't even tell him about what happened that summer; all he knows is I met you in Paris, and that we've been talking since then..."

"Go let him in," he grunted.

I hugged him, passed by him, thanked him. For an eternal second, my arms around him, I asked myself what would happen if I didn't open the door, what would happen if I stayed with Rhys forever, just touching him, feeling him, listening to him breathe. Creating an *us*. Was that even possible, or was it just a dream, an ideal, like touching the moon?

But then I returned to reality.

And I let go of him and walked out of my office.

84

Rhys

THE HARDEST THING I'D EVER done in my fucking life was putting up with that awful meal in the private dining room of a fancy restaurant with tiny portions of bullshit. The situation was killing me. Everything was killing me. The way I'd felt in those months, lonelier than ever, more lost than I'd ever been. My stomach shrank when I saw James wrapping his arms around her, resting a hand on her knee, gawking at her like an idiot. I think that's the first time I ever felt real envy, the twisted kind that fucks you up inside. Envy of stability, of how clearly I saw what I could have had if I'd known how to do things right.

"Ginger told me you're putting out a record."

"Yeah, that's the plan. If I can ever finish."

"I don't understand much about electronic music. It just sounds like noise to me. But I guess it's not easy; there must be a knack to it, like everything. It's interesting."

I nodded, distracted, trying to figure out what the hell this slop on the plate in front of me was. I'd ordered something with potatoes, and either they were invisible or they were green. I could feel Ginger's eyes piercing me. Pleading. Shouting in silence. If only I knew her less and couldn't read her face...

But I couldn't fake it, I just couldn't.

I wanted to go.

Disappear.

Turn to smoke.

Nothing.

"I'll be back in a minute."

I got up and went to the bathroom. It was just as pretentious as the food. I closed the door and looked at myself a few seconds in the mirror before taking out my wallet and the baggie. I grabbed a credit card and cut a line on the red marble counter. When I came out, five minutes later, I felt cooler, more chipper, more prepared to put up with that torture.

"We were about to order dessert without you," James joked.

"Don't worry about it. I don't like to mix chocolate and lines," I murmured. I felt Ginger tense up and regretted my words. *Shit*. I wanted to see the guy in front of me as a straight-up dickhead, but really, I was the only one at the table acting like one. "The apple pie looks good though."

I decided to make an effort.

Took a deep breath.

Rubbed my nose.

Tried. Tried.

"Should we share something?" she asked James.

"Sure. Cheesecake sound good?"

"Yeah, for sure." She closed the menu, satisfied.

As we ate dessert, James and Ginger talked and talked about the

Anne Cabot case, the success of the launch, the upcoming catalogue, which she was working on now…

I tried to listen. I really did.

I don't know how long the meal dragged on, but it felt like an eternity. James said goodbye at the door to the restaurant. He had to hurry back to work. He shook my hand firmly. Told me he was happy to meet me after hearing so much about me, and hurried down the street to a taxi stand.

We stuck around a while longer. Five minutes? Ten? Maybe. Just standing there in front of one of those red phone booths you see all over London, watching the traffic pass by on the road. I had a knot in my throat.

"You've gotten some new tattoos…" Her voice was barely a whisper.

I looked at my left hand and moved my fingers. I had a musical note on my ring finger and a little anchor on the back of my hand. I looked up at her. It had never hurt so much, just the mere act of looking at her. I forced myself to breathe, but the air that reached me wasn't enough to bear it.

"What's the anchor mean?" she asked.

"Nothing. I need to go, Ginger."

"Rhys, I'm so sorry about all this…"

Her eyes were full of tears. I just wanted to escape. I couldn't console her. I just couldn't. I had to leave. I had shown up here not knowing what I was looking for, meaning to surprise her, just following an impulse. An impulse named Ginger. And there was nothing here. But that nothing was everywhere, on the island, on every continent, in the lights of every city.

"I'll write you soon, Ginger Snap."

I bent down, kissed her on the cheek—it tasted salty—and walked off down the street. I tried to breathe. Breathe. Breathe. I felt her behind me before her arms surrounded me. And I stopped. And she came around in front of me. Her eyes were red, her lower lip trembling. I could tell she was trying to find the words.

"Promise me you'll take care of yourself."

"What do you mean, Ginger?"

"Just...promise me."

"I'm fine. I'm great."

"That's not true, Rhys. And I can't stand not being able to do anything about it, feeling like it doesn't matter what I say, because all I can do is make you angry at me."

"Look, don't be sorry." I kissed her forehead and brushed her slightly shaggy hair away from her forehead. "Try and be happy, okay? He seems...like a good guy."

She nodded, still crying.

I didn't want to drag the moment on any longer. So I left her there. I walked off, getting lost among all those strangers who seemed to know where they were going, whereas I was adrift as always, wandering, stumbling, running into things, crumbling...

85

From: Ginger Davies
To: Rhys Baker
Subject: Do tell

How's everything going, Rhys? Did you make it back okay? I haven't heard from you again, so I hope so. You never did tell me about your record when you were here; is everything good with that? I suppose it isn't easy to wrap up something like that.

Keep in touch, okay?

From: Rhys Baker
To: Ginger Davies
Subject: RE: Do tell

I've been busy working on it all week. I think things are starting to gel. I don't have much time right now, Ginger. The summer season's started and this year I'm working more nights. Everything okay with you?

From: Ginger Davies
To: Rhys Baker
Subject: Crazy busy

Yeah, everything's good. I'll be working the whole summer too, even though I convinced Kate to take a few weeks off later on so she can go visit her parents back home. We're getting the winter catalogue ready, but we've done a good job planning, and I feel like we're on top of it.

Summer must be super intense there.

From: Ginger Davies
To: Rhys Baker
Subject: Gossip

You won't believe it, Rhys! I'm actually still in shock. The other day, I decided to go home because I didn't feel great, and you know what I found? My sister and Kate kissing on the sofa. FOR REAL. I couldn't have imagined that in a million years. According to Donna, it was obvious Kate leaned that way, since, looking back, she never said anything about being interested in guys, not even when we were in college. But I don't know…it still caught me by surprise. At first, it was uncomfortable, especially because I felt like they'd been hiding it from me, but then I realized they just didn't want to tell me until they knew whether or not it was serious, because they were scared it could mess things up at work.

I'm still trying to process it, but I'm happy. Now I understand why Donna was painting again so enthusiastically this past month and what was going on all those weekends when they kept asking me, all interested, if I was thinking about staying over at James's place.

They're a perfect couple.

From: Rhys Baker
To: Ginger Davies
Subject: RE: Gossip

Sometimes I read some story like that, like Logan's with Sarah or your sister's with Kate, and I almost feel like love could be easy... But I guess it just seems that way. Like in the end there's got to be a trick, a surprise ending or something.

From: Ginger Davies
To: Rhys Baker
Subject: Always

Love should be easy, Rhys.

From: Rhys Baker
To: Ginger Davies
Subject: RE: Always

Is it like that with James?

From: Ginger Davies
To: Rhys Baker

Subject: RE: RE: Always

I think so. I think that's exactly what it's like.

From: Rhys Baker
To: Ginger Davies
Subject: RE: RE: RE: Always

What do you think it would have been like with me?

From: Ginger Davies
To: Rhys Baker
Subject: I can't

Rhys, don't do this. Just don't.
    Don't make things more complicated.

From: Rhys Baker
To: Ginger Davies
Subject: RE: I can't

I didn't know things were complicated.

From: Ginger Davies
To: Rhys Baker
Subject: RE: RE: I can't

Well, they are, because I told James everything. I told him the truth. What happened in the office the day we went to lunch, and what kind of relationship you and I have had these past few years. He didn't take it great, as you can imagine. So I need…a little distance, okay? I need everything to go back to how it always was.

From: Rhys Baker
To: Ginger Davies
Subject: [No subject]

Okay.

From: Ginger Davies
To: Rhys Baker
Subject: Thanks

Thank you, Rhys, really. It's just everything's a little too much for me. Work, my nerves, all these emotions. And I really hope this thing with James works out. I know I'm selfish to be asking you this, but hopefully you can be happy for me. Can you? He's a good guy, Rhys. And we want the same things; we have similar life plans; our dreams are similar… Do you understand what I mean?

I hope you're taking care of yourself too.

Have you talked to your mom lately?

From: Rhys Baker
To: Ginger Davies
Subject: Why?

Why do you ask, Ginger? Yeah, I talk to her every week or two. And I'm taking care of myself. Did I look bad the last time I saw you?

Stop worrying about nothing.

From: Ginger Davies
To: Rhys Baker
Subject: RE: Why?

I just asked because sometimes I have the feeling that that's where the problem comes from. From your parents. It scared me to ask you, because I don't want to force you to talk about it. And you know how grateful I am that you told me you were adopted, and I'm aware of how hard that was for you. But I think you need to reflect on it. Have you ever done that?

From: Rhys Baker
To: Ginger Davies
Subject: RE: RE: Why?

Are you for real, Ginger? I don't have problems. I'm not one of those guys that need saving. Maybe I'm not fucking perfect like James, maybe I don't have my life planned out all the way up to my seventy-third birthday, but I'm fine. I know I have my faults, I accepted that a long time ago, and I realize I can't meet your expectations or be good enough for you. But that has nothing to do with my parents. And like you said, I don't enjoy talking about it, so let's drop it and go on pretending everything's okay.

86

Ginger

IT WAS A FINE NIGHT. We went to the movies to see a flick we'd heard about everywhere—the poster was even plastered all over the bus stops. We shared a medium-sized bucket of popcorn, had lots of laughs, held hands during the tense parts. Then we walked, fingers intertwined, through the city, crossing Hyde Park.

"Have I told you how much I like being with you?" he asked, pulling me close.

I smiled. I could smell the fabric softener on his jacket. Summer had arrived, and every branch on the trees around us was bursting with leaves. I stared into the sky as we walked to the park's exit, and looked at the shimmering moon, which seemed to gaze down at me from above. It's funny how something so simple, something that's always there, can remind you so much of another person. For me, the moon would always be Rhys. Waning, full, shielded by clouds, it always remained, fixed in the heights.

"What are you thinking about?" James's breath tickled my cheeks.

"Nothing. Just how calm the night is."

I didn't want to talk about Rhys, the moon, or anything that even reminded me of him. Not when James had taken it so hard after I told him Rhys wasn't just some friend, that our relationship was full of forks and dead ends. Rhys was acting weird lately, sometimes calling me drunk in the middle of the night, arguing with me in bitter emails. The bitterness was spreading. As much as we were trying to pretend otherwise, things would never be the same after the summer we'd spent together. Those months had been beautiful, more magical than anything I'd ever lived, but they'd also produced new versions of us that didn't fit together as well as before.

"You hungry? Should we grab a bite?"

"Sure. I know a pizzeria close to here."

"Let's do it." He smiled.

We sat down and ordered a pizza with salmon and cream cheese to share, plus a couple of appetizers. He grabbed my hand whenever he had the chance. I liked that. His attentiveness. How he couldn't stop looking at me and didn't bother to hide it. With James, things were simple: no darkened windows I had to try and peek around, no fears, no risks.

"How long have we been going out, Ginger?"

"Why do you ask?" I laughed, because he seemed so serious all of a sudden, staring at me as if there were no one else there.

"No reason. Just wondering..."

"Come on, spit it out!" I was still smiling.

"It's just that, since your sister and Kate are serious now, I was thinking maybe it wouldn't be such a crazy idea if you brought some of your things to my place. After all, you spend almost every weekend there; you've already got a drawer in the dresser..."

My heart was beating fast and hard. I bent over the table.

"Are you asking me to move in with you, James?"

"It's crazy, right? After just a few months…"

"No! No! I mean, no, it's not crazy." But he'd made me nervous. It was too soon, wasn't it, but what the hell? I liked James. I liked the way I felt when I was with him, without tension, without a flood of emotions battering me back and forth. He was sweet. Caring. Attentive. In all the time we'd been seeing each other, we hadn't argued even once. And he was right, I was spending more and more time at his place, which was just ten minutes from my office on the Tube. "It's not like we just met each other, right?"

"That's what I was thinking."

"Sure. It was years ago when we first met at that party, remember? You asked me to tell you a joke in exchange for a beer."

"How could I ever forget that?" He smiled, looking excited. "Then I kissed you on the porch swing right there at my parents' house. I was dying to do it. The same way I'm dying to build a future with you now. Don't you feel like it's fate almost? Not that I believe in that, but…we're looking for the same thing, we have similar goals. Every night when we say goodbye, I wish we didn't have to."

His words moved me. And I thought—I wished, but just for a moment—if only Rhys had known what he was looking for before. Then our paths might have crossed forever, but softly rather than like a collision. With James, it was so easy, so natural to talk about my dreams, my goals, my plans, my future.

And I wanted that. I wanted to move forward. I wanted more.

I looked at our hands, holding each other.

"Let's do it," I whispered.

James smiled and gave me a kiss.

87

From: Rhys Baker
To: Ginger Davies
Subject: Just thinking

I know you told me you were planning on working the whole summer this year, but why don't you take a couple of days off? You're your own boss. You could come here and get some rest. It'll be fun, Ginger. Like last year. But we won't spend all day in bed together like last time, since there's someone in your life or whatever.

Anyway, let me know. I'd like to see you.

From: Ginger Davies
To: Rhys Baker
Subject: RE: Just thinking

I'd like to see you too, but it can't happen. I'm only taking two days off because James asked me to go to his grandmother's birthday party. It's in the suburbs, and his whole family gathers every year to celebrate. We'll probably spend the weekend out there.

From: Rhys Baker
To: Ginger Davies
Subject: RE: RE: Just thinking

Wow. Family gatherings? Weekends in the country? I see this is getting serious. Tell me more. Will you do five o'clock tea? Are they going to teach you to crochet?

From: Ginger Davies
To: Rhys Baker
Subject: RE: RE: RE: Just thinking

If you're trying to be funny, it's not working.

And yes, it's serious. Serious enough that James asked me a few weeks ago to move in with him and I said yes. You may as well know I'd also love to learn to crochet; I'm sure I'd find it fascinating. It's probably super relaxing.

From: Rhys Baker
To: Ginger Davies
Subject: I don't get it

You're going to live with him? Well then...

I guess I should congratulate you? I'm happy for you, Ginger. It seems like you're accomplishing everything you set out to do years ago. I don't understand the rush though. On your part or on James's. But whatever. Good. Great. Everything's great.

Enjoy your weekend in the country.

And give my best to James's grandmother.

From: Rhys Baker
To: Ginger Davies
Subject: I don't get it

Are you back from your little adventure? How was the family gathering? I haven't heard from you in a week. Here everything's the same old same old, nothing really to tell.

From: Ginger Davies
To: Rhys Baker
Subject: I like the country

It was amazing. James's family is so charming! Every single one of them: his sister, his cousins, his parents, his grandmother... I don't know, they just made me feel at home. And I forgot how relaxing it was to spend some time outside the city. I think I want something like that in the future: a house somewhere calm where I can go for vacation. And do nothing, just watch the hours pass, sleep after each meal, read under an apple tree in the shade...

From: Rhys Baker
To: Ginger Davies

Subject: Reflections

Aren't you awful young to be wishing for that?

From: Ginger Davies
To: Rhys Baker
Subject: RE: Reflections

Aren't you a little old to be living the life you're leading?

From: Rhys Baker
To: Ginger Davies
Subject: RE: RE: Reflections

What's that supposed to mean?

From: Ginger Davies
To: Rhys Baker
Subject: RE: RE: RE: Reflections

You know perfectly well, Rhys. You need to hit the brakes sometime, and that's about more than your age. It makes you angry to
hear this, but I get the feeling you're not exactly doing great, that
you're not yourself, and that worries me. Seeing you so cynical.
Almost like someone else.

From: Rhys Baker
To: Ginger Davies

Subject: RE: RE: RE: RE: Reflections

I'm surprised to hear you say that given what your favorite book is. "All grown-ups were once children—although few of them remember it." I have the feeling sometimes that you're no longer the girl who used to press her nose into the window of the pastry shop. And another thing: you don't know me as well as you think, Ginger.

From: Ginger Davies
To: Rhys Baker
Subject: RE: RE: RE: RE: RE: Reflections

You're wrong there, Rhys. Sorry, but I do know you. And I may as well answer your quote with another one: "It is much more difficult to judge oneself than to judge others. If you succeed in judging yourself rightly, then you are indeed a man of true wisdom."

From: Rhys Baker
To: Ginger Davies
Subject: Congratulations!

Happy birthday, Rhys. Thirty. My lord. How time passes. I guess you're still angry at me (this time I don't know why), but I still hope you're having a great day and that you make a nice wish when you blow out the candles.

Kisses (sincerely) and hugs.

88

Ginger

THE PHONE ON THE TABLE vibrated, and I reached out to silence it before James woke up, but I was too late. He turned on the lamp on the nightstand and sat up in bed, rubbing his eyes. He looked tired.

"Who's calling at two in the morning?"

"Sorry. It's Rhys."

"What's he want now?"

"I don't know. Maybe something's up."

James rolled his eyes just as the phone lit up and started vibrating again. I took a deep breath, got up, tied my robe, and answered, walking downstairs from the bedroom to the kitchen. It was already starting to fill up with boxes of my things.

"Rhys, are you okay?" I sat on the windowsill. Outside, the moon shone over the treetops. "Can you hear me?" Music was blasting on the other end of the line.

"Hey, Ginger Snap!" he shouted in a nasal voice.

"It's two in the morning; I hope you've got a good excuse for this."

"I love you. That should be enough, right?" I could hear his distorted laughter, cutting off every time he moved the phone. "Ginger, Ginger..."

That was the first time he'd ever said it to me. *I love you.* Just like that. No runaround. It should have been nice, but instead it was almost sad. I could feel my eyes burn. I thought of what I'd whispered in his ear that night when I told him I was in love with him and that he shined so bright he made everything else vanish. That had been true, but as the months passed, it was less and less so. The guy now yelling over the phone wasn't the same Rhys I'd admired so much.

"You can't do this." I was shaking.

"You're my birthday present though. I was remembering what last year on this day was like. You remember too, don't you?"

"Rhys, I'm hanging up."

My tears were dripping over my knuckles.

And my knuckles were white from clutching the phone.

And my heart was shriveling as it heard his words.

"We had dinner outside, and you hugged me in the middle of the street—I still walk that street sometimes when I feel lonely—and you told me you were in love with me."

"Rhys, stop, please..."

"And then we went back to the apartment and fucked."

"You need to go home."

"But the party just started..."

"Not for you. That much I can tell."

"Ginger, you ought to be here." He pulled the phone away from his ear a second to shout to the waiter to bring him another drink.

"We'd have fun. Enjoy ourselves. No worries, no plans. The way things ought to be. You and me versus the world."

"Rhys, you're getting out of control."

"I miss you, Ginger..."

"You need to stop." I struggled to maintain my serenity, pinched the bridge of my nose, sighed. "How can you not realize it? I've got to go."

He said something else too, but I hung up and turned my phone off before sobbing into my hand. If only I could have pretended he didn't affect me. Or that I didn't feel anything for him anymore. Or that I could just go on without him. But none of that was true. It was devastating. Like trying to walk one way while he was pulling me back toward the place I'd decided to leave behind. I couldn't go that fast. I couldn't keep looking ahead like that. I couldn't watch him fall. And everything was about to change.

Now... I couldn't let myself hesitate.

I went back to bed a little while later. I hugged James. I knew he would be awake. He rubbed my shoulders. It was comforting, that calm, that stability.

"Things can't go on like this, Ginger."

"I know. I'll take care of it."

"Okay. Get some rest then."

89

From: Ginger Davies

To: Rhys Baker

Subject: I'm so sorry

I don't know how to start this message. I don't know if the right words exist to tell you what I have to say. And maybe I'm making the biggest mistake of my life. Maybe in a few years, I'll look back and regret it…but I can't go on like this. I just can't. I will always love you, but at the moment, I need a little space. Or more. I need us not to talk to each other for a while.

You can't go on being my priority, even if I allowed it in the past. Sometimes I feel like I lost you a long time ago, when I left last summer. Ever since then, I've been trying to make things go back to the way they were, avoiding the subjects I know we always argue over, pretending everything's cool between us… but it's not true. Nothing's cool.

And now everything's changed…

I'm pregnant, Rhys.

James and I are expecting a baby.

I've been writing and erasing and rewriting this email for days. Because I know when I send it, I'll lose a part of myself. An important one. My best friend. But I think, even if you can't understand it right now, that I'm doing us both a favor. Because you can never move forward if you're constantly looking back, and I can't let myself harbor doubts right now, because this baby…knowing it exists, knowing it's growing inside me, is the most beautiful thing that's ever happened to me…

I hope one day you can forgive me.

And I hope you take care of yourself. And find yourself.

I love you, Rhys. So much.

Part 6

—

"A sheep—if it eats little bushes, does it eat flowers too?"

The Little Prince

Part 6

90

From: Rhys Baker

To: Ginger Davies

Subject: Even if you don't read this

I know it's been months since you've read an email from me, but I still wanted to write you. Maybe you do read my messages. Maybe my emails don't go straight to spam the way my calls go straight to voicemail. Ginger, I know I fucked up, I do, but I miss you. I've fucked up lots of times, honestly. It scares me to think of all the times you've forgiven me over the years.

You were the best thing in my life.

From: Rhys Baker

To: Ginger Davies

Subject: Even if you don't read this

What's up, Ginger? Are you still mad? Hasn't enough time passed? That's what you said, that you needed some time. Well, let's go. Everything can go back to how it was now. And I'm happy... Honestly, I'm happy to hear about the baby. For you. I know you wanted that. How far along are you? Five months, six?

My album came out this week, and I'm... I don't know what I'm feeling. Fucked up. Euphoric. Honestly, it's the same euphoria as when I'm high. But whatever. Ginger, who am I supposed to talk to about the things that really matter if you aren't here?

From: Rhys Baker
To: Ginger Davies
Subject: Even if you don't read this

Happy birthday, Ginger Snap. I hope you're well.

From: Rhys Baker
To: Ginger Davies
Subject: Even if you don't read this

Honestly, though, it's still hard for me to believe you're going to be a mother. It's strange to imagine. At the same time, I can just see you holding a baby in your arms and leaning your cheek against his (or hers), and the picture is almost real.

From: Rhys Baker
To: Ginger Davies
Subject: Even if you don't read this

How's your new year? Good, I guess. Probably you've got a

huge belly and you're smiling. I can't stop thinking about it, Ginger. I can't. It's not because I'm drunk right now; it's because I hit a wall months ago, and I still haven't gotten better. Everything's so crazy. There was a moment when I wished the baby was mine. I keep seeing pregnant women on the street—have they always been there? Were there so many huge bellies before? I don't remember that. And children. Children crying everywhere. I don't know, Ginger. Maybe I need another drink. What if I've been wrong my whole life? What if I still have no fucking idea who I am, what I'm looking for, or what I want? I'm tired of feeling like this. So tired.

From: Rhys Baker
To: Ginger Davies
Subject: Even if you don't read this

Do you realize we missed our friendiversary? I remember the first time I read that word. I thought it was funny. You've always been the funniest girl I knew, even when you aren't trying. I hope everything's okay.

From: Rhys Baker
To: Ginger Davies
Subject: Even if you don't read this

Did you listen to the album? I like to think you have, because it's playing everywhere. Ginger, I think everyone I've ever met in my thirty years of life has gotten in touch with me, even people

I went to preschool with, except you. What's up? Why can't you give me a sign that you're alive, at least? It's been almost a year. A fucking year, Ginger. It's torture. I've got the urge to just show up at your office. I reread your email a million times. Time, you said. You need some time not talking to me. I thought that meant a few months. I don't know what it is you want, Ginger. But give me another chance. I promise I won't fuck it up. I'll even be friends with James if that will make you happy.

I want to meet your baby. It kills me when I think you've had it, and I don't even know its name, even though you're the most important person in my life. How did we let all this happen? When did everything we'd shared stop being enough?

From: Rhys Baker
To: Ginger Davies
Subject: Even if you don't read this

Sometimes I don't know if I love you or hate you. I just don't know. I try to forget you, the months pass, and right when I think I've done it, I think of you again. Just because. Some memory returns. And it's like starting from zero.

From: Rhys Baker
To: Ginger Davies
Subject: Even if you don't read this

In case you were wondering, my birthday was crazy. I got a house in a fancy neighborhood in Ibiza. You should see it. It has glass walls, and you can see the sunset from the sofa while you're having your beer. We decided to throw a party. I don't know how many people showed up. Dozens, a hundred people maybe, or maybe more. I have lots of friends here now. I guess I needed to find a substitute for you. My birthday last year sucked, and I didn't want a repeat this year. Remember the first present you gave me, late, when I turned twenty-seven? I do. I almost tossed it in the trash the other day. Your favorite book. *The Little Prince*. You wrote in the front:

For Rhys, the boy I share my apartment on the moon with, because "he was only a fox like a hundred thousand other foxes. But I have made him my friend, and now he is unique in all the world."

I guess at some point I stopped being a fox like all the other foxes, and so did you. That's how things go, right? People are important for a time, even essential, and then one day they up and disappear into nothing. Friendships are volatile, I guess.

91

Ginger

I LOOKED AWAY FROM THE red light and into the interior of my windshield. It was raining buckets, and the wipers were straining back and forth, *tic, tac, tic, tac*, in a simple monotonous rhythm. Just like all those people crossing the street on this ordinary street in North Harrow. A dance of open umbrellas amid the screech of tires and the gurgling of gutters. I asked myself what their lives must be like. Were they happy? Had they lived their dreams, or were they the type who'd decided that giving your dreams up was what truly freed you? Had they fallen madly in love? I let go of the wheel when I felt the damp on my cheeks and looked for a tissue.

I took a deep breath, trying to shrug off the disappointment.

I had the feeling I was spending my days rowing against the current. And I was tired. My muscles were throbbing from the effort. My heart was cold from asking him so many times to *be reasonable*, and for once, just once, I needed to listen to the voice echoing in my head. It couldn't be that hard.

I shivered when the radio announcer named the upcoming song and the first notes played. Rhys. All of him reflected in the sound.

I couldn't get away from it, no matter how much I tried; it was everywhere. I turned off the radio when the cars behind me started honking. The light had turned green. I blew my nose and stomped the accelerator.

92

Rhys

I DIDN'T REMEMBER THEIR NAMES, but they were pretty, nice, and happy to keep me company for a night. Two girls, one on either side of me in the booth, laughing at something or other as one of them stroked my thigh, getting dangerously close to my zipper. The other one told me she wanted a drink.

I took a deep breath, a little confused. I don't know what I'd taken that night, but it was making me see everything blurry and sometimes double. I took out my wallet and dropped a couple of bills on the table. As I was closing it, I noticed a photo sticking out a little bit. I grabbed it, tried to focus, tried…to concentrate on the moment. On Ginger's face next to mine in the photo booth. Her dazzling smile. So pretty. Prettier than anyone else's in the world. Lower down, our lips together. Goddammit. I couldn't even remember what it was like to kiss her, what it was like to be inside her. How long ago was that? Almost three years? Maybe. And the memories were growing vaguer, as if the color was draining out of them.

I put the photo back in my wallet as I felt unknown lips on my neck, going up my jaw, finding my mouth, seductive, tasting of gin. I let myself go, the way I always did now.

Especially this past month.

Since the news came…

From: Rhys Baker

To: Ginger Davies

Subject: Even if you don't read this

My father's sick. Cancer. He's started chemo, at least that's what my mom said the last time we talked. Can you believe it? Him. Of all people. Maybe you don't understand what I mean, but you would if you knew him. He's the kind of guy nothing ever affects. Proud. Serious. Smart. He graduated from Harvard with honors, just like my grandfather, my great-grandfather, and who knows how many generations before. The Bakers have gone there since it was founded, until I broke the tradition. He's an imposing man. Remember when you told me you were glad Kate was going to help out at the publisher because you'd pee yourself in meetings? Well, my dad's one of those guys who terrifies the people he negotiates with. He's six-three, he is always in good shape as I remember, and when he shakes a guy's hand, he squeezes hard and lets them know he's no one to play with. He's got presence, you know?

And he seemed invincible. What a word, right? *Invincible.*
Why do they even have that word in the dictionary? Is there
anything it actually applies to? I doubt it. Everything dies, everything's dust, everything gets forgotten in time. Nothing remains,
nothing triumphs.

From: Rhys Baker
To: Ginger Davies
Subject: Even if you don't read this

I don't even know what I'm feeling, Ginger. And you're not here
to scream at me all the truths no one else dares to utter. I don't
know, I can't get this fucking feeling out of my chest, this pressure… There are nights when I feel like I'm going to drown. I'm
not myself. Or maybe I am, more than ever. I don't know, that's
the problem. If at some point I thought I'd managed to get to
know myself, that I had answers to all the questions I'd been
asking myself, well… I was wrong. And the more I think about
that, the worse I feel.

It's like being lost and alone on an asteroid no one's ever
heard of, at some point of the galaxy beyond exploration, far
from any other human being.

From: Rhys Baker
To: Ginger Davies
Subject: Even if you don't read this

There's no way you're reading this, right, Ginger? There's no way you're actually reading this and closing every message when you're done. That's not you. It never has been. At times, I wanted to think so, especially at first, when you said you needed time... I know now that meant something else. That you needed to be away from me entirely. And I get it. It makes sense. I guess if I hadn't fucked everything up, you'd still be there on the other side of the screen. You know I imagine you sometimes? I see a girl with a baby carriage, and I imagine you walking next to James or at the publisher or getting home each night, making dinner, laughing, having a glass of white wine, lying on the sofa at the end of the day, reading something, and then getting in bed with him.

When I see all this, I realize I screwed up. But you can't go back in time and take your knowledge from the present with you, right? Because if you could, it would all be so fucking much easier... So many things would change. Things about you. Or the day I argued with my father. It's funny. How a few words or an apparently meaningless decision can turn your entire life upside down... We should be terrified to even walk through the world, knowing we're hanging by such a thin thread. You lose your balance for a second, just one, and you fall flat on the ground. I'm rambling. But I guess it doesn't matter, since I doubt anyone's even reading this fucking message.

From: Rhys Baker
To: Ginger Davies
Subject: Even if you don't read this

They want me to put out another album soon. I said yes. I didn't feel anything at all. No joy, no excitement. I'm not sure if the problem's me. But it usually is.

I think this is something else I'd change if I could go back.

I'd like to create, compose, but for others maybe, instead of for me. You always knew that, right? That I'd find that truly fulfilling, that those were the moments when I was happy, shutting myself up in the studio and forgetting to even eat.

But everything's different now.

It feels like it has been for a long time.

From: Rhys Baker

To: Ginger Davies

Subject: Even if you don't read this

Happy birthday, Ginger Snap.

And Merry Christmas.

From: Rhys Baker

To: Ginger Davies

Subject: Even if you don't read this

What are you doing right now, Ginger?

Without you, our friendiversary's not too thrilling.

Even the word's not as funny as it used to be.

From: Rhys Baker

To: Ginger Davies

Subject: Even if you don't read this

I'm going to tell you a secret. You were right. I hurt people every time I feel attacked, every time something hurts me. It's the only way I know how to react. It's like something pokes me and I leap up in a blind fury. I'm selfish. Proud. Too proud. Not with you, with you I learned to say sorry, because I was so scared of losing you.

But it didn't matter in the end. I suppose just repeating "I'm sorry" over and over can't change things. A mistake is still a mistake.

From: Rhys Baker
To: Ginger Davies
Subject: Even if you don't read this

My father's dying.

94

Rhys

I MOVED HEAVEN AND EARTH to get that number. I dialed it and walked back and forth in the living room of my home in Ibiza, staring at the sea. The morning sun glowed through the windows and reflected off the water of the pool in the garden. The place was idyllic, perfect, but never in my life had I felt so alone, even surrounded by all those people: new friends who idolized me, girls I didn't even have to try with, hangers-on who didn't know me...

I turned back around when I heard someone pick up.

"Yeah?" a hoarse voice said.

"Axel Nguyen?" I asked.

"Yeah. Who am I speaking with?"

"Rhys Baker. I don't know if you remember me. I was living in Byron Bay a few years ago, and you did the illustration for a single that..."

"I know who you are. Long time, no hear."

"I need to talk to you about a couple of things."

"It's a good time. Shoot."

"The first thing's a proposal; the second's a favor." I bit my thumb, uncertain, knowing what I had in mind was crazy.

He giggled. "A proposal sounds better than a favor. Let's start with that."

"I've got another album coming out soon. I don't know if you know, but things have gone well for me since my single came out. Very well, in fact. I've been talking with the producer, and we want you to do the cover. I have something pretty clear in mind. I can pay. Just name your price if you're up for it."

"Sounds promising. What's the favor?"

I ran my hand through my hair and took a breath. "Remember where I used to live? On the same road as you, which leads out of town. House number fourteen. I was renting there. Well, I left something. I mean, after I left, a package arrived, and I never got it."

"You're kidding, right? You want me to go look for it?"

"I'd like you to go to that house, ring the doorbell, and if anyone's living there, ask them about it, in case whoever came after me got it…"

Silence. A pause. He was thinking, I supposed. "What's in the package?"

"I don't know."

"What do you mean, you don't know?"

"It was a birthday present."

"Why's it so important after all these years?"

"Axel, shit…" I was losing my patience. "It was a birthday gift, okay? From a girl. Someone special. When I met you to talk about the cover, you told me something. You said…we all have an anchor, maybe a person, maybe a place, maybe something else. Well, she's my anchor."

Axel sighed and dug his finger into the wound. "You can't ask the girl who gave it to you?"

"I didn't understand until it was too late."

"I'll go look for it. I'll give you a call in a couple of days."

He hung up. I stood there a few seconds longer clutching the phone to my ear, the sun soaking that empty living room, and I felt paralyzed when I saw my mom had called while I was talking, and I wasn't sure I could call back. I took a deep breath. Tried to calm down. I really did.

I turned on the stereo and heard "Without You." I lay on the wooden floor, feeling my chest rising and falling with every breath. After that came "Levels," and then "Something Like This." Every song took me away from the noise, from myself.

95

Ginger

I DROPPED THE MANUSCRIPT I was reading on the night-stand and took off the glasses I had started using a few months ago, especially toward the end of the day. For a few seconds, the silence in the room closed in on me. Then, for no reason, as I'd done many times before, I looked at my laptop in its case, resting against the feet of the nightstand. It would be so easy to reach out, open it, set it on my knees as I had for years, open the folder I'd forwarded all his messages to... I curled up and lay down. Sighed. Resisted temptation. I couldn't go back. Not now, with everything hanging by a thread and me having no idea where my life was going. Not when I knew that he was still walking a straight line in the opposite direction, putting more and more distance between us. I had seen him. He was unavoidable. All I had to do was search for his name and look at all the results, photos of him at festivals, songs...

And yet still I fantasized that there was something left of that guy named Rhys who I had met one winter night in Paris and danced with by the Seine before eating cup noodles in his attic.

But that's all it was: a fantasy.

96

Rhys

THE NEW OWNERS GOT THE package while they were moving in. They didn't know anyone named Ginger Davies, but they unwrapped it anyway, cut the ribbons, tore the tape, opened the box. After looking at the gift with a shrug, they gave it to their little daughter, but she was grown up now and wouldn't miss it.

When I got the parcel from Axel, I waited a while before opening it. My head hurt. The day before, I found myself standing between two cars and vomiting, right there in the street, with Alec laughing beside me. We were both high on the same shit. A few hours later, I still hadn't slept, my whole body ached, and I couldn't get the bitter taste of cocaine off my tongue.

I hated opening the thing when I felt so out of it, but I did.

It was another book. *Peter Pan.* Illustrated, the edges of the pages gold, hardcover. I could feel the ink of the letters when I ran my hand over the cover. I did this a few times, then opened it, and froze when I recognized her handwriting.

For the boy who doesn't need wings to fly to the moon.

I slammed it shut and poured myself a drink.

97

From: Rhys Baker
To: Ginger Davies
Subject: Even if you don't read this

He's going to die. There's no way forward. And I'm paralyzed.
I shouldn't still love him so much, should I? I shouldn't. Not
after everything he said. Those words still hurt. That was one of
the hardest moments of my life, coming back after leaving my
mother when I found out I was adopted, even though that was
the moment she needed me most. I came back, and he…he
told me: *Obviously some things run in the blood.* I hated him. I
don't know how to explain how badly that hurt me, at a moment
when I felt more lost than ever, not knowing who I was or where I
came from. And there was more. He told me he'd never wanted
to adopt, that he only agreed to because my mother couldn't
have kids and he couldn't stand seeing her so alone. We came
to blows. He was the person I loved most in the world, even
more than her, but in one second, it all crumbled. It just went to

shit. All those days I waited for him by the door just to see him come home from work. The way I always used to try to imitate him. Sundays, trying to impress him. The hours we spent putting together all those goddamn models…

I realized in that moment that my whole life, my whole childhood, was a lie. I've thought it over many, many times as the years have passed…and I can't believe he was just that good a faker. I can't. Because he was a good father. Proud, sure. We had that in common. But still…for a long time, it hurt me even to talk about him. My mother told me at some point he wanted to see me, just to clear things up, but I couldn't, Ginger. I feel like with him I just turn back into a boy incapable of protecting himself.

I don't know… I can't even think.

I wish I could explain myself better.

But you're not even going to read this.

I always knew I'd make the same mistakes as him if I became a father. Pride. Wounding others because I couldn't stand to be hurt myself. Not being able to untangle my emotions. That's why I could never see him again, even though he asked me to. He told my mother he wants me to come home, Ginger. To say goodbye to him. And I'm not ready. To see him, to accept that he's going to die. I can't, after all this time. Because it still hurts.

Goddammit. I need another drink. Just one more.

From: Rhys Baker
To: Ginger Davies
Subject: Even if you don't read this

I understood today, Ginger. All at once, like one of those revelations that comes to you when you least expect it. I was lying on the sofa. Not lying—splayed out. In the same position I flopped down in. I was looking at the ceiling as the sun rose on the other side of the window, and everything was spinning around me. I was trying to decide whether to have another drink or puke. And then it hit me. I'm the rose.

I never was the Little Prince or the narrator, and definitely not the fox. No. I was the fucking rose. Fickle, selfish, proud, full of thorns. And you spent years watering me and caring for me even though sometimes I pricked you when you got too close. And you don't know how much I regret it, Ginger. I'm sorry I hurt you, and I'm sorry I hurt myself. I'm sorry I didn't know how to do things differently. I'm sorry I'm a disaster. If you ever read this, I want you to know I understand why you had to get away from me when you realized the world was full of rosebushes full of flowers and that actually I was never special.

98

Rhys

A PERSON GETS USED TO being lost. It's like wandering through space, floating in the void. At first it upsets you, you scramble to find solid ground, to find yourself, but at some point the vertigo goes away and you think, *Well, it's not so bad living in the immense dark emptiness.* You can close your eyes, forget what it felt like to be anchored to something, to someone, to the world.

You can simply stop being.

99

Ginger

I MANAGED TO GET MY phone out of my gigantic bag, almost juggling it. I picked up as I was pushing aside the curtains of the old kitchen, done in a very charming vintage style. I looked out onto St. Ives Bay just as the unknown voice uttered something in Spanish, in loose phrases, a bit of which I was able to grasp:

"Es usted familiar de Rhys Baker?"

"Excuse me? Are you asking…"

"Espere un momento."

"Hello?" I looked at the phone.

A second later, another voice came on. "Am I speaking with Ginger Davies?"

"Yes. Who is this?"

I had a bad feeling as I heard the woman draw in a breath, speaking English with a strong Spanish accent in a neutral but delicate tone…

"The patient had you in his phone as his emergency contact. He's at Can Misses Hospital. He fell into an alcoholic coma."

I gripped the wooden counter, feeling my legs shake. My

heart... I felt him in my heart. It was beating strong, loud, erratically.

My heart...always making decisions for me.

Always betraying my efforts to forget.

"Is he okay?"

"He's stable."

"I'll come as soon as I can."

Part 7

—

HOPE. LIFE. PROMISES.

"It is the time you have wasted for your rose
that makes your rose so important."

The Little Prince

100

—

Ginger

I DON'T KNOW HOW I managed to get to his room. I was trembling. I couldn't even hear anything over my heartbeat. I took a few steps nervously. I had a knot in my throat.

I saw him. He was lying in bed. Awake. His eyes turned away from the window and toward me. He hadn't been expecting me. His jaw tensed. His shoulders turned rigid. His chest rose as he took a breath. And then...then...it was as if the two years apart had vanished in the blink of an eye. I dropped my purse on the ground, ran toward him, and hugged him in tears. We said nothing. We just held each other. I let his scent envelop me, the scent that was still familiar, the warm skin of his neck against my cheek.

"I can't believe you're here..."

"Why wouldn't I be?"

"I don't know... I really don't..."

"They called me," I told him.

I stood back to look at him. He was confused. His brow was furrowed, his lips dry, his face thinner since the last time we'd seen each other. I ran a hand over his forehead, pushing aside a few locks of hair. He stared at me, uncertain, trying to tell himself I really was there, that this was real, that I had taken the first flight out for him.

"Ginger..." He grabbed my wrist.

"Don't worry. I'm not going anywhere."

"Okay." He took a deep breath.

"I can't stay for too long though. I left Leon in reception. The nurse told me the doctor will be by soon, and they'll let you go. And I'll be waiting for you downstairs."

"Leon?" he asked in barely a whisper.

"My son, Rhys."

"Leon..." He slowly savored the name.

I stroked his hair again, hoping he wouldn't notice how I was trembling. All I could think of as I looked at him was that there were emotions more powerful than a loaded weapon.

"Rhys, do you get it?"

He nodded, but he wasn't sure and seemed a little disconcerted. I bent over, kissed his cheek, and walked out. Only then did I close my eyes. I sat down for a few seconds in one of the chairs further down the hall, near the elevators. I was exhausted. Seeing him had been almost too much to take. All those feelings I'd kept dormant, covered in dust, in the back of a drawer, had exploded into the air. I could feel them all returning as his eyes stared through me. And yet I wasn't sure what they were. Joy? Bitterness? Insecurity? In that hospital bed, Rhys seemed like the same man as always, serene, his looks unchanged, but I wasn't sure if he really was the same person who had written me for years, who had been my best friend, the guy I fell in and out of love with, who made everything shine brighter and then decided to destroy everything. The guy who, despite all that, had meant enough to me that I hadn't hesitated to catch a flight to Ibiza with a one-year-old child, even with everything it had involved. I hadn't needed a second to decide. Nothing.

And that was scary too.

101

Rhys

I WAS MOVED WHEN I saw her, but I managed to wait until the doctor came to discharge me. More than an hour had passed, and the whole time, I asked myself whether this was real or whether I was still high and dreaming. It seemed real though. Her hair was different, with highlights, and something in the way she touched me told me this couldn't just be a fantasy.

And then there was that name. *Leon.*

Maybe that was what made me throw on my clothes so fast, grab my things, sign my papers as quickly as I could. Even if I still felt like I'd been hit by a truck, I wanted to see her again, wanted to see them, and I ran down the stairs, too impatient to wait for the elevator. When I got outside, the early summer sun was glowing high in the cloudless sky. I half closed my eyes.

I saw them from far off. Ginger was sitting on a bench under the shade of a tree a few yards away. I was nailed to the spot for a second, watching the baby she held on her knees try to pull her hair before she managed to catch his little hands. She was smiling. I gathered my courage and walked over, taking one step after another, feeling guided along, unable to take my eyes off of her.

Ginger stood when she saw me.

"You're out," she said nervously.

"Yeah." I looked at the child, and he looked at me. His eyes were brown, his lashes long, his skin so white I was afraid the sun would burn him. He smiled and flapped his hand, trying to reach me. "Hey, Leon."

He laughed. I thought of how nice it would be to have a life like that, with your mother's arms around you, without worries, without fears, without burdens. He seemed so happy...

"We should go, Rhys. I should have fed him already. Do you live far from here? I rented a car at the airport; I needed it to bring the carriage."

"Sure. Let's go. We're not far."

The trip was strange. Strange because I still felt so calm next to Ginger, as if there never had been any distance, like that first night in Paris when I had that weird feeling I'd known her all my life even though we'd just met. There was something deep there. Something between us that remained intact despite all we'd done, all that had been destroyed in those years of comings and goings, falling into and out of love, all those things. When I looked at her profile, gripping the wheel, complaining about having to drive on the wrong side of the road, I couldn't figure out what it was I felt.

There was also something new there under that strange sensation of normality on the surface. The soft gurgling from the back seat, which lasted until Leon fell asleep, just before we reached my home. I kept looking at him in the rearview mirror, turning sometimes, curious, distracted, unnerved. Even when we were in the living room and I was showing her around, I kept checking on him. Ginger left the carriage next to the beige sofa. After she saw the place, she smiled.

"Things are obviously going well for you."

"You didn't know...?" I tried.

"I did. I knew something. Or more than that. I tried to avoid it. But you were on the radio at all hours, you know, especially a few months back, and... I don't know, Rhys."

After a pause, I asked, "Why'd you try to avoid it?"

"You know. It wasn't easy."

Then I dared to ask the question I'd wanted to ask since I first saw her, the same one I was scared to ask but had to know the answer to.

"Does James know you're here?"

Looking away, she responded: "Yeah. I told him when I got here."

"Not when you left?"

"We were on vacation in St. Ives. Leon and me. Just the two of us." She rubbed her arms and looked over at the carriage where the little boy was sleeping, then back at me. "It didn't work. We tried, but..." Her voice cracked.

I came closer and held her. She was still so small in my arms. And yet she was a million times stronger than me. We had taken different roads. She'd moved on; I'd moved backward. She'd grown; I'd gotten lost.

"Easy," I whispered.

"You shouldn't be the one consoling me in this situation." I wanted to keep holding her, but she made some space. Now that she was back, she was here, I couldn't stand the idea of her leaving again. "I should be mad at you, Rhys. I was on my way to the airport. I wanted to wring your neck. Scream at you... But then I read your messages. I'm so sorry."

"Ginger..."

"I'm sorry about your father. About everything."

"It's not your fault."

"I'm sorry I was such a bad friend. The worst friend in the world. That is my fault. But it was a bad time. I didn't feel ready to reach out to you again, and as the months passed, it just got more and more complicated."

I squeezed the bridge of my nose between two fingers. "We should get some rest and then catch up. I'm going to take a shower while you feed him, and then, I don't know, we can grab dinner or something."

She nodded, nibbling her lower lip, and I tried not to watch her too long. Before she could wake her baby, I grabbed her wrist and pulled her close, almost touching—close, the way we'd always been, despite all those miles, despite the obstacles. "That fucked me up. You not talking to me fucked me up bad. But I understand. I'd have understood if you hadn't caught the plane. I don't deserve having you here."

"Don't say that."

"You were right."

"Rhys..."

"I lost control."

She shook her hand and rested a hand on my chest. It was warm. And it brought me peace. "Everything that's lost can be found."

"But it's the searching that's so hard for me."

She smiled. Gorgeous. The same smile that had lingered in my memory for so long. I wanted to stare into it forever, but I turned and walked up the white marble staircase instead. Once in the shower, hot water flowing over my face, surrounded by mist, I felt less dirty, less contaminated. The echoes of that night of music and shadows that had taken me to the limit faded away with the realization that Ginger was just a few feet away. So close, and yet so far...

102

Ginger

IT WAS HARD TO FIND a simple little spoon in that modern minimalist kitchen. It didn't even have handles on the drawers. It seemed like it had never been used. Holding Leon in my arms and feeding him a late lunch, I looked at the high ceilings, the impersonal furnishings. I'd never have thought such a house could belong to Rhys. I'd known him as a person who could live anywhere in the world: in a wooden bouse by the ocean in Australia, which he must have adored; in an attic in Paris with a view of the moon; in an apartment in Ibiza, simple, but nice and comfortable. But where he lived now, this house…it was for someone else.

It terrified me to think that he had changed. Too much, maybe. That the way I'd trembled when we touched wasn't enough. That we couldn't just pretend those two years had never happened. And that even so, I still loved him in an irrational, crazy way I couldn't understand…

I looked at the shelf near the TV, full of books. I knew all of them well. I could recognize them by the spines. They were the ones I'd published those past two years. Organized in order of publication.

Without a speck of dust. Well cared for, proudly displayed, and they made me blink as I tried to suppress my tears, imagining him buying them every month.

I remembered his emails. The ones I'd read waiting to take off, with Leon sleeping in my arms. In those messages...he was him. Completely. Anxious, lost, angry at times, insecure at others, destroyed, sensitive, open, depressed.

Rhys. Just Rhys. No filters. No armor.

103

Rhys

MY HAIR WAS STILL WET when I walked downstairs in gray sweatpants and a T-shirt. Ginger looked up and smiled at me, nervous.

"You mind if I shower too?"

"No, go ahead. I'll keep an eye on him."

She kissed Leon on the forehead. He was still in the carriage. Then she grabbed her handbag and went upstairs. I sat on the sofa in the same room where I'd spent the past year and a half, but now everything felt different. Fuller. Warmer. Leon looked at me, and I looked at him. I took a deep breath. I wasn't sure what to do with a baby. This was the closest I could remember being to one. I jiggled one of the toys hanging down over his head, and he laughed, moving his arms, trying to grab it. I pulled it away a little, and he reached higher. Maybe this wasn't so hard. Maybe we could get to know each other, like each other, even if I had no idea how.

I thought that, at least, until he started crying.

At first, it was just pouting. His lips crinkled and he moaned, but then he closed his eyes, clenched his fists, and shouted so loud he scared me.

"Hey, Leon, look." I shook his rattle.

He didn't care. And he didn't like the funny faces I made either.

"Shit. No, fuck, I shouldn't have said that." I bit my lip. "Hopefully the thing about your brain being like a sponge is just a myth. Wait a second."

I hurried upstairs and knocked on the bathroom door. I heard Ginger turn off the water and couldn't help but imagine her naked. That still stung me. My lust. My desire.

"Rhys? What's up?"

"Leon won't stop crying. Can you hurry?"

"Pick him up. He loves to be carried around."

"I can't do that!"

"Rhys, I've got shampoo all in my hair. Just do it. You bend over, take him out of the carriage, and sit on the couch. It's easy. He'll stop crying, I promise."

I ground my teeth as I walked off. He was still crying downstairs, his eyes humid. He was a sly little boy. I could tell he was trying to arouse my sympathy. I picked him up and held him to my chest. I was scared of everything: him falling, me holding him too tight, just everything. I walked him close to the window, and he was hypnotized as he looked at the pool as the sun glimmered on the surface of the water. When he got tired of it, I sat on the sofa with him in my lap, and he stretched out, relaxed.

He grabbed the pacifier hanging around his neck and put it in his mouth himself. I smiled. We stared at each other a while. And in that instant, there alone, observing each other in silence, him sucking on his pacifier, me cradling him, I remembered the message I'd written Ginger a year ago. She'd probably just read it that very same day. I told her in it that I sometimes wished the baby she was expecting was mine. That I wished everything had been different, as if it was a parallel reality. Later I thought I'd lost my mind in that moment, but if I had…then I was losing it again.

I reached out with my free hand and rubbed his cheek. He didn't react—he went on staring at me as before. I wondered what it would be like to live like that, blindly trusting in any stranger who just came along and picked you up, so relaxed I could fall asleep without fear or terror, without a head full of doubt, without all those threads getting twisted up and complicating things as I grew.

"You all right?" Ginger asked.

I stopped rubbing his cheek and looked away. She approached uncertainly but smiled when she saw Leon had fallen asleep. She sat beside me on the sofa. The two of us here, as if it was the most natural thing in the world, almost like a routine. I expelled a breath I didn't realize I'd been holding in.

"Yeah, he calmed right down."

"I told you. All he wants is to be held. I've spoiled him." She reached over. "You want to hand him off to me? He won't even notice."

"No, he's fine."

I relaxed, leaning back into the sofa. Ginger did too, pulling her legs up beneath her and resting her head on my shoulder. I don't know how long the three of us stayed like that. Just breathing. In silence. Without saying a word. But it was perfect. It was what I needed to start to process everything, to comprehend what I'd done the other night, all that I could have lost, how Ginger and her life had changed… We were no longer the people we'd been. But it didn't matter. It wasn't worse; it was just different. A newness within that familiar feeling that surrounded me when she was near.

104

—

Ginger

WE MADE DINNER NOT LONG after putting Leon down in the guest bedroom, pushing the bed against the wall. It was a simple meal: spaghetti with sauce from a jar. When I kept bugging him, Rhys finally admitted with a laugh that he'd barely even used his kitchen.

"All this is just…" I looked around.

"What?" he asked, sitting down.

"It's just not you. I don't like it."

"Yeah." He sighed and twirled his noodles around his fork.

We didn't talk about anything that mattered during dinner. I just told him stuff about Leon: that he'd be starting day care soon; that he'd already taken his first steps (with a bit of help), but that he still preferred crawling and dragging himself around; that he was in love with Donna and a stuffed elephant he always slept with… Rhys smiled, eyes glistening, as he listened and asked questions.

I don't know which of us said we should go out to the yard after dinner. We lay on the damp grass by the pool under a tree with twisted branches, a mimosa, maybe. Rhys had his arms folded behind his head and was staring into the dark sky while our bare feet touched.

Crickets could be heard in the background. I realized that, for the first time since we saw each other at the hospital, silence wasn't enough.

"What happened to you, Rhys?"

"I don't know. I'm sorry."

Continuing despite my fears, I asked, "Did you want to end it all?"

"No. Jesus, Ginger, no."

He turned to me. His eyes were bright, nervous, staring straight into mine. He looked surprised by my question, but I hadn't been able to suppress it after reading all those messages in one go and seeing him so lost, like a little boy.

Because that's what he was. In some way, Rhys still had a child's soul. Despite the darkness in him. Despite the way he glowed. Despite how together he seemed to the people who didn't know him. A Peter Pan in Never Never Land. A Little Prince on his asteroid. I could see what was missing in him, his weaknesses, his fear of confronting his father.

"Things just got out of hand. I wasn't thinking that night. I hadn't been thinking for a long time. I was up against the limit."

"Why'd it happen, Rhys?"

"I don't know…"

"I should have been there to help you."

"You tried."

"Not enough."

"I never let you help me."

"And I hated that part of you."

"I know. It's just that the emptiness…" He brought a hand to his heart and looked up in the sky. "I feel it right here. Always. And I can't handle it. And then, when I'm in the spiral, it's like I don't feel anything. Nothing good, nothing bad. Just nothing."

I turned and sank my fingers into his hair, just for the pleasure of doing so, of feeling us connected again physically, knowing he was close to me, real. "You never thought that maybe there's no need to fill in the emptiness?"

"What do you mean?"

"Maybe the emptiness just is. Like the holes in Swiss cheese. You don't look at them and think you need to fill them. They don't need to be filled in to make things better."

"Maybe I'm like that, like a piece of Swiss cheese."

"Sure. Or like the moon, Rhys."

"Why the moon?"

"It's full of craters, but they're pretty, aren't they? Way more so than if its surface was just smooth. You're like the moon. All of us are—we're all imperfect. But so what? We can live with that. We should live with that."

"Come here." He hugged me.

We stayed like that a few seconds, holding each other as if the world would fall apart if we ever let each other go, as if his body pressing into mine were the only thing that brought order to the universe, held the chaos at bay, maintained calm.

"Promise me you won't do that again," I whispered, trying not to cry. "And don't lie to me like you did that day when you left the restaurant. Don't you dare."

"I swear I won't, Ginger. I really swear it."

I looked at him, smiling nervously, because his hands on my waist were burning hot, and his breath, so close, was tempting me.

"I saw you have all my books…"

"I read them too," he said with a chuckle.

"For real? You read them all?"

"Of course! Who do you take me for? I also… I tried to imagine why you chose them, why you decided it was important for each of those stories to be told."

"Don't make me cry, Rhys."

He smiled slyly and looked down at me, turning inward slightly. My head was resting on his shoulder. "What happened with James?"

"You waited long enough…"

"It was killing me," he admitted, and despite everything, I smiled. "I was dying to ask you. But if you don't want to tell me…"

"No, that's not it. It just hurt. Not because of us, but because of Leon. I kept thinking about him, and that made me feel guilty. I guess it didn't work because we just weren't in love. We did love each other. And that was nice at first. But later, the feeling wasn't strong enough. It wasn't how it had to be. It wasn't everything it should be."

"How should it be?"

As he asked that, his long, warm fingers played with mine on the dew-covered grass, and my heart beat faster.

"Rhys, you know the answer to that question."

"I want you to tell me."

"I don't know."

"You do though. You told me once." His thumb rubbed the back of my hand. "*It's feeling a tingle in your stomach when you see them. Not being able to stop looking at them. Missing them even though they're right there. Wanting to touch them at all hours, talking about any- and everything, feeling like you lose all sense of time when you're together. Noticing the details. Wanting to know everything about them, even the stupid stuff. You know what, Rhys? I think it's actually like being permanently on the moon. With a smile on your face. Without fear."*

I didn't want him to see me trembling.

"How can you remember so perfectly everything I wrote?"

"I've reread it lots of times."

"Still..."

"And back then, I was on the moon."

"Rhys..."

"No. I fucked it up, Ginger. For years I've been stumbling over the same obstacle, and I'm the one who put it there. I was wrong. And now..."

"Everything's changed," I managed to say.

"Not the important things. Not us."

"Two years have passed, Rhys."

"And yet I feel like it's just been a few months since I said goodbye to you at the end of the summer we spent together, because in all the time since, I've felt nothing. It's as if I didn't exist. Ginger..." He reached up to stroke my cheek, and I flinched. I could tell he was nervous, uncertain. His fingers traced the outline of my lips. "Don't you feel anything anymore? Don't you feel me?"

What could I tell him? Yes? That he was one of the reasons my relationship with James had fallen apart? That no other man could come out on top when I remembered everything he had made me feel, how well we knew each other, for better and for worse, and how unconditionally I loved him, tenderly, but also like an addict? It was true what I had said about that long-ago night, that he shined so brightly I could see nothing else…

He must not have understood my silence.

But in my heart, I wished that he had.

His lips touched mine. That's all—just a touch. It was almost nothing, but I felt it the way I'd never felt anything else. Reticent, unsure…from Rhys, it felt almost dainty, because I remembered him as savage, intense, hungry. Anything but tender.

"Let's try, Ginger," he whispered against my lips before kissing them again, slowly, softly. "I'll give you everything you want. You and Leon. I should have from the first day I met you. I thought about it too. I swear I did. At the airport in Paris, when you were about to turn around and get in line. You were just a kid. And I wanted to kiss you so bad. And I should have. And, dammit, I never should have told you not to wait for me after what happened on the Ferris wheel. I should have told you I'd come back in a few months after signing that contract to go to Australia…"

"Rhys, don't do this."

"And then came the worst part. That summer."

"We can't change what happened."

"I was crazy about you. I was so in love, I got angry at myself and at you, at both of us, the closer we got to your departure. I didn't dare put myself out there. It was like I had vertigo. I should have gone with you, because if I'm honest, there was nothing I really cared about keeping me here. Just a bunch of smoke and mirrors…"

"Rhys, stop torturing yourself like this." I wrapped my arm around his waist.

"All I want is to be with you and to compose. Wherever. In London. And I'll buy a house in Australia, a little old one we can renovate, and we can take our vacations there. We can have a cat…"

It sounded perfect. Magical. But distant.

"Rhys, look at me. Breathe. Take a deep breath."

He did. He breathed in several times, not taking his eyes off me, telling me so much in the silence broken by the beating of two hearts.

"I don't want to lose another second."

"I know." We were so close.

"You're my anchor. I needed time to understand that. But remember how you asked me about this tattoo when we saw each other in London last time? Well, I got it for you."

I saw it despite the darkness. A little anchor on the back of his hand, near the half moon and the musical note. I ran my fingers over it and wanted to cry. I realized that everything was different here, tonight, under the stars. We were ourselves, but different. We were ourselves beyond lust, beyond desire. We were what was left afterward, under all those layers that come together sometimes but other times get mixed up and cover things. We were trust, care, friendship, love, knowing each other.

But we weren't in the right moment.

"You didn't answer my question."

"Which?" I asked.

"If you still feel me…"

"You know I do, Rhys. You know I always will."

"Then…"

We couldn't stop touching each other, even if just subtly. My fingers in his hair, his hand on my face, his arms around me…

"You need to put yourself back together right now," I said. His expression was bitter, so I grabbed his hand. He could barely look me in the eye. "I love you, Rhys. But I want you to be okay. And you need to go see your dad. You know that, right? You need to because I know you, and I know if you don't, you'll regret it for the rest of your life."

Rhys lay back, looked into the sky, and rubbed his face with his hands. I watched his chest rise and fall as he sighed and rested a hand over his heart.

"I'll be there on the other side of the screen."

"I'm going to fucking need you…"

"I know."

"Shit."

"What are you so afraid of?"

"I don't know. Him saying something that hurts me again. Or not knowing how to forgive him or ask for forgiveness. I talked about this with my mother…" He shook his head. "Until pretty recently, she thought I didn't know. That was the one thing my father asked me before I walked out the door. Not to tell her. And I didn't. I don't know why. I guess because my mother had such a hard time when she was sick, and I didn't want to pour salt in the wound. I know, Ginger. It's been like a snowball, just getting bigger and bigger. When I was a kid, I didn't understand how families could spend so many years together and just up and stop talking, but then I grew up, and things got complicated. And pride came in. Mine. His. And the years passed, and then I got what we're looking at now. Something just completely shattered."

"You can still fix it."

"He's dying, Ginger."

"Exactly. For that very reason."

"What if it doesn't work out?"

"Well, Rhys, then at least you tried."

"I missed you so much," he told me.

"I missed you too."

I rested my head on his chest. He kissed my forehead, then looked back up into the sky, and I did too. The moon was a slender sickle, barely visible.

"The third book I decided to publish," I went on, "was about the tie between two people. I remember this one phrase about how it didn't matter how much time had passed, how many changes the people went through in their lives, that bond was still there. A thread that trembled, got pushed and pulled, frayed, but never broke. Maybe that's what the thread that unites us is like, Rhys."

"I hope so, Ginger. I really do." He squeezed me, then whispered in my ear one of my favorite phrases from *The Little Prince*: "*I wonder whether the stars are set alight in heaven so that one day each one of us may find his own again.*"

105

Ginger

WE SPENT THE NEXT TWO days in a bubble. We only went out in the evening, to take a walk on the beach as the sun was hiding behind the horizon. We'd have an ice cream on a patio somewhere. The rest of the time, we enjoyed ourselves as if we were on vacation and the years before had been a fleeting mirage.

In the mornings, Rhys would take Leon to the pool. The boy splashed, smiled, and laughed. He loved the water. I would lie on a towel in the grass and pretend to read, but really I was just watching them. I couldn't help it.

I couldn't help it at night either when Rhys would read him *Peter Pan* out loud after dinner before putting him to bed. Leon would breathe evenly, relaxed, as he looked at the two of us sitting next to him.

"You know he can't understand anything you're saying, right?

"He'll retain something," Rhys replied.

"Rhys, he's a year old." I laughed.

He ignored me and opened the book. He read for a long time, maybe for Leon or maybe for himself, because once the baby was asleep, he continued awhile longer, following the lines with his finger the way children do, so absorbed I didn't dare interrupt him. I recognized that edition, the golden edges of the pages, the hardcover, but I didn't say anything until we were back in the living room.

"I thought it never reached you."

"It didn't. I managed to get it back later."

"Later? When?"

"It's a long story. Forget about it and come here." He pulled me, but I tripped and wound up sitting on his lap on the sofa. I didn't get up as we stared at each other. Then Rhys leaned his forehead against mine and closed his eyes. "How many times have we said goodbye, Ginger?" he asked, and his warm breath made me tremble.

Goodbye. We would hear that word again the next day, when he left us at the airport at noon. I shook my head. This was different than it had been last time, less intense, but more painful in a way I wouldn't know how to describe. Sadder.

"This is the fifth one, I think..."

"And maybe the last."

"Maybe..."

We were so close that I barely had to move to find his lips, graze them, savor them again. Rhys grunted, leaned back, and reached up my shirt. And this time I was the one who lost control. Who needed it more than him, sooner. I felt for his belt buckle as he bit me on the neck, leaving marks on my skin. I pulled his shirt over his head and straddled him. I don't know how we got the rest of our clothes off. All I remember is...what I felt. Touches. His fingertips pushing between my legs. My sex seeking his, taking him in. My hands in his hair. Me riding him back and forth. Strength. Intensity. Moaning into his mouth, unable to abandon his lips until I had reached the sky with my fingertips.

Sweating. Holding him.

And kissing him the whole night through.

106

From: Ginger Davies
To: Rhys Baker
Subject: We've arrived

We got back to London a few hours ago. We're fine. Leon got a little antsy and was crying. He's not used to travel, but he'll get some sleep tonight, and he'll be fine.

It's hard to say what it feels like, writing you an email, Rhys. It's so weird and so natural at the same time. Sitting here in bed right now, with Leon resting next to me in his cradle, I've been remembering when I used to write you in my dorm room. It seems like so long ago, but really, it hasn't been that much time, right? How long? Seven years? Give or take. I guess we're the ones who are constantly changing, and sometimes you don't get around to assimilating everything. I remember the old days sometimes. They make me nostalgic. I wish we could write an email to ourselves in the past, you know? Then everything would be so simple. But I guess that would make life boring.

So anyway, I'm up to my old nonsense here.

Tell me how things are with you.

From: Rhys Baker

To: Ginger Davies

Subject: RE: We've arrived

You don't know how bad I wish I was there recreating this scene: you lying in bed, probably with a book or manuscript on your nightstand, right? And Leon next to you, close. I don't know, maybe it's better if I don't know what you're doing when you're so far away.

I spent the day packing my bags, talking with the real estate agent who's going to sell my house for me, and dealing with some loose threads for the album, which will be out in a few months. I'm catching a plane to NYC, and I'll fly home from there. I'm fucking nervous, Ginger, even if I should have gotten used to the idea by now. It's just hard after all these years.

If we really could send an email to ourselves in the past, the way you said, I think mine would be so long, I'd get bored reading it. Remember, I was an idiot back then. I still am, actually. Joking aside, I'd just have too much to tell myself.

When your email arrived, I want you to know I just sat there looking at it in my inbox for a while before opening it, enjoying the feeling of getting another message from you after so long. For me, you're still that same girl who used to write me every night from her dorm room...

From: Ginger Davies

To: Rhys Baker

Subject: RE: RE: We've arrived

Don't make me get all emotional.

It's normal for you to be nervous, Rhys. You will be until you see him, talk about things, and get that weight off your back. Everything will be fine. I know it. If he wants to see you, if you're important to him right now, that has to mean something. We could have wound up like that, you know? Not talking for a bunch of different reasons, and then in the end losing touch. It happens all the time. Time passes and it gets harder, I know that; it happened to me too. When we weren't talking, I still thought about you all the time, I wondered what you were doing, and I thought about contacting you, but I'd always put it off till the next day. And then the next day I'd do the same thing again. And eventually the distance itself became an insurmountable obstacle.

Let me know when you land, okay?

Kisses (sincere ones).

From: Rhys Baker

To: Ginger Davies

Subject: Just now

I just landed in New York.

I'll write you when I can, Ginger Snap.

107

Rhys

NOTHING HAD CHANGED, AND YET everything had. At least when I looked harder and noticed the details. The rosebush was no longer in front of the window, the garden seemed neglected, the paint on the columns out front had faded, and the wind had blown the leaves across the porch steps. Nobody had bothered to rake them on the random Wednesday I decided to go home.

I still had the keys my mom had given me the last time I visited, but I didn't dare use them. Maybe I didn't think I deserved to. I rang the doorbell and waited until she opened up and greeted me with a fragile smile and a warm hug. She smelled the same as always. That comforted me. Still recognizing that scent.

"My little boy…" she took my arm.

"Where is he?" I asked nervously.

"He's sleeping. He usually tries to rest before lunch. Come to the kitchen. You must be starving. I'll make you something."

I nodded, but before I could step forward, she hugged me again, and we stayed like that in silence for a few seconds. Later, she opened the refrigerator with shaking hands, and I noticed new wrinkles on her face, a dullness in her eyes. They were tired, her body was thin and shrunken, and yet she still seemed full of strength and energy. Not the kind someone's born with, but the kind a person finds because they have to.

"You want chicken? Vegetable soup?"

"Mom, maybe we should…"

"Or something sweet?"

I took a deep breath and shut the fridge. We looked at each other.

"I'm not hungry. And we need to talk."

"I don't know if I can."

She started wringing her hands, and I grabbed them and felt her tremble. Looking down at her, seeing her so short beneath me, her misty eyes looking up into mine, I started to see everything differently. From her perspective, as someone who had been beside me for so many days, even before I learned to walk, someone who had cared for me when I was sick, who had celebrated all those birthdays with me…

She tried to get past me, but I stopped her.

"I'm sorry, Mom."

"Rhys, it's fine."

"I shouldn't have left. Forgive me." I felt the words turning to mush, like always, but I forced myself to let them out: "When I found out, I was just… I was lost at the moment, and I didn't know how to take it. I'm glad Dad didn't tell you why I left. You didn't deserve that."

"I should have told you before."

"It doesn't matter. Nothing would have changed."

"You had a right to know." She wiped her cheeks. "But I never found the right time. When you were little, I thought you wouldn't understand. And then you grew up and got older, and you were lost, and I was scared to give you another reason to distance yourself from us."

"Mom, everything's okay."

Her eyes were shining, full of tears that she must have been holding back for years. She took a deep breath and brought her hand shakily to her lips. "I used to look at you and think you were like a grenade on the verge of exploding. I was scared that anything I did would be catastrophic. And I didn't know what to do to help you."

"I did feel on the verge of exploding a lot of the time."

"Still, I messed up."

"We both did."

She reached out and stroked my cheek. "You're my son, Rhys. You are."

"I know I am," I whispered.

She was thinking over what she had to say. "Your father told me what he said to you before he asked me to tell you to come see him. I don't know how he managed to keep it to himself for so long, to live with that secret, but you know how proud he is. You're the same way. You're alike in that sense. It's just something inside you. You don't know how many times I used to tell you when you were a kid that you needed to express your feelings, that crying was liberating... You know he didn't regret it, right?"

I felt as if I was struggling to breathe. "I'll talk to him..." Already I wanted to leave.

"It broke his heart when he found out you had left because you learned you were adopted. When I was in the hospital, you were the only person he had to lean on, and when you came back, he was so angry, so disappointed... He's never been one to just swallow his anger or his pain. But your father loves you more than anyone, Rhys..."

Attacking before he could get hurt too badly. I knew that tactic well. But it had only brought me problems, disappointment, and mistakes.

I tried to put the pain aside, the discomfort weighing on my chest when I remembered the words he'd uttered about what runs in the blood. The rage that filled me that day that now seemed so distant. I felt like a plant that had grown somewhere for years, sometimes straighter, sometimes more tangled, that someone had torn out by the roots and thrown aside. And that pain remained there in a place I refused to look at because I felt weak, small. Like a nobody. Like someone who had no place in the world that was his.

I looked at my mother. So patient. So solid.

"That's not all he said," I told her. "He also said he had never wanted to adopt, that he did it for you, because he didn't want to see you unhappy."

"It's true. He was against the idea at first. He had doubts. But they all disappeared when he took you in his arms, Rhys. He just said what he said to hurt you. It's horrible, but it's true... You hurt him, and he wanted to hurt you back. He should have realized that you were young and unstable. The conditions weren't the same."

I rubbed my chin and tried to calm myself down.

"How is he?" I asked.

"He's got his good days and his bad days."

"Has he gotten better at all?"

"No, Rhys. He's not going to get better."

"What about his medication?"

"They're painkillers, that's all." She cut me off. "Eat something and take a shower. You look tired. I'll clean your father up when he wakes up. You know how vain he is."

She said this with a smile, as if she no longer cared to struggle against the situation, as if she wasn't even upset that the person she'd shared her whole life with would die soon. I couldn't help asking, "How do you do it, Mom?"

She shook her head and sighed. "I needed a few months, but once you accept reality, you start seeing things in different ways. I have two options: crawl in bed and cry, or get up and try to enjoy the time we have together, even if the conditions aren't ideal."

She left the kitchen with her head held high. For the next few hours, I thought about what she said. As I took my hot shower, as I unpacked my bags, as I tried to get comfortable in my old room with all the memories those four walls had preserved.

I left my laptop on the bed, thinking I'd write Ginger to let her know I'd made it home, but I was too upset...

I rubbed my face and fell on the mattress.

It didn't seem real that I had been a little child in this bed, which was now almost too small for me—my feet scraped the wooden frame at the bottom. It was funny to realize that places didn't change, memory didn't change, even events didn't change—it was just us who did, molding ourselves, rising up, falling, turning into different people inside and out.

I lay there until my mother knocked to let me know I could go see him. Even then, I needed a moment to get up. Three minutes, maybe more. I didn't think about anything as I moved through the house I knew so well, toward his office, where he was waiting for me. I guess he chose it because it was where he felt most powerful, most secure, his best version of himself. When I was little, he used to always tell me not to go in there, and I never listened; I'd scuttle through the door, sit on the floor under the dark-wood desk, and wait in silence for him to come and find me. He'd click his tongue, shake his head, decide he'd lost that battle, and let me stay, playing on the burgundy carpet while he tried to finish whatever work he'd brought home with him.

But now I didn't want to go in.

I did though. I pushed the door, which was already half-open, and stepped inside. I thought at first the office was empty, but then I saw his slim, slouching figure in the wing chair next to the bookshelf.

It felt like a slap in the face to see him there.

To see...what looked like another person, but with his stare. His face was aged, his body weak and haggard, his hands trembling as they pushed onto the arms of his leather chair to try to stand.

I couldn't talk. I couldn't even move.

Not, at least, until I saw that he couldn't stand. Then I walked toward him with my heart in my throat and my eyes burning, and I grabbed him around the waist to help him up. He weighed nothing. I let him go when I realized he could hold himself there, and we looked at each other. Just a few inches apart. For the first time in more than seven long years. An eternity. Or perhaps just the blink of an eye, depending on your perspective.

I had imagined that moment thousands of times. But it was always the same. We met, we talked, I threw back in his face what he'd said to me, told him how much he'd hurt me, told him he'd never loved me, and we ended up shouting.

But nothing like that happened.

We just looked at each other.

And then the words emerged with no effort, as if I'd been meditating on them for years, as if they'd been there, caught in my throat, so deeply anchored inside me that they didn't even surprise me when they emerged. And they were sincere.

"I'm sorry, Dad."

His eyes were gleaming.

"I'm sorry too."

108

From: Ginger Davies
To: Rhys Baker
Subject: I hope you're okay

I'm assuming you reached home yesterday. And that it must have been a hard day, tiring, what with the travel and all the mixed feelings… I hope everything went well, Rhys. I can't stop thinking about you. I've had my fingers crossed all day. Write me when you can. And if you need to talk, you know where I am.

I've got tons of work at the publisher after my days out of town, but whatever, it was worth it. I think Leon misses your pool. Last night, he cried when I took him out of the tub, and he'd been there for half an hour. He loves water. Even more now, thanks to you. I need to sign him up for swimming lessons.

Kisses, Rhys. Take care.

From: Rhys Baker
To: Ginger Davies

Subject: I'm fine

I needed to find a calm moment to write you. It's 2:00 a.m. here, and...everything's fine, Ginger. Honestly. I still feel a little confused, there's a lot here to take in, but it's all gone easier than I'd imagined. You know that feeling when you've tossed something around in your head over and over and it just keeps getting bigger till you can't even grasp it? Then it turns out to be almost nothing. I don't know.

The important thing is that when I saw him...

When I saw him, I forgot all the bad things.

Weird, right?

Nourishing myself on that anger for so long, and then just letting it go from one second to the next... I wonder if I'll ever understand myself. What's happening with me? Like with Leon. There's no logical way to understand it.

When you stopped talking to me, there were times when I couldn't sleep, and I'd reread our emails. I remember now something you said a long time ago: "I think you're the most contradictory, unpredictable person I know. I wonder if that should scare me." All I could ask you then is why you should be scared. What didn't occur to me was that I was the one who should be scared. Because if I can't predict how I feel, if I contradict myself so much that I can't even trust my own beliefs and values, how could anyone else trust me? How did you do it?

I think you're the most contradictory, unpredictable person I know. I wonder if that should scare me.

From: Ginger Davies
To: Rhys Baker
Subject: Trust

Because trust is like that sometimes. It's blind, instinctual. Sometimes I don't even know how the other person is going to act, but I just believe whatever they do will be right, even if they make mistakes, even if they stumble. I would do anything for you. I hope you feel the same way about me.

You don't know how happy I am that you could forget the bad and make room for the good. Your father must be happy to have you there with him. And your mother. Something else, Rhys, since I know you…don't feel guilty or worry about how you should have done this sooner. In a perfect world, maybe it's true. Not in our world. And it's nice no matter what. Like the moon, remember? Even with all its craters.

From: Rhys Baker
To: Ginger Davies
Subject: RE: Trust

Remind me what my life would be without your words giving it a whole new meaning. You're right, Ginger. I'm learning to walk on the moon without stumbling. It would be way easier if it were a perfectly smooth surface, but… I think it's just a matter of practicing. And it's not so bad. Not so bad at all.

It's a little like being a teenager again.

From: Ginger Davies
To: Rhys Baker
Subject: RE: RE: Trust

Did you ever stop being a teenager though? I'm laughing at you right now, Rhys. And I should stop, because I'm in the middle of a publishing meeting pretending to type something important into my computer while Kate takes care of everything. By the way, she and my sister are getting married next summer. You're invited to the wedding of the year (and I hope you'll accept, because I feel a terrible need to see you in a suit and have you as my plus-one).

From: Rhys Baker
To: Ginger Davies
Subject: RE: RE: RE: Trust

Very funny, Ginger. You got me.

Congratulate them for me. Of course I'll be there. I would never miss out on watching you drool all over yourself when you see me walk in.

From: Ginger Davies
To: Rhys Baker
Subject: RE: RE: RE: RE: Trust

You're pathetic, Rhys.

From: Rhys Baker

To: Ginger Davies
Subject: RE: RE: RE: RE: RE: Trust

I missed this.

From: Ginger Davies
To: Rhys Baker
Subject: RE: RE: RE: RE: RE: RE: Trust

Me too 🙂

109

Rhys

I'D BEEN HOME ALMOST TWO weeks before I realized I'd only drunk one beer since I got there. I realized it one afternoon as I was opening a can before sitting down with my father on our back porch. We were each in our chairs watching the hours pass in silence as a cold breeze blew.

I didn't remember the last time I'd felt so good. I didn't remember feeling so clean. I didn't remember what it was to simply be with myself, with nothing to distract me, hype me up, or put me to sleep. It seemed easy now, with all the music behind me. I could hear myself in the silence.

We'd established a kind of routine. After that first, emotion-filled day, we didn't talk again about the past. We didn't dig any deeper. We didn't bother about what he'd done or what he'd said to me; we preferred to think about the years we had spent together. It was different, but it certainly wasn't worse. I slept well, as long as I wasn't up till the crack of dawn talking to Ginger. I'd get up relatively early and have breakfast with Dad in the kitchen, just like when I was little, watching him read the paper and complain every time we told him to eat a little more. *The world is going to hell in a handbasket*, he'd say—he'd said that as long as I could remember. I told him that one day as I was pouring milk over my cereal, and he just smiled and nodded before resuming his tirade.

Then I'd go with Mom to get groceries or run errands. I tried to take care of the cooking while she helped Dad shower, but I always did something wrong—I'd lose track of time, or the meat would be raw, or the potatoes a little undercooked. They would chuckle about it as they ate. It was fine.

I'd clear the table, talk about whatever with my mother while he slept, and in the evening, when Dad came downstairs to take his medicine after sundown, we'd go sit on the porch. We wouldn't do anything, just sit there until the mosquitos started buzzing around us and Mom would shout that dinner was served.

The afternoon my father and I had a beer, I remembered a melody, one that would be on the radio soon, when the new single came out. I tapped my fingers softly on the arm of the chair with printed cushions my mother had sewn.

My father looked at my hand.

"I see you've got more scribbles on you," he mumbled.

"They're called tattoos." I was amused, not offended. "You like them?" I asked.

"No." He was blunt, as always. "What do they mean?"

"Stuff." I shrugged and took a sip of my beer.

"Come on, don't make me beg. I get the musical note. But that other thing, what is it? A banana? A smile?"

"It's the moon. It's her. So's this one." I turned my hand to show him the anchor.

"Who's she?"

"Ginger."

"She's special, I guess."

"Yeah."

"Is it serious?"

"It's complicated."

He raised his eyebrows. "More complicated than me dying?"

"Fuck, Dad, no..."

"Then it's not complicated."

"Yeah, I guess you're right."

He nodded, satisfied, and looked straight ahead. I observed him for a few seconds, thinking about how everything had changed. I don't know who I owed this shift in perspective to, if it was that life had made him smaller, or if I felt stronger, bigger, more mature since the last time we'd seen each other, before I left. But I was certain it was different. Nice, but also sad. I remembered what Ginger had told me about the vision we have of our parents when we're little, how we think they're superheroes. And then life takes a turn, and they're anything but. We get stronger, and we witness how they grow weaker, more delicate, more imperfect.

"Stop looking at me like that," he grunted.

"I'm not looking at you any way."

"I know when you're lying, Rhys. Tell me about her. Or tell me about your music if that's easier. Tell me about stuff, your plans, what you're going to do in the future..."

I meditated a few moments, then took a drink.

"I don't really know what I'm going to do in the future, but I know I need a break. I'd like to try to approach things from a different angle. Devote some time to behind-the-scenes stuff, production, composition…" It sounded good saying it aloud— perfect, actually. "The next album's already done. The first single will be out soon. You want to see the cover?"

"Of course." He nodded.

I looked on my phone for the image Axel had sent me and showed it to him. He looked at it, concentrating for a few seconds. Then he smiled.

"You're putting yourself out there."

I nodded and set my phone aside. "As far as *she* goes… I think you'd like her."

He must have been surprised I didn't try to avoid the subject.

"What's she like?" he asked tentatively.

"A talker. Smart. Pretty. Sweet. She's the most amusing girl I've ever known, but I don't think she does it on purpose. Or maybe I'm the only one who sees her that way. She's patient, but she doesn't back down when she's mad. She knows how to say no."

"Good. You need a stern hand."

"Screw you." I laughed. He did too.

"You know it's true," he responded.

"She's got a kid. Leon. He's one."

He turned to me nervously. "Is it…is it yours…?"

"No. I wish."

"You wish? Who'd have ever thought you'd say something like that?"

"I know. Life, right?"

"It would be boring if it was any other way."

"I guess it would." I sighed a long sigh.

110

From: Ginger Davies

To: Rhys Baker

Subject: Got a question

There's something I've been thinking about these past few weeks, and I can't get it out of my head. I've read it over and over, and I just don't know what to think. In one of the last emails you sent me, you talked about yourself, how contradictory you were, how unpredictable, and you said something about Leon. That logically, you shouldn't feel what you were feeling. What did you mean? I need to know.

From: Rhys Baker

To: Ginger Davies

Subject: RE: Got a question

Relax, Ginger. What were you thinking? Something bad? All I meant was, if I hadn't been a total disaster, if I hadn't spent my whole life running into a wall, if I had just stuck to the straight and narrow, Leon wouldn't have affected me the way he did. But that wasn't the case. I think of him almost the way I think of you. (Now, now, don't get jealous, Ginger Snap.) He's...perfect. You were right, babies smell wonderful. That reminds me, you've hardly told me anything about him, about how everything happened. You just showed up with a baby in your arms, and I missed out on the two years in between. Be nice and bring me up to date.

From: Rhys Baker
To: Ginger Davies
Subject: I am nice

There's not much to tell, Rhys. You didn't exactly give me a wealth of details about what you were doing in all that time either, though I'm smart enough to take a guess...

James and I tried to have a baby right away. Sometimes I think it was the desire to be parents that pushed us to keep trying rather than any real romantic feelings toward each other. It seems crazy, right? But if I'm honest, I think that was it. The pregnancy was easy. I didn't really get morning sickness or any other pains, so I could focus on my work and my yoga classes (which I need to get back into). I was so busy, it flew past. James was working all the time then too. And one day, it was like Leon was just there.

He was a big boy—more than seven pounds. I can't tell you how much it hurt, pushing him out. It was worth the effort though. As soon as I had him in my arms, all the blood, sweat, and tears were forgotten, and I just looked into his little face. It was the most wonderful moment in my life.

I need to let you go, Rhys. He's up and he won't stop crying. I hope you're good, despite everything you're having to deal with there. Kisses. Lots of them.

From: Rhys Baker
To: Ginger Davies
Subject: RE: I am nice

I wish I hadn't missed that moment, Ginger. I'd have loved to be by your side. Seriously, I should have been there, in the waiting room. Just like I should have been here, at home, all those Christmases, birthdays, any other time I could have gotten away. I know you told me not to feel bad, but I have this feeling still, stuck there, this feeling I missed important things that can never be repeated. Why? For nothing. I think about all we talked about, the things I did during those two years, and the only thing that I can come up with is that I recorded an album and a single. What else? The rest is just emptiness. I met a lot of girls, went out a lot of nights, filled my phone contacts with a bunch of people who don't know me and I don't want to know. And I bought a house I don't really like.

Yeah. So things here are going well. We've got a kind of routine, except when Dad has a bad day. Otherwise, it feels like I've traveled back in time. I sleep like a baby. I'm eating better. My mom won't shut up about my diet. I'm feeling relaxed. Next week we're releasing our first single to try to drum up some interest, but I'm not doing any promo. I've decided to focus on the stuff I actually like.

From: Ginger Davies
To: Rhys Baker
Subject: Mistakes

Rhys, it's inevitable to think sometimes you've made mistakes, but what really matters is you're there now, where you need to be. And those two years didn't change anything between us— not anything important, at any rate. Maybe we needed them. Did you ever think that? Maybe you needed to hit bottom to realize what you really wanted. Maybe I needed to get away from you to make my own mistakes. Because I did, you know that, right? I did make mistakes. We'd all like to get into a time machine and change what we've done.

But let's talk about your new interests…

What is the stuff you actually like?

From: Rhys Baker
To: Ginger Davies
Subject: Things

You, more than anything.

From: Ginger Davies
To: Rhys Baker

Subject: RE: Things

Stop being an idiot.

From: Rhys Baker
To: Ginger Davies
Subject: RE: RE: Things

I'm afraid that's a tall order...

Seriously though, I was talking about work, music. I don't want to keep doing stuff I don't like. And I think I can make my own choices now. By the way, keep your ears open. The new song comes out tomorrow.

I'm excited to hear what you think. Kisses.

111

Rhys

I HAD A HELL OF an idea. It occurred to me while I was shopping with my mom, carrying the bags to the car. I saw my reflection in the store window and noticed something behind it. Two hours later, my father and I were next to each other at the coffee table reading the instructions to a model of the London Bridge, getting ready to indulge in a hobby we'd abandoned for years. He was surprised when he saw the box, but right away, he asked my mother to bring him his reading glasses.

And there we were, organizing the pieces. I remembered the first rule he always told me when I was little: *Order comes first, Rhys; everything else is second.* I was taking the glue, the paints, and some tools out of a little bag when my phone rang. I ignored it, as I had for weeks.

"Shouldn't you pick that up?" my father asked.

"It's not important," I lied, feigning indifference.

"Rhys, don't avoid things. Really, don't."

It sucked that he knew me so well, even if he'd barely seen me for a decade. I took a deep breath, got up, a little irritated, and answered on my way out to the porch. It was Daniel, the label's PR chief.

"I've been trying to get ahold of you for days," he complained. "Where the hell have you been, Rhys? Are you crazy? The single's coming out tomorrow, and you're missing in action!"

"So?" I leaned against the wall. I could see my father frowning as he read the instructions, his glasses perched on the tip of his nose.

I don't know why, but at this moment, the least opportune moment conceivable, with someone yelling at me on the other end of the phone, it struck me that he wasn't old enough to die. That he deserved to live much longer.

"Are you listening to me, Rhys, dammit?"

"I'm not going on tour."

"I've already signed the contracts."

"Well, call and cancel."

"I can't."

"I already told Paul I wasn't up for a bunch of commitments and radio interviews and festivals. If he didn't communicate that to you, it's not my problem."

"Of course he told me, but I assumed he was kidding."

"I've got to go; I'm busy."

"Are you trying to bury your career?"

"No, just refocus it."

"Fuck me, Rhys. Listen..."

I hung up. I stayed out there a while longer, watching my father through the dining room window, so concentrated on his model, so ready to start it, and, if we were lucky, to finish it too. I smiled for the first time in days. Then I went inside, sat down, and returned to what I was doing before I got up.

"Did you work it out?" he asked.

"More or less." I shrugged.

"Was it that girl of yours? Ginger?"

"Nah. We hardly call each other."

"Did you piss her off again?"

"No, Dad." I laughed. "We normally email each other at night. Don't look at me like that. It's comfortable, and I have more time to think about what I really want to say…"

"Yeah, us Bakers, our mouths get us into trouble."

My mother came in just then to see how we were.

"Why don't you grab a chair and stick around?" Dad said. She nodded, seeing his pleading eyes. "We're going to need help if we have any hope of ever finishing. Rhys bought an *easy* one," he said sarcastically.

That was far from the truth, and I laughed again, noticing his frustration.

"I didn't want you to just breeze through it."

"I'll get my revenge."

112

Ginger

I'D HAD A HARD DAY at work, had just given Leon his bath, and was making dinner when I remembered that Rhys's new song came out today. I put aside the blender and wiped my hands with a rag as I ran to get my phone. I cursed myself for forgetting what he'd told me the day before. When I opened my music app, it was already in the top hundred. I held my breath when I saw the title. I recognized it. Years before, for my birthday, he had given me a song with the same name: "*Ginger*." I could feel my hands tremble as I hit Play. And I heard that familiar melody, the one I'd listened to thousands of times as I went to sleep curled up in bed, thinking of him, wondering what he was doing now...

But this time, there was something more, something different. His voice cracking, hoarse, in a bass tone that didn't change even during the chorus. A voice talking about anchors, roses on solitary asteroids, Peter Pan, shared moons, a complicated girl, and a guy who wound up under a pile of rubble while she freed herself and turned into a butterfly.

I looked at the cover of the new album. It was called *Ginger*, just like the song. The name was surrounded by winding vines of flowers, which also enveloped the drawing underneath of a human heart, a real one, full of scars, some closed, some fresh, and the flowers had thorns next to the petals that were prettiest and shined brightest.

I listened to it again, in tears. It was perfect.

Leon pounded on the tray of his high chair.

"You like it? It's Rhys…"

He gurgled something incomprehensible, but kept smiling while the music played in the house I'd rented some time back. I bent over, kissed his forehead, and went to find my laptop.

———

113

From: Ginger Davies
To: Rhys Baker
Subject: You're crazy

I can't believe it, Rhys. Really. It was... I don't know. When I
saw the song title, my heart almost stopped, and hearing you
sing...it's the most incredible thing I've ever heard. Maybe I'm
not being objective, but who cares? It was so beautiful... I don't
even know what to say. You've left me speechless.

Leon loved it.

Thank you, thank you, thank you.

From: Rhys Baker
To: Ginger Davies
Subject: RE: You're crazy

If I left you speechless, then it was worth it.

I'm exhausted. Yesterday, I started putting together a model with my father, the kind we used to do when I was a kid. You can't imagine his endurance. He'll stuff himself with painkillers if he needs to, to make it to the point where I'm so confused, I can't tell the pieces apart. And then he laughs at me. This is now the second night he's tortured me this way. My mother helps out, but after thirty minutes, she can't hang anymore. We still have lots of work to do.

I'm glad you liked the song.

From: Ginger Davies
To: Rhys Baker
Subject: RE: RE: You're crazy

That's so great, Rhys. You were right, your dad seems to be as proud and headstrong as you. Send me a photo of the model when you're done. I don't have much time to write today because James is coming to dinner, but I'll write you tomorrow from the office.

BTW, I'm blowing up the album cover, and I'm going to frame it and hang it up. I don't care if I look like a crazed fan.

From: Rhys Baker
To: Ginger Davies
Subject: RE: RE: RE: You're crazy

Does James come often for dinner? You never gave me the details about what happened with him. We barely had time for anything those three days in Ibiza.

From: Ginger Davies
To: Rhys Baker
Subject: Organization

We keep it flexible. I have custody because James is busy, and sometimes his cases drag on till late at night. Normally he takes the kid two weekends a month, but he often stops by my parents' to pick him up on days when he finishes early. And then once in a while, he'll come by for dinner or just to see him for a bit. He's a good dad. And we get along.

We have an understanding, even if it wasn't enough to make our relationship work. I told you, I think what we had in common was that desire to settle down, find stability, have children. But it was a mistake. I can't regret it because now I have Leon. I'm looking up right now, and I see him curled in his cradle, hugging that stuffed elephant he never lets go. But when night fell and we finished dinner, James and I were sitting there on the sofa, and we just didn't have much to say to each other.

We talked about how things were going at work, our plans for the kid, and that was it. You know something? If I hadn't spent that summer with you, if I hadn't learned exactly what it meant to be on the moon with someone, in love, I'd have probably thought that was normal, the same "normal" most couples have. But in my heart, I was painfully aware that there was more out there. And I hated you a little bit.

Just a little. Selfishly.

Sometimes I'd think, *If Rhys had never crossed my path... maybe I could be happy with James.* I know now that's not true.

But I think I was trying to deceive myself. We both were. He and I are happier now that we're apart.

From: Rhys Baker
To: Ginger Davies
Subject: RE: Organization

Maybe it doesn't count for much now, but let me say this: I'm glad I crossed your path. And that you crossed mine.

We're still working on the model.

We should be done soon.

From: Ginger Davies
To: Rhys Baker
Subject: Routine

What a day. I was arguing with this unbearable author, the parking meter took my money, Leon threw up on me on the way home, and I left my groceries at Donna and Kate's place. Sometimes I forget what my life was like when I didn't have so much to do. How could I get so freaked out back then over a couple of stupid tests?

I hope your day's been better than mine.

And that your model's coming along.

From: Rhys Baker
To: Ginger Davies
Subject: Bad news

I'm writing you quickly from my phone, Ginger.

We're at the hospital. Dad took a turn for the worse last night.

From: Ginger Davies
To: Rhys Baker
Subject: RE: Bad news

I'm so sorry, Rhys.

Let me know as soon as you find out something.

From: Ginger Davies
To: Rhys Baker
Subject: RE: RE: Bad news

They're going to keep him at the hospital. He's been assigned a room. He keeps complaining and saying he wants to go home, but the doctor told me he doesn't see him getting released anytime soon.

I think he's dying, Ginger.

I doubt he'll leave here alive.

I don't know how I feel.

114

Ginger

HE PICKED UP ON THE third ring. I heard his breathing.

"Rhys, I'm so sorry," I whispered.

"I should have come earlier."

"Don't say that. We talked about this. The important thing now is you being there with him. It could have been worse. You could still be in Ibiza, directionless…"

"I just came here to see him die."

"I know it's hard, Rhys…"

"Every five minutes, I get this urge to turn and run, and I suppress it and make myself stay there with him while he's suffering in his room, and we call the nurse to get him more painkillers. But the impulse is still there, even if I can't give in. He told me something. That I needed to stay strong when this happened and take care of my mother. I don't know."

"You're doing it. You're doing a good job."

"If only it wasn't so difficult."

"Did they tell you anything else?"

"Just that he doesn't have much time left."

"I'm so sorry... Call me whenever you need to, okay? It doesn't matter what time. If you ever feel like you need a break, I'm here."

"Thanks, Ginger," he whispered.

115

From: Rhys Baker
To: Ginger Davies
Subject: [No subject]

My father died this morning.

 We came home so my mother could lie down for a while. She needs the rest. I'm taking care of all the details…

 I just wanted you to know. We'll talk soon.

From: Ginger Davies
To: Rhys Baker
Subject: RE: [No subject]

Rhys, I'm so sorry. I wish I could be there for you. I'd give you a big hug and take care of everything. I'm sorry you have to go through this alone. I keep thinking about you. How's your mother? How are you? Call me when you feel like it.

 Kisses.

116

Rhys

THE FUNERAL WAS QUICK BUT emotional. My mother was there next to me. All Dad's work colleagues came, plus his friends and some neighbors. I barely understood what anyone was saying. I hadn't slept for two days, and all I could do was stare at the coffin, which would soon be underground. I cried for the first time in years. And I understood that no matter what happened, the bonds that tied you to a person never broke. That stuck in my mind, even as we got home, I made my mother a cup of herbal tea, and she fell asleep on the couch.

I had spent half my life asking myself the same questions, looking for something, trying to fill in the void…

And it turned out everything was much simpler.

I went on thinking, sitting at the coffee table next to the model we hadn't managed to finish. The afternoon sun shone through the window. I couldn't think of anything else as I went on building it, piece by piece…

117

From: Ginger Davies

To: Rhys Baker

Subject: Worried

I'm worried, Rhys. I haven't heard from you since the funeral. I thought about calling, but I didn't want to bother you at such a private time as this. Write me, please. Even just to tell me that you're okay, that you're handling things.

From: Rhys Baker

To: Ginger Davies

Subject: RE: Worried

Sorry, Ginger. Things have been complicated around here. I'm fine. Both of us are. Given the situation, I mean. After the funeral, I slept fifteen hours straight, and then I tried to put the paperwork in order to make things easier for Mom, just stupid stuff like changing the name on the bills and the accounts…

I keep thinking about things. Everything.

Why do people feel so lost, Ginger? Why do we have this feeling we need to find a purpose, a goal, something more? I think I've realized something. I think I've just been walking in circles for a long time, chasing after something. And maybe I know what that is. It's me, Ginger. I've been spinning round and round for years, thinking too much, barely living when I thought I was grabbing hold of life.

From: Ginger Davies
To: Rhys Baker
Subject: There's more

I understand what you mean, and maybe you're right, but there have also been lots of good things, Rhys. You're not just shadows; you're also light. And it doesn't matter when we realize something, what matters is that we do. Everyone has experiences like this. And they never end. How's your mother? What are you going to do now?

From: Rhys Baker
To: Ginger Davies
Subject: RE: There's more

She's sad, but how else would she be? It's normal, right? I don't know what I'm going to do. I feel adrift. I can't leave her alone, even if she says I should go. I spend the whole day just wandering around the house, working on this stupid model, thinking about things…

From: Ginger Davies
To: Rhys Baker
Subject: RE: RE: There's more

Everything passes, Rhys. It just takes time. Maybe you need this pause in your life to decide what it is you want to do. You've got a blank page in front of you, right? Once, a long time ago, you told me that. And it worked for me.

From: Ginger Davies
To: Rhys Baker
Subject: RE: RE: RE: There's more

There's a difference: you're a very smart girl.

From: Ginger Davies
To: Rhys Baker
Subject: Look for another excuse

That one's not going to cut it.

From: Rhys Baker
To: Ginger Davies
Subject: Seriously

You need to learn to accept a compliment.

But you're right, Ginger. The future is a blank page. By the way, I finished the model last night. I don't know if I'm happy or sad about it. It was nice to finish something we started together, but at the same time, I feel like it distances me from this place somehow. And my mother seems like she's trying to push me out. I know she's doing it for me, but I can't help feeling guilty when I think of going, even if I come back more often. I don't want to make the same mistakes with her I made with my father.

From: Ginger Davies
To: Rhys Baker
Subject: You won't

Don't worry about that. You won't. I'm certain of it.
Your album's a hit.

From: Rhys Baker
To: Ginger Davies
Subject: My mother

I guess it is.

I've spent the last few weeks helping Mom out in the garden, but this morning she ditched me to do to a pastry class run by our HOA. I'm starting to feel out of place. Almost like I'm not needed here. I don't know if she's just trying to encourage me to get on with my life, or if she needs the space to get used to the idea of being alone. What do you think? We've barely talked about him. About death. I'm worried that she's doing terrible deep inside and just won't tell me.

From: Ginger Davies
To: Rhys Baker
Subject: RE: My mother

You want me to be totally honest?

From: Rhys Baker
To: Ginger Davies
Subject: RE: RE: My mother

I have a feeling that means you're going to hurt me.
     But yes, Ginger, I want you to be honest.

From: Ginger Davies
To: Rhys Baker
Subject: RE: RE: RE: My mother

I think your mother accepted the situation a long time ago. I think it hurts her that your dad's gone, I'm sure she misses him, and of course she'll need time to get over the loss. But she's been preparing for this for a long time, Rhys. I have the feeling she's a strong woman. If she could deal with everything on her own for that long, I doubt she needs you now. What I think is you're the one who needs her. That deep down, you're the one who can't turn the page. And that's fine. You will, and you don't need to put a date on it. You're going to have your good and bad days. Some people need years to talk about a tragedy without bursting into tears, and some people get over things in a matter of weeks. Your mother is trying to put all this behind her. You should probably do the same.

From: Rhys Baker
To: Ginger Davies
Subject: Maybe…

Maybe you're right. Maybe it's a mix of things: my fear of taking a new step, the feeling that I'm just spinning around in circles, this idea that I haven't yet found my place. Last night, I was looking at this old globe that I have in my room. And you know, I didn't feel like going anywhere at all. I mean, there was one place, but it's not exactly a place. But if it was, it would be the most beautiful one I've ever seen. And that's why I'm scared. I'm scared if I go there, I'll ruin it, like I'm not good enough to be there.

From: Ginger Davies
To: Rhys Baker
Subject: RE: Maybe…

I understand. Some places are more complicated than others. Because of the terrain. Especially if you've been up high, if you've been climbing the hill for a long time, and you know how painful it will be if you fall…

From: Rhys Baker
To: Ginger Davies

Subject: RE: RE: Maybe...

But sometimes it's worth the risk.

From: Ginger Davies
To: Rhys Baker
Subject: RE: RE: RE: Maybe...

What if that place isn't everything you thought it would be when you finally reach the top? Everything you hoped for? What if it doesn't make you happy?

From: Rhys Baker
To: Ginger Davies
Subject: Practicing

I'm learning not to ask myself things I can't answer. It doesn't make things worse; it just demands more courage, like learning to jump even if you have vertigo. Maybe it'll be okay. Maybe it'll be the very thing I need right now. Maybe I would let a thousand years pass if I kept looking for the perfect situation, waiting for the planets to align or whatever. I'm starting to be a big believer in living every day as if it were my last. I'm tired of waiting for things that never come and ignoring the ones that are right there in front of me.

From: Rhys Baker
To: Ginger Davies

Subject: Love and madness

I can't sleep. And I can't stop thinking about you. About us. Maybe that's why I just did something crazy. I think it's worth it though. Because this one time, years ago, I met a girl who was lost in Paris, and she stole my heart, and I can't forget her. She was a little crazy, she talked nonstop, sometimes she rained on my parade, but still, she was perfect. Perfect in the way that you can talk to a person forever and not get tired of them, and her laugh was the prettiest sound in the world, and everything about her just mattered to me. And she gave me an old book where I found the wisest and most beautiful words in the world: "It is only with the heart that one can see rightly; what is essential is invisible to the eye."

So I think I should tell this girl that next Friday at eleven at night, I'll be waiting for her in the place where we danced for the first time.

And I hope she will remember the boy who taught her to use the ticket machine for the metro and whispered in her ear that if she wanted, she could touch the moon with her fingers.

118

Rhys

WHO AM I? WHERE AM I *from? What am I doing here? Why am I in this world?* Those are the questions we should all ask ourselves at least once in life. And then there's the crucial one, the one that weighs the heaviest: Is finding the answers that important? Do we need to find them to be happy?

One day, I decided I didn't.

One day, I stopped looking.

Who am I? No idea. Sometimes I'm charming, sometimes idiotic, sometimes selfish, sometimes gentle, sometimes cowardly, sometimes brave, sometimes all of that and none of it. Where am I from? I guess I come from the sperm of some stranger that fertilized the egg of another stranger. But basically, I'm from my home, from sunny Tennessee. From my parents, my real parents, who were by my side every day, through the good times and bad, through pride and secrets and love and forgiveness. What am I doing here? Living. Like a bee. Living, living, living. Why am I in this world? No idea. And I stopped trying to figure it out. I just wanted to be. To lie down in the green fields, fill my lungs with the cold air of winter, see the sea someday, read some book Ginger chose, blast music through my headphones with my eyes closed, eat a giant plate of spaghetti with extra cheese.

And be with myself.

And be with her.

119

Ginger

NOT ONLY ARE WE WHAT we do; we're also what we don't do. What we say and what we silence. We are the questions we don't dare to ask, and the answers that will never come and will float there forever, blown about by fear and uncertainty. We are the subtlety of a gaze, the intimacy of a soft caress, the curve of an honest smile. We are sweet moments, bitter instances, sorrowful nights. We are details. We are real.

But beyond everything else, we are the decisions we make. In all their dimensions. With every choice, we take a step forward and abandon something along the way. Or we take a step back, and we abandon whatever was to come. We walk among alternatives, choosing some, rejecting others, and in this way marking our destiny. We always lose something, even when we win, but that doesn't matter. What really matters is being able to make a decision, and to do so freely: to bet on a dream, for ourselves or someone else, never doubting, never afraid, with willpower, with passion.

(Somewhere between Paris and the Moon)

HE'S LEANING ON HIS ELBOWS on the wall overlooking the Seine and staring at the Eiffel Tower rising up on the other side. It's warm. He was there years ago on a winter night, but now the breeze is mild, the tourists are walking past, they continue up the sidewalk, and he can smell the food from a nearby restaurant.

He got there a half hour early, but it doesn't matter. He's nervous. He's tapping his fingers on the balustrade to the rhythm of a song he knows well, one he heard a long time ago in the same city, one that starts with the beating of a heart. It plays on the radio often now. He sighs, impatient. Tries not to think about the possibility that she won't show, especially when he remembers all the obstacles they've had to get past, the times he tripped over his own feet, the words he shouldn't have kept to himself.

She walks in a straight line. A long time ago, she decided that when life offered her a chance to take a turn, she only would if it was worth it, if she was happy to before she even knew what lay around the corner. She must have chosen this path long ago, even when she didn't imagine it would land her on a roller coaster the day she wrote her email address on the hand of the boy who accompanied her to the airport.

She sees him.

She trembles. She smiles.

He's looking at the reflection of the moon in the river. She walks over slowly, happy because he's gained a little weight, he looks like a better version of himself, and he can't stop tapping his fingers to a rhythm only he hears.

She doesn't call his name. Doesn't warn him. She wraps an arm around his waist from behind and feels him flinch and then relax. She leans her cheek on his back, holding him. Breathes deep, breathes in his scent. She doesn't want to let him go, but she can't help it when he turns, seeking her lips. A soft kiss, deep, sweet. The only way a person can kiss someone who's been dangling upside down from the moon without even thinking about vertigo.

She holds her breath when they pull apart.

They look at each other, feel each other, in silence.

"I was waiting for you to dance."

"We're getting older…"

He ignores her. He does exactly the same thing he did years ago. Puts his phone on the wall just as "Je T'aime…Moi Non Plus" starts to play. He takes her hand and holds it to his chest, trying to bring her as close to him as possible. She blushes when she realizes people are looking at them and whispering and giggling. He doesn't care. He just smiles, looking at her, soaking her in as the melody enwraps them.

"Je t'aime, je t'aime. Tu es la vague, moi l'île nue. Tu vas, tu vas et tu viens." He bends over to whisper it in her ear. She shivers as all the memories rise up. *I love you, I love you. You are the wave; I'm the naked island. You come, you come, and you go…*

He hugs her. They stop dancing. He sinks his face into her hair and strokes her cheek with a trembling hand. He can't let her go. He's scared to, even if he knows that this time, everything's different, and that when the night reaches its end, they won't walk off in different directions.

She stands on her toes. Her lips search for him, find him.

"Ginger, tell me where we are right now."

"We're on the moon. Always on the moon."

Acknowledgments

This book wouldn't exist without all the readers who have accompanied me through the years and helped me grow, let me dream with my eyes open, and given me wings. Thank you for continuing to read my stories, for seeking refuge in books, and for believing in love.

Thanks to my publishers, Planeta in Spain and Sourcebooks in the United States. You do an incomparable job.

To Pablo, for taking my hand and walking in the same direction.

To my literary sisters, the ones who are there every day. They know who they are. I'm so lucky to have you and to share the beauty of writing with you. I hope we can always preserve our faith, even with our nerves and doubts—that would be a good sign!

To Dani, I love you more than chocolate.

To my family for always supporting me.

To J, for going to the moon with me many years ago, hanging from it upside down with a huge smile, without fear. I was so lucky to run into you on that random night.

To Leo, my little prince.

About the Author

Alice Kellen is an international bestselling author of romantic fiction. She writes stories with universal crossover themes such as love, friendship, insecurities, loss, and longing for a brighter future, connecting with younger and older readers alike. She lives in Valencia, Spain, with her family.

Website: alicekellen.com
Facebook: 7AliceKellen
Instagram: @alicekellen_
TikTok: @alicekellen_